Covenant the Unbeliever

"The books are filled with wondrous beings. There is a special warmth in Donaldson's feeling for the Land, and for the power and life inherent to it. Because his eye for detail is good and his feeling for the Land authentic, the Land is as real and substantial as the more prosaic ground we walk upon."
—*Chicago Tribune Book World*

"Here is classical fantasy with just enough of the modern to give it an added dimension. The background is carefully built, the writing has a sweep of grandeur, the imaginative factors display a depth that is seldom seen."
—Clifford D. Simak

"Stephen R. Donaldson meets the novelist's major challenge—fashioning a whole new fantasy world of his own to share with readers who esteem creative imagination."
—Robert Bloch

By Stephen R. Donaldson
Published by Ballantine Books:

THE CHRONICLES OF THOMAS COVENANT

Book One: Lord Foul's Bane
Book Two: The Illearth War
Book Three: The Power That Preserves

THE SECOND CHRONICLES OF THOMAS CONVENANT

Book One: The Wounded Land
Book Two: The One Tree
Book Three: White Gold Wielder

THE THIRD SUMMONING

For a time, Lord Mhoram stood strengthless, even forgetting to sing. But the other Lords had taken up the song, and their staffs vitalized the summoning. When his eyes regained their sight, he beheld Thomas Covenant, Unbeliever and white-gold wielder, standing half substantial in the light before him.

But the apparition did not incarnate itself. Covenant refused to cross over to physical presence. In a voice that barely existed, he cried, "Not now! Let me go! Send me back! She needs me!"

The sight of the Unbeliever's suffering shocked Mhoram. Covenant's body was bruised and battered and his mouth was caked with ugly blood. But as bad as his physical injuries were, they paled beside his psychic distress.

"Covenant!" Mhoram groaned. "Oh, Covenant!" He could not hold back his weeping. "You are in hell. Your world is a hell!"

The Chronicles of Thomas

The Chronicles of Thomas Covenant the Unbeliever

The Power that Preserves

STEPHEN R. DONALDSON

A Del Rey Book

BALLANTINE BOOKS • NEW YORK

For James R. Donaldson, M.D.,
whose life expressed compassion and commitment
more eloquently than any words

Contents

What Has Gone Before

THOMAS COVENANT is a happy and successful author until an unfelt infection leads to the amputation of two fingers. Then he learns he has leprosy. The disease is arrested at a leprosarium, but he returns home to find himself an outcast. His wife has divorced him, and his neighbors shun him in ignorant fear.

Lonely and bitter, he goes to town. There, just after meeting a strange beggar, he stumbles in front of a police car. He revives in a strange world where the evil voice of Lord Foul orders that he take a message of doom to the Lords of the Land. High on a mountain, at Kevin's Watch, a young girl named Lena finds him and takes him to her home. There he is considered a reincarnation of a legendary hero, Berek Half-hand, and his white gold wedding ring is considered a talisman of great power.

Lena treats him with a mud called hurtloam, which seems to arrest his leprosy. This sudden healing is more than he can handle, and, losing control of himself, he rapes Lena. Despite this, her mother Atiaran saves him from Lena's lover, Triock, and agrees to guide him to Revelstone, home of the Lords. She tells him of the ancient war between the Old Lords and Foul, which ended in millennia of desecration for the Land.

Covenant cannot believe in the Land, where stone and wood are made to give heat and light by magic. He becomes the Unbeliever because he dares not relax the discipline that a leper needs in order to survive. The Land seems a delirious escape from reality.

Through the help of Saltheart Foamfollower, a

friendly Giant, Covenant reaches Revelstone. There the Lords accept him and name him ur-Lord. They are dismayed when he gives them Foul's message that an evil Cavewight holds the powerful Staff of Law. They no longer have even the powers of the Old Lords whom Foul overcame; of the Seven Wards of lore, they have only the first.

They must seek the Staff, held in the caverns under Mount Thunder. Covenant goes with them, guarded by Bannor, one of the Bloodguard who have kept a Vow for long ages to guard the Lords. They go south, attacked by Foul's minions, to the Plains of Ra. There the Ramen serve the Ranyhyn, the great free horses. The Ranyhyn bow to the power of Covenant's ring, and he orders that one horse shall go to Lena to do her will once a year.

The Lords ride to Mount Thunder. After many encounters with evil creatures and dark magic, High Lord Prothall wrests the Staff from Drool, the Cavewight. They escape when Covenant manages to use the power of his ring—without understanding how.

As the Lords flee, Covenant begins to fade. He wakes in a hospital bed; only a few hours have elapsed since his accident. His leprosy has come back, supporting his belief that the Land is a delusion. He is discharged from the hospital and returns home.

But after a month, his loneliness drives him to a nightclub, where a singer calls him Berek. Before he can confront her, the over zealous sheriff forces him to return home. Later his wife calls him, but before he can reply, he stumbles and knocks himself out.

Again he is in the Land—but there forty years have passed. The High Lord is now Elena, Covenant's daughter by Lena. She harbors no ill will, however, and a warm relationship grows between them. But the Lords are desperate. Foul has found the Illearth Stone, source of great evil power; now he is preparing to attack. The army of the Lords—commanded by Hile Troy, who seems to be from Covenant's "real" Earth—appears too small to meet the challenge.

A force of Bloodguard and Lords are sent to

Coercri, city of the Giants, to gain allies for the war. But there they find that Foul has killed the Giants— all but three whose bodies have been taken over by Ravers, the evil spirits of Foul's ancient lieutenants. The Bloodguard and Lords are attacked by one Giant-Raver but manage to kill him, at least in bodily form. The Bloodguard unfortunately take the piece of the Illearth Stone the Raver carried, intending to return it to the Lords.

Some of the other Lords travel to Revelwood, a city in a vast tree where the Lore is taught. From there, Hile Troy takes his army south, accompanied by Lord Mhoram. In a desperate attempt, he meets the army of Lord Foul, commanded by another Giant-Raver. Troy is forced to flee. Finally he retreats to Garroting Deep, where the last of the ancient, sentient trees are guarded by Caerroil Wildwood, a powerful Forestal. Wildwood saves the last of Troy's army and destroys the enemy. He hangs the Raver, forcing the evil spirit to suffer and leave the Giant body.

Meanwhile, Elena has taken Covenant and their Bloodguard toward the mysterious *Melenkurion* Skyweir, a great mountain near Garroting Deep. They are led by Amok, a strange servant of Kevin's Lore, who can guide them to the ancient mysteries. They find a way into the heart of the mountain, where Amok ages and vanishes. Elena, against the pleas of Covenant, drinks from the water Amok has shown her. In doing so, she gains the Power of Command. Arrogantly, she summons the spirit of Lord Kevin and commands that he destroy Foul. But Foul overcomes Kevin's shade easily, and Kevin then turns against Elena and the Staff of Law, eventually killing her.

Covenant and Bannor escape down a river that flows out of the mountain. Covenant is sick with self-loathing and grief, blaming himself for Elena's death. They meet Troy and Lord Mhoram near Garroting Deep.

Caerroil Wildwood sends Mhoram home, but he turns Hile Troy into a tree, to become an apprentice Forestal. And Covenant again fades from the Land.

He recovers consciousness in his home. His leprosy

is again in his body, his forehead is wounded from his fall, and his wife has long since hung up. And now he must face the knowledge that his impotence has left the Land open to destruction, without most of the army and without the power of the Staff of Law.

This is a brief summary of *Lord Foul's Bane* and *The Illearth War*, the first two Chronicles of Thomas Covenant, the Unbeliever.

Be true, Unbeliever

Map by Lynn K. Plagge

ONE: The Danger in Dreams

THOMAS COVENANT was talking in his sleep. At times he knew what he was doing; the broken pieces of his voice penetrated his stupor dimly, like flickers of innocence. But he could not rouse himself— the weight of his exhaustion was too great. He babbled like millions of people before him, whole or ill, true or false. But in his case there was no one to hear. He would not have been more alone if he had been the last dreamer left alive.

When the shrill demand of the phone cut through him, he woke up wailing.

For a moment after he threw himself upright in bed, he could not distinguish between the phone and his own flat terror; both echoed like torment through the fog in his head. Then the phone rang again. It pulled him sweating out of bed, compelled him to shamble like a derelict into the living room, forced him to pick up the receiver. His numb, disease-cold fingers fumbled over the black plastic, and when he finally gained a grip on it, he held it to the side of his head like a pistol.

He had nothing to say to it, so he waited in blankness for the person at the other end of the line to speak.

A woman's voice asked uncertainly, "Mr. Covenant? Thomas Covenant?"

"Yes," he murmured, then stopped, vaguely surprised by all the things he had with that one word admitted to be true.

"Ah, Mr. Covenant," the voice said. "Megan Roman calling." When he said nothing, she added with a touch of acerbity, "Your lawyer. Remember?"

1

But he did not remember; he knew nothing about lawyers. Numb mist confused all the links of his memory. Despite the metallic distortion of the connection, her voice sounded distantly familiar; but he could not identify it.

She went on, "Mr. Covenant, I've been your lawyer for two years now. What's the matter with you? Are you all right?"

The familiarity of her voice disturbed him. He did not want to remember who she was. Dully, he murmured, "It doesn't have anything to do with me."

"Are you kidding? I wouldn't have called if it didn't have to do with you. I wouldn't have anything to do with it if it weren't your business." Irritation and discomfort scraped together in her tone.

"No." He did not want to remember. For his own benefit, he strained to articulate, "The Law doesn't have anything to do with me. She broke it. Anyway, I— It can't touch me."

"You better believe it can touch you. And you better listen to me. I don't know what's wrong with you, but—"

He interrupted her. He was too close to remembering her voice. "No," he said again. "It doesn't bind me. I'm—outside. Separate. It can't touch me. Law is"—he paused for a moment, groped through the fog for what he wanted to say—"not the opposite of Despite."

Then in spite of himself he recognized her voice. Through the disembodied inaccuracy of the phone line, he identified her.

Elena.

A sickness of defeat took the resistance out of him.

She was saying, "—what you're talking about. I'm your lawyer, Megan Roman. And if you think the law can't touch you, you'd better listen to me. That's what I'm calling about."

"Yes," he said hopelessly.

"Listen, Mr. Covenant." She gave her irritation a free hand. "I don't exactly like being your lawyer. Just thinking about you makes me squirm. But I've never backed down on a client before, and I don't mean to start with you. Now pull yourself together and listen to me."

"Yes." Elena? he moaned dumbly. Elena? What have I done to you?

"All right. Here's the situation. That—unfortunate escapade of yours—Saturday night—has brought matters to a head. It— Did you have to go to a nightclub, Mr. Covenant? A nightclub, of all places?"

"I didn't mean it." He could think of no other words for his contrition.

"Well, it's done now. Sheriff Lytton is up in arms. You've given him something he can use against you. He spent Sunday evening and this morning talking to a lot of people around here. And the people he talked to talked to other people. The township council met at noon.

"Mr. Covenant, this probably wouldn't have happened if everyone didn't remember the last time you came to town. There was a lot of talk then, but it'd calmed down for the most part. Now it's stirred up again. People want action.

"The council intends to give them action. Our scrupulous local government is going to have your property rezoned. Haven Farm will probably be zoned industrial. Residential use will be prohibited. Once that's done, you can be forced to move. You'll probably get a fair price for the Farm—but you won't find any other place to live in this county."

"It's my fault," he said. "I had the power, and I didn't know how to use it." His bones were full to the marrow with old hate and death.

"What? Are you listening to me? Mr. Covenant, you're my client—for whatever that's worth. I don't intend to stand by and let this happen to you. Sick or not, you've got the same civil rights as anyone else. And there are laws to protect private citizens from—persecution. We can fight. Now I want"—against the metallic background noise of the phone, he could hear her gathering her courage—"I want you to come to my office. Today. We'll dig into the situation—arrange to appeal the decision, or file suit against it—something. We'll discuss all the ramifications, and plan a strategy. All right?"

The sense of deliberate risk in her tone penetrated him for a moment. He said, "I'm a leper. They can't touch me."

"They'll throw you out on your ear! Damn it, Covenant—you don't seem to understand what's going on here. You are going to lose your home. It can be fought—but you're the client, and I can't fight it without you."

But her vehemence made his attention retreat. Vague recollections of Elena swirled in him as he said, "That's not a good answer." Absently, he removed the receiver from his ear and returned it to its cradle.

For a long time, he stood gazing at the black instrument. Something in its irremediable pitch and shape reminded him that his head hurt.

Something important had happened to him.

As if for the first time, he heard the lawyer saying, *Sunday evening and this morning.* He turned woodenly and looked at the wall clock. At first he could not bring his eyes into focus on it; it stared back at him as if it were going blind. But at last he made out the time. The afternoon sun outside his windows confirmed it.

He had slept for more than thirty hours.

Elena? he thought. That could not have been Elena on the phone. Elena was dead. His daughter was dead. It was his fault.

His forehead began to throb. The pain rasped his mind like a bright, brutal light. He ducked his head to try to evade it.

Elena had not even existed. She had never existed. He had dreamed the whole thing.

Elena! he moaned. Turning, he wandered weakly back toward his bed.

As he moved, the fog turned crimson in his brain.

When he entered the bedroom, his eyes widened at the sight of his pillow; and he stopped. The pillow-case was stained with black splotches. They looked like rot, some species of fungus gnawing away at the white cleanliness of the linen.

Instinctively, he raised a hand to his forehead. But his numb fingers could tell him nothing. The illness that seemed to fill the whole inside of his skull began laughing. His empty guts squirmed with nausea. Holding his forehead in both hands, he lurched into the bathroom.

In the mirror over the sink, he saw the wound on his forehead.

For an instant, he saw nothing of himself but the wound. It looked like leprosy, like an invisible hand of leprosy clenching the skin of his forehead. Black crusted blood clung to the ragged edges of the cut, mottling his pale flesh like deep gangrene; and blood and fluid seeped through cracks in the heavy scabs. He seemed to feel the infection festering its way straight through his skull into his brain. It hurt his gaze as if it already reeked of disease and ugly death.

Trembling fiercely, he spun the faucets to fill the sink. While water frothed into the basin, he hurried to lather his hands.

But when he noticed his white gold ring hanging loosely on his wedding finger, he stopped. He remembered the hot power which had pulsed through that metal in his dream. He could hear Bannor, the Bloodguard who had kept him alive, saying, *Save her! You must!*—hear himself reply, *I cannot!* He could hear Hile Troy's shout, *Leper! You're too selfish to love anyone but yourself.* He winced as he remembered the blow which had laid open his forehead.

Elena had died because of him.

She had never existed.

She had fallen into that crevice, fighting desperately against the specter of mad Kevin Landwaster, whom she had Commanded from his grave. She had fallen and died. The Staff of Law had been lost. He had not so much as lifted his hand to save her.

She had never even existed. He had dreamed her while he lay unconscious after having hit his head on the edge of the coffee table.

Torn between conflicting horrors. he stared at his wound as if it were an outcry against him, a two-edged denunciation. From the mirror it shouted to him that the prophecy of his illness had come to pass.

Moaning, he pushed away, and rushed back toward the phone. With soapy, dripping hands, he fumbled at it, struggled to dial the number of Joan's parents. She might be staying with them. She had been his wife; he needed to talk to her.

But halfway through the number, he threw down the receiver. In his memory, he could see her standing chaste and therefore merciless before him. She still believed that he had refused to talk to her when she had called him Saturday night. She would not forgive him for the rebuff he had helplessly dealt her.

How could he tell her that he needed to be forgiven for allowing another woman to die in his dreams?

Yet he needed someone—needed someone to whom he could cry out, Help me!

He had gone so far down the road to a leper's end that he could not pull himself back alone.

But he could not call the doctors at the leprosarium. They would return him to Louisiana. They would treat him and train him and counsel him. They would put him back into life as if his illness were all that mattered, as if wisdom were only skin-deep—as if grief and remorse and horror were nothing but illusions, tricks done with mirrors, irrelevant to chrome and porcelain and clean, white, stiff hospital sheets and fluorescent lights.

They would abandon him to the unreality of his passion.

He found that he was gasping hoarsely, panting as if the air in the room were too rancid for his lungs.

He needed—needed.

Dialing convulsively, he called Information and got the number of the nightclub where he had gone drinking Saturday night.

When he reached that number, the woman who answered the phone told him in a bored voice that Susie Thurston had left the nightclub. Before he could think to ask, the woman told him where the singer's next engagement was.

He called Information again, then put a long-distance call through to the place where Susie Thurston was now scheduled to perform. The switchboard of this club connected him without question to her dressing room.

As soon as he heard her low, waifish voice, he panted thickly, "Why did you do it? Did he put you up to it? How did he do it? I want to know—"

She interrupted him roughly. "Who are you? I don't know what the hell you're talking about. Who do you think you are? I didn't do nothing to you."

"Saturday night. You did it to me Saturday night."

"Buster, I don't know you from Adam. I didn't do nothing to you. Just drop dead, will you? Get off my phone."

"You did it Saturday night. He put you up to it. You called me 'Berek.'" Berek Halfhand—the long-dead hero in his dream. The people in his dream, the people of the Land, had believed him to be Berek Halfhand reborn—believed that because leprosy had claimed the last two fingers of his right hand. "That crazy old beggar told you to call me Berek, and you did it."

She was silent for a long moment before she said, "Oh, it's you. You're that guy—the people at the club said you were a leper."

"You called me Berek," Covenant croaked as if he were strangling on the sepulchral air of the house.

"A leper," she breathed. "Oh, hell! I might've kissed you. Buster, you sure had me fooled. You look a hell of a lot like a friend of mine."

"Berek," Covenant groaned.

"What—'Bere*k*'? You heard me wrong. I said, 'Berrett.' Berrett Williams is a friend of mine. He and I go 'way back. I learned a lot from him. But he was three-quarters crocked all the time. Anyway, he was sort of a clown. Coming to hear me without saying a thing about it is the sort of thing he'd do. And you looked—"

"He put you up to it. That old beggar made you do it. He's trying to do something to me."

"Buster, you got leprosy of the brain. I don't know no beggars. I got enough useless old men of my own.

Say, maybe you are Berrett Williams. This sounds like one of his jokes. Berrett, damn you, if you're setting me up for something—"

Nausea clenched in Covenant again. He hung up the phone and hunched over his stomach. But he was too empty to vomit; he had not eaten for forty-eight hours. He gouged the sweat out of his eyes with his numb fingertips, and dialed Information again.

The half-dried soap on his fingers made his eyes sting and blur as he got the number he wanted and put through another long-distance call.

When the crisp military voice said, "Department of Defense," he blinked at the moisture which filled his eyes like shame, and responded, "Let me talk to Hile Troy." Troy had been in his dream, too. But the man had insisted that he was real, an inhabitant of the real world, not a figment of Covenant's nightmare.

"Hile Troy? One moment, sir." Covenant heard the riffling of pages briefly. Then the voice said, "Sir, I have no listing for anyone by that name."

"Hile Troy," Covenant repeated. "He works in one of your—in one of your think tanks. He had an accident. If he isn't dead, he should be back to work by now."

The military voice lost some of its crispness. "Sir, if he's employed here as you say—then he's security personnel. I couldn't contact him for you, even if he were listed here."

"Just get him to the phone," Covenant moaned. "He'll talk to me."

"What is your name, sir?"

"He'll talk to me."

"Perhaps he will. I still need to know your name."

"Oh, hell!" Covenant wiped his eyes on the back of his hand, then said abjectly, "I'm Thomas Covenant."

"Yes, sir. I'll connect you to Major Rolle. He may be able to help you."

The line clicked into silence. In the background, Covenant could hear a running series of metallic snicks like the ticking of a deathwatch. Pressure mounted in him. The wound on his forehead throbbed like a scream. He clasped the receiver to his head, and hugged himself with his free arm, straining for self-control. When the line came to life again, he could hardly keep from howling at it.

"Mr. Covenant?" a bland, insinuating voice said. "I'm Major Rolle. We're having trouble locating the person you wish to speak to. This is a large department—you understand. Could you tell me more about him?"

"His name is Hile Troy. He works in one of your think tanks. He's blind." The words trembled between Covenant's lips as if he were freezing.

"Blind, you say? Mr. Covenant, you mentioned an accident. Can you tell me what happened to this Hile Troy?"

"Just let me talk to him. Is he there or not?"

The major hesitated, then said, "Mr. Covenant, we have no blind men in this department. Could you give me the source of your information? I'm afraid you're the victim of—"

Abruptly, Covenant was shouting, raging. "He fell out of a window when his apartment caught fire, and he was killed! He never even existed!"

With a savage heave, he tore the phone cord from its socket, then turned and hurled it at the clock on the living-room wall. The phone struck the clock and bounced to the floor as if it were impervious to injury, but the clock shattered and fell in pieces.

"He's been dead for days! He never existed!"

In a paroxysm of fury, he lashed out and kicked the coffee table with one numb booted foot. The table flipped over, broke the frame of Joan's picture as it jolted across the rug. He kicked it again, breaking one of its legs. Then he knocked over the sofa, and leaped past it to the bookcases. One after another, he heaved them to the floor.

In moments, the neat leper's order of the room had degenerated into dangerous chaos. At once, he rushed back to the bedroom. With stumbling fingers, he tore the penknife out of his pocket, opened it, and used it to shred the bloodstained pillow. Then, while the feathers settled like guilty snow over the bed and bureaus, he thrust the knife back into his pocket and slammed out of the house.

He went down into the woods behind Haven Farm at a run, hurrying toward the secluded hut which held his office. If he could not speak of his distress, perhaps he could write it down. As he flashed along the path, his fingers were already twitching to type out: Help me help help help! But when he reached the hut, he found that it looked as if he had already been there. Its door had been torn from its hinges, and inside the hulks of his typewriters lay battered amid the litter of his files and papers. The ruin was smeared with excrement, and the small rooms stank of urine.

At first, he stared at the wreckage as if he had caught himself in an act of amnesia. He could not remember having done thís. But he knew he had not done it; it was vandalism, an attack on him like the burning of his stables days or weeks ago. The unexpected damage stunned him. For an odd instant, he forgot what he had just done to his house. I am not a violent man, he thought dumbly. I'm not.

Then the constricted space of the hut seemed to spring at him from all the walls. A suffocating sensation clamped his chest. For the third time, he ached to vomit, and could not.

Gasping between clenched teeth, he fled into the woods.

He moved aimlessly at first, drove the inanition of his bones as fast as he could deep into the woodland with no aim except flight. But as sunset filled the hills, cluttered the trails with dusk, he bent his steps toward the town. The thought of people drew him like a lure. While he stumbled through the twilit spring evening, odd, irrational surges of hope jabbed his heart. At erratic intervals, he thought that the mere sight of a forthright, unrecriminating face would steady him, bring the extremities of his plight back within his grasp.

He feared to see such a face. The implicit judgment of its health would be beyond his endurance.

Yet he jerked unevenly on through the woods like a moth fluttering in half-voluntary pursuit of immolation. He could not resist the cold siren of people, the allure and pain of his common mortal blood. Help! He winced as each cruel hope struck him. Help me!

But when he neared the town—when he broke out of the woods in back of the scattered old homes which surrounded like a defensive perimeter the business core of the small town—he could not muster the courage to approach any closer. The bright-lit windows and porches and driveways seemed impassable: he would have to brave too much illumination, too much exposure, to reach any door, whether or not it would welcome him. Night was the only cover he had left for his terrible vulnerability.

Whimpering in frustration and need, he tried to force himself forward. He moved from house to house, searching for one, any one, which might offer him some faint possibility of consolation. But the lights refused him. The sheer indecency of thrusting himself upon unwitting people in their homes joined his fear to keep him back. He could not impose on the men and women who lived in sanctuary behind the brightness. He could not carry the weight of any more victims.

In this way—dodging and ducking around the outskirts of the community like a futile ghost, a ghoul impotent to horrify—he passed the houses, and then returned as he had come, made his scattered way back to Haven Farm like a dry leaf, brittle to the breaking point, and apt for fire.

At acute times during the next three days, he wanted to burn his house down, put it to the torch— make it the pyre or charnel of his uncleanness. And in many less savage moods, he ached to simply slit his wrists—open his veins and let the slow misery of his collapse drain away. But he could not muster the resolution for either act. Torn between horrors, he seemed to have lost the power of decision. The little strength of will that remained to him he spent in denying himself food and rest.

He went without food because he had fasted once before, and that hunger had helped to carry him

through a forest of self-deceptions to a realization of
the appalling thing he had done to Lena, Elena's
mother. Now he wanted to do the same; he wanted to
cut through all excuses, justifications, digressions, defenses, and meet his condition on its darkest terms. If
he failed to do this, then any conclusion he reached
would be betrayed from birth, like Elena, by the inadequacy of his rectitude or comprehension.

But he fought his bone-deep need for rest because
he was afraid of what might happen to him if he slept.
He had learned that the innocent did not sleep. Guilt
began in dreams.

Neither of these abnegations surpassed him. The
nausea lurking constantly in the pit of his stomach
helped him to keep from food. And the fever of his
plight did not let him go. It held and rubbed him like
a harness; he seemed to have the galls of it on his
soul. Whenever the penury of his resources threatened him, he gusted out of his house like a lost wind,
and scudded through the hills for miles up and down
the wooded length of Righters Creek. And when he
could not rouse himself with exertion, he lay down
across the broken furniture in his living room, so that
if he dozed he would be too uncomfortable to rest
deeply enough for dreams.

In the process, he did nothing to care for his illness.
His VSE—the Visual Surveillance of Extremities on
which his struggle against leprosy depended—and
other self-protective habits he neglected as if they had
lost all meaning for him. He did not take the medica-
tion which had at one time arrested the spreading of
his disease. His forehead festered; cold numbness
gnawed its slow way up the nerves of his hands and
feet. He accepted such things, ignored his danger. It
was condign; he deserved it.

Nevertheless, he fell into the same fey mood every
evening. In the gloom of twilight, his need for people
became unendurable; it drew him spitting and gnash-
ing his teeth to the outer darkness beyond the home
lights of the town. Night after night he tried to drive
himself to the door of a home, any home. But he
could not raise his courage high enough to accost the

lights. People within a stone's throw of him remained as unattainable as if they occupied another world. Each night he was thrown back for companionship on the unrelieved aspect of his own weakness—and on the throbbing ache which filled his skull as the infection in his forehead grew.

Elena had died because of him. She was his daughter, and he had loved her. Yet he had trapped her into death.

She had never even existed.

He could find no answer to it.

Then, Thursday night, the pattern of his decline was broken for him. In the process of his futile ghosting, he became aware of sounds on the dark breeze. A tone rose and fell like a voice in oratory, and between its stanzas he heard singing. Disembodied in the darkness, the voices had a tattered, mournful air, like an invitation to a gathering of damned souls— verses and chorus responding in dolor to each other. Elena had been a singer, daughter of a family of singers. Fumbling his way through the benighted outskirts of the town, he followed the reft sorrow of the music.

It led him past the houses, around the town, down the road to the barren field which served as a parade ground whenever the town celebrated a patriotic occasion. A few people were still hurrying toward the field as if they were late, and Covenant avoided them by staying off the road. When he reached the parade ground, he found that a huge tent had been erected in its center. All the sides of the tent were rolled up, so that the light of pressure lanterns shone vividly from under the canvas.

People filled the tent. They were just sitting down on benches after singing, and during the movement, several ushers guided the latecomers to the last empty seats. The benches faced in tight rows toward a wide platform at the front of the tent, where three men sat. They were behind a heavy pulpit, and behind them stood a makeshift altar, hastily hammered together out of pine boards, and bleakly adorned by a few crooked candles and a dull, battered gold cross.

As the people settled themselves on the benches,

one of the men on the platform—a short fleshy man dressed in a black suit and a dull white shirt—got to his feet and stepped to the pulpit. In a sonorous, compelling voice, he said, "Let us pray."

All the people bowed their heads. Covenant was on the verge of turning away in disgust, but the quiet confidence of the man's tone stayed him. He listened unwillingly as the man folded his hands on the pulpit and prayed gently:

"Dear Jesus, our Lord and Saviour—please look down on the souls that have come together here. Look into their hearts, Lord—see the pain, and the hurt, and the loneliness, and the sorrow—yes, and the sin—and the hunger for You in their hearts. Comfort them, Lord. Help them, heal them. Teach them the peace and the miracle of prayer in Thy true name. Amen."

Together, the people responded, "Amen."

The man's voice tugged at Covenant. He heard something in it that sounded like sincerity, like simple compassion. He could not be sure; he seemed to have learned what little he knew about sincerity in dreams. But he did not move away. Instead, while the people raised their heads from prayer, he moved cautiously forward into the light, went close enough to the tent to read a large sign posted at the side of the road. It said:

The EASTER HEALTH Crusade—
Dr. B. Sam Johnson
revivalist and healer
tonight through Sunday
only.

On the platform, another man approached the pulpit. He wore a clerical collar, and a silver cross hung from his neck. He pushed his heavy glasses up on his nose, and beamed out over the people. "I'm pleased as punch," he said, "to have Dr. Johnson and Matthew Logan here. They're known everywhere in the state for their rich ministry to the spiritual needs of people like us. I don't need to tell you how much we need reviving here—how many of us need to recover that healing faith, especially in this Easter season. Dr. Johnson and Mr. Logan are going to help us return to the matchless Grace of God."

The short man dressed in black stood up again and said, "Thank you, sir." The minister hesitated, then left the pulpit as if he had been dismissed—cut off in the opening stages of a fulsome introduction—and Dr. Johnson went on smoothly: "My friends, here's my dear brother in Christ, Matthew Logan. You've heard his wonderful, wonderful singing. Now he'll read the Divine Word of God for us. Brother Logan."

As he stepped to the pulpit, Matthew Logan's powerful frame towered over Dr. Johnson. Though he seemed to have no neck at all, the head resting on his broad shoulders was half a yard above his partner's. He flipped authoritatively through a massive black Bible on the pulpit, found his place, and bowed his head to read as if in deference to the Word of God.

He began without introduction:

"'But if you will not hearken to me, and will not do all these commandments, but break my covenant, I will do this to you: I will appoint over you sudden terror, consumption, and fever that waste the eyes and cause life to pine away. And you shall sow your seed in vain, for your enemies shall eat it; those who hate you shall rule over you, and you shall flee when none pursues you. I will make your heavens like iron and your earth like brass; and your strength shall be spent in vain, for your land shall not yield its increase, and the trees of the land shall not yield their fruit.

"'Then if you walk contrary to me, and will not hearken to me, I will bring more plagues upon you, sevenfold as many as your sins. And I will let loose the wild beasts among you, which shall rob you of your children, and destroy your cattle, and make you few in number, so that your ways shall become desolate. I also will walk contrary to you, and I will bring a sword upon you, and shall execute vengeance for the covenant; and if you gather within your cities I will send pestilence among you, and you shall be delivered into the hand of the enemy.'"

As Matthew Logan rolled out the words, Covenant felt their spell falling on him. The promise of punishment caught at his heart; it snared him as if it had been lying in ambush for his gray, gaunt soul. Stiffly, involuntarily, he moved toward the tent as the curse drew him to itself.

" 'And if in spite of this you will not hearken to me, but walk contrary to me, then I will walk contrary to you in fury, and chastise you myself sevenfold for your sins. You shall eat the flesh of your sons, and you shall eat the flesh of your daughters. My soul will abhor you. I will lay your cities waste. I will scatter you among the nations, and I will unsheathe the sword after you; and your land shall be a desolation, and your cities shall be a waste.

" 'Then the land shall pay for its sabbaths as long as it lies desolate.' "

Covenant ducked under an edge of the canvas and found himself standing beside an usher at the rear of the tent. The usher eyed him distrustfully, but made no move to offer him a seat. High on the platform at the other end, Matthew Logan stood like a savage patriarch leveling retribution at the bent, vulnerable heads below him. The curse gathered a storm in Covenant, and he feared that he would cry out before it ended. But Matthew Logan stopped where he was and flipped through the Bible again. When he found his new place, he read more quietly:

" 'Whoever, therefore, eats the bread or drinks the cup of the Lord in an unworthy manner will be guilty of profaning the body and blood of the Lord. Anyone who eats and drinks without discerning the body eats and drinks judgment upon himself. That is why many of you are weak and ill, and some have died. But if we judged ourselves truly, we should not be judged. But when we are judged by the Lord, we are chastened so that we may not be condemned along with the world.' "

Slapping the Bible closed, he returned stolidly to his seat.

At once, Dr. B. Sam Johnson was on his feet. Now he seemed to bristle with energy; he could not wait to begin speaking. His jowls quivered with excitement as he addressed his audience.

"My friends, how marvelous are the Words of God! How quick to touch the heart. How comforting to the sick, the downtrodden, the weak. And how easily they make even the purest of us squirm. Listen, my friends! Listen to the Word of the Apocalypse:

" 'To the thirsty I will give water without price from the fountain of the water of life. He who conquers shall have this heritage, and I will be his God and he shall be my son. But as for the cowardly, the unbelievers, the polluted, as for murderers, fornicators, sorcerers, idolaters, and all liars, their lot shall be in the lake that burns with fire and brimstone, which is the second death.'

"Marvelous, marvelous Words of God. Here in one short passage we hear the two great messages of the Bible, the Law and the Gospel, the Old Covenant and the New. Brother Logan read to you first from the Old Testament, from the twenty-sixth chapter of Leviticus. Did you hear him, my friends? Did you listen with all the ears of your heart? That is the voice of God, Almighty God. He doesn't mince words, my friends. He doesn't beat around the bush. He doesn't hide things in fine names and fancy language. No! He says, if you sin, if you break My Law, I will terrify you and make you sick. I will make the land barren and attack you with plagues and pestilence. And if you still sin, I will make cannibals and cripples out of you. 'Then the land shall pay for its sabbaths as long as it lies desolate.'

"And do you know what the Law is, my friends? I can summarize it for you in the Words of the Apocalypse. 'Thou shalt not be cowardly, or unbelieving, or polluted.' Never mind murder, fornication, sorcery, idolatry, lies. We're all *good* people here. We don't do things like *that*. But have you ever been afraid? Have you ever faltered just a bit in your faith? Have you ever failed to keep yourself clean in heart and mind? 'Then the land shall pay for its sabbaths as long as it lies desolate.' The Apostle Paul calls a spade a spade. He says, 'That is why many of you are weak and ill, and some have died.' But Jesus goes further. He says, 'Depart from me, you cursed, into the eternal fire prepared for the devil and his angels.'

"Do I hear you protesting? Do I hear some of you saying to yourselves, 'No one can be that good. I'm human. I can't be perfect.' You're right! Of course, you're right. But the Law of God doesn't care for your excuses. If you're lame, if you've got arthritis, if you're going blind or your heart is failing, if you're crippled, if you've got multiple sclerosis or diabetes or any other of those fancy names for sin, you can be sure that the curse of God is on you. But if you're healthy, don't think you're safe! You're just lucky that God hasn't decided to 'walk contrary to you in fury.' You can't be perfect, my friends. And the Law doesn't care how hard you tried. Instead of telling yourself what a valiant try you made, listen to the Bible. The Old Covenant says to you as plain as day, 'The leper who has the disease shall wear torn clothes and let the hair of his head hang loose, and he shall cover his upper lip and cry, "Unclean, unclean." ' "

He held his audience in the palm of his hand now. The orotund resonance of his voice swept them all together in one ranked assembly of mortality and weakness. Even Covenant forgot himself, forgot that he was an intruder in this canvas tabernacle; he heard so many personal echoes and gleams in the peroration that he could not resist it. He was willing to believe that he was accursed.

"Ah, my friends," Dr. Johnson went on smoothly, "it's a dark day for us when illness strikes, when pain or dismemberment or bereavement afflict us, and we can no longer pretend we're clean. But I haven't told you about the Gospel yet. Do you remember Christ saying, 'He who loses his life for my sake shall find it'? Did you hear Paul say, 'When we are judged by the Lord, we are chastened so that we may not be condemned along with the world'? Did you hear the writer of the Apocalypse say, 'He who conquers shall have this heritage, and I will be his God and he shall be my son'? There's another side, my friends. The law is only half of God's holy message. The other half is chastening, heritage, forgiveness, healing—the Mercy that matches God's Righteousness. Do I have to remind you that the Son of God healed everyone who asked Him? Even lepers? Do I have to remind you that He hung on a cross erected in the midst of misery and shame to pay the price of our sin for us? Do I have to remind you that the nails tore His hands and feet? That the spear pierced His side? That He was dead for three days? Dead and in hell?

"My friends, He did it for only one reason. He did it to pay for all our cowardly, unbelieving, unclean sabbaths, so that we could be healed. And all you have to do to get healed is to believe it, and accept it, and love Him for it. All you have to do is say with the man whose child was dying, 'I believe; help my unbelief!' Five little words, my friends. When they come from the heart, they're enough to pay for the whole Kingdom of Righteousness."

As if on cue, Matthew Logan stood up and began singing in soft descant, "Blessed assurance, Jesus is mine." Against this background, Dr. Johnson folded his hands and said, "My friends, pray with me."

At once, every head in the audience dropped. Covenant, too, bowed. But the wound on his forehead burned extravagantly in that position. He looked up again as Dr. Johnson said, "Close your eyes, my friends. Shut out your neighbors, your children, your parents, your mate. Shut out every distraction. Look inward, my friends. Look deep inside yourselves, and see the sickness there. Hear the voice of God saying, 'Thou art weighed in the balance, and found wanting.' Pray with me in your hearts.

"Dear holy Jesus, Thou art our only hope. Only Thy Divine Mercy can heal the disease which riddles our courage, rots the fiber of our faith, dirties us in Thy sight. Only Thou canst touch the sickness which destroys peace, and cure it. We lay bare our hearts to Thee, Lord. Help us to find the courage for those five difficult, difficult words, 'I believe; help my unbelief!' Dear Lord, please give us the courage to be healed."

Without a break, he raised his arms over the audience and continued, "Do you feel His spirit, my friends? Do you feel it in your hearts? Do you feel the finger of His Righteousness probing the sick spot in your soul and body? If you do, come forward now, and let me pray for health with you."

He bowed his head in silent supplication while he waited for the repentant to heed his call. But Covenant was already on his way down the aisle. The usher made a furtive movement to stop him, then backed off as several members of the audience looked up. Covenant stalked feverishly the length of the tent, climbed the rough wooden steps to the platform, and stopped facing Dr. Johnson. His eyes glistered as he said in a raw whisper, "Help me."

The man was shorter than he had appeared to be from the audience. His black suit was shiny, and his shirt soiled from long use. He had not shaved recently; stiff, grizzled whiskers roughened his jowls and cheeks. His face wore an uncertain aspect—almost an expression of alarm—as Covenant confronted him, but he quickly masked it with blandness, and said in a tone of easy sonority, "Help you, son? Only God can help you. But I will joyfully add my prayers to the cry of any contrite heart." He placed a hand firmly on Covenant's shoulder. "Kneel, son, and pray with me. Let's ask the Lord for help together."

Covenant wanted to kneel, wanted to submit to the commanding spell of Dr. Johnson's hand and voice. But his knees were locked with urgency and inanition. The pain in his forehead flamed like acid gnawing at his brain. He felt that if he bent at all he would collapse completely. "Help me," he whispered again. "I can't stand it."

Dr. Johnson's face became stern at Covenant's resistance. "Are you repentant, son?" he asked gravely. "Have you found the sick spot of sin in your soul? Do you truly ache for Almighty God's Divine Mercy?"

"I am sick," Covenant responded as if he were answering a litany. "I have committed crimes."

"And do you repent? Can you say those five difficult words with all the honest pain of your heart?"

Covenant's jaw locked involuntarily. Through

clenched teeth, he said as if he were whimpering, "Help my unbelief."

"Son, that's not enough. You know that's not enough." Dr. Johnson's sternness changed to righteous judgment. "Do not dare to mock God. He will cast you out forever. Do you believe? Do you believe in God's own health?"

"I do"—Covenant struggled to move his jaw, but his teeth clung together as if they had been fused by despair—"I do not believe."

Behind him, Matthew Logan stopped singing his descant. The abrupt silence echoed in Covenant's ears like ridicule. Abjectly, he breathed, "I'm a leper."

He could tell by the curious, expectant faces in the first rows of the audience that the people had not heard him, did not recognize him. He was not surprised; he felt that he had been altered past all recognition by his delusions. And even in his long-past days of health he had never been associated with the more religious townspeople. But Dr. Johnson heard. His eyes bulged dangerously in their sockets, and he spoke so softly that his words barely reached Covenant. "I don't know who put you up to this but you won't get away with it."

With hardly a pause, he began speaking for the people in the tent again. "Poor man, you're delirious. That cut is infected, and it's given you a bad fever." His public voice was redolent with sympathy. "I grieve for you, son. But it will take a great power of prayer to clear your mind so that the voice of God can reach you. Brother Logan, would you take this poor sick man aside and pray with him? If God blesses your efforts to lift his fever, he may yet come to repentance."

Matthew Logan's massive hands closed like clamps on Covenant's biceps. The fingers ground into him as if they meant to crush his bones. He found himself propelled forward, almost carried down the steps and along the aisle. Behind him, Dr. Johnson was saying, "My friends, will you pray with me for this poor suffering soul? Will you sing and pray for his healing with me?"

In a covered whisper, Matthew Logan said near Covenant's ear, "We haven't taken the offering yet. If you do anything else to interrupt, I'll break both your arms."

"Don't touch me!" Covenant snarled. The big man's treatment tapped a resource of rage which had been dammed in him for a long time. He tried to struggle against Logan's grasp. "Get your hands off me."

Then they reached the end of the aisle and ducked under the canvas out into the night. With an effortless heave, Brother Logan threw Covenant from him. Covenant stumbled and fell on the bare dirt of the parade ground. When he looked up, the big man was standing with fists on hips like a dark colossus between him and the light of the tent.

Covenant climbed painfully to his feet, pulled what little dignity he could find about his shoulders, and moved away.

As he shambled into the darkness, he heard the people singing, "Blessed Assurance." And a moment later, a pathetic childish voice cried, "Lord, I'm lame! Please heal me!"

Covenant dropped to his knees and retched dryly. Some time passed before he could get up again and flee the cruel song.

He went homeward along the main road, defying the townspeople to hurt him further. But all the businesses were closed, and the street was deserted. He walked like a flicker of darkness under the pale yellow streetlamps, past the high, belittling giant-heads on the columns of the courthouse—made his way unmolested out the end of town toward Haven Farm.

The two miles to the Farm passed like all his hikes —measured out in fragments by the rhythm of his strides, a scudding, mechanical rhythm like the ticking of overstressed clockwork. The mainspring of his movement had been wound too tight; it was turning too fast, rushing to collapse. But a change had taken place in the force which drove him.

He had remembered hate.

He was spinning wild schemes for vengeance in his head when he finally reached the long driveway leading into Haven Farm. There in the cold starlight he saw a heavy sack sitting by his mailbox. A moment passed before he remembered that the sack contained food; the local grocery store delivered to him twice a week rather than face the risk that he might choose to do his shopping in person; and yesterday—Wednesday—had been one of the delivery days. But he had been so occupied with his restless fasting that he had forgotten.

He picked up the sack without stopping to wonder why he bothered, and carried it down the driveway toward his house.

But when he looked into the sack in the bright light of his kitchen, he found he had decided to eat. Vengeance required strength; there was nothing he could do to strike back against his tormentors if he were too weak to hold himself erect. He took a package of buns from the sack.

The wrapping of the buns had been neatly cut on one side, but he ignored the thin slit. He tore off the plastic and threw it aside. The buns were dry and stiff from their exposure to the air. He took one and held it in the palm of his hand, gazed down at it as if it were a skull he had robbed from some old grave. The sight of the bread sickened him. Part of him longed for the clean death of starvation, and he felt that he could not lift his hand, could not complete his decision of retribution.

Savagely, he jerked the bun to his mouth and bit into it.

Something sharp caught between his lower lip and upper gum. Before he could stop biting, it cut him deeply. A keen shard of pain stabbed into his face. Gasping, he snatched back the bun.

It was covered with blood. Blood ran like saliva down his chin.

When he tore open the bun with his hands, he found a tarnished razor blade in it.

At first, he was too astonished to react. The rusty blade seemed beyond comprehension; he could hardly believe the blood that smeared his hands and dropped to the floor from his jaw. Numbly, he let the bun fall from his fingers. Then he turned and made his way into the littered wreckage of his living room.

His eyes were irresistibly drawn to Joan's picture. It lay faceup under the remains of the coffee table, and the glass of its frame was webbed with cracks. He pushed the table aside, picked up the picture. Joan smiled at him from behind the cracks as if she had been caught in a net of mortality and did not know it.

He began to laugh.

He started softly, but soon scaled upward into manic howling. Water ran from his eyes like tears, but still he laughed, laughed as if he were about to shatter. His bursts spattered blood over his hands and Joan's picture and the ruined room.

Abruptly, he threw down the picture and ran from it. He did not want Joan to witness his hysteria. Laughing madly, he rushed from the house into the woods, determined even while he lost control of himself to take his final breakdown as far away from Haven Farm as possible.

When he reached Righters Creek, he turned and followed it upstream into the hills, away from the dangerous lure of people as fast as his numb, awkward feet could carry him—laughing desperately all the while.

Sometime during the night, he tripped; and when he found himself on the ground, he leaned against a tree to rest for a moment. At once, he fell asleep, and did not awaken until the morning sun was shining full in his face.

For a time, he did not remember who or where he was. The hot white light of the sun burned everything out of his mind; his eyes were so dazzled that he could not make out his surroundings. But when he heard the thin, wordless cry of fear, he began to chuckle. He was too weak to laugh loudly, but he chuckled as if that were the only thing left in him.

The thin cry repeated itself. Inspired by it, he managed a fuller laugh, and started to struggle to his feet. But the effort weakened him. He had to stop laughing to catch his breath. Then he heard the cry again, a child's shriek of terror. Supporting himself on the tree, he looked around, peering through his sun blindness at the dim shapes of the woods.

Gradually, he became able to see. He was perched high on a hill in the woods. Most of the branches and bushes were bursting with green spring leaves. A few yards from him, Righters Creek tumbled gaily down the rocky hillside and wandered like a playful silver trail away among the trees. Most of the hill below him was free of brush because of the rockiness of the soil; nothing obscured his downward view.

An odd splotch of color at the bottom of the hill caught his attention. With an effort, he focused his eyes on it. It was cloth, a light blue dress worn by a child—a little girl perhaps four or five years old. She stood half turned toward him, with her back pressed against the black, straight trunk of a tall tree. She seemed to be trying to push herself into the wood, but the indifferent trunk refused to admit her.

She was screaming continuously now, and her cries begged at the anguish in his mind. As she yelled, she stared in unmasked terror at the ground two or three feet in front of her. For a moment, Covenant could not see what she was looking at. But then his ears discerned the low buzzing noise, and he picked out the ominous brown shaking of the rattle.

The timber rattler was coiled less than a yard from the girl's bare legs. Its head bobbed as if it were searching for the perfect place to strike.

He recognized her terror now. Before the shout had a chance to burst past his blood-caked lips, he pushed himself away from the tree and started running down the hill.

The slope seemed interminably long, and his legs were hardly strong enough to sustain him. At each downward plunge, his muscles gave, and he almost fell to his knees. But the child's irrefusable fear held him up. He did not look at the snake. He fixed his eyes on her bare shins, concentrated himself on the importance of reaching her before the rattler's fangs jabbed into her flesh. The rest of her was blurred in his sight, as if she did not exist apart from her peril.

With each shrill cry, she begged him to hurry.

But he was not watching his footing. Before he had covered half the distance, he tripped—pitched head-long down the hill, tumbled and bounced over the rough rocks. For an instant, he protected himself with his arms. But then his head smacked against a broad facet of stone in the hillside.

He seemed to fall into the stone, as if he were burying his face in darkness. The hard surface of it broke over him like a wave; he could feel himself plunging deep into the rock's granite essence.

No! he cried. No! Not now!

He fought it with every jot of his strength. But it surpassed him. He sank into it as if he were drowning in stone.

TWO: Variol-son

HIGH LORD MHORAM sat in his private chambers deep in Revelstone. The unadorned gut-rock walls around him were warmly lit by small urns of graveling in each corner of the room, and the faint aroma of newly broken earth from the lore-glowing stones wrapped comfortably around him. But still he could feel the preternatural winter which was upon the Land. Despite the brave hearth fires set everywhere by the Hirebrands and Gravelingases of Lord's Keep, a bitter chill seeped noticeably through the mountain granite of the city. High Lord Mhoram felt it. He could sense its effect on the physical mood of the great Giant-wrought Keep. On an almost subliminal level, Revelstone was huddling against the cold.

Already, the first natural turnings of winter toward spring were a full cycle of the moon late. The middle night of spring was only fourteen days away, and still ice clung to the Land.

Outside the wedge-shaped mountain plateau of the Keep, there was not much snow; the air was too cold for snow. It blew at Revelstone on a jagged, uncharacteristic wind out of the east, kicking a thin skiff of snow across the foothills of the plateau, blinding all the windows of the Keep under deep inches of frost and immobilizing with ice the lake at the foot of Furl Falls. Mhoram did not need to smell the Despite which hurled that wind across the Land to know its source.

It came from Ridjeck Thome, Foul's Creche.

As the High Lord sat in his chambers, with his elbows braced on the stone table and his chin propped on one palm, he was aware of that wind hissing through the background of his thoughts. Ten years ago, he would have said that it was impossible; the natural weather patterns of the Land could not be so wrenched apart. Even five years ago, after he had had time to assess and reassess the loss of the Staff of Law, he would have doubted that the Illearth Stone could make Lord Foul so powerful. But now he knew better, understood more.

High Lord Elena's battle with dead Kevin Landwaster had taken place seven years ago. The Staff of Law must have been destroyed in that struggle. Without the Staff's innate support for the natural order of the Earth, one great obstacle was gone from the path of the Despiser's corrupting power. And the Law of Death had been broken; Elena had summoned Old Lord Kevin from beyond the grave. Mhoram could not begin to measure all the terrible implications of that rupture.

He blinked, and his gold-flecked eyes shifted into focus on the carving which stood on the table two feet from the flat blade of his nose. The bone of the carving gleamed whitely in the light of the fire-stones. It was a marrowmeld sculpture, the last of Elena's *anundivian yajña* work. Bannor of the Bloodguard had preserved it, and had given it to Mhoram when they had come together on Gallows Howe in Garroting Deep. It was a finely detailed bust, a sculpting of a lean, gaunt, impenetrable face, and its lines were tense with prophetic purpose. After Mhoram and the survivors of the Warward had returned to Revelstone from Garroting Deep, Bannor had explained the history of the bone sculpture.

In fact, he had explained it in unaccustomed detail. His habitual Bloodguard reticence had given way almost to prolixity; and the fullness of his description had provided Mhoram with a first hint of the fundamental alteration which had taken place in the Bloodguard. And in turn that description had led circuitously to the great change in Mhoram's own life. By a curious logic of its own, it had put an end to the High Lord's power of prevision.

He was no longer seer and oracle to the Council of Lords. Because of what he had learned, he caught no more glimpses of the future in dreams, read no more hints of distant happenings in the dance of the fire. The secret knowledge which he had gained so intuitively from the marrowmeld sculpture had blinded the eyes of his prescience.

It had done other things to him as well. It had afflicted him with more hope and fear than he had ever felt before. And it had partly estranged him from his fellow Lords; in a sense, it had estranged him from all the people of Revelstone. When he walked the halls of the Keep, he could see in the sympathy and pain and doubt and wonder of their glances that they perceived his separateness, his voluntary isolation. But he suffered more from the breach which now obtained between him and the other Lords—Callindrill Faermate, Amatin daughter of Matin, Trevor son of Groyle, and Loerya Trevor-mate. In all their work together, in all the intercourse of their daily lives, even in all the mind melding which was the great strength of the new Lords, he was forced to hold that sickening hope and fear apart, away from them. For he had not told them his secret.

He had not told them, though he had no justification for his silence except dread.

Intuitively, by steps which he could hardly articulate, Elena's marrowmeld sculpture had taught him the secret of the Ritual of Desecration.

He felt that there was enough hope and fear in the knowledge to last him a lifetime.

In the back of his mind, he believed that Bannor had wanted him to have this knowledge and had not been able to utter it directly. The Bloodguard Vow had restricted Bannor in so many ways. But during the single year of his tenure as First Mark, he had expressed more than any Bloodguard before him his solicitude for the survival of the Lords.

High Lord Mhoram winced unconsciously at the memory. The secret he now held had been expensive in more ways than one.

There was hope in the knowledge because it answered the quintessential failure which had plagued the new Lords from the beginning—from the days in which they had accepted the First Ward of Kevin's Lore from the Giants, and had sworn the Oath of Peace. If it were used, the knowledge promised to unlock the power which had remained sealed in the Wards despite the best efforts of so many generations of Lords and students at the Loresraat. It promised mastery of Kevin's Lore. It might even show ur-Lord Thomas Covenant how to use the wild magic in his white gold ring.

But Mhoram had learned that the very thing which made Kevin's Lore powerful for good also made it powerful for ill. If Kevin son of Loric had not had that particular capacity for power, he would not have been able to Desecrate the Land.

If Mhoram shared his knowledge, any Lord who wished to reinvoke the Ritual would not be forced to rely upon an instinctive distrust of life.

That knowledge violated the Oath of Peace. To his horror, Mhoram had come to perceive that the Oath itself was the essential blindness, the incapacity which had prevented the new Lords from penetrating to the heart of Kevin's Lore. When the first new Lords, and all the Land with them, had taken the Oath, articulated their highest ideal and deepest commitment by forswearing all violent, destructive passions, all human instincts for murder and ravage and contempt—when they had bound themselves with the Oath, they had unwittingly numbed themselves to the basic vitality of the Old Lords' power. Therefore High Lord Mhoram feared to share his secret. It was a strength which could only be used if the wielders denied the most basic promise of their lives. It was a weapon which could only be used by a person who had cast down all defenses against despair.

And the temptation to use that weapon would be strong, perhaps irrefusable. Mhoram did not need oracular dreams to foresee the peril which Lord Foul the Despiser was preparing for the defenders of the Land. He could feel it in the frigid winter wind. And he knew that Trothgard was already under attack. The siege of Revelwood was under way even while he sat in his private quarters, staring morosely at a marrowmeld sculpture.

He could taste in his own mouth the desperation which had led High Lord Kevin to Kiril Threndor and the Ritual of Desecration. Power was dreadful and treacherous. When it was not great enough to accomplish its wielder's desires, it turned against the hands which held it. High Lord Elena's fate only repeated the lesson of Kevin Landwaster; he had possessed far more power than the new Lords could ever hope for, now that the Staff of Law was gone; and all his might had achieved nothing but his own ineluctable despair and the ruin of the Land. Mhoram feared to share that danger by revealing his secret. He was appalled to think he was in such peril himself.

Yet this withholding of knowledge ran against every grain of his character. He believed intensely that the refusal to share knowledge demeaned both the denier and the denied. By keeping the secret to himself, he prevented Callindrill and Amatin and Trevor and Loerya and every Lorewarden or student of the Staff from finding within themselves the strength to refuse Desecration; he placed himself falsely in the position of a judge who had weighed them and found them wanting. For this reason ten years ago he had argued passionately against the Council's decision to withhold from Hile Troy the knowledge of Elena's parentage. That decision had lessened Troy's control over his own fate. Yet how could he, Mhoram, bear the responsibility of sharing his secret if that sharing led to the Land's destruction? Better that the evil should be done by the Despiser than by a Lord.

When he heard the abrupt knock at his door, he said, "Enter," at once. He was expecting a message, and he knew from the sound of the knock who his visitor was. He did not look up from his contemplation of the sculpture as Warmark Quaan strode into the chamber and presented himself at the table.

But Quaan remained silent, and Mhoram sensed that the old Warmark was waiting to meet his gaze. With an inward sigh, the High Lord raised his head. In Quaan's age- and sun-weathered face, he read that the news was not what they had hoped it would be.

Mhoram did not offer Quaan a seat; he could see that the Warmark preferred to stand. They had sat together often enough in the past. After all the experiences they had shared, they were old comrades— though Quaan, who was twenty years younger than Mhoram, looked twenty years older. And the High Lord frequently found Quaan's blunt, soldierly candor soothing. Quaan was a follower of the Sword who had no desire to know any secrets of the Staff.

Despite his seventy years, Quaan carried proudly the insignia of his office: the yellow breastplate with its twin black diagonal slashes, the yellow headband, and the ebony sword. His gnarled hands hung at his sides as if they were ready to snatch up weapons at any moment. But his pale eyes were disquieted.

Mhoram met the Warmark's gaze steadily and said, "Well, my friend?"

"High Lord," Quaan said brusquely, "the Loresraat has come."

Mhoram could see that the Warmark had more to say than this. His eyes asked Quaan to continue.

"All the Lorewardens and students have made the

journey from Trothgard safely," Quaan responded. "The libraries of the Loresraat and the Wards have been brought here intact. All the visitors and those made homeless by the march of Satansfist's army through the Center Plains have come seeking sanctuary. Revelwood is besieged."

He stopped again, and Mhoram asked quietly, "What word do the Lorewardens bring of that army?"

"It is—vast, High Lord. It assaults the Valley of Two Rivers like a sea. The Giant-Raver Satansfist bears with him the—the same power which we saw in Fleshharrower at the battle of Doriendor Corishev. He easily overcame the river fords of the Rill and Llurallin. Revelwood will soon fall to him."

The High Lord put a measure of sternness in his voice to counter Quaan's dismay. "We were forewarned, Warmark. When the Giant-Raver and his horde climbed Landsdrop to the north of the Plains of Ra, the Ramen sent word to us. Therefore the Loresraat has been preserved."

Quaan braced one hand on his sword and said, "Lord Callindrill has remained in Revelwood."

Mhoram winced in painful surprise.

"He has remained to defend the tree city. With him are five Eoward commanded by Hiltmark Amorine—also Sword-Elder Drinishok and Staff-Elder Asuraka."

After the first jolt of the news, the High Lord's gold-flecked irises concentrated dangerously. "Warmark, the Council commanded that Revelwood should be defended only by those of the *lillianrill* who could not bear to abandon it. The Council commanded that the battle for the Land should take place here"—he slapped the table with his palm—"where we can exact the greatest possible price for our lives."

"You and I are not at Revelwood," Quaan replied bluntly. "Who there could command Lord Callindrill to turn aside from his purpose? Amorine could not— you know this. They are bound together by the costs they bore at Doriendor Corishev. Nor could she leave him alone. Nor could she refuse the aid of the Elders."

His voice was sharp in Hiltmark Amorine's defense,

but he stopped when Mhoram with a distracted gesture waved all questions of anger aside. They remained together in silence for a moment. The High Lord felt an aching anticipation of grief, but he forced it down. His eyes wandered back to the bust on the table. Softly, he said, "Has this word been given to Faer Callindrill-mate?"

"Corimini the Eldest of the Loresraat went to her at once. Callindrill studied with him, and he has known them both for many years. He apologized for not first paying his respects to the High Lord."

Mhoram shrugged away the need for any apology. His helplessness to reach Callindrill hurt him. He was six days from Revelwood by horse. And he could not call upon the Ranyhyn. The Despiser's army had effectively cut Revelstone off from the Plains of Ra; any Ranyhyn that tried to answer a summons would almost certainly be slaughtered and eaten. All the High Lord could do was wait—and pray that Callindrill and his companions fled Revelwood before Satansfist encircled them. Two thousand warriors and the Hiltmark of the Warward, two of the leaders of the Lorewardens, one Lord—it was a terrible price to pay for Callindrill's bravado.

But even as he thought this, Mhoram knew that Callindrill was not acting out of bravado. The Lord simply could not endure the thought that Revelwood might perish. Mhoram privately hoped Satansfist would let the tree stand—use it rather than destroy it. But Callindrill had no such hope. Ever since he had faltered during the battle of Doriendor Corishev, he had seen himself as a man who had disgraced his Lord's duty, failed to meet the challenge of the Land's need. He had seen himself as a coward. And now Revelwood, the fairest work of the new Lords, was under attack. Mhoram sighed again, and gently touched the bone of the marrowmeld with his fingers.

In the back of his mind, he was readying his decision.

"Quaan, my friend," he mused grimly, "what have we accomplished in seven years?"

As if this signaled an end to the formal side of

their conversation, Quaan lowered himself into a chair opposite Mhoram, and allowed his square shoulders to sag fractionally. "We have prepared for the siege of Revelstone with all our strength. We have restored the Warward somewhat—the ten Eowards which survived have been increased to twenty-five. We have brought the people of the Center Plains here, out of Satansfist's way. We have stored food, weapons, supplies. The Gray Slayer will require more than a sea of ur-viles and Cavewights to break our hold here."

"He has more, Quaan." Mhoram continued to stroke the strangely revealing face of the *anundivian yajña* bust. "And we have lost the Bloodguard."

"Through no fault of ours." Quaan's pain at the loss made him sound indignant. He had fought side-by-side with the Bloodguard more than any other warrior in the Land. "We could not have known at that time, when the mission to Seareach was given to Korik and the Bloodguard, that the Gray Slayer would attack the Giants with the Illearth Stone. We could not have known that Korik would defeat a Raver and would attempt to bring a piece of the Stone here."

"We could not have known," Mhoram echoed hollowly. After all, the end of his oracular dreams was not a great loss. Despite the myriad terrors he had beheld, he had not glimpsed or guessed at Lord Foul's attack on the Giants in time. "My friend, do you remember what Bannor told us concerning this sculpture?"

"High Lord?"

"He reported that Elena daughter of Lena carved it of Thomas Covenant, Unbeliever and white gold wielder—and that ur-Lord Covenant mistook it for the face of a Bloodguard." Bannor had also reported that Covenant had forced him to tell Elena the name of the Power hidden in the Seventh Ward, so that she could meet the conditions for approaching that Power. But Mhoram was interested for the moment in the resemblance which High Lord Elena had worked into her carving. That had been the starting point, the beginning from which he had traveled to reach his secret knowledge. "She was a true Craftmaster of the bone-sculpting skill. She would not unwittingly have made such confusion possible."

Quaan shrugged.

Mhoran smiled fondly at the Warmark's unwillingness to hazard opinions beyond his competence. "My friend," he said, "I saw the resemblance, but could not decipher it. Ahanna daughter of Hanna aided me. Though she does not know the marrowmeld skill, she has an artist's eye. She perceived the meaning which Elena made here.

"Quaan, the resemblance is that both ur-Lord Covenant the Unbeliever and Bannor of the Bloodguard require absolute answers to their own lives. With the Bloodguard it was their Vow. They demanded of themselves either pure, flawless service forever or no service at all. And the Unbeliever demands—"

"He demands," Quaan said sourly, "that his world is real and ours is not."

Another smile eased Mhoram's somberness, then faded. "This demand for absolute answers is dangerous. Kevin, too, required either victory or destruction."

The Warmark met Mhoram's gaze grimly for a moment before he said, "Then do not resummon the Unbeliever. High Lord, he will lay waste the Land to preserve his 'real' world."

Mhoram cocked an eyebrow at Quaan, and his crooked lips tightened. He knew that the Warmark had never trusted Covenant, yet in this time of crisis any doubt was more important, less answerable. But before he could reply, urgent knuckles pounded at his door. The tight voice of a sentry hissed, "High Lord, come swiftly! High Lord!"

Immediately, Mhoram stood and moved toward the door. As he strode, he banished all his reveries, and brought his senses into focus on the ambience of Revelstone, searching it for the cause of the sentry's distress.

Quaan, reaching the door a step ahead of him, thrust it open. Mhoram hastened out into the bright, round courtyard.

The whole high cavern of the court was clearly illuminated by the pale-yellow light which shone up through the stone floor, but Mhoram did not need to look up to any of the projecting coigns in the cavern walls to see why the sentry had called him. Lord Amatin stood in the center of the floor's inextinguishable light. She faced him with her back to her own chambers, as if she had been on her way toward him when the distress had come upon her.

In her hands she gripped the *lomillialor* communication rod which the Loresraat had given to Revelstone seven years ago.

She looked like a dark shadow against the bright floor, and in her hands the High Wood burned flamelessly, like a slit opening into a furnace. Small cold balls of sparks dropped in spurts from the wood. Mhoram understood instantly that she was receiving a message from whomever it was who held the other communication rod, the one at Revelwood.

He snatched up his long, iron-heeled staff from its tripod outside his door and strode across the courtyard to Amatin. He knew from experience that the sending or receiving of *lomillialor* messages was an exhausting ordeal. Amatin would want his help. She was not physically strong, and knew it; when word of the Despiser's army had reached the Lords, she had transferred to Callindrill her responsibility for Revelwood —hers because of her passionate love for lore—because she believed she lacked the sheer bodily toughness to endure prolonged strain. Yet hidden within her slight waifish frame and grave eyes was a capacity for knowledge, a devotion to study, which no other Lord could match. The High Lord had often thought that she was better equipped and less likely to uncover his secret than anyone else in the Land.

Now, silhouetted by the bright floor of the courtyard, she looked thin and frail—a mere image cast by the power in her hands. Her whole body trembled, and she held the *lomillialor* rod at arm's length as if to keep it as far from herself as possible without releasing it. She started to speak before Mhoram reached her.

"Asuraka," she gasped. "Asuraka speaks." Her voice juddered like a branch in a high wind. "Satansfist.

Fire! Fire! The tree! Ahh!" As she panted the words, she stared at Mhoram in wide dismay as if through him she could see flames chewing at the trunks of Revelwood.

Mhoram stopped within reach of the High Wood and planted his staff like a command on the floor. Pitching his voice to penetrate her transfixion, he said, "Hold fast, Amatin. I hear."

She ducked her head, trying to avoid what she saw, and words spattered past her lips as if someone had hurled a heavy boulder into the waters of her soul. "Fire! The bark burns. The wood burns. The Stone! Leaves, roots, fibers are consumed. Callindrill fights. Fights! Screams—the warriors scream. The south hall burns! Ah, my home!"

Grimly, Mhoram clenched his fist around the center of the *lomillialor* rod. The power of the message stung him, jolted him from head to foot, but he gripped the smooth wood and forced the strength of his will into it. Through it, he reached Amatin, steadied her; and with her support he reversed the flow of power through the High Wood for an instant. Against the flood of Asuraka's emotion, he hissed toward her, "Flee!"

The Staff-Elder heard. Through Amatin's lips, she cried back, "Flee? We cannot flee! Revelwood dies under us. We are surrounded. All the outer branches burn. Two trunks are aflame to their tops. Screams! Screams. Lord Callindrill stands in the *viancome* and fights. The central trunks burn. The net of the *viancome* burns. Callindrill!"

"Water!" Mhoram dashed his words at Asuraka through the communication rod. "Call the rivers! Flood the valley!"

For a moment, the pressure from Asuraka sagged, as if she had turned away from her rod. Mhoram breathed urgently, "Asuraka! Staff-Elder!" He feared that she had fallen in the fire. When she resumed her message, she felt distant, desolate.

"Lord Callindrill called the rivers—earlier. Satansfist turned the flood aside. He—the Illearth Stone—" A new note of horror came into the weak voice which shuddered between Amatin's lips. "He resurrected the old death of Kurash Plenethor. Blasted rock and blood and bones and burned earth rose up through the ground. With old waste he walled Revelwood, and turned the water. How is it possible? Is Time broken? With one stroke of the Stone centuries of healing are rent asunder."

Suddenly, Amatin stiffened in one shrill cry: "Callindrill!"

The next instant, the *lomillialor* fell silent; the power dropped from it like a stricken bird. Lord Amatin staggered, almost fell to her knees. Mhoram caught her forearm to help her keep her feet.

In the abrupt silence, the courtyard felt as dead and cold as a tomb. The atmosphere flocked with echoes of anguish like the noiseless beating of black wings. Mhoram's knuckles where he gripped his staff were strained and white.

Then Amatin shuddered, took hold of herself. The High Lord stepped back and made himself aware of the other people in the court. He could feel their presences. Quaan stood a few paces behind him, and several sentries were scattered around the rim of the shining floor. A handful of spectators watched fearfully from the railed coigns in the walls of the cavity. But the High Lord turned from them all to his left, where Corimini the Eldest of the Loresraat stood with Faer Callindrill-mate. The Eldest held each of Faer's shoulders with an old wrinkled hand. Tears glistened under his heavy eyelids, and his long white beard quivered in grief. But Faer's bluff face was as blank and pale as bone sculpture.

"Is he dead, then, High Lord?" she asked softly.

"Death reaps the beauty of the world," replied Mhoram.

"He burned."

"Satansfist is a Raver. He hates all green growing things. I was a fool to hope that Revelwood might be spared."

"Burned," she repeated.

"Yes, Faer." He could find no words adequate for

the ache in his heart. "He fought to preserve Revel-wood."

"High Lord, there was doubt in him—here." She pointed to her bosom. "He forgot himself."

Mhoram heard the truth in her voice. But he could not let her bare statement pass. "Perhaps. He did not forget the Land."

With a low moan, Lord Amatin turned and hastened painfully back to her chambers. But Faer paid no attention to her. Without meeting Mhoram's intent gaze, she asked, "Is it possible?"

He had no answer for that question. Instead, he replied as if she had repeated Asuraka's cry. "The Law of Death had been broken. Who can say what is possible now?"

"Revelwood," groaned Corimini. His voice trembled with age and sorrow. "He died bravely."

"He forgot himself." Faer moved out of the Eldest's hands as if she had no use for his consolation. Turning away from the High Lord, she walked stiffly back to her rooms. After a moment, Corimini followed, blinking uselessly against his tears.

With an effort, Mhoram loosened his grip on his staff, flexed his clawed fingers.

Firmly, deliberately, he made his decision.

His lips were tight and hard as he faced Quaan. "Summon the Council," he said as if he expected the Warmark to protest. "Invite the Lorewardens, and any of the *rhadhamaerl* and *lillianrill* who desire to come. We can no longer delay."

Quaan did not mistake Mhoram's tone. He saluted the High Lord crisply, and at once began shouting orders to the sentries.

Mhoram did not wait for the Warmark to finish. Taking his staff in his right hand, he strode off the bright floor and down the hallway which separated the apartments of the Lords from the rest of Revel-stone. He nodded to the guards at the far end of the hall, but did not stop to answer their inquiring faces. Everybody he encountered had felt the disturbance of Revelstone's ambience, and their eyes thronged with anxiety. But he ignored them. They would have their answers soon enough. Sternly, he began to climb up through the levels of Lord's Keep toward the Close.

Haste mounted around him as word of Asuraka's message spread through the walls of the city. The usual busyness of life which pulsed in the rock, concerting the rhythms of the Keep's inhabitants, gave way to an impression of focus, as if Revelstone itself were telling the people what had happened and how to respond. In this same way, the mountain rock had helped to order the lives of its denizens for generations, centuries.

Deep in his aching heart, Mhoram knew that even this rock could come to an end. In all the ages of its existence, it had never been besieged. But Lord Foul was powerful enough now. He could tear these massive walls down, reduce the Land's last bastion to rubble. And he would begin the attempt soon.

This, at least, Callindrill had understood clearly. The time had come for desperate hazards. And the High Lord was full to bursting with the damage Satansfist had already done in his long march from Ridjeck Thome. He had chosen his own risk.

He hoped to turn the breaking of the Law of Death to the Land's advantage.

He found himself hurrying, though he knew he would have to wait when he reached the Close. The pressure of decision impelled him. Yet when Trell hailed him from a side passage, he stopped at once, and turned to meet the approach of the big Gravelingas. Trell Atiaran-mate had claims which Mhoram could neither deny nor evade.

Trell was traditionally dressed as a Stonedownor— over his light brown pants he wore a short tunic with his family symbol, a white leaf pattern, woven into its shoulders—and he had the broad, muscular frame which characterized the people of the rock villages; but the Stonedownors were usually short, and Trell was tall. He created an impression of immense physical strength, which was only augmented by his great skill in the *rhadhamaerl* lore.

He approached the High Lord with his head lowered in an attitude of shyness, but Mhoram knew that it was not embarrassment which caused Trell to avoid meeting the eyes of other people. Another explanation glowered behind the thick intensity of Trell's red and gray beard and the graveling ruddiness of his features. Involuntarily, Mhoram shivered as if the wind of winter had found its way through Revelstone to his heart.

Like the other *rhadhamaerl,* Trell had given his whole life to the service of stone. But he had lost his wife and daughter and granddaughter because of Thomas Covenant. The simple sight of Covenant seven years ago had driven him to damage the rock of the Keep; he had gouged his fingers into the granite as if it were nothing more than stiff clay.

He avoided other people's eyes in an effort to conceal the conflicting hate and hurt which knotted themselves within him.

He usually kept to himself, immersing himself in the stone labors of the Keep. But now he accosted the High Lord with an air of grim purpose.

He said, "You go to the Close, High Lord." Despite the severity of his mien, his voice held an odd note of supplication.

"Yes," Mhoram answered.

"Why?"

"Trell Atiaran-mate, you know why. You are not deaf to the Land's need."

Flatly, Trell said, "Do not."

Mhoram shook his head gently. "You know that I must make this attempt."

Trell pushed this statement aside with a jerk of his shoulders, and repeated, "Do not."

"Trell, I am High Lord of the Council of Revelstone. I must do what I can."

"You will denounce—you will denounce the fall of Elena my daughter's daughter."

"Denounce?" Trell's assertion surprised the High Lord. He cocked an eyebrow and waited for the Gravelingas to explain.

"Yes!" Trell averred. His voice sounded awkward, as if in the long, low subterranean songs of his *rhadhamaerl* service he had lost his familiarity with

human speech; and he looked as if he were resisting
an impulse to shout. "Atiaran my wife said—she said
that it is the responsibility of the living to justify the
sacrifices of the dead. Otherwise their deaths have no
meaning. You will undo the meaning Elena earned.
You must not—approve her death."

Mhoram heard the truth in Trell's words. His decision might well imply an affirmation, or at least an
acceptance, of Elena's fall under *Melenkurion* Skyweir; and that would be bitter bread for Trell's distress to swallow. Perhaps this explained the inchoate
fear which he sensed behind Trell's speech. But
Mhoram's duty to the Land bound him straitly. So
that Trell could not mistake him, he said, "I must
make this attempt." Then he added gently, "High
Lord Elena broke the Law of Death. In what way
can I approve?"

Trell's gaze moved around the walls, avoiding the
face of the High Lord, and his heavy hands clutched
his hips as if to prevent themselves from striking out
—as if he did not trust what his hands might do if he
failed to hold them down. "Do you love the Land?" he
said in a thick voice. "You will destroy it."

Then he met Mhoram's gaze, and his sore eyes
gleamed with moist fire. "It would have been better if
I had"— abruptly, his hands tore loose from his sides,
slapped together in front of him, and his shoulders
hunched like a strangler's—"crushed Lena my own
daughter at birth."

"No!" Mhoram affirmed softly. "No." He yearned
to put his arms around Trell, to console the Gravelingas in some way. But he did not know how to untie
Trell's distress; he was unable to loosen his own secret
dilemma. "Hold Peace, Trell," he murmured. "Remember the Oath." He could think of nothing else to
say.

"Peace?" Trell echoed in ridicule or grief. He no
longer seemed to see the High Lord. "Atiaran believed
in Peace. There is no Peace." Turning vaguely from
Mhoram, he walked away down the side passage from
which he had come.

Mhoram stared after him down the passage for a

long moment. Duty and caution told him that he should have warriors assigned to watch the Gravelingas. But he could not bear to torment Trell with such an expression of distrust; that judgment might weaken the last clutch of Trell's self-control. And he, Mhoram, had seen men and women rise to victory from anguish as bad as Trell's.

Yet the Gravelingas had not looked like a man who could wrest new wholeness out of the ruins of his old life. Mhoram was taking a grave risk by not acting in some way. As he started again toward the Close, the weight of his responsibilities bore heavily on him. He did not feel equal to the multitude of dooms he carried.

The Lords possessed nothing of their own with which to fight the long cruel winter that fettered the Land.

He strode down a long, torchlit corridor, climbed a spiral stairway, and approached one of the Lords' private entrances to the Close. Outside the door, he paused to gauge the number of people who had already gathered for the Council, and after a moment he heard Lord Amatin coming up the stair behind him. He waited for her. When she reached the landing where he stood, he saw that her eyes were red-rimmed, her forlorn mouth aggravated by tension. He was tempted to speak to her now, but he decided instead to deal with her feelings before the Council. If he were ever to reveal his secret knowledge, he would first have to prepare the ground for it. With a quiet, sympathetic smile, he opened the door for her and followed her into the Close.

From the door, he and Amatin went down the steps to the Lords' table, which stood below the level of the tiered galleries in the high, round council hall. The hall was lit by four huge, lore-burning *lillianrill* torches set into the walls above the galleries, and by an open pit of graveling in the base of the Close, below and within the wide *C* of the table. Stone chairs for the Lords and their special guests waited around the outer edge of the table, facing in toward the open floor and the graveling pit; and at the head of the table was the high-backed seat of the High Lord.

On the floor of the Close beside the graveling pit was a round stone table with a short silver sword stabbed halfway to the hilt in its center. This was the *krill* of Loric, left where Covenant had driven it seven years ago. In that time, the Lords had found no way to remove it from the stone. They left it in the Close so that anyone who wished to study the *krill* could do so freely. But nothing had changed except the clear white gem around which the guards and haft of the two-edged blade were forged.

When Mhoram and Callindrill had returned from their plunge into Garroting Deep, they had found the gem lightless, dead. The hot fire which Covenant had set within it had gone out.

It stood near the graveling like an icon of the Lords' futility, but Mhoram kept his thoughts away from it. He did not need to look around to learn who was already present in the Close; the perfect acoustics of the hall carried every low noise and utterance to his ears. In the first row of the gallery, above and behind the seats of the Lords, sat warriors, Hafts of the Warward, occupying the former places of the Bloodguard. The two Hearthralls, Tohrm the Gravelingas and Borillar the Hirebrand, sat with Warmark Quaan in their formal positions high in the gallery behind the High Lord's chair. Several Lorewardens had taken seats in tiers above the table; the weary dust of their flight from Revelwood was still on them, but they were too taut with the news of the tree's fall to miss this Council. And with them were virtually all the *lillianrill* of Lord's Keep. The burning of a tree struck at the very hearts of the Hirebrands, and they watched the High Lord's approach with pain in their eyes.

Mhoram reached his seat but did not sit down immediately. As Lord Amatin moved to her place on the right side of the table, he felt a sharp pang at sight of the stone seat which Callindrill should have filled. And he could sense the remembered presence of the others who had occupied the High Lord's chair: Variol, Prothall, Osondrea, and Elena among the new

Lords, Kevin, Loric, and Damelon of the Old. Their individual greatness and courage humbled him, made him realize how small a figure he was to bear such losses and duties. He stood on the brink of the Land's doom without Variol's foresight or Prothall's ascetic strength or Osondrea's dour intransigence or Elena's fire; and he had not power enough to match the frailest Lord in the weakest Council led by Kevin or Loric or Damelon or Berek Heartthew the Lord-Fatherer. Yet none of the remaining Lords could take his place. Amatin lacked physical toughness. Trevor did not believe in his own stature; he felt that he was not the equal of his fellow Lords. And Loerya was torn between her love for the Land and her desire to protect her own family. Mhoram knew that more than once she had almost asked him to release her from her Lordship, so that she could flee with her daughters into the relative sanctuary of the Westron Mountains.

With Callindrill gone, High Lord Mhoram was more alone than he had ever been before.

He had to force himself to pull out his chair and sit down.

He waited for Trevor and Loerya in a private reverie, gathering his fortitude. Finally, the main doors of the Close opened opposite him, and the two Lords started down the broad steps, accompanying Eldest Corimini. He moved with slow difficulty, as if the end of Revelwood had exhausted the last elasticity of his thews, leaving him at the mercy of his age; and Trevor and Loerya supported him gently on either side. They helped him to a chair down the table from Amatin, then walked around and took their places on the High Lord's left.

When they were seated, the Close grew quiet. All talking stopped, and after a brief shuffle of feet and positions, silence filled the warm yellow light of the torches and graveling. Mhoram could hear nothing but the low susurration of hushed breathing. Slowly, he looked around the table and the galleries. Every eye in the chamber was on him. Stiffening himself, he placed his staff flat on the table before him, and stood up.

"Friends and servants of the Land," he said steadily, "be welcome to the Council of Lords. I am Mhoram son of Variol, High Lord by the choice of the Council. There are dire matters upon us, and we must take action against them. But first we must welcome the Lorewardens of the Loresraat. Corimini, Eldest of the Loresraat, be at home in Lord's Keep with all your people. You have brought the great school of lore safely to Revelstone. How may we honor you?"

Corimini rose infirmly to his feet as if to meet the High Lord's salutation, but the diffusion of his gaze showed that his mind was elsewhere. "Faer," he began in a tremulous old voice, "Faer begs me to apologize for the absence of Callindrill her husband. He will be unable to attend the Council." Dislocation gathered in his tone while he spoke, and his voice trailed off as if he had forgotten what he meant to say. Slowly, his thoughts slipped out of contact with his situation. As he stood before the Council, the power of the lore which had preserved him for so long from the effects of age seemed to fail within him. After a moment, he sat down, murmuring aimlessly to himself, wandering in his mind like a man striving to comprehend a language he no longer knew. At last he found the word, "Revelwood." He repeated it several times, searching to understand it. Softly he began to weep.

Tears burned the backs of Mhoram's eyes. With a quick gesture he sent two of the Lorewardens to Corimini's aid. They lifted him from his seat and bore him between them up the stairs toward the high wooden doors. "Take him to the Healers," Mhoram said thickly. "Find Peace for him. He has served the Land with courage and devotion and wisdom for more years than any other now living."

The Lords came to their feet, and at once all the people in the Close stood. Together, they touched their right hands to their hearts, then extended the palms toward Corimini in a traditional salute. "Hail, Corimini," they said, "Eldest of the Loresraat. Be at Peace."

The two Lorewardens took Corimini from the

Close, and the doors shut behind them. Sadly, the people in the galleries reseated themselves. The Lords looked toward Mhoram with mourning in their eyes, and Loerya said stiffly, "This is an ill omen."

Mhoram gripped himself with a stern hand. "All omens are ill in these times. Despite is abroad in the Land. For that reason we are Lords. The Land would not require us if there were no harm at work against it."

Without meeting Mhoram's gaze, Amatin replied, "If that is our purpose, then we do not serve it." Her anger and pain combined to give her a tone of defiance. She held her palms flat on the table and watched them as if she were trying to push them through the stone. "Only Callindrill of all the Lords lifted his hand in Revelwood's defense. He burned in my place."

"No!" the High Lord snapped at once. He had hoped to deal with the issues before the Council on other terms, but now that Amatin had spoken, he could not back away. "No, Lord Amatin. You cannot take upon your shoulders responsibility for the death of Callindrill Faer-mate. He died in his own place, by his own choice. When you believed that you were no longer the Lord best suited to watch over Revelwood, you expressed your belief to the Council. The Council accepted your belief and asked Lord Callindrill to take that burden upon himself.

"At the same time, the Council decided that the defenders of the Land should not spend themselves in a costly and bootless battle for Revelwood." As he spoke, the tightness around his eyes expressed how hard, how poignantly hard, that decision had been to make. "The home of the Loresraat was not made for war, and could not be well defended. The Council decided for the sake of the Land that we must save our strength, put it to its best use here. Callindrill chose" —the authority of Mhoram's tone faltered for an instant—"Lord Callindrill Faer-mate chose otherwise. There is no blame for you in this."

He saw the protest in her eyes and hastened to answer her. He did not want to hear her thought uttered aloud. "Further, I tell you that there is no blame for us in the wisdom or folly, victory or defeat, of the way we have elected to defend the Land. We are not the Creators of the Earth. Its final end is not on our heads. We are creations, like the Land itself. We are accountable for nothing but the purity of our service. When we have given our best wisdom and our utterest strength to the defense of the Land, then no voice can raise accusation against us. Life or death, good or ill —victory or destruction—we are not required to solve these riddles. Let the Creator answer for the doom of his creation."

Amatin stared at him hotly, and he could feel her probing the estranged, secret place in his heart. Speaking barely above a whisper, she said, "Do you blame Callindrill then? There is no 'best wisdom' in his death."

The misdirection of her effort to understand him pained the High Lord, but he answered her openly. "You are not deaf to me, Lord Amatin. I loved Callindrill Faer-mate like a brother. I have no wisdom or strength or willingness to blame him."

"You are the High Lord. What does your wisdom teach you?"

"I am the High Lord," Mhoram affirmed simply. "I have no time for blame."

Abruptly, Loerya joined the probing. "And if there is no Creator? Or if the creation is untended?"

"Then who is there to reproach us? We provide the meaning of our own lives. If we serve the Land purely to the furthest limit of our abilities, what more can we ask of ourselves?"

Trevor answered, "Victory, High Lord. If we fail, the Land itself reproaches us. It will be made waste. We are its last preservers."

The force of this thrust smote Mhoram. He found that he still lacked the courage to retort nakedly, *Better failure than desecration.* Instead, he turned the thrust with a wry smile and said, "The last, Lord Trevor? No. The *Haruchai* yet live within their mountain fastness. In their way, they know the name of the Earthpower more surely than any Lord. Ramen and Ranyhyn yet live. Many people of the South and North Plains yet live. Many of the Unfettered yet live. Caerroil Wildwood, Forestal of Garroting Deep, has not passed away. And somewhere beyond the Sunbirth Sea is the homeland of the Giants—yes, and of the *Elohim* and *Bhrathair,* of whom the Giants sang. They will resist Lord Foul's hold upon the Earth."

"But the Land, High Lord! The Land will be lost! The despiser will wrack it from end to end."

At once Mhoram breathed intensely, "By the Seven! Not while one flicker of love or faith remains alive!"

His eyes burned into Trevor's until the Lord's protest receded. Then he turned to Loerya. But in her he could see the discomfortable fear for her daughters at work, and he refrained from touching her torn feelings. Instead, he looked toward Amatin and was relieved to see that much of her anger had fallen away. She regarded him with an expression of hope. She had found something in him that she needed. Softly, she said, "High Lord, you have discovered a way in which we may act against this doom."

The High Lord tightened his hold upon himself. "There is a way." Raising his head, he addressed all the people in the Close. "My friends, Satansfist Raver has burned Revelwood. Trothgard is now in his hands. Soon he will begin to march upon us. Scant days remain before the siege of Revelstone begins. We can no longer delay." The gold in his eyes flared as he said, "We must attempt to summon the Unbeliever."

At this, a stark silence filled the Close. Mhoram could feel waves of surprise and excitement and dread pouring down on him from the galleries. Warmark Quaan's passionate objection struck across his shoulders. But he waited in the silence until Lord Loerya found her voice to say, "That is impossible. The Staff of Law has been lost. We have no means for such a summoning." The soft timbre of her voice barely covered its hard core.

Still Mhoram waited, looking toward the other Lords for answers to Loerya's claim. After a long moment, Trevor said hesitantly, "But the Law of Death has been broken."

"And if the Staff has been destroyed," Amatin added quickly, "then the Earthpower which it held and focused has been released upon the Land. Perhaps it is accessible to us."

"And we must make the attempt," said Mhoram. "For good or ill, the Unbeliever is inextricably linked to the Land's doom. If he is not here, he cannot defend the Land."

"Or destroy it!" Quaan rasped.

Before Mhoram could respond, Hearthrall Borillar was on his feet. He said in a rush, "The Unbeliever will save the Land."

Quaan growled, "This is odd confidence, Hearthrall."

"He will save," Borillar said as if he were surprised at his own temerity. Seven years ago, when he had met Covenant, he had been the youngest Hirebrand ever to take the office of Hearthrall. He had been acutely aware of his inexperience, and he was still deferential—a fact which amused his friend and fellow Hearthrall, Tohrm. "When I met the Unbeliever, I was young and timid—afraid." Tohrm grinned impishly at the implication that Borillar was no longer young and timid. "Ur-Lord Covenant spoke kindly to me."

He sat down again, blushing in embarrassment. But no one except Tohrm smiled, and Tohrm's smile was always irrepressible. It expressed only amused fondness, not mockery. The pitch of Borillar's conviction seemed to reproach the doubts in the Close. When Lord Loerya spoke again, her tone had changed. With a searching look at the young Hearthrall, she said, "How shall we make this attempt?"

Mhoram gravely nodded his thanks to Borillar, then turned back to the Lords. "I will essay the summoning. If my strength fails, aid me." The Lords nodded mutely. With a final look around the Close, he sat down, bowed his head, and opened his mind to the melding of the Lords.

He did so, knowing that he would have to hold back

part of himself, prevent Trevor and Loerya and Amatin from seeing into his secret. He was taking a great risk. He needed the consolation, the sharing of strength and support, which a complete mind melding could give; yet any private weakness might expose the knowledge he withheld. And in the melding his fellow Lords could see that he did withhold something. Therefore it was an expensive rite. Each meld drained him because he could only protect his secret by giving fortitude rather than receiving it. But he believed in the meld. Of all the lore of the new Lords, only this belonged solely to them; the rest had come to them through the Wards of Kevin Landwaster. And when it was practiced purely, melding brought the health and heart of any Lord to the aid of all the others.

As long as the High Lord possessed any pulse of life or thew of strength, he could not refuse to share them.

At last, the contact was broken. For a moment, Mhoram felt that he was hardly strong enough to stand; the needs of the other Lords, and their concern for him, remained on his shoulders like an unnatural burden. But he understood himself well enough to know that in some ways he did not have the ability to surrender. Instead, he had an instinct for absolute exertions which frightened him whenever he thought of the Ritual of Desecration. After a momentary rest, he rose to his feet and took up his staff. Bearing it like a standard, he walked around the table to the stairs and started down toward the open floor around the graveling pit.

As Mhoram reached the floor, Tohrm came down out of the gallery to join him. The Gravelingas's eyes were bright with humor, and he grinned as he said, "You will need far sight to behold the Unbeliever." Then he winked as if this were a jest. "The gulf between worlds is dark, and darkness withers the heart. I will provide more light."

The High Lord smiled his thanks, and the Hearthrall stepped briskly to one side of the graveling pit. He bent toward the fire-stones, and at once seemed to forget the other people in the Close. Without another look at his audience, he softly began to sing.

In a low rocky language known only to those who shared the *rhadhamaerl* lore, he hymned an invocation to the fire-stones, encouraging them, stoking them, calling to life their latent power. And the red-gold glow of the graveling reflected like a response from his face. After a moment, Mhoram could see the brightness growing. The reddish hue faded from the gold; the gold turned purer, whiter, hotter; and the new-earth aroma of the graveling rose up like incense in the Close.

In silence, the three Lords stood, and the rest of the people joined them in a mute expression of respect for the *rhadhamaerl* and the Earthpower. Before them, the radiance of the pit mounted until Tohrm himself was pale in the light.

With a slow, stately movement, High Lord Mhoram lifted his staff, held it in both hands level with his forehead.

The summoning song of the Unbeliever began to run in his mind as he focused his thoughts on the power of his staff. One by one, he eliminated the people in the Close, and then the Close itself, from his awareness. He poured himself into the straight, smooth wood of his staff until he was conscious of nothing but the song and the light—and the illimitable implications of the Earthpower beating like ichor in the immense mountain-stone around him. Then he gathered as many strands of the pulse as he could hold together in the hands of his staff, and rode them outward through the warp and weft of Revelstone's existence. And as he rode, he sang to himself:

There is wild magic graven in every rock,
contained for white gold to unleash or control—
gold, rare metal, not born of the Land,
nor ruled, limited, subdued
by the Law with which the Land was created—
but keystone rather, pivot, crux
for the anarchy out of which Time was made.

The strands carried him out through the malevolent
wind, so that his spirit shivered against gusts of spite;
but his consciousness passed beyond them swiftly,
passed beyond all air and wood and water and stone
until he seemed to be spinning through the quintessential fabric of which actuality was made. For an interval without dimension in time and space, he lost
track of himself. He felt that he was floating beyond
the limits of creation. But the song and the light held
him, steadied him. Soon his thoughts pointed like a
compass to the lodestone of the white gold.

Then he caught a glimpse of Thomas Covenant's
ring. It was unmistakable; the Unbeliever's presence
covered the chaste circlet like an aura, bound it,
sealed up its power. And the aura itself ached with
anguish.

High Lord Mhoram reached toward that presence
and began to sing:

> Be true, Unbeliever—
> Answer the call.
> Life is the Giver:
> Death ends all.
> The promise is truth,
> And banes disperse
> With promise kept:
> But soul's deep curse
> On broken faith
> And faithless thrall,
> For doom of darkness
> Covers all.
> Be true, Unbeliever—
> Answer the call.
> Be true.

He caught hold of Covenant with his song and started
back toward the Close.

The efficacy of the song took much of the burden
from him, left him free to return swiftly to himself.
As he opened his eyes to the dazzling light, he almost
fell to his knees. Sudden exhaustion washed over him;
he felt severely attenuated, as if his soul had been

stretched to cover too great a distance. For a time, he stood strengthless, even forgetting to sing. But the other Lords had taken up the song for him, and in the place of his power their staffs vitalized the summoning.

When his eyes regained their sight, he beheld Thomas Covenant, Unbeliever and white gold wielder, standing half substantial in the light before him.

But the apparition came no closer, did not incarnate itself. Covenant remained on the verge of physical presence; he refused to cross over. In a voice that barely existed, he cried, "Not now! Let me go!"

The sight of the Unbeliever's suffering shocked Mhoram. Covenant was starving, he desperately needed rest, he had a deep and seriously untended wound on his forehead. His whole body was bruised and battered as if he had been stoned, and one side of his mouth was caked with ugly blood. But as bad as his physical injuries were, they paled beside his psychic distress. Appalled resistance oozed from him like the sweat of pain, and a fierce fire of will held him unincarnate. As he fought the completion of his summoning, he reminded Mhoram forcibly of *dukkha,* the poor Waynhim upon which Lord Foul had practiced so many torments with the Illearth Stone. He resisted as if the Lords were coercing him into a vat of acid and virulent horror.

"Covenant!" Mhoram groaned. "Oh, Covenant." In his fatigue, he feared that he would not be able to hold back his weeping. "You are in hell. Your world is a hell."

Covenant flinched. The High Lord's voice seemed to buffet him physically. But an instant later he demanded again, "Send me back! She needs me!"

"We need you also," murmured Mhoram. He felt frail, sinewless, as if he lacked the thews and ligaments to keep himself erect. He understood now why he had been able to summon Covenant without the Staff of Law, and that understanding was like a hole of grief knocked in the side of his being. He seemed to feel himself spilling away.

"She needs me!" Covenant repeated. The effort of

speech made blood trickle from his mouth. "Mhoram, can't you hear me?"

That appeal touched something in Mhoram. He was the High Lord; he could not, must not, fall short of the demands placed upon him. He forced himself to meet Covenant's feverish gaze.

"I hear you, Unbeliever," he said. His voice became stronger as he spoke. "I am Mhoram son of Variol, High Lord by the choice of the Council. We need you also. I have summoned you to help us face the Land's last need. The prophecy which Lord Foul the Despiser gave you to pronounce upon the Land has come to pass. If we fall, he will have the command of life and death in his hand, and the universe will be a hell forever. Ur-Lord Covenant, help us! It is I, Mhoram son of Variol, who beseech you."

The words struck Covenant in flurries. He staggered and quailed under the sound of Mhoram's voice. But his aghast resistance did not falter. When he regained his balance, he shouted again, "She needs me, I tell you! That rattlesnake is going to bite her! If you take me now, I can't help her."

In the back of his mind, Mhoram marveled that Covenant could so grimly deny the summoning without employing the power of his ring. Yet that capacity for refusal accorded with Mhoram's secret knowledge. Hope and fear struggled in the High Lord, and he had difficulty keeping his voice steady.

"Covenant—my friend—please hear me. Hear the Land's need in my voice. We cannot hold you. You have the white gold—you have the power to refuse us. The Law of Death does not bind you. Please hear me. I will not require much time. After I have spoken, if you still choose to depart—I will recant the summoning. I will—I will tell you how to make use of your white gold to deny us."

Again, Covenant recoiled from the assault of sound. But when he had recovered, he did not repeat his demand. Instead, he said harshly, "Talk fast. This is my only chance—the only chance to get out of a delusion is at the beginning. I've got to help her."

High Lord Mhoram clenched himself, mustered all

his love and fear for the Land, put it into his voice. "Ur-Lord, seven years have passed since we stood together on Gallows Howe. In that time we have recovered from some of our losses. But since—since the Staff of Law was lost—the Despiser has been much more free. He has built a new army as vast as the sea, and has marched against us. Already he has destroyed Revelwood. Satansfist Raver has burned Revelwood and slain Lord Callindrill. In a very few days, the siege of Lord's Keep will begin.

"But that does not complete the tale of our trouble. Seven years ago, we might have held Revelstone against any foe for seasons together. Even without the Staff of Law, we might have defended ourselves well. But—my friend, hear me—we have lost the Bloodguard."

Covenant cowered as if he were being pounded by a rockfall, but Mhoram did not stop. "When Korik of the Bloodguard led his mission to the Giants of Seareach, great evils claimed the lives of the Lords Hyrim and Shetra. Without them—" Mhoram hesitated. He remembered Covenant's friendship with the Giant, Saltheart Foamfollower. He could not bear to torment Covenant by telling him of the Giants' bloody fate. "Without them to advise him, Korik and two comrades captured a fragment of the Illearth Stone. He did not recognize his danger. The three Bloodguard bore the fragment with them, thinking to carry it to Lord's Keep.

"But the Illearth Stone is a terrible wrong in the Land. The three Bloodguard were not forewarned— and the Stone enslaved them. Under its power, they bore their fragment to Foul's Creche. They believed that they would fight the Despiser. But he made them his own." Again, Mhoram forbore to tell the whole story. He could not say to Covenant that the Bloodguard Vow had been subtly betrayed by the breaking of the Law of Death—or that the fine metal of the Bloodguard rectitude had been crucially tarnished when Covenant had forced Bannor to reveal the name of the Power of Command. "Then he"—Mhoram still winced whenever he remembered what had happened—"he sent the three to attack Revelstone. Korik, Sill, and Doar marched here with green fire in their eyes and Corruption in their hearts. They killed many farmers and warriors before we comprehended what had been done to them.

"Then First Mark Bannor and Terrel and Runnik of the Bloodguard went to do battle with the three. They slew Korik and Sill and Doar their comrades, and brought their bodies to the Keep. In that way, we found"—Mhoram swallowed thickly—"we found that Lord Foul had cut off the last two fingers from the right hand of each of the three."

Covenant cried out in pain, but Mhoram drove his point home hoarsely. "He damaged each Bloodguard to resemble you."

"Stop!" Covenant groaned. "Stop. I can't stand it."

Still the High Lord continued. "When First Mark Bannor saw how Korik and his comrades had been corrupted despite their Vow, he and all the Bloodguard abandoned their service. They returned to the mountain home of the *Haruchai*. He said that they had been conquered by Corruption, and could no longer serve any Vow.

"My friend, without them—without the Staff of Law—without any immense army or dour-handed allies—we will surely fall. Only the wild magic can now come between us and Lord Foul's hunger."

As Mhoram finished, Covenant's eyes looked as bleak as a wilderland. The heat of his fever seemed to make any tears impossible. His resistance sagged briefly, and for an instant he almost allowed his translation into the Close to be completed. But then he raised his head to look at other memories. His refusal stiffened; he moved back until he almost vanished in the bright graveling light. "Mhoram, I can't," he said as distantly as if he were choking. "I can't. The snake— That little girl is all alone. I'm responsible for her. There's no one to help the child but me."

From high in the opposite gallery, Mhoram felt a surge of anger as Quaan's old indignation at Covenant flared into speech. "By the Seven!" he barked. "He speaks of responsibility." Quaan had watched himself become old and helpless to save the Land, while Covenant neither aged nor acted. He spoke with a warrior's sense of death, a warrior's sense of the value in sacrificing a few lives to save many. "Covenant, you are responsible for us!"

The Unbeliever suffered under Quaan's voice as he did under Mhoram's, but he did not turn to face the Warmark. He met Mhoram's gaze painfully and answered, "Yes, I know. I know. I am—responsible. But she needs me. There's no one else. She's part of my world, my real world. You're—not so real now. I can't give you anything now." His face twisted frantically, and his resistance mounted until it poured from him like agony. "Mhoram, if I don't get back to her she is going to die."

The desolate passion of Covenant's appeal wrung Mhoram. Unconsciously, he gnawed his lips, trying to control with physical pain the strain of his conflicting compassions. His whole life, all his long commitments, seemed rent within him. His love for the Land urged him to deny the Unbeliever, to struggle now as if he were wrestling for possession of Covenant's soul. But from the same wellspring of his self arose an opposite urge, a refusal to derogate Covenant's sovereignty, Covenant's right to choose his own fate. For a time, the High Lord hesitated, trapped in the contradiction. Then slowly he lifted his head and spoke to the people in the Close as well as to Thomas Covenant.

"No one may be compelled to fight the Despiser. He is resisted willingly, or not at all. Unbeliever, I release you. You turn from us to save life in your own world. We will not be undone by such motives. And if darkness should fall upon us, still the beauty of the Land endures. If we are a dream—and you the dreamer— then the Land is imperishable, for you will not forget.

"Be not afraid, ur-Lord Thomas Covenant. Go in Peace."

He felt a pressure of protest from Lord Loerya and some of the other spectators, but he overruled them with a commanding gesture. One by one, the Lords withdrew the power of their staffs while Tohrm lowered the graveling fire. Covenant began to fade as if he were dissolving in the abyss beyond the arch of Time.

Then High Lord Mhoram recollected his promise to reveal the secret of the wild magic. He did not know whether or not Covenant could still hear him, but he whispered after the fading form, *"You* are the white gold."

A moment later, he knew that the Unbeliever was gone. All sense of resistance and power had left the air, and the light of the graveling had declined to a more normal level. For the first time since the summoning began, Mhoram saw the shapes and faces of the people around him. But the sight did not last. Tears blinded him, and he leaned weakly on his staff as if only its stern wood could uphold him.

He was full of grief over the strange ease with which he had summoned the Unbeliever. Without the Staff of Law, he should not have been able to call Covenant alone; yet he had succeeded. He knew why. Covenant had been so vulnerable to the summons because he was dying.

Through his sorrow, he heard Trevor say, "High Lord—the *krill*—the gem of the *krill* came to life. It burned as it did when the Unbeliever first placed it within the table."

Mhoram blinked back his tears. Leaning heavily on his staff, he moved to the table. In its center, Loric's *krill* stood like a dead cross—as opaque and fireless as if it had lost all possibility of light. A rage of grief came over Mhoram. With one hand, he grasped the hilt of the silver sword.

A fleeting blue gleam flickered across its gem, then vanished.

"It has no life now," he said dully.

Then he left the Close and went to the sacred enclosure to sing for Covenant and Callindrill and the Land.

THREE: The Rescue

A cold wind blew through Covenant's soul as he struggled up out of the rock. It chilled him as if the marrow of his bones had been laid bare to an exhalation of cruel ice—cruel and sardonic, tinged with that faint yet bottomless green travail which was the antithesis of green things growing. But slowly it left him, slid away into another dimension. He became more conscious of the stone. Its granite impenetrability thickened around him; he began to feel that he was suffocating.

He flailed his arms and legs, tried to reach toward the surface. But for a time he could not even be sure that his limbs were moving. Then a series of jolts began to hurt his joints. He sensed through his elbows and knees that he was thrashing against something hard.

He was pounding his arms and legs at the hillside. Behind the muffled thuds and slaps he made, he could hear running water. The sun shone objectively somewhere beyond him. He jerked up his head.

At first, he could not orient himself. A stream splashed vividly across his sight; he felt that he was peering at it from above, that the slope down which it ran was canted impossibly under him. But at last he realized that he was not looking downward. He lay horizontally across the slope. The hill rose above him on the right, dropped away on the left.

He turned his head to search for the girl and the snake.

His eyes refused to focus. Something pale gleamed in front of his face, prevented him from seeing down the hill.

A thin, childish voice near him said, "Mister? Are you okay, mister? You fell down."

He was trying to see too far away. With an effort, he screwed his gaze closer, and at last found himself staring from a distance of a few inches at a bare shin. In the sunlight, it gleamed as pure and pale as if it had been anointed with chrism. But already it showed a slight swelling. And in the center of the swelling were two small red marks like paired pinpricks.

"Mister?" the child said again. "Are you okay? The snake bit me. My leg hurts."

The frigid winter he had left behind seemed to leap at him from the depths of his mind. He began to shiver. But he forced himself to disregard the cold, bent all his attention toward those two red fang marks. Without taking his eyes off them, he climbed into a sitting position. His bruises groaned at him, and his forehead throbbed sickly, but he ignored all the pain, discounted it as if it had nothing to do with him. His trembling hands drew the little girl toward him.

Snakebite, he thought numbly. How do you treat snakebite?

"All right," he said, then stopped. His voice shook unreassuringly, and his throat felt too dry to be controlled. He did not seem to know any comforting words. He swallowed hoarsely and hugged the child's thin bones to his chest. "All right. You're going to be all right. I'm here. I'll help you."

He sounded grotesque to himself—ghoulish and useless. The cut in his lip and gum interfered with his articulation. But he ignored that, too. He could not afford the energy to worry about such things. A haze of fever parched his thoughts, and he needed all his strength to fight it, recollect the treatment for snakebite.

He stared at the fang marks until he remembered.

Stop the circulation, he said to himself as if he were stupid. Cut. Get out the poison.

Jerking himself into movement, he fumbled for his penknife.

When he got it out, he dropped it on the ground beside him, and hunted through the debris which littered his brain for something which he could use as a tourniquet. His belt would not do, he had no way to fasten it tightly enough. The child's dress had no belt. Her shoelaces did not look long enough.

"My leg hurts," she said plaintively. "I want my mommy."

"Where is she?" muttered Covenant.

"That way." She pointed vaguely downstream. "A long way. Daddy spanked me and I snuck away."

Covenant clutched the girl with one arm to keep her from moving, and thus hastened the spread of the venom. With his free hand, he tore at the lace of his left boot. But it was badly frayed and snapped in his hand. Hellfire! he groaned in chagrin. He was taking too long. Trembling, he started on the right bootlace.

After a moment, he succeeded in removing it intact.

"All right," he said unclearly. "I've got—got to do something about that bite. First I have to tie off your leg—so the poison won't spread. Then I have to cut your leg a little. That way the poison can get out, and it won't hurt you so much." He strove to sound calm. "Are you brave today?"

She replied solemnly, "Daddy spanked me and I didn't cry. I ran away." He heard no trace of her earlier terror.

"Good girl," he mumbled. He could not delay any longer; the swelling over her skin had increased noticeably, and a faint, blackish hue had started to stain her pale flesh. He wrapped his bootlace around her wounded leg above the knee.

"Stand on your other leg, so this one can relax."

When she obeyed, he pulled the lace tight until she let out a low gasp of pain. Then he tied it off. "Good girl," he said again. "You're very brave today."

With uncertain hands, he picked up his penknife and opened it.

For a time, he quailed at the prospect of cutting her. He was shivering too badly; the sun's warmth went nowhere near the chill in his bones. But the livid fang marks compelled him. Gently, he lifted the child and seated her on his lap. With his left hand, he raised her leg until its swelling was only ten or twelve inches from his face. His penknife he gripped inadequately with the two fingers and thumb of his right hand.

"If you don't look, you might not even feel it," he said, and hoped he was not lying.

She acted as if the mere presence of an adult banished all her fears. "I'm not afraid," she replied proudly. "I'm brave today." But when Covenant turned so that his right shoulder came between her face and the sight of her leg, she caught her hands in his shirt and pressed her face against him.

In the back of his mind, he could hear Mhoram saying, *We have lost the Bloodguard. Lost the Bloodguard. Lost.* Oh, Bannor! he moaned silently. Was it that bad?

He clenched his teeth until his jaws ached, and the wound on his forehead pounded. The pain steadied him. It held him like a spike driven through his brain, affixing him to the task of the fang marks.

With an abrupt movement, he slashed twice, cut an X across the swelling between the two red marks.

The child let out a low cry, and went rigid, clinging to him fervidly.

For an instant he stared in horror at the violent red blood which welled out of the cuts and ran across the pale leg. Then he dropped the knife as if it had burned him. Gripping her leg in both hands, he bent his mouth to the fang marks and sucked.

The strain of stretching his lips tight over her shin made his mouth wound sting, and his blood mingled with hers as it trickled across the darkening stain of the swelling. But he ignored that as well. With all his strength, he sucked at the cuts. When he stopped to breathe, he rubbed the child's leg, trying to squeeze all her blood toward the cuts. Then he sucked again.

A nauseating dizziness caught hold of his head and made it spin. He stopped, afraid that he would faint. "All right," he panted. "I'm finished. You're going to be all right." After a moment, he realized that the child was whimpering softly into the back of his shoulder. Quickly, he turned, put his arms around her, hugged her to him. "You're going to be all right," he repeated thickly. "I'll take you to your mommy now." He did not believe that he had the strength to stand, much less to carry her any distance at all.

But he knew that she still needed treatment; he could hardly have removed all the venom. And the cuts he had inflicted would have to be tended. She could not afford his weakness. With an effort that almost undid him, he lurched painfully to his feet, and stood listing on the hillside as if he were about to capsize.

The child sniffled miserably in his arms. He could not bear to look at her, for fear that she would meet his gaze with reproach. He stared down the hill while he struggled to scourge or beg himself into a condition of fortitude.

Through her tears, the child said, "Your mouth's bleeding."

"Yes, I know," he mumbled. But that pain was no worse than the ache in his forehead, or the hurt of his bruises. And all of it was only pain. It was temporary; it would soon fall under the pall of his leprosy. The ice in his bones made him feel that the numbness of his hands and feet was already spreading. Pain was no excuse for weakness.

Slowly, he unlocked one knee, let his weight start forward. Like a poorly articulated puppet, he lumbered woodenly down the hillside.

By the time he reached the tree—it stood black and straight like a signpost indicating the place where the child had been bitten—he had almost fallen three times. His boots were trying to trip him; without laces to hold them to his feet, they cluttered every step he took. For a moment, he leaned against the tree, trying to steady himself. Then he kicked off his boots. He

did not need them. His feet were too numb to feel
the damage of hiking barefoot.

"You ready?" he breathed. "Here we go." But he
was not sure he made any sound. In the fever which
clouded his thoughts, he found himself thinking that
life was poorly designed; burdens were placed on the
wrong people. For some obscure reason, he believed
that in Bannor's place he could have found some other
answer to Korik's corruption. And Bannor would have
been equal many times over to the physical task of
saving this child.

Then he remembered that Mhoram had not told
him any news of the Giants in connection with Korik's
mission. Sparked by the association, a vision of Gallows Howe cut through his haze. He saw again a
Giant dangling from the gibbet of the Forestal.

What had happened to the Giants?

Gaping mutely as if the woods and the stream and
the little girl in his arms astonished him, he pushed
away from the black tree and began shambling along
Righters Creek in the general direction of the town.

As he moved, he forced open his caked lips to cry
aloud, "Help!"

The child had said that her parents were a long way
away, but he did not know what distances meant to
her. He did not know whether or not her parents were
anywhere near the Creek. He did not even know how
far he was from Haven Farm; the whole previous night
was a blank hurt in his mind. But the banks of the
stream offered him the most accessible route toward
town, and he could think of nothing to do but move
in that direction. The girl's pain was increasing. Her
leg was blacker every time he looked at it, and she
winced and whimpered at every jolt of his stiff stride.
At intervals she moaned for her parents, and every
moan made him gasp out like the jab of a goad,
"Help!"

But his voice seemed to have no authority, no
carrying power; it dropped into silence after him like
a stillborn. And the effort of shouting aggravated the
injury to his mouth. Soon he could feel his lip swelling
like the girl's leg, growing dark and taut and heavy

with pain. He hugged her closer to him and croaked in grim, forlorn insistence, "Help! Help me!"

Gradually, the heat of the sun made him sweat. It stung his forehead until his eyes blurred. But it did not touch the cold in his bones. His shivering mounted. Dizziness dismembered his balance, made him reel through the woods as if he were being driven by a tattered gale. Whenever he stepped on a pointed rock or branch, it gouged far enough up into his arches to hurt him. Several times, his joints folded sharply, and he plunged to his knees. But each time, the dark wound he carried pulled him upright again, and sent him forward, mumbling past his thick lip, "Help me."

His own swelling seemed to take over his face like a tumor. Hot lances of pain thrust from it through his head every time the ground jarred him. As time passed, he could feel his heart itself trembling, quivering between each beat as it labored to carry the strain. The haze of his fever thickened until at odd moments he feared that he had lost his sight. In the blur, he quailed away from the dazzles of sunlight which sprang at him off the stream; but when the creek passed through shadows, it looked so cool and healing that he could hardly restrain himself from stumbling into it, burying his face in its anodyne.

Yet all the while he knew he could not deviate from the strait path of his trek. If he failed to find help for the child, then everything he had already done for her would be useless, bereft of meaning. He could not stop. Her wound would not tolerate his futility. He saw too much of his lost son Roger in her bare shin. Despite the nails of pain which crucified him, he lurched onward.

Then in the distance he heard shouts, like people wailing for someone lost. He jerked to a swaying halt on stiff legs, and tried to look around. But he seemed to have lost control of his head. It wobbled vainly on his neck, as if the weight of his swelling threw it out of joint, and he was unable to face it in the direction of the shouts.

In his arms, the girl whimpered pitifully, "Mommy. Daddy."

He fought his black tight pain to frame the word, *Help*. But no sound came between his lips. He forced his vocal cords to make some kind of noise.

"Help me."

It was no louder than a whisper.

A sound like hoarse sobs shook him, but he could not tell whether they came from him or from the girl. Weakly, almost blindly, he straightened his arms, lifted the child outward as if he were offering her to the shouts.

They became a woman's voice and took on words. "Karen! Here she is! Over here! Oh, Karen! my baby!" Running came toward him through the leaves and branches; it sounded like the blade of a winter wind cutting at him from the depths of his fever. At last he was able to see the people. A woman hurried down the side of a hill, and a man ran anxiously after her. "Karen!" the woman cried.

The child reached out toward the woman and sobbed, "Mommy! Mommy!"

An instant later, the burden was snatched from Covenant's arms. "Karen. Oh, my baby," the woman moaned as she hugged the child. "We were so frightened. Why did you run away? Are you all right?" Without a glance at Covenant, she said, "Where did you find her? She ran away this morning, and we've been frightened half to death." As if this needed some explanation, she went on, "We're camping over there a ways. Dave has Good Friday off, and we decided to camp out. We never thought she would run away."

The man caught up with her, and she started speaking to the child again. "Oh, you naughty, naughty girl. Are you all right? Let me look at you."

The girl kept sobbing in pain and relief as the woman held her at arm's length to inspect her. At once, the woman saw the tourniquet and the swelling and the cuts. She gave a low scream, and looked at Covenant for the first time.

"What happened?" she demanded. "What've you done to her?" Suddenly, she stopped. A look of horror stretched her face. She backed away toward the man and screamed at him, "Dave! It's that leper! That Covenant!"

"What?" the man gasped. Righteous indignation rushed up in him. "You bastard!" he spat belligerently, and started toward Covenant.

Covenant thought that the man was going to hit him; he seemed to feel the blow coming at him from a great distance. Watching it, he lost his balance, stumbled backward a step, and sat down heavily. Red pain flooded across his sight. When it cleared, he was vaguely surprised to find that he was not being kicked. But the man had stopped a dozen feet away; he stood with his fists clenched, trying not to show that he was afraid to come closer.

Covenant struggled to speak, explain that the child still needed help. But a long, stunned moment passed before he was able to dredge words past his lips. Then he said in a tone of detachment completely at variance with the way he looked and felt, "Snakebite. Timber rattler. Help her."

The effort exhausted him; he could not go on. He lapsed into silence, and sat still as if he were hopelessly waiting for an avalanche to fall on him. The man and woman began to recede from him, lose solidity, as if they were dissolving in the acid of his prostration. Vaguely, he heard the child moan, "The snake bit me, Mommy. My leg hurts."

He realized that he still had not seen the child's face. But he had lost his chance. He had exercised too strenuously with snake venom in his blood. By degrees, he was slipping into shock.

"All right, Mhoram," he mumbled wanly. "Come and get me. It's over now."

He did not know whether he had spoken aloud. He could not hear himself. The ground under him had begun to ripple. Waves rolled through the hillside, tossing the small raft of hard soil on which he sat. He clung to it as long as he could, but the earthen seas were too rough. Soon he lost his balance and tumbled backward into the ground as if it were an undug grave.

FOUR: Siege

TWELVE days after the last charred trunks of Revelwood were consumed, reduced to ashes and trampled underfoot, Satansfist Raver, the right hand of the Gray Slayer, brought his vast, dolorous army to the stone gates of Lord's Keep. He approached slowly, though his hordes tugged forward like leashed wolves; he restrained the ravening of the ur-viles and Cave-wights and creatures he commanded so that all the inhabitants of Trothgard, and of the lands between Revelwood and the North Plains, would have time to seek safety in the Keep. This he did because he wished all the humans he meant to slay to be gathered in one place. Every increase in the Keep's population would weaken its endurance by eating its stores of food. And crowds of people would be more susceptible than trained warriors or Lords to the fear he bore.

He was sure of the outcome of his siege. His army was not as immense as the one which *moksha* Flesh-harrower his brother had lost in Garroting Deep. In order to secure his hold upon the regions he had already mastered, he had left scores of thousands of his creatures behind along the Roamsedge River, throughout the valley which formed the south border of Andelain, and across the Center Plains. But the Despiser had lost little more than a third of his forces in that earlier war. And instead of wolves and *kresh* and unwieldy *griffins*, Satansfist had with him more of the

lore-cunning, roynish, black, eyeless ur-viles, and more
of the atrocious creatures which Lord Foul had raised
up from the Great Swamp, Lifeswallower, from Sarangrave Flat, from the Spoiled Plains and the bosque of
the Ruinwash—raised up and demented with the power
of the Illearth Stone. In addition, the Giant-Raver had
at his back a power of which the Lords of Revelstone
had no conception. Therefore he was willing to prolong his approach to the Keep, so that he could hasten
its eventual and irreparable collapse.

Then, early on the twelfth day, a sky-shaking howl
shot through his hordes as they caught their first sight
of the mountain plateau of Revelstone. Thousands of
his creatures started to rush madly toward it through
the foothills, but he knocked them back with the flail
of his power. Ruling his army with a green scourge, he
spent the whole day making his approach, placing his
forces in position. When daylight at last drained away
into night, his army was wrapped around the entire
promontory of Revelstone, from the westmost edge
of its south wall to the cliffs of the plateau on the
northwest. His encampment locked the Keep in a wide,
round formation, sealing it from either flight or rescue,
from forages for food or missions to unknown allies.
And that night, Satansfist feasted on the flesh of prisoners who had been captured during his long march
from Landsdrop.

If any eyes in Revelstone had been able to penetrate the unbroken mass of clouds which frowned now
constantly over the Land, they would have seen that
this night was the dark of the moon on the middle
night of spring. The Despiser's preternatural winter
had clenched the Land for forty-two days.

Satansfist had followed precisely the design which
his master had given him for his march through the
Upper Land.

The next morning, he went to face the watchtower
which fronted the long walls of Revelstone at their
wedge point. He paid no attention to the intricate Giantish labor which had produced the pattern of coigns
and oriels and walks and battlements in the smooth
cliff-walls; that part of him which could have re-

sponded to the sight had long ago been extinguished by the occupying Raver. Without a second glance at the walls, or at the warriors who sentried the crenellated parapets, he strode around the promontory until he stood before the great stone gates in the base of the tower on its southeast side—the only entrance into Lord's Keep.

He was not surprised to find that the gates were open. Though the Giantish passion for stonework had been quelled in his blood, he retained his knowledge of the Keep. He knew that as long as those massive, interlocking gates remained intact, they could close upon command, trapping anyone who dared enter the tunnel under the tower. While in the tunnel, attackers would be exposed to counterattack from defensive windows built into the roof of the passage. And beyond the tunnel was nothing but a courtyard, open only to the sky, and then another set of gates even stronger than the first. The tower itself could not be entered except by suspended crosswalks from the main Keep, or through two small doors from the courtyard. Lord's Keep had been well made. The Giant-Raver did not accept the dare of the open gates.

Instead, he placed himself just close enough to the tower to taunt skilled archers, and shouted up at the stone walls in a voice that vibrated with malice and glee. "Hail, Lords! Worthy Lords! Show yourselves, Lordlings! Leave off cowering in your useless warrens, and speak with me. Behold! I come courteously to accept your surrender!"

There was no answer. The tower, only half as high as the main Keep behind it, stood with its windows and battlements as silent as if it were uninhabited. A whimpering growl passed among the army as the creatures begged for a chance to charge through the open gates.

"Hear me, little Lords!" he shouted. "See the toils of my strength wrapped around you. I hold your last lives in the palm of my hand. There is no hope for you unless you surrender yourselves and all to the mercy of the Despiser." Jeering barks from the ur-viles greeted this, and Satansfist grinned. "Speak, Lordlings! Speak or die!"

A moment later two figures appeared atop the tower —one a warrior and the other a blue-robed Lord whom Satansfist recognized. At first they ignored the Giant. They went to the flagpole, and together raised High Lord's Furl, the azure oriflamme of the Council. Only after it was fluttering defiantly in the gelid wind did they step to the parapet and face Satansfist.

"I hear you!" the Lord snapped. "I hear you, *samadhi* Raver. I know you, Sheol Satansfist. And you know me. I am Mhoram son of Variol, High Lord by the choice of the Council. Depart, Raver! Take your ill hordes with you. You have touched me. You know that I will not be daunted."

Fury glinted in the Giant's eyes at the memory Mhoram invoked, but he placed his hand over the livid fragment of the Stone hidden under his jerkin, and gave Mhoram a sarcastic bow. "I know you, Mhoram," he replied. "When I placed my hand upon you in the labyrinth of Kurash Qwellinir, I knew you. You were too blind with folly and ignorance to feel a wise despair. Therefore I permitted your life—so that you would live to better knowledge. Are you yet blind? Have you no eyes to see that your effectless end at my hand is as sure as the arch of Time? Have you forgotten the Giants? Have you forgotten the Bloodguard? In the name of the Despiser, I will certainly crush you where you cower!"

"Empty words," Mhoram retorted. "Bravado is easily uttered—but you will find it difficult of proof. *Melenkurion abatha!* Raver, begone! Return to your forsaken master before the Creator forgets restraint, and wreaks a timeless vengeance upon you."

The Giant laughed harshly. "Do not comfort yourself with lies, Lordling. The arch of Time will be broken if the Creator seeks to strike through it—and then Lord Foul the Despiser, Satansheart and Soulcrusher, Corruption and Render, will be unloosed upon the universe! If the Creator dares to lift his hand, my brothers and I will feast upon his very soul! Surrender, fool! Learn to be daunted while groveling may still preserve your life. Perhaps you will be permitted to serve me as my hand slave."

"Never!" High Lord Mhoram cried boldly. "We will never bow to you while one pulse of faith still beats in the Land. The Earthpower is yet strong to resist you. We will seek it until we have found the means to cast down you and your master and all his works. Your victories are hollow while one soul remains with breath enough to cry out against you!" Raising his staff, he whirled it so that blue fire danced in the air about his head. "Begone. *samadhi* Raver! *Melenkurion abatha! Duroc minas mill khabaal!* We will never surrender!"

Below him, Satansfist flinched under the power of the words. But an instant later, he sprang forward. snatching at his jerkin. With his piece of the Illearth Stone clenched and steaming in his fist, he hurled a gout of emerald force up at the High Lord. At the same time, hundreds of creatures broke from their ranks and charged toward the open gates.

But Mhoram deflected the blast with his staff, sent it into the air over his head, where his own fiery power attacked it and consumed it. Then he ducked behind the concealment of the parapet. Over his shoulder, he called to Warmark Quaan, "Seal the gates! Order the archers to slay any creatures which gain the courtyard. We cannot deal gently with this foe."

Quaan was already on his way down the stairs into the complex passages of the tower, shouting orders as he ran to oversee the fray. Mhoram looked downward to assure himself that Satansfist had not passed through the gates. Then he hastened after Quaan.

From the highest of the crosswalks above the courtyard, he surveyed the skirmish. Strong Woodhelvennin archers drove their shafts into the milling creatures from the battlements on both sides of the court, and the sound of weapons echoed out of the tunnel. In moments, the fighting would be done. Gritting his teeth over the shed blood, Mhoram left the conclusion of the skirmish in Quaan's competent hands, and crossed the wooden span to the main Keep, where his fellow Lords awaited him.

As he met the somber eyes of Trevor, Loerya, and

Amatin, a sudden weariness came over him. Satansfist's threats came so close to the truth. He and his companions were inadequate for the task of using even those few powers and mysteries which they possessed. And he was no nearer to a resolution of his secret knowledge than he had been when he had summoned and lost Thomas Covenant. He sighed, allowed his shoulders to sag. To explain himself, he said, "I had not thought there were so many ur-viles in all the world." But the words were only tangential to what he felt.

Yet he could not afford such weariness. He was the High Lord. Trevor, Loerya, and Amatin had their own uncertainties, their own needs, which he could not refuse; he had already done them enough damage in the private dilemma of his heart. Drawing himself erect, he told them what he had seen and heard of the Raver and Lord Foul's army.

When he was done, Amatin smiled wryly. "You affronted *samadhi* Raver. That was boldly done, High Lord."

"I did not wish to comfort him with the thought that we believe him safe."

At this, Loerya's gaze winced. "Is he so safe?" she asked painfully.

Mhoram hardened. "He is not safe while there is heart or bone or Earthpower to oppose him. I only say that I know not how he may be fought. Let him discover my ignorance for himself."

As she had so often in the past, Loerya once again attempted to probe his secret. "Yet you have touched Loric's *krill* and given it life. Your hand drew a gleam of blue from the gem. Is there no hope in this? The legends say that the *krill* of Loric Vilesilencer was potent against the peril of the Demondim."

"A gleam," Mhoram replied. Even in the privacy of his own knowledge, he feared the strange power which had enabled him to spark the *krill*'s opaque jewel. He lacked the courage to explain the source of his strength. "What will that avail?"

In response, Loerya's face thronged with demands and protests, but before she could voice them, a shout from the courtyard drew the Lords' attention downward. Warmark Quaan stood on the flagstones amid the corpses. When Mhoram answered him, he saluted mutely with his sword.

Mhoram returned the salute, acknowledging Quaan's victory. But he could not keep the hue of sadness from his voice as he said, "We have shed the first blood in this siege. Thus even those who oppose ill must wreak harm upon the victims of ill. Bear their bodies to the upland hills and burn them with purging fires, so that their flesh may recover its innocence in ashes. Then scatter their ashes over Furl Falls, as a sign to all the Land that we abhor the Despiser's wrong, not the slaves which he has made to serve his wrong."

The Warmark scowled, loath to honor his enemies with such courtesy. But he promptly gave the orders to carry out Mhoram's instructions. Sagging again, Mhoram turned back to his fellow Lords. To forestall any further probing, he said, "The Giant knows he cannot breach these walls with sword and spears. But he will not stand idle, waiting for hunger to do his work. He is too avid for blood. He will attempt us. We must be prepared. We must stand constant watch within the tower—to counter any force which he may bring against us."

Lord Trevor, eager for any responsibility which he believed to be within his ability, said, "I will watch."

With a nod, Mhoram accepted. "Summon one of us when you are weary. And summon us all when Satansfist chooses to act. We must see him at work, so that we may learn our defense." Then he turned to a warrior standing nearby. "Warhaft, bear word to the Hearthralls Tohrm and Borillar. Ask the Hirebrands and Gravelingases of Lord's Keep to share the watch of the Lords. They also must learn our defense."

The warrior saluted and walked briskly away. Mhoram placed a hand on Trevor's shoulder, gripped it firmly for a moment. Then, with one backward look at the winter-stricken sky, he left the balcony and went to his chambers.

He intended to rest, but the sight of Elena's marrowmeld sculpture standing restlessly on his table disturbed him. It had the fanatic, vulnerable look of a man, chosen to be a prophet, who entirely mistakes his errand—who, instead of speaking to glad ears the words of hope with which he was entrusted, spends his time preaching woe and retribution to a wilderland. Looking at the bust, Mhoram had to force himself to remember that Covenant had rejected the Land to save a child in his own world. And the Unbeliever's ability to refuse help to tens of thousands of lives—to the Land itself—for the sake of one life was a capacity which could not be easily judged. Mhoram believed that large balances might be tipped by the weight of one life. Yet the face of the sculpture seemed at this moment taut with misapprehended purpose—crowded with all the people who would die so that one young girl might live.

As he gazed at this rendition of Covenant's fate, High Lord Mhoram experienced again the sudden passion which had enabled him to draw a gleam from Loric's *krill*. Danger filled his eyes, and he snatched up the sculpture as if he meant to shout at it. But then the hard lines of his mouth bent, and he sighed at himself. With conflicting intensities in his face, he bore the *anundivian yajña* work to the Hall of Gifts, where he placed it in a position of honor high on one of the rude, rootlike pillars of the cavern. After that, he returned to his chambers and slept.

He was awakened shortly after noon by Trevor's summons. His dreamless slumber vanished instantly, and he was on his way out of his rooms before the young warrior who brought the message was able to knock a second time. He hastened up out of the recesses of Revelstone toward the battlements over the gates of the main Keep, where he chanced upon Hearthrall Tohrm. Together, they crossed to the tower and climbed the stairs to its top. There they found Trevor Loerya-mate with Warmark Quaan and Hirebrand Borillar.

Quaan stood between the Lord and the Hearthrall like an anchor to their separate tensions. Trevor's whole face was clenched white with apprehension, and Borillar's hands trembled on his staff with mixed dread and determination; but Quaan held his arms folded across his chest and frowned stolidly downward as if he had lost the capacity to be surprised by anything any servant of the Gray Slayer did. As the High Lord joined them, the old Warmark pointed with one tanned, muscular arm, and his rigid finger guided Mhoram's eyes like an accusation to a gathering of ur-viles before the gates of the tower.

The ur-viles were within arrow reach, but a line of red-eyed Cavewights bearing wooden shields protected them by intercepting the occasional shafts which Quaan's warriors loosed from the windows of the tower. Behind this cover, the ur-viles were building.

They worked with deft speed, and their construction quickly took shape in their midst. Soon Mhoram saw that they were making a catapult.

Despite the freezing ire of Foul's wind, his hands began to sweat on his staff. As the ur-viles looped heavy ropes around the sprocketed winches at the back of the machine, lashed the ropes to the stiff throwing-arm, and sealed with flashes of black power a large, ominous iron cup to the end of the arm, he found himself tensing, calling all his lore and strength into readiness. He knew instinctively that the attackers did not intend to hurl rocks at Revelstone.

The Demondim-spawn worked without instructions from Satansfist. He watched from a distance, but neither spoke nor moved. A score of them clambered over the catapult—adjusting, tightening, sealing it—and High Lord Mhoram marveled grimly that they could build so well without eyes. But they showed no need for eyes; noses were as discerning as vision. In a short time the finished catapult stood erect before Revelstone's tower.

Then barking shouts chorused through the encampment, and a hundred ur-viles ran forward to the machine. On either side, a score of them formed wedges to concentrate their power and placed themselves so that their loremasters stood at the winches. Using their iron staves, the two loremasters began turning the sprockets, thus tightening the ropes and slowly bending the catapult's arm backward. The catapult dwarfed the creatures, but by focusing their strength in wedges, they were able to crank the winches and bend the arm. And while this was being done, the other ur-viles came together and made an immense wedge behind the catapult. Against the background of the frozen snow-scud, they looked like a spear point aimed at the heart of the Keep.

With part of his mind, Mhoram observed that Lord Amatin now stood beside him. He glanced around for Loerya and saw her on a balcony of the main Keep. He waved his approval to her; if any holocaust struck the watchtower, all the Lords would not be lost. Then he cocked an eyebrow at Quaan, and when the War-mark nodded to indicate that the warriors were ready for any sudden orders, High Lord Mhoram returned his attention to the ur-viles.

As the arm of the catapult was drawn back, Grav-elingas Tohrm knelt at the parapet, spreading his arms and pressing his palms against the slow curve of the wall. In a dim, alien voice, he began to sing a song of granite endurance to the stone.

Then the arm reached its fullest arc. Quivering as if it were about to splinter, it strained toward the tower. At once, it was locked into place with iron hooks. Its wide cup had been brought down to chest level directly in front of the loremaster who apexed the largest wedge.

With a ringing clang, the loremaster struck its stave against the cup. Strength surged through scores of black shoulders; they emanated power as the loremas-ter labored over the cup. And thick, cruel fluid, as fiery as the vitriol which consumes flesh and obsidian and teak alike, splashed coruscating darkly from the stave into the waiting cup.

The High Lord had seen human bodies fall into ash at the least touch of fluid like that. He turned to warn Quaan. But the old Warmark needed no warning; he also had watched warriors die in Demondim acid. Be-fore Mhoram could speak, Quaan was shouting down the stairwell into the tower, ordering his warriors away from all the exposed windows and battlements.

At Mhoram's side, Lord Amatin's slight form began

to shiver in the wind. She held her staff braced before her as if she were trying to ward the cold away.

Slowly, the loremaster's fluid filled the cup. It splashed and spouted like black lava, throwing midnight sparks into the air; but the lore of the ur-viles contained it, held its dark force together, prevented it from shattering the catapult.

Then the cup was full.

The ur-viles did not hesitate. With a hoarse, hungry cry, they knocked free the restraining hooks.

The arm arced viciously forward, slapped with flat vehemence against the stop at the end of its throw.

A black gout of vitriol as large as a Stonedownor home sprang through the air and crashed against the tower a few dozen feet below the topmost parapet.

As the acid struck stone, it erupted. In lightless incandescence, it burned at the mountain rock like the flare of a dark sun. Tohrm cried out in pain, and the stone's agony howled under Mhoram's feet. He leaped forward. With Trevor and Amatin beside him, he called blue Lords-fire from his staff and flung it down against the vitriol.

Together, the three staffs flamed hotly to counter the acid. And because the ur-viles could not replenish it, it fell apart in moments—dropped like pieces of hate from the wall, and seared the ground before it was extinguished.

It left behind a long scar of corrosion in the stone. But it had not broken through the wall.

With a groan, Tohrm sagged away from the parapet. Sweat ran down his face, confusing his tears so that Mhoram could not tell whether the Gravelingas wept from pain or grief or rage. *"Melenkurion abatha!"* he cried thickly. "Ah, Revelstone!"

The ur-viles were already cranking their catapult into position for another throw.

For an instant, Mhoram felt stunned and helpless. With such catapults, so many thousands of ur-viles might be able to tear Lord's Keep down piece by piece, reduce it to dead rubble. But then his instinct for resistance came to life within him. To Trevor and

Amatin he snapped, "Those blasts must not touch the Keep. Join me. We will shape a Forbidding."

Even as they moved away from him on either side to prepare between them as wide a defense as possible, he knew that these tactics would not suffice. Three Lords might be able to deflect the greatest harm of a few attacks, but they could not repulse the assault of fifteen or twenty thousand ur-viles. "Tohrm!" he commanded sharply. "Borillar!"

At once, Hearthrall Tohrm began calling for more Gravelingases. But Borillar hesitated, searching around him uncertainly as if the urgency of the situation interfered with his thinking, hid his own lore from him.

"Calmly, Hirebrand," Mhoram said to steady him. "The catapults are of wood."

Abruptly, Borillar spun and dashed away. As he passed Warmark Quaan, he cried, "Archers!" Then he was yelling toward the main Keep, "Hirebrands! Bring *lor-liarill!* We will make arrows!"

In a dangerously short time, the ur-viles had cocked their machine, and were filling its cup with their black vitriol. They fired their next throw scant moments after Tohrm's *rhadhamaerl* reinforcements had positioned themselves to support the stone.

At Mhoram's command, the Lords struck against the arcing gout of acid before it reached the tower. Their staffs flashed as they threw up a wall of fire across the acid's path.

The fluid hit their fire with a force which shredded their Forbidding. The black acid shot through their power to slam against the tower wall. But the attack had spent much of its virulence. When it reached the stone, Tohrm and his fellow Gravelingases were able to withstand it.

It shattered against the strength which they called up in the rock, and fell flaming viciously to the ground, leaving behind dark stains on the wall but no serious damage.

Tohrm turned to meet High Lord Mhoram's gaze. Hot anger and exertion flushed the Hearthrall's face, but he bared his teeth in a grin which promised much for the defense of Revelstone.

Then three of Quaan's archers joined the Lords, followed closely by two Hirebrands. The archers were tall Woodhelvennin warriors, whose slimness of form belied the strength of their bows. Warmark Quaan acknowledged them, and asked Borillar what he wanted them to do. In response, Borillar accepted from the Hirebrands six long, thin arrows. These were delicately rune-carved, despite their slenderness; their tips were sharpened to keen points; and their ends were fletched with light brown feathers. The Hearthrall gave two of them to each archer, saying as he did so, "This is *lor-liarill,* the rare wood called by the Giants of Seareach 'Gildenlode.' They—"

"We are Woodhelvennin," the woman who led the archers said bluntly. *"Lor-liarill* is known to us."

"Loose them well," returned Borillar. "There are no others prepared. Strike first at the Cavewights."

The woman looked at Quaan to see if he had any orders for her, but he waved her and her companions to the parapet. With smooth competence, the three archers nocked arrows, bent bows, and took aim at the catapult.

Already, the ur-viles had pulled back its arm, and were busy rabidly refilling its iron cup.

Through his teeth, Quaan said, "Strike now."

Together, three bowstrings thrummed.

Immediately, the defending Cavewights jerked up their shields, caught the arrows out of the air.

The instant the arrows bit wood, they exploded into flame. The force of their impact spread fire over the shields, threw blazing shreds and splinters down onto the Cavewights. Yelping in surprise and pain, the dull-witted, gangling creatures dropped their shields and jumped away from the fire.

At once, the archers struck again. Their shafts sped through the air and hit the catapult's throwing arm, just below the cup. The *lor-liarill* detonated instantly, setting the black acid afire. In sudden conflagration, the fluid's power smashed the catapult, scattered blazing wood in all directions. A score of ur-viles and several Cavewrights fell, and the rest went scrambling beyond arrow range, leaving the pieces of the machine to burn themselves out.

With a fierce grin, the Woodhelvennin woman turned to Borillar and said, "The *lillianrill* make dour shafts, Hearthrall."

Borillar strove to appear dispassionate, as if he were accustomed to such success, but he had to swallow twice before he could find his voice to say, "So it would appear."

High Lord Mhoram placed a hand of praise on the Hearthrall's shoulder. "Hirebrand, is there more *lorliarill* which may be formed into such arrows?"

Borillar nodded like a veteran. "There is more. All the Gildenlode keels and rudders which were made for the Giants—before— That wood may be reshaped."

"Ask the Hirebrands to begin at once," said Mhoram quietly.

Smiling broadly, Tohrm moved to stand beside Borillar. "Hearthrall, you have outdone me," he said in a teasing tone. "The *rhadhamaerl* will not rest until they have found a way to match this triumph of yours."

At this, Borillar's dispassion broke into a look of wide pleasure. Arm in arm, he and Tohrm left the tower, followed by the other Hirebrands and Gravelingases.

After bowing under a few curt words of praise from Quaan, the archers left also. He and the three Lords were left alone on the tower, gazing somberly into each other's eyes.

Finally, Quaan spoke the thought that was in all their faces. "It is a small victory. Larger catapults may strike from beyond the reach of arrows. Larger wedges may make power enough to breach the walls. If several catapults are brought to the attack together, we will be sorely pressed to resist even the first throws."

"And the Illearth Stone has not yet spoken against us," Mhoram murmured. He could still feel the force which had rent his defense tingling in his wrists and elbows. As an afterthought, he added, "Except in the voice of this cruel wind and winter."

For a moment, he melded his mind with Trevor and Amatin, sharing his strength with them, and reminding them of their own resources. Then, with a sigh, Lord Amatin said, "I am of Woodhelvennin blood. I will assist Hearthrall Borillar in the making of these shafts. It will be slow work, and many of the *lillianrill* have other tasks."

"And I will go to Tohrm," Trevor said. "I have no lore to match the *rhadhamaerl*. But it may be that a counter to this Demondim-bane can be found in the fire-stones."

Mhoram approved silently, put his arm around the two Lords and hugged them. "I will stand watch," he said, "and summon Loerya when I am weary." Then he sent Quaan with them from the tower, so that the Warmark could ready his warriors for all the work they might have to do if the walls were harmed. Alone, the High Lord stood and faced the dark encampment of Satansfist's hordes—stood below the snapping Furl, which was already ragged in the sharp wind, planted the iron heel of his staff on the stone, and faced the encircling enemy as if his were the hand which held the outcome of the siege.

In the gray dimness toward evening, the ur-viles built another catapult. Beyond the reach of arrows, they constructed a stronger machine, one capable of throwing their power across the additional ground. But High Lord Mhoram summoned no aid. When the black spew of corrosion was launched, it had farther to travel; it was beyond the command of its makers for a longer time. Mhoram's blue power lashed out at it as it reached the top of its arc. A fervid lightning of Lords-fire bolted into the vitriol, weakened its momentum, caused it to fall short. Splashing angrily, effectlessly, it crashed to the earth, and burned a morbid hole like a charnel pit in the frozen dirt.

The ur-viles withdrew, returned to the garish watch fires which burned throughout the army for the sake of the misborn creatures that needed light. After a time, Mhoram rubbed the strain from his forehead, and called Lord Loerya to take his place.

During the blind night, three more catapults were built in the safety of distance, then brought forward to attack Revelstone. None of them assaulted the tower; two of them threw at the walls of the main Keep from the north, one from the south. But each time the defenders were able to react quickly. The loremasters' exertion of power as they cocked the machines radiated a palpable impression up at the battlements, and this emanation warned the Keep of each new assault. Archers waiting with *lor-liarill* arrows raced to respond.

They gained light to aim with by driving arrows into the ground near the catapults; in the sudden revealing fires, they destroyed two of the new threats as they had destroyed the first. But the third remained beyond bowshot, and attacked the south wall from a position out of Loerya's reach. Yet this assault was defeated also. In a moment of inspiration, the Haft commanding the archers ordered them to direct their shafts at the acid as it arced toward the Keep. The archers fired a dozen shafts in rapid succession into the gout of fluid, and succeeded in breaking it apart, so that it spattered against the stone in weaker pieces and did little harm.

Fortunately, there were no more attacks that night. All the new Gildenlode arrows had been used, and the process of making more was slow and difficult. Throughout the next day also there were no attacks, though the sentries could see ur-viles building catapults in the distance. No move was made against Revelstone until deep in the chattering darkness of midnight. Then alarms rang through the Keep, calling all its defenders from their work or rest. In the windtorn light of arrows aflame like torches in the frozen earth, the Lords and Hirebrands and Gravelingases and warriors and Lorewardens saw ten catapults being cranked into position beyond the range of the archers.

Orders hummed through the stone of the Keep. Men and women dashed to take their places. In moments, a Lord or a team of defenders stood opposite each catapult. As the cups were filled, Revelstone braced itself for the onslaught of power.

At the flash of a dank green signal from Satansfist, the ten catapults threw.

The defense outlined Revelstone in light, cast so much bright orange, yellow, and blue fire from the walls that the whole plateau blazed in the darkness like a conflagration of defiance. Working together from the tower, Mhoram and Amatin threw bolts of power which cast down two of the vitriol attacks. From the plateau atop Revelstone, the Lords Trevor and Loerya used their advantage of height to help them each deflect one cupful of corrosion into the ground.

Two of the remaining attacks were torn apart by Hearthrall Borillar's arrows. Using a piece of *orcrest* given to them by Hearthrall Tohrm, and a *lomillialor* rod obtained from Lord Amatin, teams of Lorewardens erected barriers which consumed most of the virulence in two assaults, prevented them from doing any irrecoverable damage.

Gravelingases met the last two throws of the urviles. With one partner, Tohrm had positioned himself on a balcony directly in front of one catapult. They stood on either side of a stone vat of graveling, and sang a deep *rhadhamaerl* song which slowly brought their mortal flesh into harmony with the mounting radiance of the fire-stones. While the ur-viles filled the cup of the machine, Tohrm and his companion thrust their arms into the graveling, pushed their lore-preserved hands deep among the fire-stones near the sides of the vat. There they waited in the golden heat, singing their earthish song until the catapult threw and the vitriol sprang toward them.

In the last instant, they heaved a double armful of graveling up at the black gout. The two powers collided scant feet above their heads, and the force of the impact knocked them flat on the balcony. The wet corrosion of the acid turned the graveling instantly to cinders, but in turn the *rhadhamaerl* might of the fire-stones burned away the acid before the least drop of it touched Tohrm or Revelstone.

The other pair of Gravelingases were not so successful. They mistimed their countering heave, and as a result their graveling only stopped half the vitriol. Both men died in fluid fire which destroyed a wide section of the balcony.

But instead of striking again, launching more attacks to wear down the defenses of the Keep, the ur-viles abandoned their catapults and withdrew—apparently satisfied with what they had learned about Revelstone's mettle.

High Lord Mhoram watched them go with surprise in his face and cold dread in his heart. Surely the ur-viles had not been intimidated by the defense. If Satansfist chose now to change his tactics, it was because he had measured the weakness of Revelstone, and knew a better way to capitalize on it.

The next morning, Mhoram saw the commencement of Satansfist's new strategy, but for two days after that he did not comprehend it. The Raver's hordes moved closer to Revelstone, placed themselves hardly a hundred yards from the walls, and faced the plateau as if they expected its defenders to leap willingly into their jaws. The ur-viles moved among the slavering creatures and Cavewights, and formed scores of wedges which seemed to point toward the very heart of Revelstone. And behind them Satansfist stood in a broad piece of open ground, openly wielding his Stone for the first time. But he launched no physical onslaught, offered the Keep no opportunity to strike or be stricken. Instead, his creatures dropped to their hands and knees, and glared hungrily at Revelstone like crouching preyers. The ur-vile loremasters set the tips of their staves in the ground, began a barking ululation or invocation which carried in shreds to the Keep through the tearing wind. And *samadhi* Raver, Sheol and Satansfist, squeezed his fragment of the Illearth Stone so that it ran with steam like boiling ice.

As Mhoram watched, he could feel the upsurge of power on all sides; the exertion of might radiated at him until the skin of his cheeks stung under it, despite the raw chill of the wind. But the besiegers took no other action. They held their positions in fierce concentration, scowling murderously as if they were envisioning the blood of their victims.

Slowly, tortuously, they began to have an effect upon the ground of the foothills. From the unflickering green blaze of the Stone, a rank emerald hue spread to the dirt around Satansfist's feet and throbbed in the soil. It encircled him, pulsing like a fetid heart, then sent crooked offshoots like green veins through the ground toward Revelstone. These grew with each savage throb, branched out until they reached the backs of the crouching hordes. At that point, red pain sickly tinged with green blossomed from the embedded tips of the loremasters' staves. Like Satansfist's emerald, the ill red grew in the ground like arteries or roots of hurt. It shone through the gray ice on the earth without melting it, and expanded with each throb of *samadhi*'s central power until all of Revelstone was ringed in pulsing veins.

The process of this growth was slow and deadly; by nightfall, the red-green harm was not far past the feet of the ur-viles; and after a long, lurid darkness, dawn found the veins just halfway to the walls. But it was implacable and sure. Mhoram could conceive no defense against it because he did not know what it was.

During the next two days, the dread of it spread over Lord's Keep. People began to talk in whispers. Men and women hurried from place to place as if they feared that the city stone were turning against them. Children whimpered inexplicably, and winced at the sight of well-known faces. A thick atmosphere of fear and incomprehension hovered in Revelstone like the spread wings of an alighting vulture. Yet Mhoram did not grasp what was being done to the city until the evening of the third day. Then by chance he approached Warmark Quaan unseen and unheard, and at the touch of his hand on Quaan's shoulder, the Warmark reeled away in panic, clawing at his sword. When his eyes finally recognized the High Lord, his face filled with a gray ash of misery, and he trembled like an overwhelmed novice.

With a groan of insight, Mhoram understood Revelstone's plight. Dread of the unknown was only the surface of the peril. As he threw his arms around Quaan's trembling, he saw that the red-green veins of power in the ground were not a physical danger; rather, they were a vehicle for the raw emotional force of the Despiser's malice—a direct attack on the Keep's will, a corrosive hurled against the moral fabric of Revelstone's resistance.

Fear was growing like a fatal disease in the heart of Lord's Keep. Under the influence of those lurid veins, the courage of the city was beginning to rot.

It had no defense. The *lillianrill* and *rhadhamaerl* could build vast warming fires within the walls. The Lorewardens could sing in voices that shook helplessly brave songs of encouragement and victory. The Warward could drill and train until the warriors had neither leisure nor stamina for fear. The Lords could flit throughout the city like blue ravens, carrying the light of courage and support and intransigence wherever they went, from gray day to blind night to gray day again. The Keep was not idle. As time dragged its dread-aggravated length along, moved through its skeletal round with an almost audible clatter of flesh-less bones, everything that could be done was done. The Lords took to moving everywhere with their staffs alight, so that their bright azure could resist the erosion of Revelstone's spirit. But still the veined, bloody harm in the ground multiplied its aegis over the city. The malignance of tenscore thousand evil hearts stifled all opposition.

Soon even the mountain rock of the plateau seemed to be whimpering in silent fear. Within five days, some families locked themselves in their rooms and refused to come out; they feared to be abroad in the city. Others fled to the apparent safety of the upland hills. Mad fights broke out in the kitchens, where any cook or food handler could snatch up a knife to slash at sudden gusts of terror. To prevent such outbursts, Warmark Quaan had to station Eoman in every kitchen and refectory.

But though he drove them as if he had a gaunt specter of horror clinging to his shoulders, he could not keep even his warriors from panic. This fact he was finally forced to report to the High Lord, and after hearing it, Mhoram went to stand his watch on the tower. Alone there, he faced the night which fell as heavily as the scree of despair against the back of his neck, faced the unglimmering emerald loathsomeness of the Stone, faced the sick, red-green veined fire —and hugged his own dread within the silence of his heart. If he had not been so desperate, he might have wept in sympathy for Kevin Landwaster, whose dilemma he now understood with a keenness that cut him to the bone of his soul.

Sometime later—after the darkness had added all its chill to Lord Foul's winter, and the watch fires of the encampment had paled to mere sparks beside *samadhi* Raver's loud, strong lust for death, Loerya Trevor-mate came to the tower, bearing with her a small pot of graveling which she placed before her when she sat on the stone, so that the glow lit her drawn face. The uplift of her visage cast her eyes into shadow, but still Mhoram could see that they were raw with tears.

"My daughters"—her voice seemed to choke her— "my children—they— You know them, High Lord," she said as if she were pleading. "Are they not children to make a parent proud?"

"Be proud," Mhoram replied gently. "Parents and children are a pride to each other."

"You know them, High Lord," she insisted. "My joy in them has been large enough to be pain. They— High Lord, they will no longer eat. They fear the food —they see poison in the food. This evil maddens them."

"We are all maddened, Loerya. We must endure."

"How endure? Without hope—? High Lord, it were better if I had not borne children."

Gently, quietly, Mhoram answered a different question. "We cannot march out to fight this evil. If we leave these walls, we are ended. There is no other hold for us. We must endure."

In a voice suffused with weeping, Loerya said, "High Lord, summon the Unbeliever."

"Ah, sister Loerya—that I cannot do. You know I

cannot. You know that I chose rightly when I released Thomas Covenant to the demands of his own world. Whatever other follies have twisted the true course of my life, that choice was not folly."

"Mhoram!" she beseeched thickly.

"No. Loerya, think what you ask. The Unbeliever desired to save a life in his world. But time moves in other ways there. Seven and forty years have passed since he came first to Revelstone, yet in that time he has not aged even three cycles of the moon. Perhaps only moments have gone by for him since his last summoning. If he were called again now, perhaps he would still be prevented from saving the young child who needs him."

At the mention of a child, sudden anger twisted Loerya's face. "Summon him!" she hissed. "What are his nameless children to me? By the Seven, Mhoram! Summon—!"

"No." Mhoram interrupted her, but his voice did not lose its gentleness. "I will not. He must have the freedom of his own fate—it is his right. We have no right to take it from him—no, even the Land's utterest need does not justify such an act. He holds the white gold. Let him come to the Land if he wills. I will not gainsay the one true bravery of my unwise life."

Loerya's anger collapsed as swiftly as it had come. Wringing her hands over the graveling as if even the hope of warmth had gone out of them, she moaned, "This evening my youngest—Yolenid—she is hardly more than a baby—she shrieked at the sight of me." With an effort, she raised her streaming eyes to the High Lord, and whispered, "How endure?"

Though his own heart wept for her, Mhoram met her gaze. "The alternative is Desecration." As he looked into the ragged extremity of her face, he felt his own need crying out, urging him to share his perilous secret. For a moment that made his pulse hammer apprehensively in his temples, he knew that he would answer Loerya if she asked him. To warn her, he breathed softly, "Power is a dreadful thing."

A spark of inchoate hope lit her eyes. She climbed unsteadily to her feet, brought her face closer to his

and searched him. The first opening of a meld drained
the surfaces of his mind. But what she saw or felt in
him stopped her. His cold doubt quenched the light
in her eyes, and she receded from him. In an awkward voice that carried only a faint vibration of bitterness, she said, "No, Mhoram. I will not ask. I trust
you or no one. You will speak when your heart is
ready."

Gratitude burned under Mhoram's eyelids. With a
crooked smile, he said, "You are courageous, sister
Loerya."

"No." She picked up her graveling pot and moved
away from him. "Though it is no fault of theirs, my
daughters make me craven." Without a backward
glance, she left the High Lord alone in the lurid night.

Hugging his staff against his chest, he turned and
faced once more the flawless green wrong of the
Raver's Stone. As his eyes met that baleful light, he
straightened his shoulders, drew himself erect, so that
he stood upright like a marker or witness to Revelstone's inviolate rock.

FIVE: Lomillialor

THE weight of mortality which entombed
Covenant seemed to press him deeper and deeper into
the obdurate stuff of the ground. He felt that he had
given up breathing—that the rock and soil through
which he sank sealed him off from all respiration—
but the lack of air gave him no distress; he had no

more need for the sweaty labor of breathing. He was plunging irresistibly, motionlessly downward, like a man falling into his fate.

Around him, the black earth changed slowly to mist and cold. It lost none of its solidity, none of its airless weight, but its substance altered, became by gradual increments a pitch-dark fog as massive and unanswerable as the pith of granite. With it, the cold increased. Cold and winter and mist wound about him like cerements.

He had no sense of duration, but at some point he became aware of a chill breeze in the mist. It eased some of the pressure on him, loosened his cerements. Then an abrupt rift appeared some distance away. Through the gap, he saw a fathomless night sky, unredeemed by any stars. And from the rift shone a slice of green light as cold and compelling as the cruelest emerald.

The cloud rift rode the breeze until it crossed over him. As it passed, he saw standing behind the heavy clouds a full moon livid with green force, an emerald orb radiating ill through the heavens. The sick green light caught at him. When the rift which exposed it blew by him and away into the distance, he felt himself respond. The authority, the sovereignty, of the moon could not be denied: he began to flow volitionlessly through the mist in the wake of the rift.

But another force intervened. For an instant, he thought he could smell the aroma of a tree's heart sap, and pieces of song touched him through the cold: *be true . . . answer . . . soul's deep curse . . .*

He clung to them, and their potent appeal anchored him. The darkness of the mist locked around him again, and he went sinking in the direction of the song.

Now the cold stiffened under him, so that he felt he was descending on a slab, with the breeze blowing over him. He was too chilled to move, and only the sensation of air in his chest told him that he was breathing again. His ribs and diaphragm worked, pumped air in and out of his lungs automatically. Then he noticed another change in the mist. The blank, wet, blowing

night took on another dimension, an outer limit; it
gave the impression that it clung privately to him,
leaving the rest of the world in sunlight. Despite the
cloud, he could sense the possibility of brightness in
the cold breeze beyond him. And the frigid slab grew
harder and harder under him, until he felt he was
lying on a catafalque with a cairn of personal darkness piled over him.

The familiar song left him there. For a time, he
heard nothing but the hum of the breeze and the
hoarse, lisping sound made by his breath as it labored past his swollen lip and gum. He was freezing
slowly, sinking into icy union with the stone under his
back. Then a voice near him panted, "By the Seven!
We have done it."

The speaker sounded spent with weariness and
oddly echoless, forlorn. Only the hum of the wind
supported his claim to existence; without it, he might
have been speaking alone in the uncomprehended
ether between the stars.

A light voice full of glad relief answered, "Yes, my
friend. Your lore serves us well. We have not striven
in vain these three days."

"My lore and your strength. And the *lomillialor* of
High Lord Mhoram. But see him. He is injured and
ill."

"Have I not told you that he also suffers?"

The light voice sounded familiar to Covenant. It
brought the sunshine closer, contracted the mist until
it was wholly within him, and he could feel cold
brightness on his face.

"You have told me," said the forlorn man. "And I
have told you that I should have killed him when he
was within my grasp. But all my acts go astray. Behold—even now the Unbeliever comes dying to my
call."

The second speaker replied in a tone of gentle
reproof, "My friend, you—"

But the first cut him off. "This is an ill-blown place.
We cannot help him here."

Covenant felt hands grip his shoulders. He made an
effort to open his eyes. At first he could see nothing;

the sunlight washed everything out of his sight. But then something came between him and the sun. In its shadow, he blinked at the blur which marred all his perceptions.

"He awakens," the first voice said. "Will he know me?"

"Perhaps not. You are no longer young, my friend."

"Better if he does not," the man muttered. "He will believe that I seek to succeed where I once failed. Such a man will understand retribution."

"You wrong him. I have known him more closely. Do you not see the greatness of his need for mercy?"

"I see it. And I also know him. I have lived with Thomas Covenant in my ears for seven and forty years. He receives mercy even now, whether or not he comprehends it."

"We have summoned him from his rightful world. Do you call this mercy?"

In a hard voice, the first speaker said, "I call it mercy."

After a moment, the second sighed. "Yes. And we could not have chosen otherwise. Without him, the Land dies."

"Mercy?" Covenant croaked. His mouth throbbed miserably.

"Yes!" the man bending over him averred. "We give you a new chance to resist the ill which you have allowed upon the Land."

Gradually, Covenant saw that the man had the square face and broad shoulders of a Stonedownor. His features were lost in shadow, but woven into the shoulders of his thick, fur-lined cloak was a curious pattern of crossed lightning—a pattern Covenant had seen somewhere before. But he was still too bemused with fog and shock to trace the memory.

He tried to sit up. The man helped him, braced him in that position. For a moment, his gaze wandered. He found that he was on a circular stone platform edged by a low wall. He could see nothing but sky beyond the parapet. The cold blue void held his eyes as if it were beckoning to him; it appealed to his emptiness. He had to wrestle his gaze into focus on the Stonedownor.

From this angle, the sun illuminated the man's face. With his gray-black hair and weathered cheeks, he appeared to be in his mid-sixties, but age was not his dominant feature. His visage created a self-contradictory impression. He had a hard, bitter mouth which had eaten sour bread for so long that it had forgotten the taste of sweetness, but his eyes were couched in fine lines of supplication, as if he had spent years looking skyward and begging the sun not to blind him. He was a man who had been hurt and had not easily borne the cost.

As if the words had just penetrated through his haze, Covenant heard the man say, *Should have killed him.* A man wearing a pattern of crossed lightning on his shoulders had once tried to kill Covenant—and had been prevented by Atiaran Trell-mate. She had invoked the Oath of Peace.

"Triock?" Covenant breathed hoarsely. "Triock?"

The man did not flinch from Covenant's aching gaze. "I promised that we would meet again."

Hellfire, Covenant groaned to himself. Hell and blood. Triock had been in love with Lena daughter of Atiaran before Covenant had ever met her.

He struggled to get to his feet. In the raw cold, his battered muscles could not raise him; he almost fainted at the exertion. But Triock helped him, and someone else lifted him from behind. He stood wavering, clinging helplessly to Triock's support, and looked out beyond the parapet.

The stone platform stood in empty air as if it were afloat in the sky, riding the hum of the breeze. In the direction Covenant faced, he could see straight to the farthest horizon, and that horizon was nothing but a sea of gray clouds, a waving, thick mass of blankness like a shroud over the earth. He wobbled a step closer to the parapet, and saw that the deep flood covered everything below him. The platform stood a few hundred feet above the clouds as if it were the only thing in the world on which the sun still shone.

But a promontory of mountains jutted out of the

gray sea on his left. And when he peered over his shoulder past the man who supported him from behind, he found another promontory towering over him on that side; a flat cliff-face met his view, and on either side of it a mountain range strode away into the clouds.

He was on Kevin's Watch again, standing atop a stone shaft which joined that cliff-face somewhere out of sight below him.

For a moment, he was too surprised to be dizzy. He had not expected this; he had expected to be recalled to Revelstone. Who in the Land beside the Lords had the power to summon him? When he had known Triock, the man had been a Cattleherd, not a wielder of lore. Who but the Despiser could make such a summons possible?

Then the sight of the long fall caught up with him, and vertigo took the last strength from his legs. Without the hands which held him, he would have toppled over the parapet.

"Steady, my friend," Triock's companion said reassuringly. "I will not release you. I have not forgotten your dislike of heights." He turned Covenant away from the wall, supporting him easily.

Covenant's head rolled loosely on his neck, but when the Watch stopped reeling around him, he forced himself to look toward Triock. "How?" he mumbled thickly. "Who—where did you get the power?"

Triock's lips bent in a hard smile. To his companion, he said, "Did I not say that he would understand retribution? He believes that even now I would break my Oath for him." Then he directed the bitterness of his mouth at Covenant. "Unbeliever, you have earned retribution. The loss of High Lord Elena has caused—"

"Peace, my friend," the other man said. "He has pain enough for the present. Tell him no sad stories now. We must bear him to a place where we may succor him."

Again, Triock looked at Covenant's injuries. "Yes," he sighed wearily. "Pardon me, Unbeliever. I have spent seven and forty years with people who cannot forget you. Be at rest—we will preserve you from harm as best we may. And we will answer your questions. But first we must leave this place. We are exposed here. The Gray Slayer has many eyes, and some of them may have seen the power which summoned you."

He slid a smooth wooden rod under his cloak, then said to his companion, "Rockbrother, can you bear the Unbeliever down this stair? I have rope if you desire it."

His companion laughed quietly. "My friend, I am a Giant. I have not lost my footing on stone since the first sea voyage of my manhood. Thomas Covenant will be secure with me."

A Giant? Covenant thought dumbly. For the first time, he noticed the size of the hands which supported him. They were twice as big as his. They turned him lightly, lifted him into the air as if he were weightless.

He found himself looking up into the face of Saltheart Foamfollower.

The Giant did not appear to have changed much since Covenant had last seen him. His short, stiff iron beard was grayer and longer, and deep lines of care furrowed his forehead, on which the mark of the wound he had received at the battle of Soaring Woodhelven was barely visible; but his deep-set eyes still flashed like enthusiastic gems from under the massive fortification of his brows, and his lips curled wryly around a smile of welcome. Looking at him, Covenant could think of nothing except that he had not said good-bye to the Giant when they had parted in Treacher's Gorge. Foamfollower had befriended him —and he had not even returned that friendship to the extent of one farewell. Shame pushed his eyes from Foamfollower's face. He glanced down the Giant's gnarled, oaklike frame. There he saw that Foamfollower's heavy leather jerkin and leggings were tattered and rent, and under many of the tears were battle scars, both old and new. The newest ones hurt him as if they had been cut into his own flesh.

"Foamfollower," he croaked. "I'm sorry."

The Giant replied gently, "Peace, my friend. All that is past. Do not condemn yourself."

"Hellfire." Covenant could not master his weakness. "What's happened to you?"

"Ah, that is a long tale, full of Giantish episodes and apostrophes. I will save it until we have taken you to a place where we may aid you. You are ill enough to bandy stories with death itself."

"You've been hurt," Covenant went on. But the intensity in Foamfollower's eyes stopped him.

In mock sternness, the Giant commanded, "Be silent, Unbeliever. I will listen to no sad stories in this place." Gently, he cradled the wounded man in his arms, then said to Triock, "Follow carefully, Rock-brother. Our work has only begun. If you fall, I will be hard pressed to catch you."

"Look to yourself," Triock replied gruffly. "I am not unaccustomed to stone—even stone as chill as this."

"Well, then. Let us make what haste we can. We have endured much to come so far, you and I. We must not lose the ur-Lord now."

Without waiting for an answer, he started down the rude stair of Kevin's Watch.

Covenant turned his face to the Giant's breast. The breeze had a high lonely sound as it rustled past the cliff and eddied around Foamfollower; it reminded Covenant that the Watch stood more than four thousand feet above the foothills. But Foamfollower's heart beat with forthright confidence, and his arms felt unbreakable. At each downward step, a slight jolt passed through him, as if that foot had locked itself to the stair stone. And Covenant no longer possessed even strength enough for fear. He rode numbly in the Giant's hold until the hum of the wind increased, and Foamfollower dropped one step at a time into the cold sea of clouds.

In moments, the sunlight was gone as if it had been irretrievably lost. The wind took on a raw, dry, cutting edge, too chill to be softened by moisture. Covenant and Foamfollower descended through dim vistaless air as icy as polar mist—cloud as thick and thetic as a fist clenched around the world. Under its pressure, Covenant felt icicles crawling up his spine toward the last warmth of life left in him.

Then they reached the ledge at the base of Kevin's Watch. The precipice loomed darkly beside them as Foamfollower turned to the right and moved out along the ledge, but he stepped securely, as if he had no conception of falling. And shortly he left the exposed cliff-face, began to clamber along the trail into the mountains. After that, the last tension faded from the background of Covenant's mind. His weakness opened in him like a funereal lily, and the mist drew him into a wan, slumberous daze.

For some time he lost track of where Foamfollower was going. He seemed to feel himself bleeding away into the gray air. Tranquillity like the peace of ice surrounded his heart. He no longer understood what Foamfollower was talking about when the Giant whispered urgently, "Triock, he fails. We must aid him now or not at all."

"Yes," Triock agreed. He called commandingly, "Bring blankets and graveling! He must have warmth."

"That will not suffice. He is ill and injured. He must have healing."

Triock snapped, "I see him. I am not blind."

"Then what can we do? I am helpless here—the Giants have no lore for cold. We suffer little from it."

"Rub his limbs. Put your strength into him. I must think."

Something rough began to batter Covenant, but the ice in him was impervious to it. Vaguely, he wondered why Foamfollower and Triock would not let him sleep.

"Is there no hurtloam here?" asked the Giant.

"At one time there was," Triock responded distantly. "Lena—Lena healed him in this same place—when he first came to the Land. But I am not a *rhadhamaerl*—I do not feel the secret flavors and powers of the Earth. And it is said that the hurtloam has—retreated—that it has hidden itself to escape the ill which is upon the Land. Or that this winter has slain it. We cannot succor him in that way."

"We must help him. His very bones freeze."

Covenant felt himself being shifted, felt blankets being wrapped around him. In the background of his haze, he thought he saw the kind yellow light of graveling. That pleased him; he could rest better if the gray fog did not dominate everything.

After a moment, Triock said uncertainly, "It is possible that the power of the High Wood can help him."

"Then begin!" the Giant urged.

"I am no Hirebrand. I have no *lillianrill* lore—I have only studied this matter in the Loresraat for a year—after High Lord Mhoram gave the *lomillialor* to me. I cannot control its power."

"Nevertheless! You must make the attempt."

Triock protested. "The High Wood test of truth may quench the last flicker within him. Hale and whole, he might fail such testing."

"Without it he will surely die."

Triock snarled under his breath, then said grimly, "Yes. Yes, Rockbrother. You outsee me. Keep life within him. I must prepare."

In a mood of sadness, Covenant saw that the yellow light was receding into gray around him. He did not know how he could bear to lose it. Raw, reviling fog had no right to outweigh graveling in the balance of the Land. And there was no more hurtloam. No more hurtloam, he repeated with an unexpected pang. His sorrow turned to anger. By hell! Foul, he grated mutely, you can't do this. I won't let you. The hate for which he had been groping a night and a world earlier began to return to him. With the strength of anger, he pried his eyes open.

Triock was standing over him. The Stonedownor held his *lomillialor* rod as if he meant to drive it like a spike between Covenant's eyes. In his hands, the white wood shone hotly, and steam plumed from it into the chill air. A smell of wood sap joined the loamy odor of the graveling.

Muttering words that Covenant could not understand, Triock brought the rod down until its end touched the infected fever in his forehead.

At first, he felt nothing from the contact; the *lomillialor* pulsed effectlessly on his wound as if he were immune to it. But then he was touched from another direction. An exquisite ache of heat cut through the ice in his left palm, spreading from the ring he wore. It sliced into him, then moved up through his wrist. It hurt him as if it were flaying cold and flesh off his bones, but the pain gave him a kind of savage pleasure. Soon his whole left arm was livid with excruciation. And under the heat his bruises reawoke, came back from the dead.

When the hold of the ice had been broken that far, it began to give way in other places. Warmth from the blankets reached toward his battered ribs. The joints of his legs throbbed as if they had been kicked into consciousness. In moments, his forehead remembered its anguish.

Then Triock transferred the tip of the High Wood from his forehead to the tight black swelling of his lip. At once, agony erupted within him, and he plunged into it as if it were solace.

He returned to consciousness slowly, but when he opened his eyes he knew that he had become steadier. His wounds were not healed; both his forehead and mouth ached like goads embedded in his flesh, and his body moaned with bruises. But the ice no longer gnawed his bones. The swelling of his lip was reduced, and his sight had improved, as if the lenses of his eyes had been cleaned. Yet he felt a private grief at the numbness which clung to his hands and feet. His dead nerves had not yet rediscovered the health which he had learned to expect from the Land.

But he was alive—he was in the Land—he had seen Foamfollower. He set aside the distress of his nerves for another time, and looked around him.

He lay in a small, sheer valley nestled among the mountains behind Kevin's Watch. While he had been unconscious, the enshrouding sea of clouds had receded a few hundred feet, and now light snow filled the air like murmuring. Already an inch of it blanketed him. Something in the timbre of the snow gave him the impression that the time was late afternoon. But he was not concerned about time. He had been in this valley once before, with Lena.

The memory of it contrasted starkly with what he saw. It had been a quiet, grassy place girdled with pines like tall sentinels guarding its quietude, and a sprightly brook flowing down its center. But now only bare, wasted earth showed through the thickening snow. The pines had been stripped naked and splintered by more winter than they could survive; and instead of water, a weal of ice ran through the valley like a scar already old.

Covenant wondered painfully how long this weather would last.

The implications of that question made him shiver, and he fought his tired frame into a sitting position so that he could lean closer to the pot of graveling. As he did so, he saw three figures sitting around another pot a short distance away. One of them observed his movement and spoke to the others. At once Triock stood and strode toward Covenant. He squatted near the Unbeliever, and studied him gravely before saying, "You have been grievously ill. My lore does not suffice to heal you. But I see that you are no longer dying."

"You saved me," Covenant said as bravely as he could through the pain of his mouth and his inanition.

"Perhaps. I am unsure. The wild magic has been at work in you." Covenant stared, and Triock went on: "It appeared that the *lomillialor* drew a response from the white gold of your ring. With that power, you surpass any test of truth I might give."

My ring, Covenant thought dully. But he was not ready to deal with that idea, and he set it aside also. "You saved me," he repeated. "There are things I need to know."

"Let them be. You must eat now. You have not taken food for many days." He looked around through the snow, then said, "Saltheart Foamfollower brings you *aliantha*."

Covenant heard heavy feet moving across the frozen ground. A moment later Foamfollower knelt with a quiet smile beside him. Both his hands were full of viridian treasure-berries.

Covenant looked at the *aliantha*. He felt he had

forgotten what to do with them; he had been hungry for so long that hunger had become a part of him. But he could not refuse the offer behind the Giant's kind smile. Slowly, he reached out a numb hand and took one of the treasure-berries.

When he slipped it past his lip and bit into it, the tangy salt-peach flavor which blossomed in his mouth seemed to refute all his reasons for fasting. And as he swallowed, he could feel nourishment rushing eagerly into him. He spit the seed into his palm; as if he were completing a ritual, he dropped it over his shoulder. Then he began to eat rapidly, wolfishly.

He did not stop until Foamfollower's hands were empty. Sighing as if he longed for more, he sowed the last seed behind him.

The Giant nodded approval and seated himself in a more relaxed position near the graveling. Triock followed his example. When they were both looking at him, Covenant said softly, "I won't forget this." He could not think of any other way to express his thanks.

Triock frowned sharply. He asked Foamfollower, "Does he threaten us now?"

The Giant's cavernous eyes searched Covenant's face. He smiled wanly as he replied, "The Unbeliever has a mournful turn of speech. He does not threaten —he does not threaten us."

Covenant felt a surge of grim gratitude for Foamfollower's understanding. He tried to smile in return, but the tightness of his lip prevented him. He winced at the effort, then pulled his blankets more closely around him. He sensed a depth of cold answers behind the questions he needed to ask.

But he did not know how to ask them. Triock's bitter mouth and Foamfollower's scars intruded between him and his summoners; he feared that he was to blame for the tales they might tell him if he asked. Yet he had to know the answers, had to know where he stood. The first outlines of purpose were taking shape within him. He could not forget how this valley had looked when he had first seen it. And Mhoram had pleaded with him for help.

Lamely, he began, "I didn't expect to turn up here.

I thought Mhoram was going to call me back. But even he doesn't have the Staff of Law. How—how did you do it?"

Triock answered in stiff tones, "Mhoram son of Variol, seer and oracle to the Council of Lords, came to Mithil Stonedown before the last war—the battle against Fleshharrower Raver. At that time, he gave to me the *lomillialor* rod which I have used today—and for the past three days. Because of his gift, I journeyed to the Loresraat, to study the uses of the High Wood. There I learned of High Lord Elena's fall—I—"

He paused for a moment to lash down his passion, then went on. "In the years which followed, I waited for the reason of High Lord Mhoram's gift to be made plain. During that time, I fought with my people against the marauders of the Gray Slayer. Then the Giant Saltheart Foamfollower joined us, and we fought together through the South Plains. While winter increased upon the Land, we attacked and ran and attacked again, doing what damage we could to our vast foe. But at last word came to us that Revelwood had fallen—that great Revelstone itself was besieged. We left our battles, and returned to Mithil Stonedown and Kevin's Watch. With the *lomillialor* of High Lord Mhoram, and the strength of Saltheart Foamfollower, and the lore I brought from the Loresraat, we labored for three days, and in the end brought you to the Land. It was not easily done."

Triock's flint voice sparked visions of desperation in Covenant's mind. To resist them, control them until he was ready for them, he asked, "But how? I thought only the Staff of Law—"

"Much has been broken by the fall of High Lord Elena," Triock retorted. "The Land has not yet tasted all the consequences of that evil. But the Staff made possible certain expressions of power—and limited others. Now that limit is gone. Do you not feel the malice of this winter?"

Covenant nodded with an ache in his eyes. His responsibility for Elena's end stung him, goaded him to ask another kind of question. "That doesn't tell me why you did it. After Lena—and Elena—and Atiaran"—he could not bring himself to be more specific—"and everything —you've got less reason than anyone in the world to want me back. Even Trell— Maybe Foamfollower here can forget, but you can't. If you were thinking it any louder, I could taste it."

Bitterness clenched Triock's jaws, but his reply was sharp and ready, as if he had whetted it many times. "Yet Foamfollower is persuasive. The Land is persuasive. The importance which the Lorewardens see in you is persuasive. And Lena daughter of Atiaran still lives in Mithil Stonedown. In her last years, Atiaran Trell-mate said often that it is the duty of the living to make meaningful the sacrifices of the dead. But I wish to find meaning for the sacrifices of those who live. After—after the harm which you wrought upon Lena—she hid herself so that the harm would not be known—so that you would be left free to bear your prophecy to the Lords. That sacrifice requires meaning, Unbeliever."

In spite of himself, in spite of his own expectations of hostility and recrimination, Covenant believed Triock. Elena had warned him; she had described the size of Triock's capabilities. Now he wondered where Triock found his strength. The man had been an unambitious Cattleherd. The girl he loved had been raped, and her bastard daughter had grown up to love the rapist. Yet because of them he had gone to the Loresraat, studied dangerous lore for which he had no desire or affinity. He had become a guerrilla fighter for the Land. And now he had summoned Covenant at the command of the Land's need and his own harsh sense of mercy. Thickly, Covenant muttered, "You've kept your Oath." He was thinking, I owe you for this, too, Foul.

Abruptly, Triock got to his feet. The lines around his eyes dominated his face as he scrutinized Covenant. In a low voice. he said, "What will you do?"

"Ask me later." Covenant was ashamed that he could not match Triock's gaze. "I'm not ready yet."

Instinctively, he clasped his right hand over his ring, hiding it from consideration.

"There is time," murmured Foamfollower. "You have a great need for rest."

Triock said, "Choose soon. We must be on our way at dawn." Then he moved brusquely away through the mounting snow toward his two companions by the second pot of graveling.

"He is a good man," Foamfollower said softly. "Trust him."

Oh, I trust him, Covenant thought. How can I help it?

Despite the warmth of his blankets, he began to shiver again.

As he leaned still closer to the glowing fire-stones, he noticed the look of concern on Foamfollower's face. To forestall any expression of anxiety which would remind him how little he deserved the Giant's concern, he said hastily, "I still don't know what's happened to you. The Giants were—I don't know what happened to them. And you— You've been outrageously hacked upon." In an effort to probe Foamfollower, he went on: "I'll tell you something funny. I was afraid of what you might do—after all that business in Treacher's Gorge. I was afraid you might go back to your people and—and convince them to stop fighting, give it up. What do you think? Have I finally succeeded in telling you a story you can laugh at?"

But he saw poignantly that he had not. Foamfollower bowed his head, covered his face with one hand. For a moment, the muscles of his shoulders tensed as if with his fingers he were squeezing the bones of his countenance into an attitude which he could not achieve in any other way. "Joy is in the ears that hear," he said in a voice muffled by his hand. "My ears have been too full of the noise of killing."

Then he raised his head, and his expression was calm. Only a smoldering deep within the caves of his eyes revealed that he was hurt. "I am not yet ready to laugh over this matter. Were I able to laugh, I would not feel so—driven to slay Soulcrusher's creatures."

"Foamfollower," Covenant murmured again, "what's happened to you?"

The Giant gestured helplessly with both hands, as if he could not conceive any way to tell his story. "My friend, I am what you see. Here is a tale which lies beyond even my grasp, and I am a Giant—though you will remember that my people considered me uncommonly brief of speech. Stone and Sea! Covenant, I know not what to say. You know how I fought for the Quest for the Staff of Law. When Damelon Giantfriend's prophecy for my people came to pass, I found that I could not give up this fighting. I had struck blows which would not stop. Therefore I left Seareach, so that I would at least serve the Land with my compulsion.

"But I did not go to the Lords. In my thoughts, the great rare beauty of Revelstone, Giant-wrought Lord's Keep, daunted me. I did not wish to stand in those brave halls while Soulcrusher's creatures raved in the Land. For that reason, I fight, and spend my days with people who fight. From the Northron Climbs to the Last Hills I have struck my blows. When I met Triock son of Thuler and his companions—when I learned that he holds a limb of the High Wood, descendant of the One Tree from which the Staff of Law was made—I joined him. In that way, I garnered my scars, and at last came here."

"You've been around humans too long," muttered Covenant. "You haven't told me anything. What—? How—? I don't know where to begin."

"Then do not begin, my friend. Rest." Foamfollower reached out and gently touched Covenant's shoulder. "You also have been too long among—people of another kind. You need days of rest which I fear you will not receive. You must sleep."

To his surprise, Covenant found that he was capable of sleep. Warm drowsiness seeped into him from the blankets and the graveling light, spread outward from the *aliantha* in his blood. Tomorrow he would know better what questions to ask. He lay back on the cold ground and pulled the blankets about his ears.

But as Foamfollower adjusted the blankets for him, he asked, "How much longer is this winter going to last?"

"Peace, my friend," Foamfollower replied. "The Land's spring should have been born three full moons ago."

A shudder of ice ran through Covenant. Bloody hell, Foul! he gritted. Hellfire!

But in his reclining position he could not resist his long weariness. He fell asleep almost at once, thinking, Hellfire. Hell and blood.

He lay in red, visionless slumber until sometime after dark he seemed to hear voices that awakened him slightly. Disembodied in his grogginess, they spoke across him as if he were a prostrate corpse.

"You told him little of the truth," Triock said.

And Foamfollower answered, "He has pain enough for one heart. How could I tell him?"

"He must know. He is responsible."

"No. For this he is not responsible."

"Still he must know."

"Even stone may break when it is too heavily burdened."

"Ah, Rockbrother. How will you justify yourself if he turns against the Land?"

"Peace, my friend. Do not torment me. I have already learned that I cannot be justified."

Covenant listened incomprehendingly. When the voices drifted out of his awareness, he sank into wild dreams of purpose and savage restitution.

SIX: The Defense of
Mithil Stonedown

LATER, he was shaken awake by Foamfollower. The Giant nudged his shoulder until he started up out of his blankets into the darkness. In the dim light of half-covered graveling pots, he could see that the snow had stopped, but dawn was still some time away. Night locked the valley full of black air.

He dropped back into the blankets, muttering groggily, "Go away. Let me sleep."

Foamfollower shook him again. "Arise, ur-Lord. You must eat now. We will depart soon."

"Dawn," Covenant said. The stiff soreness of his lip made him mumble as if the numbness of his hands and feet had spread to his tongue. "He said dawn."

"Yeurquin reports watch fires approaching Mithil Stonedown from the South Plains. They will not be friendly—few people of the south dare show light at night. And someone climbs toward us from the Stonedown itself. We will not remain here. Arise." He lifted Covenant into a sitting position, then thrust a flask and bowl into his hands. "Eat."

Sleepily, Covenant drank from the stone flask, and found that it contained water as icy as melted snow. The chill draft jolted him toward wakefulness. Shivering, he turned to the bowl. It contained unleavened bread and treasure-berries. He began to eat quickly to appease the cold water in his stomach.

Between bites, he asked, "If whatever they are— marauders—are coming, aren't we safe here?"

109

"Perhaps. But the Stonedownors will fight for their homes. They are Triock's people—we must aid them."

"Can't they just hide in the mountains—until the marauders go away?"

"They have done so in the past. But Mithil Stonedown has been attacked many times. The Stonedownors are sick at the damage done to their homes in these attacks. This time, they will fight."

Covenant emptied the bowl, and forced himself to drink deeply from the flask. The chill of the water made his throat ache.

"I'm no warrior."

"I remember," Foamfollower said with an ambiguous smile, as if what he remembered did not accord with Covenant's assertion. "We will keep you from harm."

He took the flask and bowl and stowed them in a large leather sack. Then from it he pulled out a heavy sheepskin jacket, which he handed to Covenant. "This will serve you well—though it is said that no apparel or blaze can wholly refute the cold of this winter." As Covenant donned the jacket, the Giant went on, "I regret that I have no better footwear for you. But the Stonedownors wear only sandals." He took from his sack a pair of thick sandals and passed them to Covenant.

When Covenant pushed back his blankets, he saw for the first time the damage he had done to his feet. They were torn and bruised from toe to heel; dry, caked blood covered them in blotches; and the remains of his socks hung from his ankles like the ragged frills of a jester. But he felt no pain; the deadness of his nerves reached deeper than these injuries. "Don't worry about it," he rasped as he pulled the socks from his ankles. "It's only leprosy."

He snatched the sandals from Foamfollower, jammed them onto his feet, and tied their thongs behind his heels. "One of these days I'll figure out why I bother to protect myself at all." But he knew why; his inchoate purpose demanded it.

"You ought to visit my world," he growled only half to the Giant. "It's painless. You won't feel a thing."

Then Triock hailed them. Foamfollower got swiftly to his feet. When Covenant climbed from the blankets, Foamfollower picked them up and pushed them into his sack. With the sack in one hand and the graveling pot in the other, he went with Covenant toward the Stonedownor.

Triock stood with three companions near the narrow ravine which was the outlet of the valley. They spoke together in low, urgent tones until Foamfollower and Covenant joined them. Then Triock said rapidly, "Rockbrother, our scouts have returned from the Plains. Slen reports that—" Abruptly he stopped himself. His mouth bent into a sardonic smile, and he said, "Pardon me. I forget my courtesy. I must make introductions."

He turned to one of his companions, a stocky old man breathing hoarsely in the cold. "Slen Terass-mate, here is ur-Lord Thomas Covenant, Unbeliever and white gold wielder. Unbeliever, here is Slen, the rarest cook in all the South Plains. Terass his wife stands among the Circle of elders of Mithil Stonedown."

Slen gave Covenant a salute which he returned awkwardly, as if the steaming of his breath and the numbness of his hands prevented him from grace. Then Triock turned to his other companions. They were a man and a woman who resembled each other like twins. They had an embattled look, as if they were familiar with bloodshed and killing at night, and their brown eyes blinked at Covenant like the orbs of people who had lost the capacity to be surprised. "Here are Yeurquin and Quirrel," said Triock. "We have fought together from the first days of this attack upon the Land.

"Unbeliever, when the Giant and I heard the word of Revelstone's siege, we were at work harrying a large band of the Slayer's creatures in the center of the South Plains. We fled from them at once, taking care to hide our trail so that they would not follow. And we left scouts to keep watch on the band. Now the scouts have returned to say that at first the band hunted us without success. But two days ago they turned suddenly and hastened straight toward the Mithil valley."

Triock paused grimly, then said, "They have felt the power of our work upon Kevin's Watch. *Melenkurion!* Some creature among them has eyes."

"Therefore we are not safe here," Foamfollower said to Covenant. "If they have truly seen the power of the High Wood, they will not rest until they have captured it for Soulcrusher—and slain its wielder."

Slen coughed a gout of steam. "We must go. We will be assailed at daybreak."

With a sharp nod, Triock agreed. "We are ready." He glanced toward Foamfollower and Covenant. "Unbeliever, we must travel afoot. The days of horseback sojourning are gone from the Land. Are you able?"

Covenant shrugged the question away. "It's a little late for us to start worrying about what I can or can't do. Foamfollower can carry me easily enough—if I slow you down."

"Well, then." Triock tightened his cloak, then picked up the graveling pot and held it over his head so that it lighted the ravine ahead of him. "Let us go."

Quirrel strode briskly ahead of them into the darkness of the ravine, and Triock preceded Slen after her. At a gesture from the Giant, Covenant followed Slen. Foamfollower came behind him with the other graveling pot, and Yeurquin brought up the rear of the group.

Before he had worked his way twenty yards down the ravine, Covenant knew that he was not yet strong enough to travel. Lassitude clogged his muscles, and what little energy he had he needed to defend himself from the penetrating cold. At first he resolved to endure despite his weakness. But by the time he had hauled himself halfway up the rift which led to the mountainside overlooking Mithil Stonedown, he understood that he could not go on without help. If he were to accomplish the purpose which grew obscurely in the back of his mind, he would have to learn how to accept help.

He leaned panting against the stone. "Foamfollower."

The Giant bent near him. "Yes, my friend."

"Foamfollower—I can't make it alone."

Chuckling gently, Foamfollower said, "Nor can I. My friend, there is comfort—in some companionships." He lifted Covenant effortlessly into his arms, carried him in a half-sitting position so that Covenant could see ahead. Though he only needed one arm to bear Covenant's weight, he put the graveling pot into Covenant's hands. The warm light revealed that Foamfollower was grinning as he said, "This is hazardous for me. It is possible that being of use may become a dangerous habit."

Gruffly, Covenant muttered, "That sounds like something I might say."

Foamfollower's grin broadened. But Triock threw back a warning scowl, and the Giant made no other response.

Moments later, Triock covered his graveling pot. At a nod from Foamfollower, Covenant did the same. The Giant placed the urn in his sack. Without any light to give them away, the group climbed out of the rift onto the exposed mountainside high above the Mithil valley.

Under the heavy darkness, they could see nothing below them but the distant watch fires smoldering like sparks in cold black tinder. Covenant could not gauge how far away the fires were, but Foamfollower said tightly, "It is a large band. They will gain the Stonedown by dawn—as Slen said."

"Then we must make haste," snapped Triock. He swung away to the left, moving swiftly along the unlit ledge.

The Giant followed at once, and his long strides easily matched Triock's trotting pace. Soon they had left the ledge, crossed from it to more gradual slopes as their trail worked downward into the valley. Slowly, Covenant could feel the air thickening. With the warmth of the graveling pot resting against his chest, he began to feel stronger. He made an effort to remember what this trail had looked like in the spring, but no memories came; he could not escape the impression of bare bleakness which shone through the night at him. He sensed that if he could have seen the unrelieved rock faces of the mountains, or the imposed lifelessness of the foothills, or the blasted tree trunks, or the Mithil River writhing in ice, he would have been dismayed. He was not yet ready for dismay.

Ahead of him, Triock began to run.

Foamfollower's jogging shook other thoughts out of Covenant's mind, and he began to concentrate in earnest on the gloomy night. By squinting grotesquely, he found that he could adjust his sight somewhat to the dark; apparently his eyes were remembering their Land-born penetration. As Foamfollower hurried him down the trail, he made out the high loom of the mountains on his left and the depth of the valley on his right. After a while, he caught vague, pale glimpses of the ice-gnarled river. Then the trail neared the end of the valley, and swung down in a wide arc toward the Mithil. When Foamfollower had completed the turn, Covenant saw the first dim lightening of dawn behind the eastern peaks.

Their pace became more urgent. As dawn leaked into the air, Covenant could see shadowy clouts of snow jumping from under the beat of Triock's feet. Foamfollower's strong respiration filled his ears, and behind it at odd intervals he heard the river straining in sharp creaks and groans against the weight of its own freezing. He began to feel a need to get down from the Giant's arms, either to separate himself from this urgency or to run toward it on his own.

Then Quirrel slowed abruptly and stopped. Triock and Foamfollower caught up with her, found her with another Stonedownor woman. The woman whispered quickly, "Triock, the people are ready. Enemies approach. They are many, but the scouts saw no Cavewights or ur-viles. How shall we fight them?"

As she spoke, Covenant dropped to the ground. He stamped his feet to speed the circulation in his knees and stepped close to Triock so that he could hear what was said.

"Someone among them has eyes," Triock responded. "They hunt the High Wood."

"So say the elders."

"We will use it to lure them. I will remain on this side of the Stonedown—away from them, so that they must search all the homes to find me. The houses will disrupt their formations, come between them. The Stonedown itself and surprise will aid us. Tell the people to conceal themselves on this side—behind the walls, in the outer houses. Go."

The woman turned and ran toward the Stonedown. Triock followed her more slowly, giving instructions to Quirrel and Yeurquin as he moved. With Foamfollower at his side, Covenant hurried after them, trying to figure out how to keep himself alive when the fighting started. Triock seemed sure that the marauders were after the *lomillialor,* but Covenant had other ideas. He was prepared to believe that this band of Foul's creatures had come for him and the white gold.

He panted his way up a long hill behind Triock, and when they topped it, he found himself overlooking the crouched stone shapes of the village. In the unhale dawn, he made out the rough, circular configuration of the Stonedown; its irregular houses, most of them flat-roofed and single-storied, stood facing inward around its open center, the gathering place for its people.

In the distance, near the mouth of the valley, were the fires of the marauders. They moved swiftly, as if they had the scent of prey in their nostrils.

Triock stopped for a moment to peer through the gloom toward them. Then he said to Foamfollower, "If this also goes astray, I leave the High Wood and the Unbeliever in your care. You must do what I cannot."

"It must not go astray," Foamfollower replied. "We cannot allow it. What is there that I could do in your stead?"

Triock jerked his head toward Covenant. "Forgive him."

Without waiting for an answer, he started at a lope down the hill.

Covenant rushed to catch up with him, but his dead feet slipped so uncertainly through the snow that he could not move fast enough. He did not overtake Triock until they were almost at the bottom of the hill. There Covenant grabbed his arm, stopped him, and panted steamily into his face, "Don't forgive me.

Don't do any more violence to yourself for me. Just give me a weapon so I can defend myself."

Triock struck Covenant's hand away. "A weapon, Unbeliever?" he barked. "Use your ring." But a moment later he controlled himself, fought down his bitterness. Softly, he said, "Covenant, perhaps one day we will come to comprehend each other, you and I." Reaching into his cloak, he drew out a stone dagger with a long blade, and handed it to Covenant gravely, as if they were comrades. Then he hastened away to join the people scurrying toward their positions on the outskirts of the village.

Covenant regarded the knife as if it were a secret asp. For a moment, he was uncertain what to do with it; now that he had a weapon, he could not imagine using it. He had had other knives, the implications of which were ambiguous. He looked questioningly up at Foamfollower, but the Giant's attention was elsewhere. He was staring intently toward the approach of the fires, and his eyes held a hot, enthusiastic gleam, as if they reflected or remembered slaughter. Covenant winced inwardly. He passed the knife back and forth between his hands, almost threw it away, then abruptly opened his jacket and slid the blade under his belt.

"Now what?" he demanded, trying to distract Foamfollower's stare. "Do we just stand here, or should we start running around in circles?"

The Giant looked down sharply and his face darkened. "They fight for their homes," he said dangerously. "If you cannot aid, at least forbear to ridicule." With a commanding gesture, he strode away between the nearest houses.

Groaning at the Giant's unfamiliar ire, Covenant followed him into the Stonedown. Most of the people had stopped moving now and were stealthily crouched behind the houses around that side of the village. They seemed to ignore Covenant, and he went by them after Foamfollower as if he were on his way to bait their trap for the marauders.

Foamfollower halted at the back of one of the inner houses. It was flat-roofed, like most of the buildings around it, and its stone eaves reached as high as the Giant's throat. When Covenant joined him, he picked up the Unbeliever and tossed him lightly onto the roof.

Covenant landed facedown in the snow. At once, he lurched sputtering to his knees, and turned angrily back toward the Giant.

"You will be safer there," Foamfollower said. He nodded toward a neighboring house. "I will ward you from here. Stay low. They are almost upon us."

Instinctively, Covenant dropped to his belly.

As if on signal, he felt a hushed silence spring up around him. No sound touched the Stonedown except the low, dislocated whistle of the wind. He felt acutely exposed on the roof. But even this height made him dizzy; he could not look or jump down. Hastily, he skittered back from the edge, then froze as he heard the noise he made. Though his movements were muffled by the snow, they sounded as loud as betrayal in the stillness. For a moment, he could not muster the courage to turn around. He feared to find cruel faces leering at him over the roof edge.

But slowly the apprehension beating in his temples eased. He began to curse himself. Spread-eagled on the roof, he worked slowly around until he was facing in toward the center of the Stonedown.

Across the valley, light bled into the air through the gray packed clouds. The clouds shut out any other sky completely, and under their cold weight the day dawned bleak and cheerless, irremediably aggrieved. The sight chilled Covenant more than black night. He could see now more clearly than he had from Kevin's Watch that this shrouded, constant gloom was unnatural, wrong—the pall of Lord Foul's maddest malice. And he was aghast at the power it implied. Foul had the might to distort the Earth's most fundamental orders. It would not exhaust him to crush one ineffectual leper. Any purpose to the contrary was mere witless buffoonery.

Covenant's hand moved toward the knife as if its stone edge could remind him of fortitude, tighten the moorings of his endurance. But a distant, clashing sound, uncertain in the wind, cast all other thoughts from his mind. After straining his ears briefly, he knew that he was hearing the approach of the marauders.

He began to shiver as he realized that they were making no effort to move quietly. The whole valley lay open before them, and they had the hungry confidence of numbers; they came up along the river clattering their weapons, defying the Stonedownors to oppose them. Cautiously, Covenant slid into a better position to see over the edge of the roof. His muscles trembled, but he locked his jaws, pressed himself flat in the snow, and peered through the dim air toward the center of the village with an intensity of concentration that made his head ache.

Soon he heard guttural shouts and the clang of iron on stone as the marauders rushed to search the first houses. Still he could see nothing; the roofline of the village blocked his view. He tried to keep his breathing low, so that exhaled vapor would not obscure his sight or reveal his position. When he turned his head to look in other directions, he found that he was clenching fistfuls of snow, squeezing them into ice. He opened his hands, forced his fingers to unclaw themselves, then braced his palms flat on the stone so that he would be ready to move.

The loud approach spread out over the far side of the village and began to move inward, working roughly parallel to the river. Instead of trying to surround and trap the Stonedownors, the marauders were performing a slow sweep of the village; disdaining surprise, they maneuvered so that the people would be forced to flee toward the narrow end of the valley. Covenant could think of no explanation for these tactics but red-eyed confidence and contempt. The marauders wanted to drive the people into the final trap of the valley's end, thus prolonging and sharpening the anticipated slaughter. Such malicious surety was frightening, but Covenant found relief in it. It was not an approach designed to capture something as reputedly powerful as white gold.

But he soon learned another explanation. As he

strained his eyes to peer through the dawn, he saw a sharp flash of green light from the far side of the village. It lasted only an instant, and in its wake a crumbling noise filled the air—a noise like the sound of boulders crushing each other. It startled him so much that he almost leaped to his feet to see what had happened. But he caught himself when he saw the first creatures enter the center of the Stonedown.

Most of them were vaguely human in outline. But their features were tormented, grotesquely arranged, as if some potent fist had clenched them at birth, twisting them beyond all recognition. Eyes were out of place, malformed; noses and mouths bulged in skin that was contorted like clay which had been squeezed between strong fingers; and in some cases all the flesh of face and scalp oozed fluid as if the entire head were a running sore. And the rest of their forms were no healthier. Some had backs bent at demented angles, others bore extra arms or legs, still others wore their heads between their shoulder blades or in the center of their chests. But one quality they shared: they all reeked of perversion as if it were the very lifeblood of their existence; and a hatred of everything hale or well curdled their sight.

Naked except for food sacks and bands to hold weapons, they came snarling and spitting into the open core of Mithil Stonedown. There they stopped until the shouts of their fellows told them that the first half of the village was under their control. Then a tall figure with a knuckled face and three massive arms barked a command to the marauders behind her. In response, a group moved into the open circle, bringing with it three prodigious creatures unlike the others.

These three were as blind and hairless as if they had been spawned from ur-viles, but they had neither ears nor noses. Their small heads sat necklessly on their immense shoulders. At the bottom of trunks as big as hogsheads, their short legs protruded like braces, and their heavy arms were long enough to reach the ground. From shoulder to fingertip, the inner surfaces of their arms were covered with suckers. Together, they seemed to ripple in Covenant's sight, as if within them they carried so much ill might that his unwarped eyes could not discern their limits.

On command, the marauders led the three to a house at the edge of the circle. They were positioned around the building, and at once they moved close to the walls, spread their arms to their fullest extent, gripped the flat rock with their suckers.

Hoarse, growling power began to mount between them. Their might reached around the house and tightened slowly like a noose.

Covenant watched them in blank dismay. He understood the marauders' tactics now; the band attacked as it did to protect these three. With a stink of attar, their power increased, tightened, growled, until he could see a hawser of green force running through them around the house, squeezing it in implacable fury. He thought that he should shout to the Stonedownors, warn them of the danger. But he was dry-mouthed and frozen with horror. He hardly knew that he had risen to his hands and knees to gain a better view of what was happening.

Moments passed. Tension crackled in the air as the stone of the house began to scream silently under the stress. Covenant gaped at it as if the mute rock were crying out to him for help.

Then the noose exploded in a flash of green force. The house crumbled inward, fell into itself until all its rooms and furnishings were buried in rubble. Its three destroyers stepped back and searched blindly around them for more stone to crush.

Abruptly, a woman screamed—a raw shout of outrage. Covenant heard her running between the houses. He leaped to his feet and saw a fleet, white-haired woman dash past the eaves of his roof with a long knife clenched in both hands. In an instant, she had raced beyond him toward the center of the Stonedown.

At once he went after her. With two quick steps, he threw himself like a bundle of disjointed limbs toward the next roof. He landed off balance, fell, and slid through the snow almost to the edge of the house. But he picked himself up and moved back to get a running start toward the next roof.

From that position, he saw the woman rush into the open circle. Her scream had alerted the marauders, but they were not ready for the speed with which she launched herself at them. As she sprang, she stabbed the long knife with all her strength, drove it hilt-deep into the breast of the three-armed creature which had been commanding the assault.

The next instant, another creature grabbed her by the hair and flung her back. She lost her knife, fell out of Covenant's sight in front of one of the houses. The marauders moved after her, swords upraised.

Covenant leaped for the next roof. He kept his balance as he landed this time, ran across the stone, and leaped again. Then he fell skidding on the roof of the house which blocked the woman from his sight. He had too much momentum now; he could not stop. In a cloud of snow, he toppled over the edge and slammed heavily to the ground beside the woman.

The impact stunned him. But his sudden appearance had surprised the attackers, and the nearest creature recoiled several steps, waving its sword defensively as if Covenant were a group of warriors. In the interval, he shook red mist from his eyes, and got gasping to his feet.

The marauders whirled their weapons, dropped into fighting crouches. But when they saw that they were threatened by only one half-stunned man, some of them spat hoarse curses at him and others began to laugh malevolently. Sheathing their weapons, several of them moved forward with an exaggerated display of caution to capture Covenant and the old woman. At this, other creatures jeered harshly, and more came into the circle to see what was happening.

Covenant's gaze dashed in all directions, hunting for a way of escape. But he could find nothing; he and the woman were alone against more than a score of the misborn creatures.

The marauders' breathing did not steam in the cold air. Though they wore nothing to protect their flesh from the cold, they seemed horribly comfortable in the preternatural winter.

They approached as if they meant to eat Covenant and the woman alive.

The woman hissed at them in revulsion, but he paid no attention to her. All of him was concentrated on escape. An odd memory tugged at the back of his mind. He remembered a time when Mhoram had made even powerless white gold useful. As the creatures crept hooting toward him, he suddenly brandished his ring and sprang forward a step, shouting, "Get back, you bloody bastards, or I'll blast you where you stand!"

Either his shout or the sight of his ring startled them; they jumped back a few paces, grabbing at their weapons.

In that instant, Covenant snatched up the woman's hand and fled. Pulling her after him, he raced to the corner of the house, swung sharply around it, and sped as fast as he could away from the open ground. He lost his hold on the woman almost at once; he could not grip her securely with his half-fingerless hand. But she was running on her own now. In a moment, she caught up with him and took hold of his arm, helped him make the next turn.

Roaring with fury, the marauders started in pursuit. But when they entered the lane between the houses, Foamfollower dove from a rooftop and crashed headlong into them like a battering ram. Constricted by the houses on either side, they could not evade him; he hit them squarely, breaking the ones nearest him and bowling the others back into the center of the Stonedown.

Then Triock, Quirrel, and Yeurquin led a dozen Stonedownors into the village across the roofs. Amid the confusion caused by the Giant's attack, the defenders fell onto the marauders like a rain of swords and javelins. Other people ran forward to engage the creatures that were still hunting among the houses. In moments, fighting raged throughout the Stonedown.

But Covenant did not stop; drawing the woman with him, he fled until he was past the last buildings. There he lengthened his stride, intending to run as far as he could up the valley. But Slen intercepted him. Panting hoarsely, Slen snapped at the woman, "Fool! You have lost sense altogether." Then he tugged at Covenant. "Come. Come."

Covenant and the woman followed him away from the river along an unmarked path into the foothills. A few hundred yards above the village, they came to a jumble of boulders—the ancient remains of a rockfall from the mountains. Slen took a cunning way in among the boulders and soon reached a large, hidden cave. Several Stonedownors stood on guard at the cave mouth, and within it the children and the ill or infirm huddled around graveling bowls.

Covenant was tempted to enter the cave and share its sanctuary. But near its mouth was a high, sloped heap of rock with a broad crown. He turned and climbed the rocks to find out if he could see the Stonedown from its top. The white-haired woman ascended lightly behind him; soon they stood together, looking down at the battle of Mithil Stonedown.

The altitude of his position surprised him. He had not realized that he had climbed so high. Vertigo made his feet feel suddenly slippery, and he recoiled from the sight. For a moment, the valley reeled around him. He could not believe that a short time ago he had been leaping across rooftops; the mere thought of such audacity seemed to sweep his balance away, leaving him at the mercy of the height. But the woman caught hold of him, supported him. And his urgent need to watch the fighting helped him to resist his dizziness. Clinging half unconsciously to the woman's shoulder, he forced himself to peer downward.

At first, the cloud-locked dimness of the day obscured the battle, prevented him from being able to distinguish what was happening. But as he concentrated, he made out the Giant.

Foamfollower dominated the melee in the Stonedown's center. He waded hugely through the marauders, heaved himself from place to place. Swinging his mighty fists like cudgels, he chopped creatures down, pounded them out of his way with blows which appeared powerful enough to tear their heads off. But he was sorely outnumbered. Though his movement prevented the marauders from hitting him with a concerted attack, they were armed and he was not. As Covenant watched, several of the creatures succeeded in knocking Foamfollower toward one of the rock destroyers.

The soft, glad tone of the woman's voice jarred painfully against his anxiety. "Thomas Covenant, I thank you," she said. "My life is yours."

Foamfollower! Covenant cried silently. "What?" He doubted that the woman had actually spoken. "I don't want your life. What in hell possessed you to run out there, anyway?"

"That is unkind," she replied quietly. "I have waited for you. I have ridden your Ranyhyn."

The meaning of what she said did not penetrate him. "Foamfollower is getting himself killed down there because of you."

"I have borne your child."

What?

Without warning, her words hit him in the face like ice water. He snatched his hand from her shoulder, jerked backward a step or two across the rock. A shift in the wind brought the clamor of battle up to him in tatters, but he did not hear it. For the first time, he looked at the woman.

She appeared to be in her mid-sixties—easily old enough to be his mother. Lines of groundless hope marked her pale skin around the blue veins in her temples, and the hair which plumed her head was no longer thick. He saw nothing to recognize in the open expectancy of her mouth, or in the bone-leanness of her body, or in her wrinkled hands. Her eyes had a curious, round, misfocused look, like the confusion of madness.

But for all their inaccuracy, they were spacious eyes, like the eyes of the women she claimed for her mother and daughter. And woven into the shoulders of her long blue robe was a pattern of white leaves.

"Do you not know me, Thomas Covenant?" she said gently. "I have not changed. They all wish me to change—Triock and Trell my father and the Circle of elders, all wish me to change. But I do not. Do I appear changed?"

"No," Covenant panted. With sour nausea in his mouth, he understood that he was looking at Lena, the woman he had violated with his lust—mother of the woman he had violated with his love—recipient of the Ranyhyn-boon he had instigated when he had violated the great horses with his false bargains. Despite her earlier fury, she looked too old, too fragile, to be touched. He forced out the words as if they appalled him. "No—change."

She smiled with relief. "I am glad. I have striven to hold true. The Unbeliever deserves no less."

"Deserves," Covenant croaked helplessly. The battle noises from Mithil Stonedown taunted him again. "Hellfire."

He coerced himself to meet her gaze, and slowly her smile turned to a look of concern. She moved forward, reached out to him. He wanted to back away, but he held still as her fingertips lightly touched his lip, then stroked a cool line around the wound on his forehead. "You have been harmed," she said. "Does the Despiser dare to assault you in your own world?"

He felt that he had to warn her away from him; the misfocus of her gaze showed that she was endangered by him. Rapidly, he whispered, "Atiaran's judgment is coming true. The Land is being destroyed, and it's my fault."

Her fingers caressed him as if they were trying to smooth a frown from his brow. "You will save the Land. You are the Unbeliever—the new Berek Half-hand of our age."

"I can't save anything—I can't even help those people down there. Foamfollower is my friend, and I can't help him. Triock—Triock has earned anything I can do, and I can't—"

"Were I a Giant," she interrupted with sudden vehemence, "I would require no aid in such a battle. And Triock—" She faltered unexpectedly, as if she had stumbled over an unwonted perception of what Triock meant to her. "He is a Cattleherd—content. He wishes— But I am unchanged. He—"

Covenant stared at the distress which strained her

face. For an instant, her eyes seemed to be on the verge of seeing clearly, and her forehead tightened under the imminence of cruel facts. "Covenant?" she whispered painfully. "Unbeliever?"

"Yes, I know," Covenant mumbled in spite of himself. "He would consider himself lucky if he got killed." As tenderly as he could, he reached out and drew her into his arms.

At once she embraced him, clung convulsively to him while a crisis within her crested, receded. But even as he gave her what comfort he could with his arms, he was looking back toward the Stonedown. The shouts and cries and clatter of the fighting outweighed his own torn emotions, his conflicting sympathy for and horror of Lena. When she stepped back from him, he had to force himself to meet the happiness which sparkled in her mistaken eyes.

"I am so glad—my eyes rejoice to behold you. I have held—I have desired to be worthy. Ah, you must meet our daughter. She will make you proud."

Elena! Covenant groaned thickly. They haven't told her—she doesn't understand— Hellfire.

For a moment, he ached under his helplessness, his inability to speak. But then a hoarse shout from the Stonedown rescued him. Looking down, he saw people standing in the center of the village with their swords and spears upraised. Beyond them, the surviving marauders fled for their lives toward the open plains. A handful of the defenders gave savage pursuit, harried the creatures to prevent as many as possible from escaping.

Immediately, Covenant started down the rocks. He heard Lena shout word of the victory to Slen and the other people at the mouth of the cave, but he did not wait for her or them. He ran down out of the foothills as if he too were fleeing—fleeing from Lena, or from his fear for Foamfollower, he did not know which. As swiftly as he could without slipping in the snow, he hurried toward Mithil Stonedown.

But when he dashed between the houses and stumbled in among the hacked corpses, he lurched to a halt. All around him the snow and stone were spattered with blood—livid incarnadine patches, heavy swaths of red-gray serum diseased by streaks of green. Stonedownors—some of them torn limb from limb—lay confused amid the litter of Lord Foul's creatures. But the perverse faces and forms of the creatures were what drew Covenant's attention. Even in death, they stank of the abomination which had been practiced upon them by their maker, and they appalled him more than ur-viles or *kresh* or discolored moons. They were so entirely the victims of Foul's contempt. The sight and smell of them made his guts heave. He dropped to his knees in the disfigured snow and vomited as if he were desperate to purge himself of his kinship with these creatures.

Lena caught up with him there. When she saw him, she gave a low cry and flung her arms around him. "What is wrong?" she moaned. "Oh, beloved, you are ill."

Her use of the word *beloved* stung him like acid flung from the far side of Elena's lost grave. It drove him reeling to his feet. Lena tried to help him, but he pushed her hands away. Into the concern of her face, he cried, "Don't touch me. Don't." Jerking brokenly, his hands gestured at the bodies around him. "They're lepers. Lepers like me. This is what Foul wants to do to everything." His mouth twisted around the words as if they shared the gall of his nausea.

Several Stonedownors had gathered near him. Triock was among them. His hands were red, and blood ran from a cut along the line of his jaw, but when he spoke, he only sounded bitterer, harder. "It boots nothing to say that they have been made to be what they are. Still they shed blood—they ravage—they destroy. They must be prevented."

"They're like me." Covenant turned panting toward Triock as if he meant to hurl himself at the Stonedownor's throat. But when he looked up he saw Foamfollower standing behind Triock. The Giant had survived a fearsome struggle. The muscles of his arms quivered with exhaustion. His leather jerkin hung from his shoulders in shreds, and all across his chest were garish red sores—wounds inflicted by the suckers of the rock destroyer. But a sated look glazed his deep-set eyes, and the vestiges of a fierce grin clung to his lips.

Covenant struggled for breath in the bloody air of the Stonedown. The sight of Foamfollower triggered a reaction he could not control. "Get your people together," he rasped at Triock. "I've decided what I'm going to do."

The hardness of Triock's mouth did not relent, but his eyes softened as he searched Covenant's gaze. "Such choices can wait a little longer," he replied stiffly. "We have other duties. We must cleanse Mithil Stonedown—rid our homes of this stain." Then he turned and walked away.

Soon all the people who were whole or strong enough were at work. First they buried their fallen friends and kindred in honorable rocky cairns high in the eastern slopes of the valley. And when that grim task was done, they gathered together all the creature corpses and carted this hacked and broken rubble downriver across the bridge to the west bank of the Mithil. There they built a pyre like a huge warning blaze to any marauders in the South Plains and burned the dead creatures until even the bones were reduced to white ash. Then they returned to the Stonedown. With clean snow, they scrubbed it from rim to center until all the blood and gore had been washed from the houses and swept from the ground of the village.

Covenant did not help them. After his recent exertions, he was too weak for such labor. But he felt cold, upright, and passionate, ballasted by the new granite of his purpose. He went with Lena, Slen, and the Circle of elders to the banks of the river, and there helped treat the injuries of the Stonedownors. He cleaned and bound wounds, removed slivers of broken weapons, amputated mangled fingers and toes. When even the elders faltered, he took the blue-hot blade and used it to clean the sores which covered Foamfollower's chest and back. His fingers trembled at the task, and his halfhand slipped on the knife's handle, but he pressed fire into the Giant's oaken muscles until all the sucker wounds had been seared.

Foamfollower took a deep breath that shuddered with pain, and said, "Thank you, my friend. That is a grateful fire. You have made it somewhat like the *caamora*." But Covenant threw down the blade without answering, and went to plunge his shaking hands into the icy waters of the Mithil. All the while, a deep rage mounted within him, grew up his soul like slow vines reaching toward savagery.

Later, when all the wounded had been given treatment, Slen and the elders cooked a meal for the whole village. Sitting in the new cleanliness of the open center, the people ate hot savory stew with unleavened bread, cheese, and dried fruit. Covenant joined them. Throughout the meal, Lena tended him like a servant. But he kept his eyes down, stared at the ground to avoid her face and all other faces; he did not wish to be distracted from the process taking place within him. With cold determination, he ate every scrap of food offered to him. He needed nourishment for his purpose.

After the meal, Triock made new arrangements for the protection of the Stonedown. He sent scouts back out to the Plains, designed tentative plans against another attack, asked for volunteers to carry word of the rock-destroying creatures to the Stonedown's nearest neighbors, thirty leagues away. Then at last he turned to the matter of Covenant's decision.

Yeurquin and Quirrel sat down on either side of Triock as he faced the village. Before he began, he glanced at Foamfollower, who stood nearby. Obliquely, Covenant observed that in place of his ruined jerkin Foamfollower now wore an armless sheepskin cloak. It did not close across his chest, but it covered his shoulders and back like a vest. He nodded in response to Triock's mute question, and Triock said, "Well, then. Let us delay no longer." In a rough, sardonic tone, he added, "We have had rest enough.

"My friends, here is ur-Lord Thomas Covenant, Unbeliever and white gold wielder. For good or ill, the Giant and I have brought him to the Land. You know the lore which has been abroad in the Land since that day seven and forty years ago when the Unbeliever first came to Mithil Stonedown from Kevin's Watch. You see that he comes in the semblance of Berek Halfhand, Heartthew and Lord-Fatherer, and bears with him the talisman of the wild magic which destroys peace. You have heard the ancient song:

> And with the one word of truth or treachery,
> he will save or damn the Earth
> because he is mad and sane,
> cold and passionate,
> lost and found.

He is among us now so that he may fulfill all his prophecies.

"My friends, a blessing in the apparel of disease may still right wrongs. And treachers in any other garb remain accursed. I know not whether we have wrought life or death for the Land in this matter. But many brave hearts have held hope in the name of the Unbeliever. The Lorewardens of the Loresraat saw omens of good in the darkest deeds which cling to Covenant's name. And it was said among them that High Lord Mhoram does not falter in his trust. Each of you must choose your own faith. I choose to support the High Lord's trust."

"I, also," said Foamfollower quietly. "I have known both Mhoram son of Variol and Thomas Covenant."

Omens, hell! Covenant muttered to himself. Rape and betrayal. He sensed that Lena was gathering herself to make some kind of avowal. To prevent her, he pushed glaring to his feet. "That's not all," he grated. "Tamarantha and Prothall and Mhoram and who knows how many others thought that I was chosen for this by the Creator or whoever's responsible in the end. Take consolation in that if you can. Never mind that it's just another way of saying I chose myself. The idea itself isn't so crazy. Creators are the most helpless people alive. They have to work through unsufferable —they have to work through tools as blunt and misbegotten and useless as myself. Believe me, it's easier just to burn the world down, reduce it to innocent or

clean or at least dead ash. Which may be what I'm
doing. How else could I—?"

With an effort, he stopped himself. He had already
iterated often enough the fundamental unbelief with
which he viewed the Land; he had no reason to repeat
that it was a delusion spawned by his abysmal incapacity for life. He had gone beyond the need for such
assertions. Now he had to face their consequences. To
begin, he broached a tangent of what was in his heart.
"Did any of you see a break in the clouds—sometime
—maybe a couple nights ago?"

Triock stiffened. "We saw," he said gruffly.

"Did you see the moon?"

"It was full."

"It was green!" Covenant spat. His vehemence
cracked his swollen lip, and a trickle of blood started
down his chin. He scrubbed the blood away with his
numb fingers, steadied himself on the stone visage of
his purpose. Ignoring the stares of the Stonedownors,
he went on, "Never mind. Never mind that. Listen. I'll
tell you what we're going to do. I'll tell you what you're
going to do."

He met Triock's gaze. Triock's lips were white with
tension, but his eyes crouched in their sockets as if
they ached to flinch away from what they beheld.
Covenant scowled into them. "You're going to find
some way to let Mhoram know I'm here."

For an instant, Triock gaped involuntarily. Then
he drew himself up as if he were about to start yelling
at Covenant. Seeing this, Foamfollower interposed,
"Ur-Lord, do you know what you ask? Revelstone is
three hundred leagues distant. In the best of times,
even a Giant could not gain the high halls of Lord's
Keep in less than fifteen days."

"And the Plains are aswarm with marauders!"
barked Triock. "From here to the joining of the Black
and Mithil rivers, a strong band might fight and dodge
its way in twenty days. But beyond—in the Center
Plains—are the fell legions of the Gray Slayer. All the
Land from Andelain to the Last Hills is under their
dominion. With twenty thousand warriors, I could not

battle my way even to the Soulsease River in twice or ten times fifty days."

Covenant began, "I don't give a bloody damn what—"

Flatly, Quirrel interrupted him. "Further, you must not call upon the Ranyhyn for aid. The creatures of the Gray Slayer prize Ranyhyn-flesh. The Ranyhyn would be taken and eaten."

"I don't care!" Covenant fumed. "It doesn't matter what you think is possible or impossible. Everything here is impossible. If we don't start doing the impossible now, it'll be too late. And Mhoram has got to know."

"Why?" Anger still crackled in Triock's voice, but he was watching Covenant closely now, scrutinizing him as if he could see something malignant growing behind Covenant's belligerence.

Under Triock's gaze, Covenant felt too ashamed to admit that he had already refused a summons from Mhoram. He could taste the outrage with which all the Stonedownors would greet such a confession. Instead, he replied, "Because it will make a difference to him. If he knows where I am—if he knows what I'm doing—it'll make a difference. He'll know what to do."

"What can he do? Revelstone is besieged by an army as unanswerable as the Desert. High Lord Mhoram and all the Council are prisoners in Lord's Keep. We are less helpless than they."

"Triock, you're making a big mistake if you ever assume that Mhoram is helpless."

"The Unbeliever speaks truly," Foamfollower said. "The son of Variol is a man of many resources. Much that may appear impossible is possible for him."

At this Triock looked at his hands, then nodded sharply. "I hear you. The High Lord must be told. But still I know not how such a thing may be accomplished. Much which may appear possible to Giants and white gold wielders is impossible for me."

"You've got one of those *lomillialor* rods," rasped Covenant. "They were made for communication."

Triock growled in exasperation. "I have told you

that I lack the lore for such work. I did not study the speaking of messages in the Loresraat."

"Then learn. By hell! Did you expect it to be easy? Learn!" Covenant knew how unfairly he was treating Triock, but the exigency of his purpose countenanced neither consideration nor failure.

For a long moment, Triock glared miserably at Covenant, and his hands twitched with anger and helplessness. But then Quirrel whispered to him, and his eyes widened hopefully. "Perhaps," he murmured. "Perhaps it may be done." He made an effort to steady himself, forced a measure of calmness into his face. "It is said" —he swallowed thickly—"it is said that an Unfettered One lives in the mountains which protect the South Plains from Garroting Deep. Uncertain word of such a One has been whispered among the southron villages for—many years. It is said that he studies the slow breathing of the mountains—or that he gazes constantly across Garroting Deep in contemplation of *Melenkurion* Skyweir—or that he lives in a high place to learn the language of the wind. If such a One lives —if he may be found—perhaps he can make use of the High Wood as I cannot."

A rustle of excitement ran through the circle at this idea. Triock took a deep breath and nodded to his companions. "I will make this attempt." Then a sardonic hue colored his voice. "If it also goes astray, I will at least know that I have striven to fulfill your choices.

"Unbeliever, what word shall I send to High Lord Mhoram and the Council of Revelstone?"

Covenant looked away, raised his face to the leaden sky. Snow had started to fall in the valley; a scattering of flakes drifted on the breeze like instants of mist, dimming the day even further. They had an early look about them, as if they presaged a heavy fall. For a moment, Covenant watched them tumble through the Stonedown. He was acutely conscious of Triock's question. It confronted him starkly, challenged the untried mettle of his purpose. And he feared to answer it. He feared to hear himself say things which were so insane. When he returned his gaze to the waiting Stonedownors, he replied obliquely, seeking fuel for his courage.

"Foamfollower, what happened to your people?"

"My friend?"

"Tell me what happened to the Giants."

Foamfollower squirmed at Covenant's scowl. "Ah, ur-Lord, there is no need for such stories now. They are long in the telling, and would better suit another time. The present is full."

"Tell me!" Covenant hissed. "Bloody hell, Foamfollower! I want to know it all! I need—everything, every damned despicable thing that Foul—"

Without warning, Triock interrupted him. "The Giants have returned to their Home beyond the Sunbirth Sea."

Covenant whirled toward Triock. The lie in his words was so palpable that it left Covenant gasping, and around him the Stonedownors gaped at Triock. But Triock met Covenant's aghast stare without flinching. The cut along his jaw emphasized his determination. In a hard, steady voice that cut through Covenant's superficial ire to the rage growing within him, Triock said, "We have sworn the Oath of Peace. Do not ask us to feed your hate. The Land will not be served by such passions."

"It's all I've got!" Covenant answered thickly. "Don't you understand? I don't have anything else. Nothing! All by itself, it has got to be enough."

Gravely, almost sorrowfully, Triock said, "Such a foe cannot be fought with hate. I know. I have felt it in my heart."

"Hellfire, Triock! Don't preach at *me*. I'm sick to death of being victimized. I'm sick of walking meekly or at least quietly and just putting my head on the block. I am going to fight this."

"Why?" Triock asked in a restrained voice. "What will you fight for?"

"Are you deaf as well as blind?" Covenant wrapped his arms around his chest to steady himself. "I hate Foul. I've had all I can stand of—"

"No. I am neither deaf nor blind. I see and hear that you intend to fight. What will you fight for? There is matter enough to occupy your hate in your own world. You are in the Land now. What will you fight for?"

Hell and blood! Covenant shouted silently. How much of me do you want? But Triock's question threw him back upon himself. He could have replied: I hate Foul because of what he's doing to the Land. But that sounded like a disclaimer of responsibility, and he was too angry to deny his own convictions. He was too angry, also, to give Triock any comforting answer. In a brittle voice, he said, "I'm going to do it for myself. So that I can at least believe in me before I lose my mind altogether."

This response silenced Triock, and after a moment Foamfollower asked painfully, "My friend, what will you do with your passion?"

Snow slowly thickened in the air. The flakes danced like motes of obscurity across Covenant's vision, and the strain of his fierce stare made his unhealed forehead throb as if his skull were crippled with cracks. But he did not relent, could not relent now. "There's only one good answer to someone like Foul." Yet in spite of his anger, he found that he could not meet Foamfollower's gaze.

"What answer?"

Involuntarily, Covenant's fingers bent into claws. "I'm going to bring Foul's Creche down around his ears."

He heard the surprise and incredulity of the Stonedownors, but he ignored them. He listened only to Foamfollower as the Giant said, "Have you learned then how to make use of the white gold?"

With all the intensity of conviction he could muster, Covenant replied, "I'll find a way."

As he spoke, he believed himself. Hatred would be enough. Foul could not take it from him, could not quench it or deflect its aim. He, Thomas Covenant, was a leper; he alone in all the Land had the moral experience or training for this task. Facing between Foamfollower and Triock, addressing them both, he said, "You can either help me or not."

Triock met him squarely. "I will not aid you. I will

undertake to send word of you to High Lord Mhoram —but I will not share in this defamation of Peace."

"It is the wild magic, Triock," Foamfollower said as if he were pleading on Covenant's behalf, "the wild magic which destroys Peace. You have heard the song. White gold surpasses all Oaths."

"Yet I will retain my own. Without the Oath, I would have slain the Unbeliever seven and forty years ago. Let him accept that, and be content."

Softly, the Giant said, "I hear you, my friend. You are worthy of the Land you serve." Then he turned to Covenant. "Ur-Lord, permit me to accompany you. I am a Giant—I may be of use. And I—I yearn to strike closer blows against the Soulcrusher who so appalled my kindred. And I know the peril. I have seen the ways in which we become what we hate. Permit me."

Before Covenant could reply, Lena jumped to her feet. "Permit me also!" she cried excitedly.

"Lena!" Triock protested.

She paid no attention to him. "I wish to accompany you. I have waited so long. I have striven to be worthy. I have mothered a High Lord and ridden a Ranyhyn. I am young and strong. Ah, I yearn to share with you. Permit me, Thomas Covenant."

The wind hummed softly between the houses, carrying the snow like haze into Covenant's eyes. The flakes flicked cold at his sore lip, but still he nodded his approval of the gathering flurries. A good snowfall would cover his trail. The snow muffled the sounds of the village, and he seemed to be speaking to himself as he said, "Let's get going. I've got debts to pay."

SEVEN: Message to Revelstone

THOUGH his jaws ached with protests, Triock gave the orders which sent several of his comrades hurrying to collect supplies for Covenant, Foamfollower, and Lena. In that moment, the giving of those orders seemed to be the hardest thing he had ever done. The restraint which had allowed Covenant to live seven and forty years ago paled by comparison. The exertions which had brought Covenant to the Land now lost their meaning. Lena Atiaran-daughter's desire to accompany the Unbeliever turned all Triock's long years of devotion to dust and loss, and all his lavish love had been wasted.

Yet he could not refuse her—could not, though he had the authority to do so. He was one of Mithil Stonedown's Circle of elders, and by old Stonedown tradition, even marriages and long journeys were subject to the approval of the Circle. Furthermore, he was the acknowledged leader of Mithil Stonedown's defense. He could have commanded Lena to stay at home, and if his reasons were valid, all the Stonedown would have fought to keep her.

His reasons were valid. Lena was old, half confused. She might hamper Covenant's movements; she might even risk his life again, as she had so recently. She would be in danger from all the enemies between Mithil Stonedown and Foul's Creche. Covenant was the one man responsible for her condition, the man who had permanently warped the channel of her life. And he, Triock son of Thuler—he loved her.

Yet he gave the orders. He had never loved Lena in a way which would have enabled him to control her. At one time, he had been ready to break his Oath of Peace for her, but throughout most of his life now he had kept it for her. He had done his utmost to raise her daughter free of shame and outrage. He could not begin now to refuse the cost of a love to which he had so entirely given himself.

Once that ordeal was over, he grew somewhat calmer. In the back of his heart, he believed that if there were any hope for the Land in Thomas Covenant, it depended upon Covenant's responses to Lena. Then his chief bitterness lay in the fact that he himself could not accompany Covenant, could not go along to watch over Lena. He had his own work to do, work which he acknowledged and approved. Through the yearning clench of his jaws, he told himself that he would have to rely on Saltheart Foamfollower.

With a brusque movement, he pushed the gray snow out of his eyes and looked toward the Giant. Foamfollower met his gaze, came over to him, and said, "Be easy at heart, my friend. You know that I am not an inconsiderable ally. I will do all I can for both."

"Take great care," Triock breathed through his teeth. "The eyes which saw our work upon Kevin's Watch are yet open. We did not close them in this battle."

Foamfollower studied this thought for a moment, then said, "If that is true, then it is you who must take the greatest care. You bear your High Wood into the hazard of the South Plains."

Triock shrugged. "High Wood or white gold—we must all tread cunningly. I can send none of my people with you."

With a nod of approval, the Giant said, "I would refuse if they were offered. You will need every sword. The mountains where you will seek this Unfettered One are many leagues distant, and you will be required to fight much of your way."

The clench of Triock's teeth made his voice rasp harshly. "I take none but Quirrel and Yeurquin with me."

Foamfollower started to protest, but Triock cut him off. "I need the speed of few companions. And Mithil Stonedown stands now in its gravest peril. For the first time, we have given open battle to the marauders. With the power we revealed on Kevin's Watch, and the strength of our victory here, we have declared beyond question that we are not mere vagabond warriors, seeking refuge in lifeless homes. We have defended our Stonedown—we are an unbeaten people. Therefore the enemy will return against us with a host to dwarf this last band. No, Rockbrother," he concluded grimly, "every war-ready hand must remain to hold what we have won—lest our foes break upon the Stonedown like a wave and leave not one home standing."

After a moment, Foamfollower sighed. "I hear you. Ah, Triock—these are grave times indeed. I will rest easier when my friend Mhoram son of Variol has received word of what we do."

"You believe I will succeed?"

"Who can if you cannot? You are hardy and knowledgeable, familiar with plains and mountains—and marauders. You have accepted the need, though your feet yearn to follow other paths. Those who pursue their heart's desire risk more subtle failures and treacheries. In some ways, it is well to leave your soul's wish in other hands." He spoke musingly, as if in his thoughts he were comparing Triock's position with his own. "You can accomplish this message purely."

"I reap one other blessing also," Triock returned through a mouthful of involuntary gall. "The burden of mercy falls on your shoulders. Perhaps you will bear it more easily."

Foamfollower sighed again, then smiled gently. "Ah, my friend, I know nothing of mercy. My own need for it is too great."

The sight of Foamfollower's smiling regret made Triock wish that he could protest against what the Giant said. But he understood only too well the com-

plex loss and rue which weighed on Foamfollower.
Instead, he returned the best smile he could manage
and saluted Foamfollower from the bottom of his
heart. Then he turned away to make his own preparations for travel.

In a short time, he packed blankets, an extra cloak,
a small stoneware pot of graveling, supplies of dried
meat, cheese, and fruit, and a knife to replace the one
he had given Covenant, in a knapsack. He took only
a few moments to whet his sword, and to secure his
lomillialor rod in the tunic belt under his cloak. Yet
when he returned to the open center of the Stonedown,
he found Covenant, Foamfollower, and Lena ready to
depart. Lena carried her own few belongings in a pack
like his; Foamfollower had all the supplies for the
three of them in his leather sack, which he slung easily
over his shoulder; and Covenant's wounded face held
a look of intentness or frustration, as if only the hurt
on his mouth kept him from complaining impatiently.
In that look, Triock caught a glimpse of how fragile
Covenant's avowed hatred was. It did not appear to be
a sustaining passion. Triock shivered. A foreboding
distrust told him that Thomas Covenant's resolve or
passion would not suffice.

But he clenched the thought to himself as he returned Foamfollower's final salute. There was nothing
he could say. And a moment later, the Giant and his
two companions had disappeared northward between
the houses. Their footmarks filled with snow and faded
from sight until Mithil Stonedown seemed to retain no
record of their passing.

Gruffly, Triock said to Yeurquin and Quirrel, "We
also must depart. We must leave this valley while the
snow holds."

His two friends nodded without question. Their
faces were empty of expression; they looked like people from whom combat had drained all other consider-
ations—carried their short javelins as if the killing of
enemies were their sole interest. From them, Triock
drew a kind of serenity. He was no High Wood
wielder to them, no bearer of burdens which would
have bent the back of a Lord. He was only a man,

fighting as best he could for the Land, without pretensions to wisdom or prophecy. This was a proper role for a Cattleherd in times of war, and he welcomed it.

Girded by the readiness of his companions, he went to the other elders and spent a short time discussing with them Mithil Stonedown's precautions against future attacks. Then he left his home to them and went out into the snow again as if it were the duty of his life.

Flanked by Quirrel and Yeurquin, he left the village by the northward road, and crossed without stealth the stone bridge to the western side of the valley. He wanted to make good time while the snow cover lasted, so he stayed on the easiest route until he neared the end of the horn of mountains which formed the Mithil valley's western wall. At that point, he moved off the road and started up into the foothills that clung around the tip of the horn.

He intended to skirt the peaks west and south almost as far as Doom's Retreat, then swing northwest toward the isolated wedge of mountains which defended the South Plains from Garroting Deep. He could not take the straight march westward. In the open Plains, he would certainly encounter marauders, and when he did, he would have to flee wherever they chased him. So he chose the rugged terrain of the foothills. The higher ground would give him both a vantage from which to watch for enemies and a cover in which to hide from them.

Yet, as he plodded upward through the snow, he feared the choice he had made. In the foothills, he would need twenty days to reach those mountains beyond Doom's Retreat; twenty days would be lost before he could begin to search for the Unfettered One. In that time, Covenant and his companions might travel all the way to Landsdrop or beyond. Then any message which the High Lord might receive would be too late; Covenant would be beyond any hand but the Gray Slayer's.

With that dread in his heart, he began the arduous work of rounding the promontory.

He and his comrades had reached the first lee beyond the horn when the snowfall ended, late that

afternoon. There he ordered a halt. Instead of running the risk of being seen—brown against the gray
slush of the snow—he made camp and let the long
weariness which had been his constant companion
since he first began fighting lull him to sleep.

Sometime after nightfall, Yeurquin awakened him.
They moved on again, chewing strips of dried meat to
keep some warmth in their bones, and washing the
salt from their throats with mouthfuls of the unsavory
snow. In the cloud-locked darkness, they made slow
progress. And every league took them farther from
the hills they knew most intimately. After a tortuous
and unsuccessful effort to scale one bluff slope, Triock
cursed the dreary clasp of the sky and turned to descend toward easier ground nearer the Plains.

For most of the night, they traveled the lower hillsides, but when they felt dawn crouching near, they
climbed again to regain their vantage. They pushed
upward until they gained a high ridge from which
they could see a long stretch of the way they had
come. There they stopped. During the gray seepage
of day into the air, they opened their smokeless graveling pots and cooked one hot meal. When they were
done, they waited until the wind had obliterated all
their tracks. Then they set watches, slept.

They followed this pattern for two more days—
down out of the foothills at dusk, long, dark night-
trek, back toward higher ground at dawn for one hot
meal and sleep—and during these three days, they
saw no sign of any life, human or animal, friend or
foe, anywhere; they were alone in the cold gray world
and the forlorn wind. Trudging as if they were half
crippled by the snow, they pressed themselves through
the chapped solitude toward Doom's Retreat. Aside
from the unpredictably crisp or muffled noises of their
own movement, they heard nothing but the overstressed cracklings of the ice and the scrapings of the
wind, fractured in their ears by the rumpled hills.

But in the dawn of the fourth day, while they
watched the wind slowly filling the footmarks of their
trail, they saw a dull, ugly, yellow movement cross
one rib of the hills below them and come hunting up-

ward in their direction. Triock counted ten in the pack.

"*Kresh!*" Yeurquin spat under his breath.

Quirrel nodded. "And hunting us. It must be that they passed downwind of us during the night."

Triock shivered. The fearsome yellow wolves were not familiar to the people of the South Plains; until the last few years, the *kresh* had lived primarily in the regions north of Ra, foraging into the North Plains when they could not get Ranyhyn-flesh. And many thousands of them had been slain in the great battle of Doom's Retreat. Yet they soon replenished their numbers, and now scavenged in every part of the Land where the hand of the Lords no longer held sway. Triock had never had to fight *kresh,* but he had seen what they could do. A year ago, one huge pack had annihilated the whole population of Gleam Stonedown, in the crystal hills near the joining of the Black and Mithil rivers; and when Triock had walked through the deserted village, he had found nothing but rent clothes and splinters of bone.

"*Melenkurion!*" he breathed as he gauged the speed of the yellow wolves. "We must climb swiftly."

As his companions slung their packs, he searched the terrain ahead for an escape or refuge. But despite their roughness, the hills and slopes showed nothing which the wolves might find impassable; and Triock knew of no defensible caves or valleys this far from Mithil Stonedown.

He turned upward. With Quirrel and Yeurquin behind him, he started along a ridge of foothills toward the mountains.

In the lee of the ridge, the snow was not thick. They made good speed as they climbed and scrambled toward the nearest mountain flank. But it rose sheerly out of the hillslope ahead, preventing escape in that direction. When the western valley beside the ridge rose up toward the mountain, Triock swung to the right and ran downward, traversed the valley, lunged through the piled snow toward the higher ground on the far side.

Before he and his companions reached the top, the leading *kresh* crested the ridge behind them and gave

out a ferocious howl. The sound hit Triock between
his shoulder blades like the flick of a flail. He stopped,
whirled to see the wolves rushing like yellow death
along the ridge hardly five hundred yards from him.

The sight made the skin of his scalp crawl, and his
cold-stiff cheeks twitched as if he were trying to bare
his teeth in fear. Without a word, he turned and attacked the climb again, threw himself through the
snow until his pulse pounded and he seemed to be
surrounded by his own gasping.

When he gained the ridge top, he paused long
enough to steady his gaze, then scanned the terrain
ahead. Beyond this rib of the foothills, all the ground
in a wide half-circle reaching to the very edge of the
mountains fell steeply away into a deep valley. The
valley was roughly conical in shape, open to the plains
only through a sheer ravine on its north side. It offered no hope to Triock's searching eyes. But clinging
to the mountain edge beyond a narrow ledge along the
lip of the valley was a broken pile of boulders, the
remains of an old rockfall. Triock's attention leaped
to see if the boulders could be reached along the
ledge.

"Go!" Quirrel muttered urgently. "I will hold
them here."

"Two javelins and one sword," Triock panted in
response. "Then they will outweigh us seven to two. I
prefer you alive." Pointing, he said, "We must cross
that ledge to the rocks. There we can strike at the
kresh from above. Come."

He started forward again, driving his tired legs as
fast as he could, and Quirrel and Yeurquin followed
on his heels. When they reached the rough ground
where the ridge blended into the cliff, they clambered
through it toward the ledge.

At the ledge, Triock hesitated. The lip of the valley
was packed in snow, and he could not tell how much
solid rock was hidden under it. But the *kresh* were
howling up the hill behind him; he had no time to
scrape the snow clear. Gritting his teeth, he pressed
himself against the cliff and started outward.

His feet felt the slickness of the ledge. Ice covered

the rock under the snow. But he had become accustomed to ice in the course of this preternatural winter. He moved with small, unabrupt steps, did not let himself slip. In moments, Quirrel and Yeurquin were on the ledge as well, and he was halfway to his destination.

Suddenly, a muffled boom like the snapping of old bones echoed off the cliff. The ledge jerked. Triock scrambled for handholds in the rock, and found none. He and his comrades were too far from safety at either end of the ledge.

An instant later, it fell under their weight. Plunging like stones in an avalanche, they tumbled helplessly down the steep side of the valley.

Triock tucked his head and knees together and rolled as best he could. The snow protected him from the impacts of the fall, but it also gave way under him, prevented him from stopping or slowing himself. He could do nothing but hug himself and fall. Dislodged by the collapse of the ledge, more snow slid into the valley with him, adding its weight to his momentum as if it were hurling him at the bottom. In wild vertigo, he lost all sense of how far he had fallen or how far he was from the bottom. When he hit level ground, the force of the jolt slammed his breath away, left him stunned while snow piled over him.

For a time, he lay smothered under the snow, but as the dizziness relaxed in his head, he began to recover. He thrust himself to his hands and knees. Gasping, he fought the darkness which swarmed his sight like clouds of bats rushing at his face. "Quirrel!" he croaked. "Yeurquin!"

With an effort, he made out Quirrel's legs protruding from the snow a short distance away. Beyond her, Yeurquin lay on his back. A bloody gash on his temple marred the blank pallor of his face. Neither of them moved.

Abruptly, Triock heard the scrabbling of claws. A savage howl like a tantara of victory snatched his gaze away from Quirrel and Yeurquin, made him look up toward the slope of the valley.

The *kresh* were charging furiously down toward

him. They had chosen a shallower and less snowbound part of the ridge side, and were racing with rapacious abandon toward their fallen prey. Their leader was hardly a dozen yards from Triock.

He moved instantly. His fighting experience took over, and he reacted without thought or hesitation. Snatching at his sword, he heaved erect, presented himself as a standing target to the first wolf. Fangs bared, red eyes blazing, it leaped for his throat. He ducked under it, twisted, and wrenched his sword into its belly.

It sailed past him and crashed into the snow, lay still as if it were impaled on the red trail of its blood. But its momentum had torn his sword from his cold hand.

He had no chance to retrieve his weapon. Already the next wolf was gathering to spring at him.

He dove out from under its leap, rolled heels over head, snapped to his feet holding his *lomillialor* rod in his hands.

The rod was not made to be a weapon; its shapers in the Loresraat had wrought that piece of High Wood for other purposes. But its power could be made to burn, and Triock had no other defense. Crying the invocation in a curious tongue understood only by the *lillianrill*, he swung the High Wood over his head and chopped it down on the skull of the nearest wolf.

At the impact, the rod burst into flame like a pitch-soaked brand, and all the wolf's fur caught fire as swiftly as tinder.

The flame of the rod lapsed immediately, but Triock shouted to it and hacked at a *kresh* bounding at his chest. Again the power flared. The wolf fell dead in screaming flames.

Another and another Triock slew. But each blast, each unwonted exertion of the High Wood's might, drained his strength. With four *kresh* sizzling in the snow around him, his breath came in ragged heaves, gaps of exhaustion veered across his sight, and fatigue clogged his limbs like iron fetters.

The five remaining wolves circled him viciously.

He could not face them all at once. Their yellow

fur bristled in violent smears across his sight; their red and horrid eyes flashed at him above their wet chops and imminent fangs. For an instant, his fighting instincts faltered.

Then a weight of compact fury struck him from behind, slammed him facedown in the trampled snow. The force of the blow stunned him, and the weight on his back pinned him. He could do nothing but hunch his shoulders against the rending poised over the back of his neck.

But the weight did not move. It lay as inert as death across his shoulder blades.

His fingers still clutched the *lomillialor*.

With a convulsive heave, he rolled to one side, tipped the heavy fur off him. It smeared him with blood—blood that ran, still pulsing, from the javelin which pierced it just behind its foreleg.

Another javelined *kresh* lay a few paces away.

The last three wolves dodged and feinted around Quirrel. She stood over Yeurquin, whirling her sword and cursing.

Triock lurched to his feet.

At the same time, Yeurquin moved, struggled to get his legs under him. Despite the wound on his temple, his hands pulled instinctively at his sword.

The sight of him made the wolves hesitate.

In that instant, Triock snatched a javelin from the nearest corpse and hurled it with the strength of triumph into the ribs of another *kresh*.

Yeurquin was unsteady on his feet; but with one lumbering hack of his sword, he managed to disable a wolf. It lurched away from him on three legs, but he caught up with it and cleft its skull.

The last *kresh* was already in full flight. It did not run yipping, with its tail between its legs, like a thrashed cur; it shot straight toward the narrow outlet of the valley as if it knew where allies were and intended to summon them.

"Quirrel!" Triock gasped.

She moved instantly. Ripping her javelin free of the nearest wolf, she balanced the short shaft across her palm, took three quick steps, and lofted it after the running *kresh*. The javelin arched so high that Triock feared it would fall short, then plunged sharply downward and caught the wolf in the back. The beast collapsed in a rolling heap, flopped several times across the snow, throwing blood in all directions, quivered, and lay still.

Triock realized dimly that he was breathing in rough sobs. He was so spent that he could hardly retain his grip on the *lomillialor*. When Quirrel came over to him, he put his arms around her, as much to gain strength from her as to express his gratitude and comradeship. She returned the clasp briefly, as if his gesture embarrassed her. Then they moved toward Yeurquin.

Mutely, they inspected and tended Yeurquin's wound. Under other circumstances, Triock would not have considered the hurt dangerous; it was clean and shallow, and the bone was unharmed. But Yeurquin still needed time to rest and heal—and Triock had no time. The plight of his message was now more urgent than ever.

He said nothing about this. While Quirrel cooked a meal, he retrieved their weapons, then buried all the *kresh* and the blood of battle under mounds of gray snow. This would not disguise what had happened from any close inspection, but Triock hoped that a chance enemy passing along the rim of the valley would not be attracted to look closer.

When he was done, he ate slowly, gathering his strength, and his eyes jumped around the valley as if he expected ur-viles or worse to rise up suddenly from the ground against him. But then his mouth locked into its habitual dour lines. He made no concessions to Yeurquin's injury; he told his companions flatly that he had decided to leave the foothills and risk cutting straight west toward the mountains where he hoped to find the Unfettered One. For such a risk, the only possibility of success lay in speed.

With their supplies repacked and their weapons cleaned, they left the valley through its narrow northward outlet at a lope.

They traveled during the day now for the sake of

speed. Half dragging Yeurquin behind them, Triock and Quirrel trotted doggedly due west, across the cold-blasted flatland toward the eastmost outcropping of the mountains. As they moved, Triock prayed for snow to cover their trail.

By the end of the next day, they caught their first glimpses of the great storm which brooded for more than a score of leagues in every direction over the approaches to Doom's Retreat.

North of that defile through the mountains, the parched ancient heat of the Southron Wastes met the Gray Slayer's winter, and the result was an immense storm, rotating against the mountain walls which blocked it on the south and west. Its outer edges concealed the forces which raged within, but even from the distance of a day's hard traveling, Triock caught hints of hurricane conditions: cycling winds that ripped along the ground as if they meant to lay bare the bones of the earth; snow as thick as night; gelid air cold enough to freeze blood in the warmest places of the heart.

It lay directly across his path.

Yet he led Quirrel and Yeurquin toward it for another day, hurried in the direction of the storm's core until its outer winds were tugging at his garments, and its first snows were packing wetly against his windward side. Yeurquin was in grim condition—blood oozed like exhaustion through the overstrained scabs of his wound, and the tough fiber of his stamina was frayed and loosened like a breaking rope. But Triock did not turn aside. He could not attempt to skirt the storm, could not swing north toward the middle of the South Plains to go around. During the first night after the battle with the *kresh,* he had seen watch fires northeast of him. They were following him. He had studied them the next night, and had perceived that they were moving straight toward him, gaining ground at an alarming rate.

Some enemy had felt his exertion of the *lomillialor.* Some enemy knew his scent now and pursued him like mounting furor.

"We cannot outrun them," Quirrel observed grimly

as they huddled together under the lip of the storm to rest and eat.

Triock said nothing. He could hear Covenant rasping, *If we don't start doing the impossible. Doing the impossible.*

A moment later, she sniffed the wind. "And I do not like the taste of this weather. There is a blizzard here—a blast raw enough to strike the flesh from our limbs."

The impossible, Triock repeated to himself. He should have said to the Unbeliever, "I was born to tend cattle. I am not a man who does impossible things." He was tired and old and unwise. He should have taken Lena and led his people toward safety deep in the Southron Range, should have chosen to renew the ancient exile rather than allow one extravagant stranger to bend all Mithil Stonedown to the shape of his terrible purpose.

Without looking at him, Quirrel said, "We must separate."

"Separate," Yeurquin groaned hollowly.

"We must confuse the trail—confuse these"—she spat fiercely along the wind—"so that you may find your way west."

Impossible. The word repeated itself like a weary litany in Triock's mind.

Quirrel raised her eyes to face him squarely. "We must."

And Yeurquin echoed, "Must."

Triock looked at her, and the wrinkles around his eyes winced as if even the skin of his face were afraid. For a moment, his jaw-worked soundlessly. Then he grimaced. "No."

Quirrel tightened in protest, and he forced himself to explain. "We would gain nothing. They do not follow our trail—they could not follow a trail so swiftly. Your trails would not turn them aside. They follow the spoor of the High Wood."

"That cannot be," she replied incredulously. "I sense nothing of it from an arm's reach away."

"You have no eyes for power. If we part, you will leave me alone against them."

"Separate," Yeurquin groaned again.

"No!" Anger filled Triock's mouth. "I need you."

"I slow you," the injured man returned emptily, fatally. His face looked pale and slack, frost-rimed, defeated.

"Come!" Triock surged to his feet, quickly gathered his supplies and threw his pack over his shoulders, then stalked away across the wind in the direction of the storm's heart. He did not look behind him. But after a moment Quirrel caught up with him on the right, and Yeurquin came shambling after him on the left. Together, they cut their way into the blizzard.

Before they had covered a league, they were stumbling against wind and snow as if the angry air were assaulting them with fine granite chips of cold. Snow piled against them, and the wind tore through their clothes as if the fabric were thinner than gauze. And in another league, they lost the light of day; the mounting snow flailed it out of the air. Quirrel tried to provide some light by uncovering a small urn of graveling, but the wind snatched the fire-stones from the urn, scattered them like a brief burning plume of gems from her hands. When they were gone, Triock could hardly make out her form huddled dimly near him, too cold even to curse what had happened. Yeurquin had dropped to the ground when they had stopped, and already he was almost buried in snow. Ahead of them—unmuffled now by the outer winds— Triock could see something of the rabid howl and scourge of the storm itself, the hurricane or blizzard shrieking at the violence of the forces which formed it.

Its fury slammed against his senses like the crumbling of a mountain. Peering at it, he knew that there was nothing erect within it, no beast or man or Giant or tree or stone; the maelstroming winds had long since leveled everything which had dared raise its head above the battered line of the ground. Triock had to protect his eyes with his hands. *Impossible* was a pale word to describe the task of walking through that storm. But it was his only defense against pursuit.

With all the strength he could muster, he lifted Yeurquin and helped the injured man lurch onward.

Black wind and sharp snow clamped down on him, stamped at him, slashed sideways to cut his legs from under him. Cold blinded him, deafened him, numbed him; he only knew that he had not lost his companions because Quirrel clutched the back of his cloak and Yeurquin sagged with growing helplessness against him. But he himself was failing, and could do nothing to prevent the loss. He could hardly breathe; the wind ripped past him so savagely that he caught only inadequate pieces of it. Yeurquin's weight seemed unendurable. He jerked woodenly to a halt. Out of a simple and unanswerable need for respite, he pushed Yeurquin away, forced him to support himself.

Yeurquin reeled, tottered a few steps along the wind, and abruptly vanished—disappeared as completely as if a sudden maw of the blizzard had swallowed him.

"Yeurquin!" Triock screamed. "Yeurquin!"

He dashed after his friend, grappling, groping frantically for him. For an instant, a dim shape scudded away just beyond his reach. "Yeurquin!" Then it was gone, scattered into the distance like a handful of brittle leaves on the raving wind.

He ran after it. He was hardly conscious of Quirrel's grip on his cloak, or of the wind yammering at his back, impelling him southward, away from his destination. Fear for Yeurquin drove every other thought from his mind. Suddenly he was no longer the bearer of impossible messages for the Lords. With a rush of passion, he became mere Triock son of Thuler, the former Cattleherd who could not bear to abandon a friend. He ran along the wind in search of Yeurquin as if his soul depended on it.

But the snow struck at his back like one vicious blow prolonged into torment; the wind yelped and yowled in his numb ears, unmoored his bearings; the cold sucked the strength out of him, weakened him as if it frosted the blood in his veins. He could not find Yeurquin. He had rushed past his friend unknowing in the darkness—or Yeurquin had somewhere found the strength to turn to one side against the wind—or the injured man had simply fallen and disappeared under the snow. Triock shouted and groped and ran, and encountered nothing but the storm. When he tried to turn his head toward Quirrel, he found that inches of ice had already formed on his shoulders, freezing his neck into that one strained position. His very sweat turned to ice on him. He could not resist the blast. If he did not keep stumbling tortuously before the wind, he would fall and never rise again.

He kept going until he had forgotten Yeurquin and Covenant and messages, forgotten everything except the exertion of his steps and Quirrel's grim grasp on his cloak. He had no conception of where he was going; he was not going anywhere except along the wind, always along the wind. Gradually the storm became silent around him as the crusting snow froze over his ears. Leagues passed unnoticed. When the ground abruptly canted upward under him, he fell to his hands and knees. A wave of numbness and lassitude ran through him as if it were springing from the frost-bite in his hands and feet.

Something shook his head, something was hitting him on the side of his head. At first, the ice protected him, then it broke away with a tearing pain as if it had taken his ear with it. The howling of wind demons rushed at him, and he almost did not hear Quirrel shout, "Hills! Foothills! Climb! Find shelter!"

He was an old man, too old for such labor.

He was a strong Stonedown Cattleherd, and did not intend to die frozen and useless. He lumbered to his feet, struggled upward.

Leaning weakly back against the wind, he ascended the ragged slope. He realized dimly that both wind and snow were less now. But still he could see nothing; now the storm itself was wrapped in night. When the slope became too steep for the wind to push him up it, he turned to the side which offered the least resistance and went on, lumbering blindly through knee-deep snow, letting the blizzard guide him wherever it chose.

Yet in spite of the night and the storm, his senses

became slowly aware of looming rock walls. The wind lost its single fury, turned to frigid gusts and eddies, and he limped between sheer, close cliffs into a valley. But the disruption of the storm's force came too late to save him. The valley floor lay waist-deep in heavy gray snow, and he was too exhausted to make much headway against it. Once again, he found he was supporting a comrade; Quirrel hung from his shoulders like spent mortality. Soon he could go no farther. He fell into a snowbank, gasping into the snow, "Fire. Must—fire."

But his hands were too frozen, his arms were too locked in ice. He could not reach his *lomillialor* rod, could never have pulled flame from it. Quirrel had already lost her graveling. And his was in his pack. It might as well have been lost also; he could not free his shoulders from the pack straps. He tried to rouse Quirrel, failed. The lower half of her face was caked in ice, and her eyelids fluttered as if she were going into shock.

"Fire," Triock rasped. He was sobbing and could not stop. Frustration and exhaustion overwhelmed him. The snow towered above him as if it would go on forever.

Tears froze his eyes shut, and when he pried them open again, he saw a yellow flame flickering its way toward him. He stared at it dumbly. It bobbed and weaved forward as if it were riding the wick of an invisible candle until it was so close to his face that he could feel its warm radiance on his eyeballs. But it had no wick. It stood in the air before his face and flickered urgently, as if it were trying to tell him something.

He could not move; he felt that ice and exhaustion had already frozen his limbs to the ground. But when he glanced away from the flame, he saw others, three or four more, dancing around him and Quirrel. One of them touched her forehead as if it were trying to catch her attention. When it failed, it flared slightly, and at once all the flames left, scurried away down the valley. Triock watched them go as if they were his last hope.

Then the cold came over him like slumber, and he began to lose consciousness. Unable to help himself, he sagged toward night. The cold and the snow and the valley faded and were replaced by vague faces— Lena, Elena, Atiaran, Trell, Saltheart Foamfollower, Thomas Covenant. They all regarded him with supplication, imploring him to do something. If he failed, their deaths would have no meaning. "Forgive me," he breathed, speaking especially to Covenant. "Forgive."

"Perhaps I shall," a distant voice replied. "It will not be easy—I do not desire these intrusions. But you bear a rare token. I see that I must at least help you."

Struggling, Triock turned his sight outward again. The air over his head was bright with dancing flames, each no larger than his hand. And among them stood a tall man dressed only in a long robe the color of granite. He met Triock's gaze awkwardly, as if he were unaccustomed to dealing with eyes other than his own. But when Triock croaked, "Help," he replied quickly, "Yes. I will help you. Have no fear."

Moving decisively, he knelt, pulled open Triock's cloak and tunic, and placed one warm palm on his chest. The man sang softly to himself, and as he did so, Triock felt a surge of heat pour into him. His pulse steadied almost at once; his breathing unclenched; with wondrous speed, the possibility of movement returned to his limbs. Then the man turned away to help Quirrel. By the time Triock was on his feet among the bobbing flames, she had regained consciousness.

He recognized the flames now; he had heard of them in some of the happiest and saddest legends of the Land. They were Wraiths. As he shook his head clear of ice, he heard through the gusting wind snatches of their light crystal song, music like the melody of perfect quartz. They danced about him as if they were asking him questions which he would never be able to understand or answer, and their lights bemused him, so that he stood entranced among them.

The tall man distracted him by helping Quirrel to her feet. Surrounded by Wraiths, he raised her, supported her until she could stand on her own. Then for a moment he looked uncomfortably back and forth between her and Triock. He seemed to be asking himself if he could justify leaving them there, not helping them further. Almost at once, however, he made his decision. The distant roar of the blizzard rose and fell as if some hungry storm-animal strove to gain access to the valley. He shivered and said, "Come. Foul's winter is no place for flesh and blood."

As the man turned to move toward the upper end of the valley, Triock said abruptly, "You are One of the Unfettered."

"Yes. Yet I aid you." His voice vanished as soon as it appeared on the tattered wind. "I was once Woodhelvennin. The hand of the Forest is upon me. And you"—he was thrusting powerfully away through the snow as if he were talking to himself, as if he had been companionless for so long that he had forgotten how people listen—"bear *lomillialor*."

Triock and Quirrel pushed after him. His gait was strong, unweary, but by following his path through the drifts, they were able to keep up with him. The Wraiths lighted their way with crystal music until Triock felt that he was moving through a pocket of Andelain, a brief eldritch incarnation of clean light and warmth amid the Gray Slayer's preternatural malevolence. In the dancing encouragement of the flames, he was able to disregard his great fatigue and follow the Unfettered One's song:

> Lone
> Unfriended
> Bondless
> Lone—
> Drink of loss until 'tis done:
> 'Til solitude has come and gone,
> And silence is communion—
> And yet
> Unfriended
> Bondless
> Lone.

Slowly, they worked their way up to the end of the

valley. It was blocked by a huge litter of boulders, but the Unfettered One led them along an intricate path through the rocks. Beyond, they entered a sheer ravine which gradually closed over their heads until they were walking into a black cave lit only by the flickering of the Wraiths. In time, the crooked length of the cave shut out all the wind and winter. Warmth grew around Triock and Quirrel, causing their garments to drip thickly. And ahead they saw more light.

Then they reached the cave end, the Unfettered One's home. Here the cave expanded to form a large chamber, and all of it was alive with light and music, as scores of Wraiths flamed and curtsied in the air. Some of them cycled through the center of the chamber, and others hung near the black walls as if to illuminate inscriptions on the gleaming facets of the stone. The floor was rude granite marked by lumps and projecting surfaces which the Unfettered One clearly used as chairs, tables, bed. But the walls and ceiling were as black as obsidian, and they were covered with reflective irregular planes like the myriad fragments of a broken mirror in which the Wraith light would have dazzled the beholders if the surfaces had not been made of black stone. As it was, the chamber was warm and evocative; it seemed a fit place for a seer to read the writing graved within the heart of the mountain.

At the mouth of the chamber, Triock and Quirrel shed their packs and cloaks, opened their ice-stiff inner garments to the warmth. Then they took their first clear look at their rescuer. He was bald except for a white fringe at the back of his head, and his mouth hid in a gnarled white beard. His eyes were so heavily couched in wrinkles that he seemed to have spent generations squinting at illegible communications; and this impression of age was both confirmed by the old pallor of his skin and denied by the upright strength of his frame. Now Triock could see that his robe had been white at one time. It had gained its dull granite color from long years of contact with the cave walls.

In his home, he seemed even more disturbed by the Stonedownors. His eyes flicked fearful and surprised glances at them—not as if he considered them evil, but rather as if he distrusted their clumsiness, as if his life lay in fragile sections on the floor and might be broken by their feet.

"I have little food," he said as he watched the puddles which Triock and Quirrel left behind. "Food also—I have no time for it." But then an old memory seemed to pass across his face—a recollection that the people of the Land did not treat their guests in this way. Triock felt suddenly sure that the One had been living in this cave before he, Triock, was born. "I am not accustomed," the man went on as if he felt he should explain himself. "One life does not suffice. When I found I could not refuse succor to the Wraiths —much time was lost. They repay me as they can, but much—much— How can I live to the end of my work? You are costly to me. Food itself is costly."

As Triock recovered himself in the cave's mouth, he remembered his message to the Lords, and his face tightened into its familiar frown. "The Gray Slayer is costly," he replied grimly.

His statement disconcerted the Unfettered One. "Yes," he mumbled. Bending quickly, he picked up a large flask of water and a covered urn containing dried fruit. "Take all you require," he said as he handed these to Triock. "I have—I have seen some of the Despiser's work. Here." He gestured vaguely at the walls of his cave.

There was little fruit in the urn, but Triock and Quirrel divided it between them. As he munched his share, Triock found he felt a great deal better. Although the meager amount of food hardly touched his hunger, his skin seemed to be absorbing nourishment as well as warmth from the Wraith light. And the radiance of the flames affected him in other ways also. Gradually the numbness of frostbite faded from his fingers and toes and ears; blood and health flowed back into them as if they had been treated with hurtloam. Even the habitual sourness which galled his mouth seemed to decline.

But his mission remained clear to him. When he was sure that Quirrel had regained her stability, he asked her to go a short way out of the tunnel to stand guard.

She responded tightly, "Will pursuit come even here?"

"Who can say?" The Unfettered One did not appear to be listening, so Triock went on: "But we must have this One's aid—and I fear he will not be persuaded easily. We must not be surprised here with the message unattempted."

Quirrel nodded, approving his caution though she clearly believed that no pursuit could have followed them through the blizzard. Without delay,. she collected her cloak and weapons and moved away down the cave until she was out of sight beyond the first bend.

The Unfettered One watched her go with a question in his face.

"She will stand guard while we talk," Triock answered.

"Do we require guarding? There are no ill creatures in these mountains—in this winter. The animals do not intrude."

"Foes pursue me," said Triock. "I bear my own ill—and the Land's need." But there he faltered and fell silent. For the first time, he realized the immensity of his situation. He was face to face with an Unfettered One and Wraiths. In this cave, accompanied by dancing flames, the One studied secret lores which might have amazed even the Lords. Awe crowded forward in Triock; his own audacity daunted him. "Unfettered One," he mumbled, "lore-servant—I do not intrude willingly. You are beyond me. Only the greatness of the need drives—"

"I have saved your life," the One said brusquely. "I know nothing of other needs."

"Then I must tell you." Triock gathered himself and began, "The Gray Slayer is abroad in the Land—"

The tall man forestalled him. "I know my work. I was given the Rites of Unfettering when Tamarantha was Staff-Elder of the Loresraat, and know nothing else. Except for the intrusion of the Wraiths—except—which I could not refuse—I have devoted my meager flesh here, so that I might work my work and see what no eyes have seen before. I know nothing else—no, not even how the Wraiths came to be driven from Andelain, though they speak of ur-viles and— Such talk intrudes."

Triock was amazed. He had not known that Tamarantha Variol-mate had ever been Staff-Elder of the Loresraat, but such a time must have been decades before Prothall became High Lord at Revelstone. This Unfettered One must have been out of touch with all the Land for the past four- or five-score years. Thickly, awefully, Triock said, "Unfettered One, what is your work?"

A grimace of distaste for explanations touched the man's face. "Words— I do not speak of it. Words falter." Abruptly, he moved to the wall and touched one of the stone facets gently, as if he were caressing it. "Stone is alive. Do you see it? You are Stonedownor— do you see it? Yes, alive—alive and alert. Attentive. Everything—everything which transpires upon or within the Earth is seen—beheld—by the Earthrock." As he spoke, enthusiasm came over him. Despite his awkwardness, he could not stop once he had begun. His head leaned close to the stone until he was peering deeply into its flat blackness. "But the—the process— the action of this seeing is slow. Lives like mine are futilely swift—Time—time!—is consumed as the seeing spreads—from the outer surfaces inward. And this time varies. Some veins pass their perception in to the mountain roots in millennia. Others require millennia of millennia.

"Here"—he gestured around him without moving from where he stood—"can be seen the entire ancient history of the Land. For one whose work is to see. In these myriad facets are a myriad perceptions of all that has occurred. All!

"It is my work to see—and to discover the order— and to preserve—so that the whole life of the Land may be known."

As he spoke, a tremor of passion shook the Unfettered One's breathing.

"Since the coming of the Wraiths, I have studied the fate of the One Forest. I have seen it since the first seed grew to become the great Tree. I have seen its awakening—its awareness—the peaceful communion of its Land-spanning consciousness. I have seen Forestals born and slain. I have seen the Colossus of the Fall exercise its interdict. The hand of the Forest is upon me. Here"—his hands touched the facet into which he stared as if the stone were full of anguish—"I see men with axes—men of the ground with blades formed from the bones of the ground—I see them cut—!"

His voice trembled vividly. "I am Woodhelvennin. In this rock I see the desecration of trees. You are Stonedownor. You bear a rare fragment of High Wood, precious *lomillialor*."

Suddenly, he turned from the wall and confronted Triock with a flush of urgent fervor, almost of desperation, in his old face. "Give it to me!" he begged. "It will help me see." He came forward until his eager hands nearly touched Triock's chest. "My life is not the equal of this rock."

Triock did not need to think or speak. If Covenant himself had been standing at his back, he would not have acted differently; he could not distrust an Unfettered One any more than he could have distrusted a Lord. Without hesitation, he drew out the High Wood rod and placed it in the tall man's hands. Then, very quietly, he said, "The foes who pursue me also seek this *lomillialor*. It is a perilous thing I have given you."

The One did not appear to hear. As his fingers closed on the wood, his eyes rolled shut, and a quiver passed through his frame; he seemed to be drinking in the High Wood's unique strength through his hands.

But then he turned outward again. With several deep breaths he steadied himself until he was gazing calmly into Triock's face.

"Perilous," he said. "I hear you. You spoke of the Land's need. Do you require aid to fight your foes?"

"I require a message." All at once, Triock's own urgency came boiling up in him, and he spouted, "The whole Land is at war! The Staff of Law has been lost again, and with it the Law of Death has been broken! Creatures that destroy stone have attacked Mithil Stonedown. Revelstone itself is besieged! I need—!"

"I hear you," the tall man repeated. His earlier awkwardness was gone; possession of the High Wood seemed to make him confident, capable. "Do not fear. I have found that I must help you also. Speak your need."

With an effort, Triock wrenched himself into a semblance of control. "You have heard the Wraiths," he rasped. "They spoke to you of ur-viles—and white gold. The bearer of that white gold is a stranger to the Land, and he has returned. The Lords do not know this. They must be told."

"Yes." The One held Triock's hot gaze. "How?"

"The Loresraat formed this High Wood so that messages may be spoken through it. I have no lore for such work. I am a Stonedownor, and my hands are not apt for wood. I—"

But the Unfettered One accepted Triock's explanation with a wave of his hand. "Who," he asked, "who in Revelstone can hear such speaking?"

"High Lord Mhoram."

"I do not know him. How can I reach him? I cannot direct my words to him if I do not know him."

Inspired by urgency, Triock answered, "He is the son of Tamarantha Variol-mate. You have known Tamarantha. The thought of her will guide you to him."

"Yes," the One mused. "It is possible. I have—I have not forgotten her."

"Tell the High Lord that Thomas Covenant has returned to the Land and seeks to attack the Gray Slayer. Tell him that Thomas Covenant has sworn to destroy Foul's Creche."

The One's eyes widened at this. But Triock went on: "The message must be spoken now. I have been pursued. A blizzard will not prevent any eyes which could see the High Wood in my grasp."

"Yes," the tall man said once more. "Very well— I will begin. Perhaps it will bring this intrusion to an end."

He turned as if dismissing Triock from his thoughts, and moved into the center of his cave. Facing the entrance of the chamber, he gathered the Wraiths around him so that he was surrounded in light, and held the *lomillialor* rod up before his face with both hands. Quietly, he began to sing—a delicate, almost wordless melody that sounded strangely like a transposition, a rendering into human tones, of the Wraith song. As he sang, he closed his eyes, and his head tilted back until his forehead was raised toward the ceiling.

"Mhoram," he murmured through the pauses in his song, "Mhoram. Son of Variol and Tamarantha. Open your heart to hear me."

Triock stared at him, tense and entranced.

"Tamarantha-son, open your heart. Mhoram."

Slowly, power began to gleam from the core of the smooth rod.

The next instant, Triock heard feet behind him. Something about them, something deadly and abominable, snatched his attention, spun him toward the entrance to the chamber.

A voice as harsh as the breaking of stone grated, "Give it up. He cannot open his heart to you. He is caught in our power and will never open his heart again."

Yeurquin stood just within the cave, eyes exalted with madness.

The sight stunned Triock. Yeurquin's frozen apparel had been partially torn from him, and wherever his flesh was bare the skin hung in frostbitten tatters. The .blizzard had clawed his face and hands to the bone. But no blood came from his wounds.

He bore Quirrel in his arms. Her head dangled abjectly from her broken neck.

When he saw Yeurquin, the Unfettered One recoiled as if he had been struck—reeled backward and staggered against the opposite wall of the cave, gaping in soundless horror.

Together, the Wraiths fled, screaming.

"Yeurquin." The death and wrong which shone from the man made Triock gag. He croaked the name as if he were strangling on it. "Yeurquin?"

Yeurquin laughed with a ragged, nauseating sound. In gleeful savagery, he dropped Quirrel to the floor and stepped past her. "We meet at last," he rasped to

Triock. "I have labored for this encounter. I think I will make you pay for that labor."

"Yeurquin?" Staggering where he stood, Triock could see that the man should have been dead; the storm damage he had suffered was too great for anyone to survive. But some force animated him, some ferocity that relished his death kept him moving. He was an incarnated nightmare.

The next moment, the Unfettered One mastered his shock, rushed forward. Wielding the *lomillialor* before him like a weapon, he cried hoarsely, "*Turiya* Raver! Tree foe! I know you—I have seen you. *Melenkurion abatha!* Leave this place. Your touch desecrates the very Earth."

Yeurquin winced under the flick of the potent words. But they did not daunt him. "Better dead feet like mine than idiocy like yours," he smirked. "I think I will not leave this place until I have tasted your blood, Unfettered wastrel. You are so quick to give your life to nothing. Now you will give it to me."

The One did not flinch. "I will give you nothing but the *lomillialor* test of truth. Even you have cause to fear that, *turiya* Raver. The High Wood will burn you to the core."

"Fool!" the Raver laughed. "You have lived here so long that you have forgotten the meaning of power!"

Fearlessly, he started toward the two men.

With a sharp cry, Triock threw off his stunned dismay. Sweeping his sword from its scabbard, he sprang at the Raver.

Yeurquin knocked him effortlessly aside, sent him careening to smack his head against the wall. Then *turiya* closed with the Unfettered One.

Pain slammed through Triock, flooded his mind with blood. Gelid agony shrieked in his chest where the Raver had struck him. But for one moment, he resisted unconsciousness, lurched to his feet. In torment, he saw *turiya* and the Unfettered One fighting back and forth, both grasping the High Wood. Then the Raver howled triumphantly. Bolts of sick, red-green power shot up through the Unfettered One's arms and shattered his chest.

When Triock plunged into darkness, the Raver had already started to dismember his victim. He was laughing all the while.

EIGHT: Winter

WITH snow swirling around him like palpable mist, Thomas Covenant left Mithil Stonedown in the company of Saltheart Foamfollower and Lena daughter of Atiaran. The sensation of purpose ran high in him—he felt that all his complex rages had at last found an effective focus—and he strode impatiently northward along the snow-clogged road as if he were no longer conscious of his still-unhealed forehead and lip, or of the damaged condition of his feet, or of fatigue. He walked leaning ahead into the wind like a fanatic.

But he was not well, could not pretend for any length of time that he was well. Snowflakes hurried around him like subtle gray chips of Lord Foul's malice, seeking to drain the heat of his life. And he felt burdened by Lena. The mother of Elena his daughter stepped proudly at his side as if his companionship honored her. Before he had traveled half a league toward the mouth of the valley, his knees were trembling, and his breath scraped unevenly past his sore lip. He was forced to stop and rest.

Foamfollower and Lena regarded him gravely, concernedly. But his former resolution to accept help had deserted him; he was too angry to be carried like a child. He rejected with a grimace the tacit offer in Foamfollower's eyes.

The Giant also was not well—his wounds gave him pain—and he appeared to understand the impulse behind Covenant's refusal. Quietly, he asked, "My friend, do you know the way"—he hesitated as if he were searching for a short name—"the way to Ridjeck Thome, Foul's Creche?"

"I'm leaving that to you."

Foamfollower frowned. "I know the way—I have it graven in my heart past all forgetting. But if we are separated—"

"I don't have a chance if we're separated," Covenant muttered mordantly. He wished that he could leave the sound of leprosy out of his voice, but the malady was too rife in him to be stifled.

"Separated? Who speaks of separation?" Lena protested before Foamfollower could reply. "Do not utter such things, Giant. We will not be separated. I have preserved—I will not part from him. You are old, Giant. You do not remember the giving of life to life in love—or you would not speak of separation."

In some way, her words twisted the deep knife of Foamfollower's hurt. "Old, yes." Yet after a moment he forced a wry grin onto his lips. "And you are altogether too young for me, fair Lena."

Covenant winced for them both. Have mercy on me, he groaned. Have mercy. He started forward again, but almost at once he tripped on a snow-hidden roughness in the road.

Lena and Foamfollower caught him from either side and upheld him.

He looked back and forth between them. "Treasureberries. I need *aliantha*."

Foamfollower nodded and moved away briskly, as if his Giantish instincts told him exactly where to find the nearest *aliantha*. But Lena retained her hold on Covenant's arm. She had not pulled the hood of her robe over her head, and her white hair hung like wet snow. She was gazing into Covenant's face as if she were famished for the sight of him.

He endured her scrutiny as long as he could. Then he carefully removed his arm from her fingers and said, "If I'm going to survive this, I'll have to learn to stand on my own."

"Why?" she asked. "All are eager to aid—and none more eager than I. You have suffered enough for your aloneness."

Because I'm all I have, he answered. But he could not say such a thing to her. He was terrified by her need for him.

When he did not reply, she glanced down for a moment, away from the fever of his gaze, then looked up again with the brightness of an idea in her eyes. "Summon the Ranyhyn."

The Ranyhyn?

"They will come to you. They come to me at your command. It has hardly been forty days since they last came. They come each year on"—she faltered, looked around at the snow with a memory of fear in her face—"on the middle night of spring." Her voice fell until Covenant could hardly hear her. "This year the winter cold in my heart would not go away. The Land forgot spring—forgot— Sunlight abandoned us. I feared—feared that the Ranyhyn would never come again—that all my dreams were folly.

"But the stallion came. Sweat and snow froze in his coat, and ice hung from his muzzle. His breath steamed as he asked me to mount him. But I thanked him from the bottom of my heart and sent him home. He brought back such thoughts of you that I could not ride."

Her eyes had left his face, and now she fell silent as if she had forgotten why she was speaking. But when she raised her head, Covenant saw that her old face was full of tears. "Oh, my dear one," she said softly, "you are weak and in pain. Summon the Ranyhyn and ride them as you deserve."

"No, Lena." He could not accept the kind of help the Ranyhyn would give him. He reached out and awkwardly brushed at her tears. His fingers felt nothing. "I made a bad bargain with them. I've made nothing but bad bargains."

"Bad?" she asked as if he amazed her. "You are Thomas Covenant the Unbeliever. How could any doing of yours be bad?"

Because it let me commit crimes.

But he could not say that aloud either. He reacted instead as if she had struck the touchstone of his fury.

"Listen, I don't know who you think I am these days; maybe you've still got Berek Halfhand on the brain. But I'm not him—I'm not any kind of hero. I'm nothing but a broken-down leper, and I'm doing this because I've had it up to here with being pushed around. With or without your company I'm going to start getting even regardless of any misbegotten whatever that tries to get in my way. I'm going to do it my own way. If you don't want to walk, you can go home."

Before she had a chance to respond, he turned away from her in shame, and found Foamfollower standing sadly beside him. "And that's another thing," he went on almost without pause. "I have also had it with your confounded misery. Either tell me the truth about what's happened to you or stop sniveling." He emphasized his last two words by grabbing treasure-berries from the Giant's open hands. "Hell and blood! I'm sick to death of this whole thing." Glaring up at the Giant's face, he jammed *aliantha* into his mouth, chewed them with an air of helpless belligerence.

"Ah, my friend," Foamfollower breathed. "This way that you have found for yourself is a cataract. I have felt it in myself. It will bear you to the edge in a rush and hurl you into abysses from which there is no recovery."

Lena's hands touched Covenant's arm again, but he threw them off. He could not face her. Still glaring at Foamfollower, he said, "You haven't told me the truth." Then he turned and stalked away through the snow. In his rage, he could not forgive himself for being so unable to distinguish between hate and grief.

Treasure-berries supplied by both Foamfollower and Lena kept him going through most of the afternoon.

But his pace remained slow and ragged. Finally his strength gave out when Foamfollower guided him off the road and eastward into the foothills beyond the mouth of the valley. By then, he was too exhausted to worry about the fact that the snowfall was ending. He simply lumbered into the lee of a hill and lay down to sleep. Later, in half-conscious moments, he discovered that the Giant was carrying him, but he was too tired to care.

He awoke sometime after dawn with a pleasant sensation of warmth on his face and a smell of cooking in his nostrils. When he opened his eyes, he saw Foamfollower crouched over a graveling pot a few feet away, preparing a meal. They were in a small ravine. The leaden skies clamped over them like a coffin lid, but the air was free of snow. Beside him, Lena lay deep in weary slumber.

Softly, Foamfollower said, "She is no longer young. And we walked until near dawn. Let her sleep." With a short gesture around the ravine, he went on: "We will not be easily discovered here. We should remain until nightfall. It is better for us to travel at night." He smiled faintly. "More rest will not harm you."

"I don't want to rest," Covenant muttered, though he felt dull with fatigue. "I want to keep moving."

"Rest," Foamfollower commanded. "You will be able to travel more swiftly when your health has improved."

Covenant acquiesced involuntarily. He lacked the energy to argue. While he waited for the meal, he inspected himself. Inwardly, he felt steadier; some of his self-possession had returned. The swelling of his lip had receded, and his forehead no longer seemed feverish. The infection in his battered feet did not appear to be spreading.

But his hands and feet were as numb as if they were being gradually gnawed off his limbs by frostbite. The backs of his knuckles and the tops of his arches retained some sensitivity, but the essential deadness was anchored in his bones. At first he tried to believe that the cause actually was frostbite. But he knew better.

His sight told him clearly that it was not ice which deadened him.

His leprosy was spreading. Under Lord Foul's dominion—under the gray malignant winter—the Land no longer had the power to give him health.

Dream health! He knew that it had always been a lie, that leprosy was incurable because dead nerves could not be regenerated, that the previous impossible aliveness of his fingers and toes was the one incontrovertible proof that the Land was a dream, a delusion. Yet the absence of that health staggered him, dismayed the secret, yearning recusancy of his immedicable flesh. Not anymore, he gaped dumbly. Now he had been bereft of that, too. The cruelty of it seemed to be more than he could bear.

"Covenant?" Foamfollower asked anxiously. "My friend?"

Covenant gaped at the Giant as well, and another realization shook him. Foamfollower was closed to him. Except for the restless grief which crouched behind the Giant's eyes, Covenant could see nothing of his inner condition, could not see whether his companion was well or ill, right or wrong. His Land-born sight or penetration had been truncated, crippled. He might as well have been back in his own blind, impervious, superficial world.

"Covenant?" Foamfollower repeated.

For a time, the fact surpassed Covenant's comprehension. He tested—yes, he could see the interminable corruption eating its ill way toward his wrists, toward his heart. He could smell the potential gangrene in his feet. He could feel the vestiges of poison in his lip, the residual fever in his forehead. He could see hints of Lena's age, Foamfollower's sorrow. He could taste the malevolence which hurled this winter across the Land —that he could perceive without question. And he had surely seen the ill in the marauders at Mithil Stonedown.

But that was no feat; their wrong was written on them so legibly that even a child could read it. Everything else was essentially closed to him. He could not discern Foamfollower's spirit, or Lena's confusion, or the snow's falseness. The stubbornness which should have been apparent in the rocky hillsides above him was invisible. Even this rare gift which the Land had twice given him was half denied him now.

"Foamfollower." He could hardly refrain from moaning. "It's not coming back. I can't—this winter —it's not coming back."

"Softly, my friend. I hear you. I"—a wry smile bent his lips—"I have seen what effect this winter has upon you. Perhaps I should be grateful that you cannot behold its effect upon me."

"What effect?" Covenant croaked.

Foamfollower shrugged as if to deprecate his own plight. "At times—when I have been too long unsheltered in this wind—I find I cannot remember certain precious Giantish tales. My friend, Giants do not forget stories."

"Hell and blood." Covenant's voice shook convulsively. But he neither cried out nor moved from his blankets. "Get that food ready," he juddered. "I've got to eat." He needed food for strength. His purpose required strength.

There was no question in him about what he meant to do. He was shackled to it as if his leprosy were an iron harness. And the hands that held the reins were in Foul's Creche.

The stew which Foamfollower handed to him he ate severely, tremorously. Then he lay back in his blankets as if he were stretching himself on a slab, and coerced himself to rest, to remain still and conserve his energy. When the warm stew, and the long debt of recuperation he owed to himself, sent him drifting toward slumber, he fell asleep still glowering thunderously at the bleak, gray, cloud-locked sky.

He awoke again toward noon and found Lena yet asleep. But she was nestling against him now, smiling faintly at her dreams. Foamfollower was no longer nearby.

Covenant glanced around and located the Giant keeping watch up near the head of the ravine. He waved when Covenant looked toward him. Covenant responded by carefully extricating himself from Lena, climbing out of his blankets. He tied his sandals securely onto his numb feet, tightened his jacket, and went to join the Giant.

From Foamfollower's position, he found that he could see over the rims of the ravine into its natural approaches. After a moment, he asked quietly, "How far did we get?" His breath steamed as if his mouth were full of smoke.

"We have rounded the northmost point of this promontory," Foamfollower replied. Nodding back over his left shoulder, he continued, "Kevin's Watch is behind us. Through these hills we can gain the Plains of Ra in three more nights."

"We should get going," muttered Covenant. "I'm in a hurry."

"Practice patience, my friend. We will gain nothing if we hasten into the arms of marauders."

Covenant looked around, then asked, "Are the Ramen letting marauders get this close to the Ranyhyn? Has something happened to them?"

"Perhaps. I have had no contact with them. But the Plains are threatened along the whole length of the Roamsedge and Landrider rivers. And the Ramen spend themselves extravagantly to preserve the great horses. Perhaps their numbers are too few for them to ward these hills."

Covenant accepted this as best he could. "Foamfollower," he murmured, "whatever happened to all that Giantish talk you used to be so famous for? You haven't actually told me what you're worried about. Is it those 'eyes' that saw you and Triock summon me? Every time I ask a question, you act as if you've got lockjaw."

With a dim smile, Foamfollower said, "I have lived a brusque life. The sound of my own voice is no longer so attractive to me."

"Is that a fact?" Covenant drawled. "I've heard worse."

"Perhaps," Foamfollower said softly. But he did not explain.

The Giant's reticence made Covenant want to ask more questions, attack his own ignorance somehow.

He was sure that the issues at stake were large, that the things he did not yet know about the Land's doom were immensely important. But he remembered the way in which he had extracted information from Bannor on the plateau of Rivenrock. He could not forget the consequences of what he had done. He left Foamfollower's secrets alone.

Down the ravine from him, Lena's slumber became more restless. He shivered to himself as she began to flinch from side to side, whimpering under her breath. An impulse urged him to go to her, prevent her from thrashing about for fear that she might break her old, frail bones; but he resisted. He could not afford all that she wanted to mean to him.

Yet when she jerked up and looked frantically around her, found that he was gone from her side—when she cried out piercingly, as if she had been abandoned—he was already halfway down the ravine toward her. Then she caught sight of him. Surging up from her blankets, she rushed to meet him, threw herself into his arms. There she clung to him so that her sobs were muffled in his shoulder.

With his right hand—its remaining fingers as numb and awkward as if they should have been amputated —he stroked her thin white hair. He tried to hold her consolingly to make up for his utter lack of comfortable words. Slowly, she regained control of herself. When he eased the pressure of his embrace, she stepped back. "Pardon me, beloved," she said contritely. "I feared that you had left me. I am weak and foolish, or I would not have forgotten that you are the Unbeliever. You deserve better trust."

Covenant shook his head dumbly, as if he wished to deny everything and did not know where or how to begin.

"But I could not bear to be without you," she went on. "In deep nights—when the cold catches at my breast until I cannot keep it out—and the mirror lies to me, saying that I have not kept myself unchanged for you—I have held to the promise of your return. I have not faltered, no! But I learned that I could not bear to be without you—not again. I have earned—I have— But I could not bear it—to sneak alone into the night and crouch in hiding as if I were ashamed —not again."

"Not again," Covenant breathed. In her old face he could see Elena clearly now, looking so beautiful and lost that his love for her wrenched his heart. "As long as I'm stuck in this thing—I won't go anywhere without you."

But she seemed to hear only his proviso, not his promise. With anguish in her face, she asked, "Must you depart?"

"Yes." The stiffness of his mouth made it difficult for him to speak gently; he could not articulate without tearing at his newly formed scabs. "I don't belong here."

She gasped at his words as if he had stabbed her with them. Her gaze fell away from his face. Panting, she murmured, "Again! I cannot—cannot— Oh, Atiaran my mother! I love him. I have given my life without regret. When I was young, I ached to follow you to the Loresraat—to succeed so boldly that you could say, 'There is the meaning of my life, there in my daughter.' I ached to marry a Lord. But I have given—"

Abruptly, she caught the front of Covenant's jacket in both hands, pulled herself close to him, thrust her gaze urgently at his face. "Thomas Covenant, will you marry me?"

Covenant gaped at her in horror.

The excitement of the idea carried her on in a rush. "Let us marry! Oh, dearest one, that would restore me. I could bear any burden. We do not need the permission of the elders—I have spoken to them many times of my desires. I know the rites, the solemn promises—I can teach you. And the Giant can witness the sharing of our lives." Before Covenant could gain any control over his face, she was pleading with him. "Oh, Unbeliever! I have borne your daughter. I have ridden the Ranyhyn that you sent to me. I have waited—! Surely I have shown the depth of my love for you. Beloved, marry me. Do not refuse."

Her appeal made him cringe, made him feel grotesque and unclean. In his pain, he wanted to turn his back on her, push her from him and walk away. Part of him was already shouting, *You're crazy, old woman! It's your daughter I love!* But he restrained himself. With his shoulders hunched like a strangler's to choke the violence of his responses, he gripped Lena's wrists and pulled her hands from his jacket. He held them up so that his fingers were directly in front of her face. "Look at my hands," he rasped. "Look at my fingers."

She stared at them wildly.

"Look at the sickness in them. They aren't just cold —they're sick, numb with sickness almost all the way across my palms. That's my disease."

"You are closed to me," she said desolately.

"That's leprosy, I tell you! It's there—even if you're blind to it, it's there. And there's only one way you can get it. Prolonged exposure. You might get it if you stayed around me long enough. And children— what's marriage without children?" He could not keep the passion out of his voice. "Children are even more susceptible. They get it more easily—children and— and old people. When I get wiped out of the Land the next time, you'll be left behind, and the only absolutely guaranteed legacy you'll have from me is leprosy. Foul will make sure of it. On top of everything else, I'll be responsible for contaminating the entire Land."

"Covenant—beloved," Lena whispered, "I beg you. Do not refuse." Her eyes swam with tears, torn by a cruel effort to see herself as she really was. "Behold, I am frail and faulty. I have neither worth nor courage to preserve myself alone. I have given— Please, Thomas Covenant." Before he could stop her, she dropped to her knees. "I beg—do not shame me in the eyes of my whole life."

His defensive rage was no match for her. He snatched her up from her knees as if he meant to break her back, but then he held her tenderly, put all the gentleness of which he was capable into his face. For an instant, he felt he had in his hands proof that he—not Lord Foul—was responsible for the misery of the Land. And he could not accept that responsibility without rejecting her. What she asked him to do was to forget—

He knew that Foamfollower was watching him. But if Triock and Mhoram and Bannor had been behind him as well—if even Trell and Atiaran had been present—he would not have changed his answer.

"No, Lena," he said softly. "I don't love you right —I don't have the right kind of love to marry you. I'd only be cheating you. You're beautiful—beautiful. Any other man wouldn't wait for you to ask him. But I'm the Unbeliever, remember? I'm here for a reason." With a sick twisting of his lips that was as close as he could come to a smile, he finished, "Berek Halfhand didn't marry his Queen, either."

His words filled him with disgust. He felt that he was telling her a lie worse than the lie of marrying her— that any comfort he might try to offer her violated the severe truth. But as she realized what he was saying, she caught hold of the idea and clasped it to her. She blinked rapidly at her tears, and the harsh effort of holding her confusion at bay faded from her face. In its place, a shy smile touched her lips. "Am I your Queen then, Unbeliever?" she asked in a tone of wonder.

Roughly, Covenant hugged her so that she could not see the savagery which white-knuckled his countenance. "Of course." He forced up the words as if they were too thick for his aching throat. "No one else is worthy."

He held her, half fearing she would collapse if he let her go, but after a long moment, she withdrew from his embrace. With a look that reminded him of her sprightly girlhood, she said, "Let us tell the Giant," as if she wished to announce something better than a betrothal.

Together, they turned and climbed arm in arm up the ravine toward Saltheart Foamfollower.

When they reached him, they found that his buttressed visage was still wet with weeping. Gray ice sheened his face, hung like beads from his stiff beard. His hands were gripped and straining across his knees.

"Foamfollower," Lena said in surprise, "this is a moment of happiness. Why do you weep?"

His hands jerked up to scrub away the ice, and when it was gone, he smiled at her with wonderful fondness. "You are too beautiful, my Queen," he told her gently. "You surpass me."

His response made her shine with pleasure. For a moment, her old flesh blushed youthfully, and she met the Giant's gaze with joy in her eyes. Then a recollection started her. "But I am remiss. I have been asleep, and you have not eaten. I must cook for you." Turning lightly, she scampered down the ravine toward Foamfollower's supplies.

The Giant glanced up at the chill sky, then looked at Covenant's gaunt face. His cavernous eyes glinted sharply, as if he understood what Covenant had been through. As gently as he had spoken to Lena, he asked, "Do you now believe in the Land?"

"I'm the Unbeliever. I don't change."

"Do you not?"

"I am going to"—Covenant's shoulders hunched—"exterminate Lord Foul the bloody Despiser. Isn't that enough for you?"

"Oh, it is enough for me," Foamfollower said with sudden vehemence. "I require nothing more. But it does not suffice for you. What do you believe—what is your faith?"

"I don't know."

Foamfollower looked away again at the weather. His heavy brows hid his eyes, but his smile seemed sad, almost hopeless. "Therefore I am afraid."

Covenant nodded grimly, as if in agreement.

Nevertheless, if Lord Foul had appeared before him at that moment, he, Thomas Covenant, Unbeliever and leper, would have tried to tear the Despiser's heart out with his bare hands.

He needed to know how to use the white wild magic gold.

But there were no answers in the meal Lena cooked for him and Foamfollower, or in the gray remainder of the afternoon, which he spent huddled over the fire-stones with Lena resting drowsily against him, or in the dank, suffering twilight that finally brought his waiting to an end. When Foamfollower led the way eastward out of the ravine, Covenant felt that he understood nothing but the wind which blew through him like scorn for the impotence of sunlight and warmth. And after that he had no more time to think about it. All his attention was occupied with the work of stumbling numbly through the benighted hills.

Traveling was difficult for him. His body's struggle to recover from injury and inanition drained his strength; the bitter cold drained his strength. He could not see where to place his feet, could not avoid tripping, falling, bruising himself on insensate dirt and rock. Yet he kept going, pushed himself after Foamfollower until the sweat froze on his forehead and his clothing grew crusted with stains of ice. His resolve held him. In time, he even became dimly grateful that his feet were numb, so that he could not feel the damage he was doing to himself.

He had no sense of duration or progress; he measured out the time in rest halts, in *aliantha* unexpectedly handed to him out of the darkness by Foamfollower. Such things sustained him. But eventually he stopped rubbing the ice from his nose and lips, from his forehead and his fanatical beard; he allowed the gray cold to hang like a mask on his features, as if he were becoming a creature of winter. And he stumbled on in the Giant's wake.

When Foamfollower stopped at last, shortly before dawn, Covenant simply dropped to the snow and fell asleep.

Later, the Giant woke him for breakfast, and he found Lena sleeping beside him, curled against the cold. Her lips were faintly tinged with blue, and she shivered from time to time, unable to get warm. Her years showed clearly now in the lines of her face and in the frail, open-mouthed rise and fall of her breathing. Covenant roused her carefully, made her eat hot food until her lips lost their cold hue and the veins in her temples became less prominent. Then, despite her protests, he put her down in blankets and lay beside her until she went back to sleep.

Sometime later, he roused himself to finish his own breakfast. Calculating backward, he guessed that the Giant had been without rest for at least the last three days and nights. So he said abruptly, "I'll let you know when I can't stay awake anymore," took the graveling pot, and moved off to find a sheltered place where he could keep watch. There he sat and watched daylight ooze into the air like seepage through the scab of an old wound.

He awoke late in the afternoon to find Foamfollower sitting beside him, and Lena preparing a meal a short distance away. He jerked erect, cursing inwardly. But his companions did not appear to have suffered from his dereliction. Foamfollower met his gaze with a smile and said, "Do not be alarmed. We have been safe enough—though I was greatly weary and slept until midday. There is a deer run north of us, and some of the tracks are fresh. Deer would not remain here in the presence of marauder spoor."

Covenant nodded. His breath steamed heavily in the cold. "Foamfollower," he muttered, "I am incredibly tired of being so bloody mortal."

But that night he found the going easier. In spite of the encroaching numbness of his hands and feet, some of his strength had returned. And as Foamfollower led him and Lena eastward, the mountains moved away from them on the south, easing the ruggedness of the hills. As a result, he was better able to keep up the pace.

Yet the relaxation of the terrain caused another problem. Since they were less protected from the wind, they often had to walk straight into the teeth of Lord Foul's winter. In that wind, Covenant's inmost clothing seemed to turn to ice, and he moved as if he were scraping his chest raw like a penitent.

Still, he had enough stamina left at the end of the night's march to take the first watch. The Giant had chosen to camp in a small hollow sheltered on the east by a low hill; and after they had eaten, Foamfollower and Lena lay down to sleep while Covenant took a position under a dead, gnarled juniper just below the crown of the knoll. From there, he looked down at his companions, resting as if they trusted him completely. He was determined not to fail them again.

Yet he knew, could not help knowing, that he was poorly equipped for such duty. The wintry truncation of his senses nagged at him as if it implied disaster—as if his inability to see, smell, hear peril would necessarily give rise to peril. And he was not mistaken. Though he was awake, almost alert—though the day had begun, filling the air with its gray, cold sludge—though the attack came from the east, upwind from him—he felt nothing until too late.

He had just finished a circuit of the hilltop, scanning the terrain around the hollow, and had returned to sit in the thin shelter of the juniper, when at last he became aware of danger. Something imminent ran along the wind; the atmosphere over the hollow became suddenly intense. The next instant, dark figures rose up out of the snow around Foamfollower and Lena. As he tried to shout a warning, the figures attacked.

He sprang to his feet, raced down into the hollow. Below him, Foamfollower surged to his knees, throwing dark brown people aside. With a low cry of anger, Lena struggled against the weight of the attackers who pinned her in her blankets. But before Covenant could get to her, someone hit him from behind, knocked him headlong into the snow.

He rolled, got his feet under him, but immediately arms caught him around the chest above the elbows. His own arms were trapped. He fought, threw himself from side to side, but his captor was far too strong; he could not break the grip. Then a flat, alien voice said into his ear, "Remain still or I will break your back."

His helplessness infuriated him. "Then break it," he panted under his breath as he struggled. "Just let her go." Lena was resisting frantically, yelping in frustration and outrage as she failed to free herself.

"Foamfollower!" Covenant shouted hoarsely.

But he saw in shocked amazement that the Giant was not fighting. His attackers stood back from him, and he sat motionless, regarding Covenant's captor gravely.

Covenant went limp with chagrin.

Roughly, the attackers pulled Lena from her blankets. They had already lashed her wrists with cords. She still struggled, but now her only aim seemed to be to break loose so that she could run to Covenant.

Then Foamfollower spoke. Levelly, dangerously, he said, "Release him." When the arms holding Covenant did not loosen, the Giant went on: "Stone and Sea! You will regret it if you have harmed him. Do you not know me?"

"The Giants are dead," the voice in Covenant's ear said dispassionately. "Only Giant-Ravers remain."

"Let me go!" Lena hissed. "Oh, look at him, you fools! *Melenkurion abatha!* Is he a Raver?" But Covenant could not tell whether she referred to Foamfollower or himself.

His captor ignored her. "We have seen—I have seen The Grieve. I have made that journey to behold the work of Ravers."

A shadow tightened in Foamfollower's eyes, but his voice did not flicker. "Distrust me, then. Look at him, as Lena daughter of Atiaran suggests. He is Thomas Covenant."

Abruptly, the strong arms spun Covenant. He found himself facing a compact man with flat eyes and a magisterial mien. The man wore nothing but a thin, short, vellum robe, as if he were impervious to the cold. In some ways he had changed; his eyebrows were stark white against his brown skin; his hair had aged to a mottled gray; and deep lines ran like the erosion of time down his cheeks past the corners of his mouth. But still Covenant recognized him.

He was Bannor of the Bloodguard.

NINE: Ramen Covert

THE sight of him stunned Covenant. Lithe, loam-colored forms, some wearing light robes shaded to match the gray-white snow, moved closer to him as if to verify his identity; a few of them muttered, "Ring-thane," in tense voices. He hardly saw them. "But Mhoram said—"

But Mhoram had said that the Bloodguard were lost.

"Ur-Lord Covenant." Bannor inclined his head in a slight bow. "Pardon my error. You are well disguised."

"Disguised?" Covenant had no conception of what Bannor was talking about. Mhoram's pain had carried so much conviction. Numbly, he glanced downward as if he expected to find two fingers missing from Bannor's right hand.

"A Stonedownor jacket. Sandals. A Giant for a companion." Bannor's impassive eyes held Covenant's face. "And you stink of infection. Only your countenance may be recognized."

"Recognized." Covenant could not stop himself. He repeated the word because it was the last thing Bannor had said. Fighting for self-control, he croaked, "Why aren't you with the Lords?"

"The Vow was Corrupted. We no longer serve the Lords."

Covenant gaped at this answer as if it were nonsense. Confusion befogged his comprehension. Had Mhoram said anything like this? He found that his knees were trembling as if the ground under him had shifted. *No longer serve the Lords,* he repeated blankly. He did not know what the words meant.

But then the sounds of Lena's struggle penetrated him. "You have harmed him," she gasped fiercely. "Release me!"

He made an effort to pull himself together. "Let her go," he said to Bannor. "Don't you understand who she is?"

"Did the Giant speak truly?"

"What? Did he what?" Covenant almost lapsed back into his stupor at the jolt of this distrust. But for Lena's sake he took a deep breath, resisted. "She is the mother of High Lord Elena," he grated. "Tell them to let her go."

Bannor glanced past Covenant at Lena, then said distantly, "The Lords spoke of her. They were unable to heal her." He shrugged slightly. "They were unable to heal many things."

Before Covenant could respond, the Bloodguard signaled to his companions. A moment later, Lena was at Covenant's side. From somewhere in her robes, she produced a stone knife and brandished it between Bannor and Covenant. "If you have harmed him," she fumed, "I will take the price of it from your skin, old man."

The Bloodguard cocked an eyebrow at her. Covenant reached for her arm to hold her back, but he was still too staggered to think of a way to calm her, reassure her. "Lena," he murmured ineffectively, "Lena." When Foamfollower joined them, Covenant's eyes appealed to the Giant for help.

"Ah, my Queen," Foamfollower said softly. "Remember your Oath of Peace."

"Peace!" Lena snapped in a brittle voice. "Speak to them of Peace. They attacked the Unbeliever."

"Yet they are not our enemies. They are the Ramen."

She jerked incredulously to face the Giant. "Ramen? The tenders of the Ranyhyn?"

Covenant stared as well. Ramen? He had unconsciously assumed that Bannor's companions were other Bloodguard. The Ramen had always secretly hated the Bloodguard because so many Ranyhyn had died while bearing the Bloodguard in battle. Ramen and Bloodguard? The ground seemed to lurch palpably under him. Nothing was as he believed it to be; everything in the Land would either astound or appall him, if only he were told the truth.

"Yes," Foamfollower replied to Lena. And now Covenant recognized the Ramen for himself. Eight of them, men and women, stood around him. They were lean, swift people, with the keen faces of hunters, and skin so deeply tanned from their years in the open air that even this winter could not pale them. Except for their scanty robes, their camouflage, they dressed in the Ramen fashion as Covenant remembered it— short shifts and tunics which left their legs and arms free; bare feet. Seven of them had the cropped hair and roped waists characteristic of Cords; and the eighth was marked as a Manethrall by the way his fighting thong tied his long black hair into one strand, and by the small, woven circlet of yellow flowers on the crown of his head.

Yet they had changed; they were not like the Ramen he had known forty-seven years ago. The easiest alteration for him to see was in their attitude toward him. During his first visit to the Land, they had looked at him in awed respect. He was the Ringthane, the man to whom the Ranyhyn had reared a hundred strong. But now their proud, severe faces regarded him with asperity backed by ready rage, as if he had violated their honor by committing some nameless perfidy.

But that was not the only change in them. As he scrutinized the uncompromising eyes around him, he became conscious of a more significant difference, something he could not define. Perhaps they carried themselves with less confidence or pride; perhaps they had been attacked so often that they had developed a habitual flinch; perhaps this ratio of seven Cords to one Manethrall, instead of three or four to one, as it should have been, indicated a crippling loss of life among their leaders, the teachers of the Ranyhyn-lore. Whatever the reason, they had a haunted look, an aspect of erosion, as if some subliminal ghoul were gnawing at the bones of their courage. Studying them, Covenant was suddenly convinced that they endured Bannor, even followed him, because they were no longer self-sure enough to refuse a Bloodguard.

After a moment, he became aware that Lena was speaking, more in confusion than in anger now. "Why did you attack us? Can you not recognize the Unbeliever? Do you not remember the Rockbrothers of the Land? Can you not see that I have ridden Ranyhyn?"

"Ridden!" spat the Manethrall.

"My Queen," Foamfollower said softly, "the Ramen do not ride."

"As for Giants," the man went on, "they betray."

"Betray?" Covenant's pulse pounded in his temples, as if he were too close to an abyss hidden in the snow.

"Twice now Giants have led Fangthane's rending armies north of the Plains of Ra. These 'Rockbrothers' have sent fangs and claws in scores of thousands to tear the flesh of Ranyhyn. Behold!" With a swift tug, he snatched his cord from his hair and grasped it taut like a garrote. "Every Ramen cord is black with blood." His knuckles tightened as if he were about to leap at the Giant. "Manhome is abandoned. Ramen and Ranyhyn are scattered. Giants!" He spat again as if the very taste of the word disgusted him.

"Yet you know me," Foamfollower said to Bannor. "You know that I am not one of the three who fell to the Ravers."

Bannor shrugged noncommittally. "Two of the three are dead. Who can say where those Ravers have gone?"

"I am a Giant, Bannor!" Foamfollower insisted in a tone of supplication, as if that fact were the only proof of his fidelity. "It was I who first brought Thomas Covenant to Revelstone."

Bannor was unmoved. "Then how is it that you are alive?"

At this, Foamfollower's eyes glinted painfully. In a

thin tone, he said, "I was absent from *Coercri*—when my kindred brought their years in Seareach to an end."

The Bloodguard cocked an eyebrow, but did not relent. After a moment, Covenant realized that the resolution of this impasse was in his hands. He was in no condition to deal with such problems, but he knew he had to say something. With an effort, he turned to Bannor. "You can't claim you don't remember me. You probably have nightmares about me, even if you don't ever sleep."

"I know you, ur-Lord Covenant." As he spoke, Bannor's nostrils flared as if they were offended by the smell of illness.

"You know me, too," Covenant said with mounting urgency to the Manethrall. "Your people call me Ringthane. The Ranyhyn reared to me."

The Manethrall looked away from Covenant's demanding gaze, and for an instant the haunted look filled his face like an ongoing tragedy. "Of the Ringthane we do not speak," he said quietly. "The Ranyhyn have chosen. It is not our place to question the choices of the Ranyhyn."

"Then back off!" Covenant did not intend to shout, but he was too full of undefined fears to contain himself. "Leave us alone! Hellfire! We've got enough trouble as it is."

His tone brought back the Manethrall's pride. Severely, the man asked, "Why have you come?"

"I haven't 'come.' I don't want to be here at all."

"What is your purpose?"

In a voice full of mordant inflections, Covenant said, "I intend to pay a little visit to Foul's Creche."

His words jolted the Cords, and their breath hissed through their teeth. The Manethrall's hands twitched on his weapon.

A flare of savage desire widened Bannor's eyes momentarily. But his flat dispassion returned at once. He shared a clear glance with the Manethrall, then said, "Ur-Lord, you and your companions must accompany us. We will take you to a place where more Ramen may give thought to you."

"Are we your prisoners?" Covenant glowered.

"Ur-Lord, no hand will be raised against you in my presence. But these matters must be given consideration."

Covenant glared hard into Bannor's expressionlessness, then turned to Foamfollower. "What do you think?"

"I do not like this treatment," Lena interjected. "Saltheart Foamfollower is a true friend of the Land. Atiaran my mother spoke of all Giants with gladness. And you are the Unbeliever, the bearer of white gold. They show disrespect. Let us leave them and go our way."

Foamfollower replied to them both, "The Ramen are not blind. Bannor is not blind. They will see me more clearly in time. And their help is worth seeking."

"All right," Covenant muttered. "I'm no good at fighting anyway." To Bannor, he said stiffly, "We'll go with you." Then, for the sake of everything that had happened between himself and the Bloodguard, he added, "No matter what else is going on here, you've saved my life too often for me to start distrusting you now."

Bannor gave Covenant another fractional bow. At once, the Manethrall snapped a few orders to the Cords. Two of them left at a flat run toward the northeast, and two more moved off to take scouting positions on either side of the company, while the rest gathered small knapsacks from hiding places around the hollow. Watching them, Covenant was amazed once again at how easily, swiftly, they could disappear into their surroundings. Even their footprints seemed to vanish before his eyes. By the time Foamfollower had packed his leather sack, they had effaced all signs of their presence from the hollow. It looked as untroubled as if they had never been there.

Before long, Covenant found himself trudging between Lena and Foamfollower in the same general direction taken by the two runners. The Manethrall and Bannor strode briskly ahead of them, and the three remaining Cords marched at their backs like guards. They seemed to be moving openly, as if they had no fear of enemies. But twice when he looked back Covenant saw the Cords erasing the traces of their passage from the gray drifts and the cold ground.

The presence of those three ready garrotes behind him only aggravated his confusion. Despite his long experience with hostility, he was not prepared for such distrust from the Ramen. Clearly, important events had taken place—events of which he had no conception. His ignorance afflicted him with a powerful sense that the fate of the Land was moving toward a crisis, a fundamental concatenation in which his own role was beclouded, obscure. The facts were being kept from him. This feeling cast the whole harsh edifice of his purpose into doubt, as if it were erected on slow quicksand. He needed to ask questions, to get answers. But the unspoken threat of those Ramen ropes disconcerted him. And Bannor—! He could not frame his questions, even to himself.

And he was tired. He had already traveled all night, had not slept since the previous afternoon. Only four days had passed since his summoning. As he labored to keep up the pace, he found that he lacked the strength of concentration to think.

Lena was in no better condition. Although she was healthier than he, she was old, and not hardened to walking. Gradually, he became as worried about her as he was weary himself. When she began to droop against him, he told Bannor flatly that he would have to rest.

They slept until midafternoon, then traveled late into the night before camping again. And the next morning, they were on their way before dawn. But Covenant and Lena did better now. The food which the Ramen gave them was hot and nourishing. And soon after gray dim day had shambled into the laden air, they reached the edge of the hills, came in sight of the Plains of Ra. At this point, they swung northward, staying in the rumbled terrain of the hills-edge rather than venturing into the bleak, winter-bitten openness of the Plains. But still they found the going easier. In time, Covenant recovered enough to begin asking questions.

As usual, he had trouble talking to Bannor. The

Bloodguard's unbreachable dispassion daunted him, often made him malicious or angry through simple frustration; such reticence seemed outrageously immune from judgment—the antithesis of leprosy. Now all the Bloodguard had abandoned the Lords, Revelstone, death refusal. Lord's Keep would fall without them. And yet Bannor was here, living and working with the Ramen. When Covenant tried to ask questions, he felt that he no longer knew the man to whom he spoke.

Bannor met his first tentative inquiries by introducing Covenant to the Ramen—Manethrall Kam, and his Cords, Whane, Lal, and Puhl—and by assuring him that they would reach their destination by evening the next day. He explained that this band of Ramen was a scouting patrol responsible for detecting marauders along the western marge of Ra; they had found Covenant and his companions by chance rather than design. When Covenant asked about Rue, the Manethrall who had brought word of Fleshharrower's army to Revelstone seven years ago, Bannor replied flatly that she had died soon after her return home. But after that, Covenant had to wrestle for what he wanted to know.

At last he could find no graceful way to frame his question. "You left the Lords," he rasped awkwardly. "Why are you here?"

"The Vow was broken. How could we remain?"

"They need you. They couldn't need you more."

"Ur-Lord, I say to you that the Vow was broken. Many things were broken. You were present. We could not—ur-Lord, I am old now. I, Bannor, First Mark of the Bloodguard. I require sleep and hot food. Though I was bred for mountains, this cold penetrates my bones. I am no fit server for Revelstone—no, nor for the Lords, though they do not equal High Lord Kevin who went before them."

"Then why are you here? Why didn't you just go home and forget it?"

Foamfollower winced at Covenant's tone, but Bannor replied evenly, "That was my purpose—when I departed Lord's Keep. But I found I could not forget.

I had ridden too many Ranyhyn. At night I saw them—
in my dreams they ran like clear skies and cleanliness.
Have you not beheld them? Without Vows or defiance
of death, they surpassed the faith of the Bloodguard.
Therefore I returned."

"Just because you were addicted to Ranyhyn? You
let the Lords and Revelstone and all go to hell and
blood, but you came here because you couldn't give up
riding Ranyhyn?"

"I do not ride."

Covenant stared at him.

"I have come to share the work of the Ramen. A
few of the *Haruchai*—I know not how many—a few
felt as I did. We had known Kevin in the youth of his
glory, and could not forget. Terrel is here, and Runnik.
There are others. We teach our skills to the Ramen,
and learn from them the tending of the great horses.
Perhaps we will learn to make peace with our failure
before we die."

Make peace, Covenant groaned. Bannor! The very
simplicity of the Bloodguard's explanation dismayed
him. So all those centuries of untainted and sleepless
service came to this.

He asked Bannor no more questions; he was afraid
of the answers.

For the rest of that day, he fell out of touch with his
purpose. Despite the concern and companionship of
Foamfollower and Lena, he walked between them in
morose separateness. Bannor's words had numbed his
heart. And he slept that night on his back with his eyes
upward, as if he did not believe that he would ever see
the sun again.

But the next morning he remembered. Shortly after
dawn, Manethrall Kam's party met another Cord. The
man was on his way to the edge of the Plains, and in
his hands he carried two small bouquets of yellow
flowers. The gray wind made their frail petals flutter
pathetically. After saluting Manethrall Kam, he strode
out into the open, shouted shrilly against the wind in a
language Covenant could not understand. He repeated
his shout, then waited with his hands extended as if he
were offering flowers to the wind.

Shortly, out of the shelter of a frozen gully came two Ranyhyn, a stallion and a mare. The stallion's chest was scored with fresh claw-marks, and the mare had a broken, hollow look, as if she had just lost her foal. Both were as gaunt as skeletons; hunger had carved the pride from their shoulders and haunches, exposed their ribs, given their emaciated muscles an abject starkness. They hardly seemed able to hold up their heads. But they nickered to the Cord. With a stumbling gait, they trotted forward, and began at once to eat the flowers he offered to them. In three bites the food was gone. He hugged them quickly, then turned away with tears in his eyes.

Without a word, Manethrall Kam gave the Cord the bedraggled circlet from his hair, so that each of the Ranyhyn could have one more bite. "That is *amanib-havam,* the healing grass of Ra," he explained stiffly to Covenant. "It is a hardy grass, not so easily daunted by this winter as the Render might wish. It will keep life in them—for another day." As he spoke, he glared redly into Covenant's face, as if the misery of these two horses were the Unbeliever's doing. With a brusque nod toward the Cord feeding the Ranyhyn, he went on: "He walked ten leagues today to bring even this much food to them." The haunted erosion filled his face; he looked like the victim of a curse. Painfully, he turned and strode away again north-ward, along the edges of the Plains.

Covenant remembered; he had no trouble remem-bering his purpose now. When he followed the Mane-thrall, he walked as if he were fighting the deadness of his feet with outrage.

In the course of that day, he saw a few more Ranyhyn. Two were uninjured, but all were gaunt, weak, humbled. All had gone a long way down the road toward starvation.

The sight of them wore heavily upon Lena. There was no confusion in the way she perceived them, no distortion or inaccuracy. Such vision consumed her. As time passed, her eyes sank back under her brows, as if they were trying to hide in her skull, and dark circles like bruises grew around the orbs. She stared brittlely

about her as if even Covenant were dim in her gaze—
as if she beheld nothing but the protruding ribs and
fleshless limbs of Ranyhyn.

Covenant held her arm as they walked, guided and
supported her as best he could. Weariness gradually
became irrelevant to him; even the keen wind, flaying
straight toward him across the Plains, seemed to lose
its importance. He stamped along behind Kam like
a wild prophet, come to forge the Ramen to his will.

They reached the outposts of Kam's destination by
midafternoon. Ahead of them, two Cords abruptly
stepped out of a barren copse of wattle, and saluted
Manethrall Kam in the Ramen fashion, with their
hands raised on either side of their heads and their
palms open, weaponless. Kam returned the bow, spoke
to the two briefly in a low, aspirated tongue, then motioned for Covenant, Lena, and Foamfollower to continue on with him. As they moved back into the hills,
he told them, "My Cords were able to summon only
three other Manethralls. But four will be enough."

"Enough?" Covenant asked.

"The Ramen will accept a judgment made by four
Manethralls."

Covenant met Kam's glare squarely. A moment
later, the Manethrall turned away with an oddly
daunted air, as if he had remembered that Covenant's
claim on him came from the Ranyhyn. Hurrying now,
he led his company upward with the gray wind cutting
at their backs.

They climbed across two steep bluffs which gave
them a panoramic view of the Plains. The hard open
ground lay ruined below them, scorched with winter
and gray snow until it looked maimed and lifeless.
But Manethrall Kam moved rapidly onward, ignoring
the sight. He took his companions past the bluffs down
into a valley cunningly hidden among rough knolls
and hilltops. This valley was largely sheltered from
the wind, and faint, cultivated patches of unripe
amanibhavam grew on its sides. Now Covenant remembered what he had heard about *amanibhavam*
during his previous visit to the Plains of Ra. This grass,

which held such a rare power of healing for horses, was poisonous to humans.

Aside from the grass, the valley contained nothing but three dead copses leaning at various points against the steepest of the slopes. Manethrall Kam walked directly toward the thickest one. As he approached, four Cords stepped out of the wood to meet him. They had a tense, frail air about them which made Covenant notice how young they were; even the two older girls seemed to have had their Cording thrust unready upon them. They saluted Kam nervously, and when he had returned their bow, they moved aside to let him enter the copse.

Covenant followed Bannor into the wood and found that at its back was a narrow rift in the hillside. The rift did not close, but its upper reaches were so crooked that Covenant could not see out the top. Under his feet, a layer of damp, dead leaves muffled his steps; he passed in silence like a shadow between the cold stone walls. A smell of musty age filled his nostrils, as if the packed leaves had been rotting in the rift for generations; and despite their wetness, he felt dim warmth radiating from them. No one spoke. Gripping Lena's chill fingers in his numb hand, he moved behind Bannor as the cleft bent irregularly from side to side on its way through the rock.

Then Manethrall Kam stopped. When Covenant caught up with him, he said softly, "We now enter the secret places of a Ramen covert. Be warned, Ringthane. If we are not taught to trust you and your companions, you will not leave this place. In all the Plains of Ra and the surrounding hills, this is the last covert.

"At one time, the Ramen held several such hidden places of refuge. In them the Manethralls tended the grievous wounds of the Ranyhyn and trained Cords in the secret rites of their Maneing. But one by one in turn each covert"—Kam fixed Covenant with a demon-ridden gaze—"has been betrayed. Though we have preserved them with our utterest skill, *kresh*—ur-viles—Cavewights—ill flesh in every shape—all have found our hidden coverts and ravaged them." He studied the Ringthane as if he were searching for some sign which would brand Covenant as the betrayer. "We will hold you here—we will kill your companions —rather than permit treachery to this place."

Without allowing Covenant time to reply, he turned on his heel and stalked around another bend in the cleft.

Covenant followed, scowling stormily. Beyond the bend, he found himself in a large chamber. The air was dim, but he could see well enough to discern several Ranyhyn standing against the walls. They were eating scant bundles of grass, and in this closed space the sharp aroma of the *amanibhavam* made his head ring. All of them were injured—some so severely that they could hardly stand. One had lost the side of its face in a fight, another still bled from a cruel fretwork of claw-marks in its flanks, and two others had broken legs which hung limply, with excruciating bone-splinters tearing the skin.

As he stared gauntly at them, they became aware of him. A restless movement passed through them, and their heads came up painfully, turning soft, miserable eyes toward him. For a long moment, they looked at him as if they should have been afraid but were too badly hurt for fear. Then, in agony, even the horses with broken legs tried to rear.

"Stop it. Stop." Covenant hardly knew that he was moaning aloud. His hands flinched in front of his face, trying to ward off an abominable vision. "I can't stand it."

Firmly, Bannor took his arm and drew him past the chamber into another passage through the rock.

After a few steps, his legs failed him. But Bannor gripped him, bore him up. Clutching with useless fingers at the Bloodguard's shoulders, he pulled himself around until he was facing Bannor. "Why?" he panted into Bannor's flat visage. "Why did they do that?"

Bannor's face and voice revealed nothing. "You are the Ringthane. They have made promises to you."

"Promises." Covenant rubbed a hand over his eyes. The promises of the Ranyhyn limped across his memory. "Hell and blood." With an effort, he pushed away from Bannor. Bracing himself against the wall of the crevice, he clenched his trembling fists as if he were trying to squeeze steadiness out of them. His fingers ached for the Despiser's throat. "They should be killed!" he raged thickly. "They should be put out of their misery! How can you be so cruel?"

Manethrall Kam spat, "Is that how it is done in your world, Ringthane?"

But Bannor replied evenly, "They are the Ranyhyn. Do not presume to offer them kindness. How can any human decide the choices of death and pain for them?"

At this, Foamfollower reached out and touched Bannor's shoulder in a gesture of respect.

Covenant's jaw muscles jumped as he bit his shouts into silence. He followed the Giant's gesture, turned, and looked grayly up at Foamfollower. Both the Giant and Bannor had witnessed his bargain with the Ranyhyn forty-seven years ago, when the great horses had first reared to him; Bannor and Foamfollower and Mhoram and Quaan might be the last remaining survivors of the Quest for the Staff of Law. But they were enough. They could accuse him. The Ramen could accuse him. He still did not know all the things of which they could accuse him.

His wedding band hung loosely on his ring finger; he had lost weight, and the white gold dangled as if it were meaningless. He needed its power. Without power, he was afraid to guess at the things which were being kept from him.

Abruptly, he stepped up to Kam, jabbed the Manethrall's chest with one stiff finger. "By hell," he muttered into Kam's glare, "if you're only doing this out of pride, I hope you rot for it. You could have taken them south into the mountains—you could have saved them from this. Pride isn't a good enough excuse."

Again the ghoul-begotten hurt darkened Kam's gaze. "It is not pride," he said softly. "The Ranyhyn do not choose to go."

Without wanting to, Covenant believed him. He could not doubt what he saw in the Manethrall. He drew back, straightened his shoulders, took a deep breath. "Then you'd better help me. Trust me whether you want to or not. I hate Foul just as much as you do."

"That may be," Kam replied, recovering his severity. "We will not contradict the Ranyhyn concerning you. I saw—I would not have believed if I had not seen. To rear! Hurt as they are! You need not fear us. But your companions are another matter. The woman"—he made an effort to speak calmly—"I do not distrust. Her love for the Manes is in her face. But this Giant—he must prove himself."

"I hear you, Manethrall," said Foamfollower quietly. "I will respect your distrust as best I can."

Kam met the Giant's look, then glanced over at Bannor. The Bloodguard shrugged impassively. Kam nodded and led the way farther down the cleft.

Before following, Covenant regained his grip on Lena's hand. She did not raise her head, and in the gloom he could see nothing of her eyes but the bruises under them. "Be brave," he said as gently as he could. "Maybe it won't all be this bad." She made no response, but when he drew her forward she did not resist. He kept her at his side, and soon they stepped together out the far end of the passage.

The cleft opened into a hidden valley which seemed spacious after the constriction of its approach. Over a flat floor of packed dirt the sheer walls rose ruggedly to a narrow swath of evening sky. The valley itself was long and deep; its crooked length formed a vague *S*, ending in another crevice in the hills. Battered rock pillars and piles stood against the walls in several places, and in the corners and crannies around these immense stones, sheltered from any snowfall through the open roof, were Ramen tents—the nomadic homes of individual families. They seemed pitifully few in the canyon.

Manethrall Kam had announced himself with a shout as he entered the valley, and when Covenant and Lena caught up with him, dozens of Ramen were already moving toward them from the tents. Covenant was struck by how much they all shared Kam's haunted air. In sharp contrast to the Ranyhyn, they were not ill-fed. The Ramen were renowned for their skill as hunters, and clearly they were better able to provide more meat for themselves than grass for the horses. Nevertheless they were suffering. Every one of them who was not either a child or infirm wore the apparel of a Cord, though even Covenant's untrained and superficial eyes could see how unready some were for the work and risk of being Cords. This fact confirmed his earlier guess that the Ramen population had been dangerously reduced, by winter or war. And they all had Kam's driven, sleepless aspect, as if they could not rest because their dreams were fraught with horror.

Now Covenant knew intuitively what it was. All of them, even the children, were haunted by the bloody visage of Ranyhyn extermination. They were afraid that the meaning, the reason, of their entire race would soon be eradicated utterly from the Land. The Ramen had always lived for the Ranyhyn, and now they believed they would only survive long enough to see the last Ranyhyn slaughtered. As long as the great horses refused to leave the Plains, the Ramen were helpless to prevent that end.

Only their stubborn, fighting pride kept them from despair.

They met Covenant, Lena, and the Giant with silence and hollow stares. Lena hardly seemed to notice them, but Foamfollower gave them a bow in the Ramen style, and Covenant took his example, though the salute exposed his ring for all to see.

Several Cords murmured at the sight of the white gold, and one of the Manethralls said grimly, "It is true, then. He has returned." When Kam told them what the wounded Ranyhyn had done, some recoiled in pained amazement, and others muttered angrily under their breath. Yet they all bowed to Covenant; the Ranyhyn had reared to him, and the Ramen could not refuse him welcome.

Then the Winhomes, the Ramen who were too young or too old or too crippled to be Cords, moved away, and the three Manethralls Kam had mentioned earlier came forward to be introduced. When they had given their names, Manethrall Jain, the grim woman who had just spoken, asked Kam, "Was it necessary to admit the Giant?"

"He's my friend," Covenant said at once. "And Bannor knows he can be trusted, even if the Blood-guard are too thickheaded to say such things out loud. I wouldn't be here if it weren't for Saltheart Foamfollower."

"You honor me too much," Foamfollower said wryly.

The Manethralls weighed Covenant's words as if his speech had more than one meaning. But Bannor said, "Saltheart Foamfollower shared the Quest for the Staff of Law with High Lord Prothall, ur-Lord Covenant, and Manethrall Lithe. At that time, he was worthy of trust. But I have seen many trusts fall into Corruption. Perhaps nothing of the old Giantish faith remains."

"You don't believe that," Covenant snapped.

Bannor raised one eyebrow. "Have you seen The Grieve, ur-Lord? Has Saltheart Foamfollower told you what occurred in the Seareach home of the Giants?"

"No."

"Then you have been too quick with your trust."

Covenant tightened his grip on himself. "Why don't you tell me about it?"

"That is not my place. I do not offer to guide you to Ridjeck Thome."

Covenant started to protest, but Foamfollower placed a restraining hand on his shoulder. In spite of the conflicting emotions which knotted the Giant's fore-head, smoldered dangerously in his cavernous eye-sockets, his voice was steady as he said, "Is it the Ramen custom to keep their guests standing cold and hungry after a long journey?"

Kam spat on the ground, but Manethrall Jain replied tautly, "No, that is not our custom. Behold." She nodded toward the head of the canyon, where the Winhomes were busy around a large fire under the overhang of one of the pillars. "The food will be pre-pared soon. It is *kresh* meat, but you may eat it in safety—it has been cooked many times." Then she took Lena's arm and said, "Come. You have suffered at the sight of the Ranyhyn. Thus you share our pain. We will do what we can to restore you." As she spoke, she guided Lena toward the fire.

Covenant was seething with frustration and dread, but he could not refuse the warmth of the campfire; his flesh needed it too badly. His fingertips and knuckles had a frostbitten look in addition to their sick numbness, and he knew that if he did not tend his feet soon he would be in danger of blood poisoning and gangrene. The effort of self-command hurt him, yet he followed Lena and Jain to the fire. As quietly as he could, he asked one of the Winhomes for hot water in which to bathe his feet.

Despite his numbness, the soaking of his feet gave him relief. The hot water helped the fire's warmth thaw out his bones. And his feet were not as badly damaged as he had feared they would be. Both were swollen with infection, but the harm was no worse than it had been several days ago. For some reason, his flesh was resisting the illness. He was glad to discover that he was in no immediate danger of losing his feet.

A short time later, the food was ready. Kam's seven Cords sat cross-legged around the fire with the four Manethralls, Bannor, Foamfollower, Lena, and Covenant, and the Winhomes set dry, brittle banana leaves in front of them as plates. Covenant found himself positioned between Lena and Bannor. A lame man muttering dimly to himself served the three of them stew and hot winter potatoes. Covenant did not relish the idea of eating *kresh*—he expected to find the meat rank and stringy—but it had been cooked so long, with such potent herbs, that only a faint bitterness remained. And it was hot. His appetite for heat seemed insatiable. He ate as if he could see long days of cold, scarce provender ahead of him.

He had good reason. Without help, he and his companions would not be able to find enough food for the journey to Foul's Creche. He seemed to remember having heard somewhere that *aliantha* did not grow in the Spoiled Plains. The hostility of the Ramen boded ill for him in more ways than one.

Though he was afraid of it, he knew he would have to penetrate to the bottom of that hostility.

He looked for an antidote to fear in food, but while he chewed and thought, he was interrupted by a strange man who strode unexpectedly into the covert. The man entered at the far end of the canyon, and moved directly, deliberately, toward the seated men and women. His dress vaguely resembled that of the Ramen; he used the same materials to make his thin shirt and pants, his cloak. But he wore the cloak hanging from his shoulders in a way that affected his freedom of movement more than any Ramen would have tolerated. And he bore no cords anywhere about him. Instead of a Ramen garrote, he carried a short spear like a staff in one hand; and under his belt he wore a sharp wooden stave.

Despite the directness with which he approached, he created an impression of uncomfortable daring, as if he had some reason to believe that the Ramen might jeer at him. His gaze flicked fearfully about him, jumping away from rather than toward what he saw.

He had an air of blood about him that Covenant could not explain. He was clean, uninjured; neither spear nor spike showed recent use. Yet something in him spoke of blood, of killing and hunger. As the man reached the fire, Covenant realized that all the Ramen were sitting stiffly in their places—not moving, not eating, not looking at the stranger. They knew this man in a way that gave them pain.

After a moment, the man said aggressively, "Do you eat without me? I, too, need food."

Manethrall Jain's eyes did not raise themselves from the ground. "You are welcome, as you know. Join us or take what food you require."

"Am I so welcome? Where are the salutes and words of greeting? Pah! You do not even gaze at me."

But when Kam glared up from under his angry brows at the stranger, the man winced and looked away.

Jain said softly, "You have drunk blood."

"Yes!" the man barked rapidly. "And you are offended. You understand nothing. If I were not the best runner and Ranyhyn-tender in the Plains of Ra, you would slay me where I stand without a moment's concern for your promises."

Darkly, Kam muttered, "We are not so swift to forget promises."

The stranger took no notice of Kam's assertion. "Now I see guests among you. The Ringthane himself. And a Giant"—he drawled acerbically—"if my eyes do not mistake. Are Ravers also welcome?"

Covenant was surprised to hear Bannor speaking before either Jain or Kam could reply. "He is Saltheart Foamfollower." The Bloodguard's alien inflection carried an odd note of intensity, as if he were communicating a crucial fact.

"Saltheart Foamfollower!" the stranger jeered. But he did not meet the Giant's gaze. "Then you are already certain that he is a Raver."

Kam said, "We are uncertain."

Still the man ignored him. "And the Ringthane— the tormentor of horses. Does he also Rave? He holds his proper place—at the right hand of a Bloodguard. This is a proud feast—all the cruelest foes of the Ranyhyn together. And welcome!"

At this, Jain's tone tightened. "You also are welcome. Join us—or take what food you require and go."

A Winhome moved hesitantly toward the stranger, carrying a leaf laden with food. He caught it from her hands brusquely. "I will go. I hear your heart deny your words. I am not proud or welcome enough to eat with such as these." At once, he turned sarcastically on his heel, strode back the way he had come. Moments later, he had left the covert as abruptly as he had entered.

Covenant stared uncomprehendingly after him, then looked toward the Manethralls for some explanation. But they sat glowering at their food as if they could not meet either his eyes or each other's. Foamfollower also showed no understanding of what had happened. Lena had not noticed it; she was half asleep where she sat. Covenant turned to Bannor.

The Bloodguard faced Covenant's question squarely, answered it with the same dispassionate intensity. "He is Pietten."

"Pietten," Covenant repeated dismally. And Foam-follower echoed thickly, "Pietten!"

"He and the Heer Llaura were saved by the Quest for the Staff of Law at the battle of Soaring Wood-helven. Do you remember? Llaura and the child Piet-ten were damaged—"

"I remember," Covenant answered bitterly. "The ur-viles did something to them. They were used to bait the trap. She—she—" The memory appalled him. Llaura had been horribly abused, and all her great courage had not sufficed to overcome what had been done to her. And the child, Pietten—the child, too, had been abused.

Across Covenant's dismay, Foamfollower said, "We bore both Heer Llaura and Pietten to the Plains of Ra and Manhome." Covenant remembered that the Giant had carried Pietten in his arms. "There, at the request of the Ringthane and—and myself—the Ramen took Llaura and Pietten into their care."

Bannor nodded. "That is the promise of which he spoke."

"Llaura?" asked Covenant weakly.

"While Pietten was yet young, she died. The harm done to her cut short her years."

"And Pietten?" Foamfollower pursued. "What did the ur-viles do to him?"

Manethrall Kam broke his silence to mutter, "He is mad."

But Jain countered grimly, "He is the best runner and Ranyhyn-tender in the Plains of Ra—as he said."

"He serves the Ranyhyn," Bannor added. "He cares for them as entirely as any Manethrall. But there is"—he searched briefly for a description—"a ferocity in his love. He—"

"He liked the taste of blood," Covenant interrupted. In his memory, he could see Pietten—hardly more than four years old—under the crimson light of the sick moon. Pietten had smeared his hands on the bloody grass, then licked his fingers and smiled.

Bannor agreed with a nod.

"He licks the wounds of the Ranyhyn to clean them!" Kam snapped in horror.

"Because of his great skill with the Ranyhyn," Bannor went on, "and because of old promises made in the days of the Quest, the Ramen share their lives and work with him. But he is feared for his wildness. Therefore he lives alone. And he abuses the Ramen as if they have outcast him."

"Yet he fights," Jain breathed a moment later. "I have seen that spear slay three *kresh* in their very death hold on a Ranyhyn."

"He fights," Kam murmured. "He is mad."

Covenant took a deep breath as if he were trying to inhale courage. "And we're responsible—Foamfollower and I—we're the ones who gave him to you, so we're responsible. Is that it?"

At the sound of his voice, Lena stirred, blinked wearily, and Foamfollower said, "No, my friend."

But Manethrall Jain answered in a haunted voice, "The Ranyhyn have chosen you. We do not ask you to save them."

And Kam added, "You may call that pride if you wish. The Ranyhyn are worthy of all pride."

"And the responsibility is mine," Foamfollower said in a tone of pain that made Covenant's hearing ache. "The blame is mine. For after the battle of Soaring Woodhelven—when all the Quest knew that some nameless harm had been done to the child—it was I who denied to him the hurtloam which might have healed him."

This also Covenant remembered. Stricken by remorse for all the Cavewights he had slain, Foamfollower had used the last of the hurtloam to ease one of the wounded creatures rather than to treat Pietten. In protest against the Giant's self-judgment, Covenant said, "You didn't *deny* it. You—"

"I did not *give* it." Foamfollower's response was as final as an ax.

"Oh, hell!" Covenant glared around the group, searching for some way in which to grasp the situation. But he did not find it.

He had unintentionally roused Lena. She pulled herself erect, and asked, "Beloved, what is amiss?"

Covenant took her hand in his numb fingers. "Don't worry about it. I'm just trying to figure out what's going on here."

"My Queen," Foamfollower interposed. He wiped his mouth, set aside the leaves which had held his meal, then climbed to his feet. Towering over the circle of Ramen, he stepped forward to stand beside the fire. "My Queen, our difficulty is that the Ramen misdoubt me. They have spoken their respect for you, Lena Atiaran-daughter, and their acceptance of ur-Lord Thomas Covenant, Unbeliever and Ringthane. But me they distrust."

Lena looked up at him. "Then they are fools," she said with dignity.

"No." Foamfollower smiled wanly. "It is true that I have been a guest at Manhome, and a companion of Manethrall Lithe on the Quest for the Staff of Law. And it is true that Bannor of the Bloodguard has known me. We fought together at the battle of Soaring Woodhelven. But they are not fools. They suffer a doom of Giants, and their distrust must be respected."

He turned to the four Manethralls. "Yet, though I acknowledge your doubt, it is hard for me to bear. My heart urges me to leave this place where I am not trusted. You could not easily stop me. But I do not go. My thoughts urge me to turn to my friend Thomas Covenant. Perhaps he would compel you to accept me. But I do not ask this of him. I must bring your acceptance upon myself. I will strive to meet your doubt—so that the enemies of the Despiser, Soulcrusher and Fangthane, may not be divided against themselves. Ask anything that you require."

The Manethralls looked sharply at each other, and Covenant felt the atmosphere over the gathering tighten. The Giant's face was ominously calm, as if he recognized a personal crisis and understood how to meet it. But Covenant did not understand. The hostility of the Ramen continued to amaze him. He ached to jump to the Giant's defense.

He refrained because he saw why Foamfollower

wanted to prove himself—and because he had a fascinated, fearful desire to see how the Giant would do it.

After a wordless consultation with the other Manethralls, Jain got to her feet and confronted Foamfollower across the fire. Unbidden, Bannor joined her. They regarded the Giant gravely for a long moment. Then Jain said, "Saltheart Foamfollower, the Render is cunning in malice. To discover him in all his secret treacheries requires an equal cunning. The Ramen have no such cunning. How is it possible for us to test you?"

"Inquire of my past," Foamfollower responded evenly. "I was absent from Giant-wrought *Coercri* when the Ravers put their hands upon my kindred. Since that time, I have roved the Land, striking—slaying marauders. I have fought at the side of the Stonedownors in defense of their homes. I—"

"They had creatures which destroyed stone!" Lena cut in with sudden vehemence. "Their great, cruel arms tore our homes to rubble. Without the Giant's strength, we could not have preserved one rock upright."

"Lena." Covenant wanted to applaud, cheer her affirmation, but he stopped her gently, squeezed her arm until she turned her angry gaze toward him. "He doesn't need our help," he said as if he were afraid her ire might break the frail bones of her face. "He can answer for himself."

Slowly, her anger turned to pain. "Why do they torment us? We seek to save the Ranyhyn also. The Ranyhyn trust us."

Covenant steadied her as best he could. "They've suffered. They've got to answer for themselves too."

"I also shared somewhat in the returning of Thomas Covenant to the Land," Foamfollower continued. "He would not sit here now, purposing to aid the Land, had I not given of my strength."

"That does not suffice," said Jain sternly. "The Render would not hesitate to kill his own for the sake of a larger goal. Perhaps you served the Stonedownors and the summoning so that this white gold might fall into Fangthane's hands."

"And you have not given an account of The

Grieve." Bannor's voice was soft, withdrawn, as if the question he raised were perilous.

But Foamfollower turned such issues aside with a jerk of his massive head. "Then discount my past—discount the scars of risk which cover my flesh. It is possible that I am a tool of the Despiser. Inquire of what you see. Behold me. Do you truly believe that a Raver might disguise himself within me?"

"How can we answer?" Jain muttered. "We have never seen you hale."

But Foamfollower was facing Bannor now, addressing his question to the Bloodguard.

Evenly, objectively, Bannor replied, "Giant, you do not appear well. Many things are obscured in this winter—but you do not appear well. There is a lust in you that I do not comprehend. It has the look of Corruption."

The Manethralls nodded in sharp agreement.

"Bannor!" Foamfollower breathed intently. His stiff calm broke momentarily, and a pang of anguish twisted his countenance. "Do not damn me with such short words. It may be that I too much resemble Pietten. I have struck blows that I cannot call back or prevent. And you have seen—there is the blood of Giants upon my head."

The blood of Giants? Covenant moaned. Foamfollower!

The next instant, Foamfollower regained mastery of himself. "But you have known me, Bannor. You can see that it is not my intent to serve the Despiser. I could not—!" The words ripped themselves savagely past his lips.

"I have known you," Bannor agreed simply. "In what way do I know you now?"

The Giant's hands twitched as if they were eager for a violent answer, but he kept his steadiness. Without dropping Bannor's gaze, he knelt by the fire. Even then he was taller than Bannor or Manethrall Jain. His muscles tensed as he leaned forward, and the orange firelight echoed dangerously out of the dark caves of his eyes.

"You have seen the *caamora,* Bannor," he said

tightly, "the Giantish ritual fire of grief. You have seen its pain. I am not prepared—this is not my time for such rituals. But I will not withdraw until you acknowledge me, Bannor of the Bloodguard."

He did not release Bannor's eyes as he thrust both his fists into the hottest coals of the campfire.

The Cords gasped at the sight, and the other Manethralls jumped up to join Jain. Covenant followed as if the Giant had snatched him erect.

Foamfollower was rigid with agony. Though the flames did not consume his flesh, they tortured him horrendously. The muscles of his forehead bulged and worked as if they were tearing his skull apart; the thews of his neck stood out like cables; sweat oozed like blood down his fire-hot cheeks; his lips drew back into a white snarl across his teeth. But his gaze did not waver. In anguish he kept up the demand of his pain.

Bannor stared back with a look of magisterial indifference on his alien mien.

The Cords were appalled. They gaped sickly at Foamfollower's hands. And the Manethralls painfully, fearfully, watched Bannor and the Giant, measuring the test of will between them. But Lena gave a low cry and hid her face in Covenant's shoulder.

Covenant, too, could not bear to see Foamfollower's hurt. He turned on Bannor and gasped into the Bloodguard's ear, "Give it up! Admit you know him. Hellfire! Bannor—you bloody egomaniac! You're so proud —after the Bloodguard failed you can't stand to admit there might be any faithfulness left anywhere. It's you or nothing. But he's a Giant, Bannor!" Bannor did not move, but a muscle quivered along his jaw. "Wasn't Elena enough for you?" Covenant hissed. "Are you trying to make *another* Kevin out of him?"

For an instant, Bannor's white eyebrows gathered into a stark frown. Then he said flatly, "Pardon me, Saltheart Foamfollower. I trust you."

Foamfollower withdrew his hands. They were rigid with pain, and he hugged them to his chest, panting hoarsely.

Bannor turned to Covenant. Something in his pose made Covenant flinch as if he expected the Bloodguard to strike him. "You also caused the fall of High Lord Elena," Bannor said brittlely. "You compelled us to reveal the unspoken name. Yet you did not bear the burden of that name yourself. Therefore the Law of Death was broken, and Elena fell. I did not reproach you then, and do not now. But I say to you: beware, ur-Lord Covenant! You hold too many dooms in your unwell hands."

"I know that," muttered Covenant. He was shaking so badly that he had to keep both arms around Lena to support himself. "I know that. It's the only thing I know for sure." He could not look at Foamfollower; he was afraid of the Giant's pain, afraid that the Giant might resent his intervention. Instead, he held onto Lena while his reaction to the strain surged into anger.

"But I've had enough of this." His voice was too violent, but he did not care. He needed some outlet for his passion. "I'm not interested in asking for help anymore. Now I'm going to *tell* you what to do. Manethrall Lithe promised that the Ramen would do whatever I wanted. You care about promises—you keep this one. I want food, all we can carry. I want guides to take us to Landsdrop as fast as possible. I want scouts to help us get across the Spoiled Plains." Words tumbled through his teeth faster than he could control them. "If Foamfollower's been crippled— By hell, you're going to make it up to him!"

"Ask for the moon," Manethrall Kam muttered.

"Don't tempt me!" Hot shouts thronged in his throat like fire; he whirled to fling flames at the Manethralls. But their haunted eyes stopped him. They did not deserve his rage. Like Bannor and Foamfollower, they were the victims of the Despiser—the victims of the things he, Thomas Covenant, had not done, had been unwilling or unable to do, for the Land. Again, he could feel the ground on which he stood tremoring.

With an effort, he turned back to Bannor, met the Bloodguard's aging gaze. "What happened to Elena wasn't your fault at all," he mumbled. "She and I— did it together. Or I did it to her." Then he pushed himself to go to Foamfollower.

But as he moved, Lena caught his arm, swung him

around. He had been bracing himself on her without paying any attention to her; now she made him look at her. "Elena—my daughter—what has happened to her?" Horror crackled in her eyes. The next instant, she was clawing at his chest with desperate fingers. "What has happened to her?"

Covenant stared at her. He had half forgotten, he had not wanted to remember that she knew nothing of Elena's end.

"He said she fell!" she cried at him. "What have you done to her?"

He held her at arm's length, backed away from her. Suddenly everything was too much for him. Lena, Foamfollower, Bannor, the Ramen—he could not keep a grip on it all at once. He turned his head toward Foamfollower, ignored Lena, and looked dumbly to the Giant for help. But Foamfollower did not even see Covenant's stricken, silent plea. He was still wrapped in his own pain, struggling to flex his wracked fingers. Covenant lowered his head and turned back toward Lena as if she were a wall against which he had to batter himself.

"She's dead," he said thickly. "It's my fault—she wouldn't have been in that mess if it hadn't been for me. I didn't save her because I didn't know how."

He heard shouts behind him, but they made no impression on him. He was watching Lena. Slowly the import of his words penetrated her. "Dead," she echoed emptily. "Fault." As Covenant watched her, the light of consciousness in her eyes seemed to falter and go out.

"Lena," he groaned. "Lena!"

Her gaze did not recognize him. She stared blankly through him as if her soul had lapsed within her.

The shouting behind him mounted. A voice nearby gasped out, "We are betrayed! Ur-viles and Cave-wights—! The sentries were slain."

The urgency in the voice reached him. He turned dully. A young Cord almost chattering with fear stood before the Manethralls and Bannor. Behind her, in the entrance to the covert, fighting had already begun.

Covenant could hear the shouts and groans of frantic hand-to-hand combat echoing out of the rift.

The next instant, a tight pack of Cavewights burst into the canyon, whirling huge broadswords in their powerful, spatulate hands. With a shrill roar, they charged the Ramen.

Before Covenant could react, Bannor caught hold of him and Lena, began to drag them both toward the other end of the valley. "Flee," he said distinctly as he impelled them forward. "The Giant and I will prevent pursuit. We will overtake you—as soon as may be. Flee north, then east."

The cliffs narrowed until Covenant and Lena stood in the mouth of another cleft through the hills. Bannor thrust them in the direction of the dark crevice. "Make haste. Keep to the left." Then he was gone, running toward the battle.

Half unconsciously, Covenant checked to be sure that he still had Triock's knife under his belt. Part of him yearned to run after Bannor, to throw himself like Bannor into the absolution of the fray—to seek forgiveness.

Clutching hard at Lena's arm, he drew her with him into the cleft.

TEN: Pariah

AFTER the first bend, even the trailing light of the campfires was cut off, and he could see nothing. Lena moved like a puppet in his grasp—empty and unadept. He wanted her to hold onto him, so that he would have both hands free; but when he wrapped her fingers around his arm, they slipped limply off again. He was forced to grope ahead with his left hand, and retain her with his maimed right. His numbness made him feel at every moment that he was about to lose her.

The shouting pursued him along the crevice, increased his sense of urgency yell by yell. He cursed furiously, trying to keep himself from becoming frantic.

When the rift divided, he followed the left wall. In a few steps, this crevice became so narrow that he had to move along it sideways, pulling Lena after him. Then it began to descend. Soon it was so steep that the moldering leaves and loam of the floor occasionally shifted under their feet. There the rift became a tunnel. The stone sealed over their heads, while the floor leveled until the ceiling was so close that it made Covenant duck for fear he might crack open his skull. The utter lightlessness of the passage dismayed him. He felt that he was groping his way blindly into the bowels of the earth, felt at every step that the tunnel might pitch him into a chasm. He no longer heard any sound from the canyon; his own loud scrabbling filled his ears. Yet he did not stop. The pressure of his urgency, the pressure of the blind stone impending over the back of his neck, compelled him onward.

Still Lena gave no sign of life. She stumbled, moved at his pull, bumped dumbly against the walls of the tunnel; but her arm in his grasp was inert. He could not even hear her breathing. He tugged her after him as if she were a mindless child.

At last the tunnel ended. Without warning, the stone vanished, and Covenant blundered into a thicket. The stems and branches lashed at him as if he were an enemy. Protecting his eyes with his forearm, he thrust ahead until he found himself on open ground, sweating in the teeth of the wind.

The night was as dank and bitter as ever, but after the pitch blackness of the tunnel he found that he could see vaguely. He and Lena stood below a high, looming bluff. Thickets and brush covered most of its base, but beyond them the ground sloped down barrenly toward the Plains of Ra.

He paused in the scything wind and tried to take stock of the situation. The tunnel from this side was well disguised by the thickets and underbrush, but still the Ramen should have posted sentries here. Where were they? He saw no one, heard nothing but the wind.

He was tempted to call out, but the frigid emptiness of the night restrained him. If the Ramen were defeated, the marauders would have no difficulty following him through the tunnel; Cavewights and ur-viles could take such passages in the dark gleefully. Ur-viles might already be watching him from the thicket.

North, then east, Bannor had said. He knew he had to start moving. But he had no supplies—no food, no bedding, no fire. Even if he were not pursued, he could hardly hope to survive in this cold. If Bannor and the Giant did not come soon, he and Lena were finished.

But Bannor had said that they would overtake him. It's too late, he muttered to steady his resolve, it's too late to start worrying about the impossible. It's all been impossible from the beginning. Just get going. At least get her out of this wind.

He put Lena on his left, wrapped his arm around her, and started north across the preternatural current of the winter.

He hurried as much as possible, supporting Lena, glancing fearfully back over his shoulder to see if they were being followed. When he reached a break in the hills on his left, he faced a difficult decision: Bannor and Foamfollower would locate him more easily if he stayed on the edge of the Plains, but if he moved up among the hills he would have a better chance of finding shelter and *aliantha*. After a painful moment, he chose the hills. He would have to trust the hunting skills of his friends; Lena was his first concern.

He labored strenuously up through the break, half carrying his companion. Once he had passed beyond the first crests, he found a shallow valley running roughly northward which provided some cover from the wind. But he did not stop; he was not far enough from the tunnel. Instead, he took Lena along the valley and into the hills beyond it.

On the way, he stumbled by chance into a battered *aliantha*. It had few berries, but its presence there reassured him somewhat. He ate two berries himself, then tried to get Lena to take the others. But she neither saw the *aliantha* nor heard his demands; all her outer senses were blank.

He ate the rest of the treasure-berries so that they would not be wasted, then left the bush behind and took Lena along and out of the valley. For a long time after that, he could not find an easy way through the hills. He struggled generally northward, searching for usable valleys or paths, but the terrain turned him insistently east, downhill toward the plains. Now the sweat was freezing in his beard again, and his muscles slowly stiffened against the icy cut of the wind. Whenever the wind hit Lena directly, she trembled. At last her need for shelter became imperative in his mind. When he saw a darker shadow which looked like a gully in the wasteland below him, he gave up on the hills and went down to it.

It had not deceived him. It was a dry arroyo with sheer sides. In places its walls were more than ten feet high. He took Lena down an uneven slope into the gully, then guided her under the lee of the opposite wall and seated her with her back against the packed dirt.

As he peered at her through the darkness, her condition scared him. She shivered constantly now, and her skin was cold and clammy. Her face held no recognition, no awareness of where she was or what was happening to her. He chafed her wrists roughly, but her arms remained limp, as if the cold had unmarrowed her bones. "Lena," he called to her hesitantly, then with more force. "Lena!" She did not answer. She sat slack against the wall as if she had decided to freeze to death rather than acknowledge the fact that the man she loved was a murderer.

"Lena!" he begged gruffly. "Don't make me do this. I don't want to do it again."

She did not respond. The irregular moan and catch

of her breathing gave no indication that she had heard him. She looked as brittle as frostbitten porcelain.

With a fierce grimace clenched on his face, he drew back his halfhand and struck her hard across the side of her head for the second time in his life.

Her head snapped soddenly to the side, swung back toward him. For an instant, her breath shuddered in her lungs, and her lips trembled as if the air hurt her mouth. Then suddenly her hands leaped out like claws. Her nails dug into the flesh of his face around his eyes. She gripped him there, gouging him, poised ready to tear his eyes out.

A sharp nausea of fear wrenched his guts, made him flinch. But he did not back away.

After a moment, she said starkly, "You slew Elena my daughter."

"Yes."

Her fingers tightened. "I could blind you."

"Yes."

"Are you not afraid?"

"I'm afraid."

Her fingers tightened again. "Then why do you not resist?" Her nails drew blood from his left cheek.

"Because I've got to talk to you—about what happened to Elena. I've got to tell you what she did—and what I did—and why I did it. You won't listen unless you decide—"

"I will not listen at all!" Her voice shook with weeping. Savagely, she snatched back her hands and returned his blow, struck his cheek with all her strength. The sting brought water to his eyes. When he blinked them clear, he saw that she had clamped her hands to her face to keep herself from sobbing aloud.

Awkwardly, he put his arms around her. She did not resist. He held her firmly while she wept, and after a time she moved her head, pressed her face into his jacket. But soon she stiffened and withdrew. She wiped her eyes, averting her face as if she were ashamed of a momentary weakness. "I do not want your comfort, Unbeliever. You have not been her father. It is a father's place to love his daughter, and

you did not love her. Do not mistake my frail grief—
I will not forget what you have done."

Covenant hugged himself in an effort to contain his
hurt. "I don't want you to forget." For that moment,
he would have been willing to lose his eyes if the pain
of blindness could have enabled him to weep. "I
don't want anyone to forget."

But he was too barren for tears; the water which
blurred his sight did not come from his heart.
Roughly, he forced himself to his feet. "Come on.
We'll freeze to death if we don't get moving."

Before she could respond, he heard feet hit the
ground behind him. He whirled, waving his hands to
ward off an attack. A dark figure stood opposite him
in the gully. It was wrapped in a cloak; he could not
discern its outlines. But it carried a spear like a staff
in its right hand.

"Pah!" the figure spat. "You would be dead five
times if I had not chosen to watch over you."

"Pietten?" Covenant asked in surprise. "What're
you doing here?" Lena was at his side, but she did not
touch him.

"You are stupid as well as unskilled," rasped
Pietten. "I saw at once that the Ramen would not
defend you. I took the task upon myself. What folly
made you deliver yourself into their hands?"

"What happened in the fight?" Questions rushed up
in Covenant. "What happened to Bannor and Foamfollower? Where are they?"

"Come!" the Woodhelvennin snapped. "Those worm-
spawn are not far behind. We must move swiftly if
you wish to live."

Covenant stared. Pietten's attitude unnerved him.
For an instant, his jaw worked uselessly. Then he repeated with a note of desperation in his voice, "What
happened to Bannor and Foamfollower?"

"You will not see them again." Pietten sounded
scornful. "You will see nothing again unless you follow me now. You have no food and no skill. Remain
here, and you will be dead before I have gone
a league." Without waiting for answer, he turned and
trotted away along the gully.

Covenant hesitated indecisively while contradictory fears clamored in him. He did not want to trust Pietten. His instincts shouted loudly, He drinks blood; Foul did something to him and he likes the taste of blood! But he and Lena were too helpless. They could not fend for themselves. Abruptly, he took Lena's arm and started after Pietten.

The Ramen-trained Woodhelvennin allowed Covenant and Lena to catch up with him, but then he set a pace for them which kept Covenant from asking any questions. Traveling swiftly, he guided them northward out of the arroyo into the open Plains, hastened them along like a man with a goal clearly visible before him. When they showed signs of tiring, he irritably found *aliantha* for them. But he revealed no weariness himself; he moved strongly, surely, reveling in the flow of his strides. And from time to time he grinned jeeringly at Covenant and Lena, mocking them for their inability to match him.

They followed him as if they were entranced, spellbound to him by the harsh winter and their extreme need. Covenant maintained the pace doggedly, and Lena labored at his side, spurning his every effort to help her. Her new, grim independence seemed to sustain her; she covered nearly two leagues before she began to weaken. Then, however, her strength rapidly deserted her.

Covenant was deeply tired himself, but he ached to aid her. When she stumbled for the third time, and could hardly regain her feet, he demanded breathlessly across the wind, "Pietten, we've got to rest. We need fire and shelter."

"You are not hardy, Ringthane," Pietten gibed. "Why do so many people fear you?"

"We can't go on like this."

"You will freeze to death if you stop here."

Painfully, Covenant mustered the strength to shout, "I know that! Are you going to help us or not?"

Pietten's voice sounded oddly cunning as he replied, "We will be safer—beyond the river. It is not far." He hurried on before Covenant could question him.

Covenant and Lena made the effort to follow him and found that he had spoken the truth. Soon they reached the banks of a dark river flowing eastward out of the hills. It lay forbiddingly across their way like a stream of black ice, but Pietten jumped into it at once and waded straight to the opposite bank. The current was stiff, but did not reach above his knees.

Cursing, Covenant watched him go. His weariness multiplied his distrust; his instinctive leper's caution was yowling inside him like a wounded animal. He did not know this river, but he guessed it was the Roamsedge, Ra's northern boundary. He feared that Bannor and Foamfollower would not expect him to leave the Plains—if they were still alive.

But he still had no choice. The Woodhelvennin was their only chance.

"Will you halt there?" Pietten scoffed at them from the far bank. "Halt and die."

Hellfire! Covenant snarled to himself. He took Lena's arm despite her angry efforts to pull away, and went down the bank into the river.

His feet felt nothing of the cold, but it burned like numb fire into his lower legs. Before he had waded a dozen yards, his knees hurt as if his calves were being shredded by the river. He tried to hurry, but the speed of the current and the unevenness of the river bottom only made him trip and stagger brokenly. He clung to Lena's arm and plowed onward with his gaze fixed on the bank ahead.

When he stumbled up out of the river, his legs ached as if they had been maimed. "Damn you, Pietten," he muttered. "Now we have got to have a fire."

Pietten bowed sardonically. "Whatever you command, Ringthane." Turning on his heel, he ran lightly away into the low hills north of the river like a sprite enticing them to perdition.

Covenant lumbered in pursuit, and when he crested the hill, he saw that Pietten had already started a fire in the hollow beyond it. Flames crackled in a dry patch of brambles and bushes. As Covenant and Lena descended toward it, the fire spread, jumping fiendishly higher and higher as it ran through the dead wood.

They hastened fervidly to the blaze. Lena's legs gave way at the last moment, and she fell to her knees as if that were the only way she could prevent herself from leaping into the flames. And Covenant spread his arms to the heat, stood on the very verge of the fire and threw open his jacket like an acolyte embracing vision. For long moments they neither spoke nor moved.

But when the warmth melted the ice to make itself felt against Covenant's forehead, started to draw the moisture in steam from his clothes, he stepped back a pace and looked about him.

Pietten was leering at him mercilessly.

He felt suddenly trapped, cornered; for reasons that he could not name, he knew he was in danger. He looked quickly toward Lena. But she was absorbed in the fire, oblivious. Unwillingly he met Pietten's gaze again. That stare held him like the eyes of a snake, trying to paralyze him. He had to resist it. Without thinking, he growled, "That was a damn stupid thing to do." He indicated the fire with a jerk of one hand. "A fire this big will throw light over the hill. We'll be seen."

"I know." Pietten licked his lips.

"You know," Covenant muttered mordantly. "Did it occur to you that this could bring a pack of marauders down on us?" He snarled the words thoughtlessly, but as soon as he had spoken them, they sent a stammer of fear through him.

"Are you not grateful?" Pietten grinned maliciously. "You command fire—fire I provide. Is that not how men show their devotion to the Ringthane?"

"What are we going to do if we're attacked? She and I are in no condition to fight."

"I know."

"You know," Covenant repeated. The upsurge of his trepidation almost made him stutter.

"But no marauders will come," the Woodhelvennin went on immediately. "I hate them. Pah! They slay Ranyhyn."

"What do you mean, they won't come? You said" —he searched his memory—"you said they weren't far behind. How in hell do you expect them to miss us in all this light?"

"I do not want them to miss us."

"What?" The fear taking shape within him made him shout. "Hellfire! Make sense!"

"Ringthane," Pietten shot back with sudden vehemence, "this night I will complete the whole sense of my life!"

The next instant he had returned to scorn. "I desire them to find us, yes! I desire them to see this blaze and come. Land friends—horse servants—pah! They torment the Ranyhyn in the name of faith. I will teach them faith." Covenant felt Lena jump to her feet behind him; he could sense the way she focused herself on Pietten. In the warmth of the fire, he finally noticed what had caught her attention. It was the smell of blood. "I desire the Giant my benefactor and Bannor the Bloodguard to stand upon this hillside and witness my faith."

"You said that they are dead!" Lena hissed. "You said that we would not see them again."

At the same time, Covenant croaked, "It was you!" His apprehensions burst into clarity. "You did it." In the lurid light of the fire, he caught his first sure glimpse of his plight. "You're the one who betrayed all those coverts!"

Lena's movement triggered him into movement. He was one step ahead of her as she threw herself at Pietten.

But Pietten was too swift for them. He aimed his spear and braced himself to impale the first attack.

Covenant leaped to a stop. Grappling frantically, he caught Lena, held her from hurling herself onto Pietten's weapon. She struggled for one mute, furious moment, then became still in his grasp. Her bedraggled white hair hung across her face like a fringe of madness. Grimly, he set her behind him.

He was trembling, but he forced himself to face Pietten. "You want them to watch while you kill us."

Pietten laughed sourly. "Do they not deserve it?"

His eyes flashed as if a lightning of murder played in back of them. "If I could have my wish, I would place the entire Ramen nation around this hollow so that they might behold my contempt for them. Ranyhyn servants! Pah! They are vermin."

"Render!" Lena spat hoarsely.

With his left hand, Covenant held her behind him. "You betrayed those coverts—you betrayed them all. You're the only one who could have done it. You killed the sentries and showed those marauders how to get in. No wonder you stink of blood."

"It pleases me."

"You betrayed the Ranyhyn!" Covenant raged. "Injured Ranyhyn got slaughtered!"

At this, Pietten jerked forward, brandished his spear viciously. "Hold your tongue, Ringthane!" he snapped. "Do not question my faith. I have fought—I would slay any living creature that raised its hands against the Ranyhyn."

"Do you call that faith? There were injured Ranyhyn in that covert, and they were butchered!"

"They were murdered by Ramen!" Pietten retorted redly. "Vermin! They pretend service to the Ranyhyn, but they do not take the Ranyhyn to the safety of the south. I hold no fealty for them." Lena tried to leap at Pietten again, but Covenant restrained her. "They are like you—and that Giant—and the Bloodguard! Pah! You feast on Ranyhyn-flesh like jackals."

With an effort, Covenant made Lena look at him. "Go!" he whispered rapidly. "Run. Get out of here. Get back across the river—try to find Bannor or Foamfollower. He doesn't care about you. He won't chase you. He wants me."

Pietten cocked his spear. "If you take one step to flee," he grated, "I will kill the Ringthane where he stands and hunt you down like a wolf."

The threat carried conviction. "All right," Covenant groaned to Lena. "All right." Glowering thunderously, he swung back toward Pietten. "Do you remember ur-viles, Pietten? Soaring Woodhelven? Fire and ur-viles? They captured you. Do you remember?"

Pietten stared back like lightning.

"They captured you. They did things to you. Just as they did to Llaura. Do you remember her? They hurt her inside so that she had to help trap the Lords. The harder she tried to break free, the worse the trap got. Do you remember? It's just like that with you. They hurt you so that you would—destroy the Ranyhyn. Listen to me! Foul knew when he started this war that he wouldn't be able to crush the Ranyhyn unless he found some way to betray the Ramen. So he hurt you. He made you do what he wants. He's using you to butcher the Ranyhyn! And he's probably given you special orders about me. What did he tell you to do with my ring?" He hurled the words at Pietten with all his strength. "How many bloody times have you been to Foul's Creche since this winter started?"

For a moment, Pietten's eyes lost their focus. Dimly, he murmured, "I must take it to him. He will use it to save the Ranyhyn." But the next instant, white fury flared in him again. "You lie! I love the Ranyhyn! You are the butchers, you and those vermin!"

"That isn't true. You know it isn't true."

"Is it not?" Pietten laughed desperately. "Do you think I am blind, Ringthane? I have learned much in —in my journeys. Do you think the Ramen hold the Ranyhyn here out of love?"

"They can't help it," Covenant replied. "The Ranyhyn refuse to go."

Pietten did not hear him. "Do you think the Blood-guard are here out of love? You are a fool! Bannor is here because he has caused the deaths of so many Ranyhyn that he has become a betrayer. He needs to betray, as he did the Lords. Oh, he fights—he has always fought. He hungers to see every Ranyhyn slain in spite of his fighting so that his need will be fed. Pah!"

Covenant tried to interrupt, protest, but Pietten rushed on: "Do you think the Giant is here out of love? You are anile—sick with trust. Foamfollower is here because he has betrayed his people. Every last Giant, every man, woman, and child of his kindred, lies dead and moldered in Seareach because he abandoned them! He fled rather than defend them. His very bones are made of treachery, and he is here because he can find no one else to betray. All his other companions are dead."

Foamfollower! Covenant cried in stricken silence. All dead? Foamfollower!

"And you, Ringthane—you are the worst of all. You surpass my contempt. You ask what I remember." His spear point waved patterns of outrage at Covenant's chest. "I remember that the Ranyhyn reared to you. I remember that I strove to stop you. But you had already chosen to betray them. You bound them with promises—promises which you knew they could not break. Therefore the Ranyhyn cannot seek the safety of the mountains. They are shackled by commitments which you forced from them, you! You are the true butcher, Ringthane. I have lived my life for the chance to slay you."

"No," Covenant gasped. "I didn't know." But he heard the truth in Pietten's accusation. Waves of crime seemed to spread from him in all directions. "I didn't know."

Bannor? he moaned. Foamfollower? A livid orange mist filled his sight like the radiance of brimstone. How could he have done so much harm? He had only wanted to survive—had only wanted to extract survival from the raw stuff of suicide and madness. The Giants!—lost like Elena. And now the Ranyhyn were being driven down the same bloody road. Foamfollower? Did I do this to you? He knew that he was defenseless, that he could have done nothing to ward off a spear thrust. But he was staring into the abyss of his own actions and could not look away.

"We're the same," he breathed without knowing what he was saying. "Foul and I are the same."

Then he became aware that hands were pulling at him. Lena had gripped his jacket and was shaking him as hard as she could. "Is it true?" she shouted at him. "Are they dying because you made them promise to visit me each year?"

He met her eyes. They were full of firelight; they

compelled him to recognize still another of his crimes. In spite of his peril, he could not refuse her the truth.

"No." His throat was clogged with grief and horror. "That's only part— Even if they went to the mountains, they could still reach you. I—I"—his voice ached thickly—"I made them promise to save me— if I ever called them. I did it for myself."

Pietten laughed.

A cry of fury and despair tore between her lips. With the strength of revulsion, she thrust Covenant from her, then started to run out of the hollow.

"Stop!" Pietten barked after her. "You cannot escape!" He turned as she ran, following her with the tip of his spear.

In the instant that Pietten cocked his arm to throw, Covenant charged. He got his hands on the spear, heaved his weight against Pietten, tried to tear the spear away. Pietten recoiled a few steps under the onslaught. They wrestled furiously. But the grip of Covenant's halfhand was too weak. With a violent wrench, Pietten twisted the spear free.

Covenant grappled for Pietten's arms. Pietten knocked him back with the butt of the spear and stabbed its point at him. Covenant threw himself to the side, managed to avoid the thrust. But he landed heavily on one foot, with the ankle bent under his weight.

Bones snapped. He heard them retorting through his flesh as he crashed to the ground, heard himself scream. Agony erupted in his leg. But he made himself roll, trying to evade the jabs of the spear.

As he flopped onto his back, he saw Pietten standing over him with the spear clenched like a spike in both hands.

Then Lena slammed into the Woodhelvennin. She launched her slight form at him with such ferocity that he fell under her, lost his grip on the spear. It landed across Covenant.

He grabbed it, tried to lever himself to his feet with it. But the pain in his ankle held him down as if his foot had been nailed to the ground. "Lena!" he shouted wildly. "No!"

Pietten threw her off him with one powerful sweep of his arm. She sprang up again and pulled a knife out of her robe. Rage contorted her fragile face as she hacked at Pietten.

He evaded her strokes, backed away quickly for an instant to gather his balance. Then, fiercely, he grinned.

"No!" Covenant shrieked.

When Lena charged again, Pietten caught her knife wrist neatly and turned the blade away from him. Slowly, he twisted her arm, forcing her down. She hammered at him with her free hand, but he held her. She could not resist his strength. She fell to her knees.

"The Ranyhyn!" she gasped to Covenant. "Call the Ranyhyn!"

"Lena!" Using the spear, he lunged to his feet, fell, tried to crawl forward.

Slowly, inexorably, Pietten bent her backward until she lay writhing on the ground. Then he pulled his sharp wooden stave from his belt. With one savage blow he stabbed her in the stomach, spiked her to the frozen earth.

Horror roared in Covenant's head. He seemed to feel himself shattering; stricken with pain, he lost consciousness momentarily.

When he opened his eyes, he found Pietten standing in front of him.

Pietten was licking the blood off his hand.

Covenant tried to raise the spear, but Pietten snatched it from him. "Now, Ringthane!" he cried ecstatically. "Now I will slay you. Kneel there—grovel before me. Bring my dreams to life. I will be fair—I will allow you a chance. From ten paces I will hurl my spear. You may dodge—if your ankle permits. Do so. I relish it."

With a grin like a snarl on his face, he strode away, turned and balanced the spear on his palm. "Do you not choose to live?" he jeered. "Kneel, then. Groveling becomes you."

Numbly, as if he did not know what he was doing,

Covenant raised the two fingers of his right hand to his mouth and let out a weak whistle.

A Ranyhyn appeared instantly over the hillcrest, and came galloping down into the hollow. It was miserably gaunt, reduced by the long winter to such inanition that only its chestnut coat seemed to hold its skeleton together. But it ran like indomitable pride straight toward Covenant.

Pietten did not appear to see it coming. He was in a personal trance, exalted by blood. Obliviously, he drew back his arm, bent his body until his muscles strained with passion—obliviously he launched the spear like a bolt of retribution at Covenant's heart.

The Ranyhyn veered, flashed between the two men, then fell tumbling like a sack of dismembered bones. When it came to rest on its side, both men saw Pietten's spear jutting from its bloodstained coat.

The sight struck Pietten like a blast of chaos. He gaped at what he had done in disbelief, as if it were inconceivable, unendurable. His shoulders sagged, eyes stared widely. He seemed to lack language for what he saw. His lips fumbled over meaningless whimpers, and the muscles of his throat jerked as if he could not swallow. If he saw Covenant crawling terribly toward him, he gave no sign. His arms dangled at his sides until Covenant reared up in front of him on one leg and drove a sharp Stonedownor knife into his chest with both hands.

Covenant delivered the blow like a double fistful of hate. Its momentum carried him forward, and he toppled across Pietten's corpse. Blood pumping from around the blade scored his jacket, slicked his hands, stained his shirt. But he paid no attention to it. That one blow seemed to have spent all his rage. He pushed himself off the body, and crawled away toward Lena, dragging his broken ankle like a millstone of pain behind him.

When he reached her, he found that she was still alive. The whole front of her robe was soaked, and blood coughed thinly between her lips; but she was still alive. He gripped the spike to draw it out. But the movement drew a gasp of pain from her. With an effort, she opened her eyes. They were clear, as if she were finally free of the confusion which had shaped her life. After a moment, she recognized Covenant, and tried to smile.

"Lena," he panted. "Lena."

"I love you," she replied in a voice wet with blood. "I have not changed."

"Lena." He struggled to return her smile, but the attempt convulsed his face as if he were about to shriek.

Her hand reached toward him, touched his forehead as if to smooth away his scowl. "Free the Ranyhyn," she whispered.

The plea took her last strength. She died with blood streaming between her lips.

Covenant stared at it as if it were vituperation. His eyes had a feverish cast, a look of having been blistered from within. No words came to his mind, but he knew what had happened. Rape, treachery, now murder—he had done them all, he had committed every crime. He had broken the promise he had made after the battle of Soaring Woodhelven, when he swore that he would not kill again. For a long moment, he regarded his numb fingers as if they were things of no importance. Only the blood on them mattered. Then he pushed himself away from Lena. Crawling like an abject passion, he moved toward the Ranyhyn.

Its muzzle was frothed with pain, and its sides heaved horridly. But it watched Covenant's approach steadily, as if for the first time in its life it was not afraid of the bearer of white gold. When he reached it, he went directly to its wound. The spear was deeply embedded; at first he did not believe he could draw it out. But he worked at it with his hands, digging his elbows into the Ranyhyn's panting ribs. At last the shaft tore free. Blood pulsed from the wound, yet the horse lurched to its feet, stood wavering weakly on splayed legs, and nuzzled him as if to tell him that it would live.

"All right," he muttered, speaking half to himself. "Go back. Go—tell all the others. Our bargain is over.

No more bargains. No more—" The fire was falling into embers, and his voice faded as if he were losing strength along with it. Dark fog blew into him along the wind. But a moment later, he rallied. "No more bargains. Tell them."

The Ranyhyn stood as if it were unwilling to leave him.

"Go on," he insisted thickly. "You're free. You've got to tell them. In the—in the name of *Kelenbhra-banal,* Father of Horses. Go."

At the sound of that name, the Ranyhyn turned painfully and started to limp out of the hollow. When it reached the crest of the hill, it stopped and faced him once more. For an instant, he thought he could see it silhouetted against the night, rearing. Then it was gone.

He did not wait, did not rest. He was past taking any account of the cost of his actions. He caught up Pietten's spear and used it as a staff to hold himself erect. His ankle screamed at him as it dragged the ground, but he set his teeth and struggled away from the fire. As soon as he left the range of its warmth, his wet clothing began to freeze.

He had no idea where he was headed, but he knew he had to go. On each breath that panted through his locked teeth, he whispered *hate* as if it were a question.

ELEVEN: The Ritual of Desecration

AFTER Loerya left him, High Lord Mhoram stayed on the tower for the rest of the night. He kept himself warm against the bitter wind by calling up a flow of power through his staff from time to time and watched in silent dread as the pronged veins of malice in the ground pulsed at Revelstone like sick, green-red lava oozing its way into the Keep's courage. The ill might which spread from *samadhi* Raver's Stone and the staves of the ur-viles lit the night garishly; and at irregular intervals, fervid sparks writhed upward when the attack met resistance in the rock of the foothills.

Though it moved slowly, the hungry agony of the attack was now only scant yards from Revelstone's walls. Through his feet, Mhoram could feel the Keep moaning in silent immobility, as if it ached to recoil from the leering threat of those veins.

But that was not why Mhoram stood throughout the long night exposed to the immedicable gall of the wind. He could have sensed the progress of the assault from anywhere in the Keep, just as he did not need his eyes to tell him how close the inhabitants of the city were to gibbering collapse. He watched because it was only by beholding Satansfist's might with all his senses, perceiving it with all his resources in all its horror, that he could deal with it.

When he was away from the sight, dread seemed to fall on him from nowhere, adumbrate against his heart like the knell of an unmotivated doom. It confused his thoughts, paralyzed his instincts. Walking through the halls of Revelstone, he saw faces gray with inarticulate terror, heard above the constant, clenched mumble of sobs children howling in panic at the sight of their parents, felt the rigid moral exhaustion of the stalwart few who kept the Keep alive—Quaan, the three Lords, most of the Lorewardens, *lillianrill,* and *rhadhamaerl.* Then he could hardly master the passion of his futility, the passion which urged him to strike at his friends because it blamed him for failing the Land. A wild hopelessness moved in him, shouldered its way toward the front of his responses. And he alone of all the Lords knew how to make such hopelessness bear fruit.

But alone on the watchtower, with Satansfist's army revealed below him, he could clarify himself, recognize what was being done to Revelstone. The winter and the attack assumed a different meaning. He no longer accused himself; he knew then that no one could be blamed for being inadequate in the face of such unanswerable malevolence. Destruction was easier than preservation, and when destruction had risen high enough, mere men and women could not be condemned if they failed to throw back the tide. Therefore he was able to resist his own capacity for desecration. His eyes burned like yellow fury at the creeping attack, but he was searching for defenses.

The aspect of the assault which most daunted him was its unwavering ferocity. He could see that the urviles maintained their part of the power by rotating their positions, allowing each wedge and loremaster to rest in turn. And he knew from experience that Lord Foul's strength—his own prodigious might making use of the Illearth Stone—was able to drive armies mad, push them to greater savagery than their flesh could bear. But Satansfist was only one Giant, one body of mortal thew and bone and blood. Even a Giant-Raver should not have been able to sustain such an extravagant exertion for so long.

In addition, while *samadhi* concentrated on his attack, he might reasonably have been expected to lose

some of his control over his army. Yet the whole
horde, legion after legion, remained poised around
Revelstone. Each creature in its own way bent the
lust of its will at the Keep. And the emerald expenditure of *samadhi's* strength never blinked. Clearly,
Lord Foul supported his army and its commander
with might so immense that it surpassed all Mhoram's
previous conceptions of power.

He could see no hope for Revelstone anywhere
except in the cost of that unwavering exertion. The
defenders would have to hope and pray that Satansfist's aegis broke before they did. If they could not
contrive to endure the Raver's attack, they were
doomed.

When Mhoram returned to the hollow stone halls in
the first, gray, dim ridicule of dawn, he was ready to
strive for that endurance.

The hushed, tight wave of panic that struck him as
he strode down the main passage into the Keep almost
broke his resolve. He could feel people grinding their
teeth in fear behind the walls on either side of him.
Shouts reached him from a far gallery; two parties
had banded together to defend themselves from each
other. Around a bend he surprised a hungry group
that was attempting to raid one of the food storerooms; the people believed that the cooks in the
refectories were preparing poison.

His anger blazed up in him, and he surged forward,
intending to strike them where they stood in their
folly. But before he reached them, they fell into panic
and fled from him as if he were a ghoul. Their retreat left two of Quaan's warriors standing guard in
front of the storeroom as if they were watching each
other rather than the supplies. Even these two
regarded Mhoram with dread.

He mastered himself, forced a smile onto his
crooked lips, said a few encouraging words to the
guards. Then he hastened away.

He saw now that Revelstone was at the flash point
of crisis. To help it, he had to provide the city with
something more than moments of temporary aid.
Grimly, he ignored the other needs, the multitudes of

fear, which cut at his awareness. As he strode along passages and down stairways, he used his staff to summon Hearthrall Tohrm and all the Gravelingases. He put his full authority into the command, so that as many *rhadhamaerl* as possible might resist their panic and answer.

When he reached the bright floor of the courtyard around which the Lords' chambers were situated, he felt a brief surge of relief to see that Tohrm and a dozen Gravelingases were already there, and more were on their way. Soon a score of the *rhadhamaerl* —nearly all the Keep's masters of stone-lore—stood on the shining rock, waiting to hear him.

For a moment, the High Lord gazed at the men, wincing inwardly at their misery. They were Gravelingases of the *rhadhamaerl,* and were being hurt through the very stone around them. Then he nodded sharply to himself. This was the right place for him to begin; if he could convince these men that they were able to resist Satansfist's ill, they would be able to do much for the rest of the city.

With an effort that strained the muscles of his face, he smiled for them. Tohrm answered with an awkward grin which quickly fell into apprehension again.

"Gravelingases," Mhoram began roughly, "we have spent too long each of us alone enduring this ill in small ways. We must put our strength together to form a large defense."

"We have obeyed your orders," one man muttered sullenly.

"That is true," Mhoram returned. "Thus far we have all given our strength to encourage the people of Revelstone. You have kept your graveling fires bright, as I commanded. But wisdom does not always come swiftly. Now I see with other eyes. I have listened more closely to the voice of the Keep. I have felt the rock itself cry out against this evil. And I say now that we must resist in other ways if Revelstone is to endure.

"We have mistaken our purpose. The Land does not live for us—we live for the Land. Gravelingases, you must turn your lore to the defense of the stone.

Here, in this place"——he touched the radiant floor
with the heel of his staff——"slumbers power that perhaps only a *rhadhamaerl* may comprehend. Make use
of it. Make use of any possible lore—do here together
whatever must be done. But find some means to seal
the heart-rock of Revelstone against this blight. The
people can provide for themselves if Revelstone remains brave."

As he spoke, he realized that he should have understood these things all along. But the fear had
numbed him, just as it had icebound the Gravelingases. And like him they now began to comprehend.
They shook themselves, struck their hands together,
looked around them with preparations rather than
dread in their eyes. Tohrm's lips twitched with their
familiar grin.

Without hesitation, High Lord Mhoram left the
Gravelingases alone to do their work. As he walked
along the tunnel away from the courtyard, he felt like
a man who had discovered a new magic.

He directed his steps toward one of the main
refectories, whose chief cook he knew to be a feisty,
food-loving man not prone to either awe or fear; and
as he moved, he sent out more summonses, this time
calling his fellow Lords and Hearthrall Borillar's Hirebrands. Amatin and Trevor answered tensely, and
Borillar sent a half-timid sign through the walls. But
a long moment passed before Loerya answered,
and when her signal came it was torpid, as if
she were dazed with dismay. Mhoram hoped that
the *rhadhamaerl* could make themselves felt soon, so
that people like Loerya might not altogether lose
heart; and he climbed up through the levels of the
Keep toward the refectory as if he were surging
through viscous dread.

But as he neared the kitchen, he saw a familiar
figure dodge away into a side passage, obviously trying to avoid him. He swung around the corner after
the man, and came face to face with Trell Atiaran-
mate.

The big man looked feverish. His graying beard
seemed to bristle hotly, his sunken cheeks were

flushed, and his dull, hectic eyes slid away from Mhoram's gaze in all directions, as if he could not control their wandering. He stood under Mhoram's scrutiny as if he might break and run at any moment.

"Trell Gravelingas," Mhoram said carefully, "the other *rhadhamaerl* are at work against this ill. They need your strength."

Trell's gaze flicked once across Mhoram's face like a lash of anger. "You wish to preserve Revelstone so that it will be intact for the Despiser's use." He filled the word *intact* with so much bitterness that it sounded like a curse.

At the accusation, Mhoram's lips tightened. "I wish to preserve the Keep for its own sake."

The roaming of Trell's eyes had an insatiable cast, as if they were afraid of going blind. "I do not work well with others," he said dimly after a moment. Then, without transition, he became urgent. "High Lord, tell me your secret."

Mhoram was taken aback. "My secret?"

"It is a secret of power. I must have power."

"For what purpose?"

At first, Trell squirmed under the question. But then his gaze hit Mhoram again. "Do you wish Revelstone intact?" Again, *intact* spat like gall past his lips. He turned sharply and strode away.

For an instant, Mhoram felt a cold hand of foreboding on the back of his neck, and he watched Trell go as if the big Gravelingas trailed plumes of calamity. But before he could grasp the perception, Revelstone's ambience of dread clouded it, obscured it. He did not dare give Trell his secret knowledge. Even a Gravelingas might be capable of invoking the Ritual of Desecration.

With an effort, he remembered his purpose, and started again toward the refectory.

Because he had been delayed, all the people he had summoned were waiting for him. They stood ineffectively among the forlorn tables in the great, empty hall, and watched his approach with trepidation, as if he were a paradoxically fatal hope, a saving doom. "High Lord," the chief cook began at once, quelling his fear with anger, "I cannot control these useless sheep disguised as cooks. Half have deserted me, and the rest will not work. They swing knives and refuse to leave the corners where they hide."

"Then we must restore their courage." Despite the scare Trell had given him, Mhoram found that he could smile more easily. He looked at the Lords and Hirebrands. "Do you not feel it?"

Amatin nodded with tears in her eyes. Trevor grinned.

A change was taking place under their feet.

It was a small change, almost subliminal. Yet soon even the Hirebrands could feel it. Without either heat or light, it warmed and lit their hearts.

On a barely palpable level, the rock of Revelstone was remembering that it was obdurate granite, not susceptible sandstone.

Mhoram knew that this change could not be felt everywhere in the Keep—that all the strength of the *rhadhamaerl* would never suffice to throw back the lurid dread of Satansfist's attack. But the Gravelingases had made a start. Now anyone who felt the alteration would know that resistance was still possible.

He let his companions taste the granite for a moment. Then he began the second part of his defense. He asked Hearthrall Borillar for all the healing wood essence—the *rillinlure*—he could provide, and sent the other Hirebrands to help the chief cook begin working again. "Cook and do not stop," he commanded. "The other refectories are paralyzed. All who seek food must find it here."

Borillar was doubtful. "Our stores of *rillinlure* will be swiftly consumed in such quantities of food. None will remain for the future of this siege."

"That is as it must be. Our error has been to conserve and portion our strength against future perils. If we fail to endure this assault, we will have no future." When Borillar still hesitated, Mhoram went on: "Do not fear, Hearthrall. Satansfist himself must rest after such an exertion of power."

After a moment, Borillar recognized the wisdom of the High Lord's decision. He left to obey, and

Mhoram turned to the other Lords. "My friends, to us falls another task. We must bring the people here so that they may eat and be restored."

"Send the Warward," said Loerya. Her pain at being away from her daughters was plainly visible in her face.

"No. Fear will cause some to resist with violence. We must call them, make them wish to come. We must put aside our own apprehension, and send a call like a melding through the Keep, so that the people will choose to answer."

"Who will defend Revelstone—while we work here?" Trevor asked.

"The peril is here. We must not waste our strength on useless watching. While this attack continues, there will be no other. Come. Join your power to mine. We, the Lords, cannot permit the Keep to be thus broken in spirit."

As he spoke, he drew a fire bright and luminescent from his staff. Tuning it to the ambience of the stone, he set it against one wall so that it ran through the rock like courage, urging all the people within its range to lift up their heads and come to the refectory.

At his back, he felt Amatin, Trevor, then Loerya following his example. Their Lords-fire joined his; their minds bent to the same task. With their help, he pushed dread away, shared his own indomitable conviction, so that the appeal which radiated from them into Revelstone carried no flaw or dross of fear.

Soon people began to answer. Hollow-eyed like the victims of nightmares, they entered the refectory— accepted steaming trays from the chief cook and the Hirebrands—sat at the tables and began to eat. And when they had eaten, they found themselves ushered to a nearby hall, where the Lorewardens enjoined them to sing boldly in the face of defeat:

> Berek! Earthfriend!—help and weal,
> Battle-aid against the foe!
>   Earth gives and answers Power's peal,
>   Ringing, Earthfriend! help and heal!
> Clean the Land from bloody death and woe!

More and more people came, drawn by the music, and the Lords, and the reaffirmation of Revelstone's granite. Supporting each other, carrying their children, dragging their friends, they fought their fear and came because the deepest impulses of their hearts responded to food, music, *rillinlure,* rock—to the Lords and the life of Revelstone.

After the first influx, the Lords took turns resting so that fatigue would not make their efforts waver. When the *rillinlure* gave out, the Hirebrands provided special fires for the returning cooks, and joined their own lore to the call of the Lords. Quaan's warriors gave up all pretense of guarding the walls, and came to help the cooks—clearing tables, cleaning pots and trays, carrying supplies from the storerooms.

Now the city had found a way to resist the dread, and it was determined to prevail. In all, less than half of Revelstone's people responded. But they were enough. They kept Lord's Keep alive when the very air they breathed reeked of malice.

For four days and four nights, High Lord Mhoram did not leave his post. He rested and ate to sustain himself, but he stayed at his station by the refectory wall. After a time, he hardly saw or heard the people moving around him. He concentrated on the stone, wrought himself to the pitch of Revelstone, to the pulse of its existence and the battle for possession of its life rock. He saw as clearly as if he were standing on the watchtower that Satansfist's livid power oozed close to the outer walls and then halted—hung poised while the Keep struggled against it. He heard the muffled groaning of the rock as it fought to remember itself. He felt the exhaustion of the Gravelingases. All these things he took into himself, and against the Despiser's wrong he placed his unbreaking will.

And he won.

Shortly before dawn on the fifth day, the onslaught broke like a tidal wave collapsing out to sea under its own weight. For a long stunned moment, Mhoram felt jubilation running through the rock under his feet and could not understand it. Around him, people gaped as if the sudden release of pressure astounded

them. Then, swept together by a common impulse, he
and everyone else dashed toward the outer battlements to look at the siege.

The ground below them steamed and quivered like
wounded flesh, but the malevolence which had
stricken it was gone. Satansfist's army lay prostrate
from overexertion in its encampments. The Giant-
Raver himself was nowhere to be seen.

Over all its walls from end to end, Revelstone
erupted in the exultation of victory. Weak, hoarse,
ragged, starving voices cheered, wept, shouted raucous
defiance as if the siege had been beaten. Mhoram
found his own vision blurred with relief. When he
turned to go back into the Keep, he discovered Loerya
behind him, weeping happily and trying to hug all
three of her daughters at once. At her side, Trevor
crowed, and tossed one of the girls giggling into the
air.

"Rest now, Mhoram," Loerya said through her joy.
"Leave the Keep to us. We know what must be done."

High Lord Mhoram nodded his mute gratitude and
went wearily away to his bed.

Yet even then he did not relax until he had felt
the Warward resume its defensive stance—felt search
parties hunting through the Keep for the most blighted
survivors of the assault—felt order slowly reform the
city like a mammoth being struggling out of chaos.
Only then did he let himself flow with the slow pulse
of the gut-rock and lose his burdens in sleep—secure
in the confidence of stone.

By the time he awoke the next morning, Lord's
Keep had been returned as much as possible to battle-
readiness. Warmark Quaan brought a tray of breakfast to him in his private quarters, and reported the
news of the city to him while he ate.

Thanks to its training, and to exceptional service
by some of the Hafts and Warhafts, the Warward had
survived essentially unscathed. The Gravelingases
were exhausted, but well. The Lorewardens and Hirebrands had suffered only chance injuries from
panic-stricken friends. But the people who had not
answered the Lords' summons had not fared so well.

Search parties had found several score dead, especially in ground-level apartments near the outer walls. Most of these people had died of thirst, but some were murdered by their fear-mad friends and neighbors. And of the hundreds of other survivors, four- or fivescore appeared irreparably insane.

After the search had ended, Lord Loerya had taken to the Healers all those who were physically and mentally damaged, as well as those who seemed to remember having committed murder. She was assisting the Healers now. In other ways, Revelstone was swiftly recovering. The Keep was intact.

Mhoram listened in silence, then waited for the old Warmark to continue. But Quaan fell studiously silent, and the High Lord was forced to ask, "What of the Raver's army?"

Quaan spat in sudden vehemence. "They have not moved."

It was true. Satansfist's hordes had retreated to their encampment and fallen into stasis as if the force which animated them had been withdrawn.

In the days that followed, they remained essentially still. They moved enough to perform the bare functions of their camp. They received dark supply wains from the south and east. From time to time, an indefinite flicker of power ran among them—a half-hearted whip keeping surly beasts under control. But none of them approached within hailing distance of the Keep. *Samadhi* Raver did not show himself. Only the unbroken girdle of the siege showed that Lord Foul had not been defeated.

For five days—ten—fifteen—the enemy lay like a dead thing around Revelstone. At first, some of the more optimistic inhabitants of the city argued that the spirit of the attackers had been broken. But Warmark Quaan did not believe this, and after one long look from the watchtower, Mhoram agreed with his old friend.

Satansfist was simply waiting for Revelstone to eat up its supplies, weaken itself, before he launched his next assault.

As the days passed, High Lord Mhoram lost his

capacity to rest. He lay tense in his chambers and listened to the mood of the city turn sour.

Slowly, day by day, Lord's Keep came to understand its predicament. The Giants who had delved Revelstone out of the mountain rock thousands of years ago, in the age of Damelon, had made it to be impregnable; and all its inhabitants had lived from birth with the belief that this intention had succeeded. The walls were granite, and the gates, unbreakable. In a crisis the fertile upland plateau could provide the Keep with food. But the Despiser's unforeseen, unforeseeable winter had laid the upland barren; crops and fruit could not grow, cattle or other animals could not live, in the brazen wind. And the storerooms had already supplied the city since the natural onset of winter.

For the first time in its long history, Revelstone's people saw that they might starve.

In the initial days of waiting, the Lords began a stricter rationing of the supplies. They reduced each person's daily share of food until everyone in Revelstone felt hungry all the time. They organized the refectories more stringently, so that food would not be wasted. But these measures were palpably inadequate. The city had many thousand inhabitants; even on minimal rations they consumed large portions of the stores every day.

Their earlier elation ran out of them like water leaking into parched sand. The wait became first stupefying, then heavy and ominous, like pent thunder, then maddening. And High Lord Mhoram found himself yearning for the next attack. He could fight back against an attack.

Gradually, the cold gray days of suspense began to weaken the Keep's discretion, its pragmatic sense. Some of the farmers—people whose lifework had been taken from them by the winter—crept out to the upland hills around Glimmermere, sneaking as if they were ashamed to be caught planting futile rows of seeds in the frozen earth.

Lord Trevor began to neglect some of his duties. At odd times, he forgot why he had become a Lord,

forgot the impulse which had made him a Lord in
defiance of his lack of belief in himself; and he
shirked normal responsibilities as if he were inexplicably afraid of failure. Loerya his wife remained
staunch in her work, but she became distracted, almost furtive, as she moved through the Keep. She
often went hungry so that her daughters could have
more food. Whenever she saw the High Lord, she
glared at him with a strange resentment in her eyes.

Like Loerya, Lord Amatin grew slowly distant. At
every free moment she plunged into a feverish study
of the First and Second Wards, searching so hard
for the unlocking of mysteries that when she went
back to her public duties her forehead looked as sore
as if she had been battering it against her table.

Several Hirebrands and Gravelingases took to
carrying fire with them wherever they went, like men
who were going incomprehensibly blind. And on the
twentieth day of the waiting, Warmark Quaan
abruptly reversed all his former decisions; without
consulting any of the Lords, he sent a party of scouts
out of the Keep toward Satansfist's camp. None of
them returned.

Still the Raver's army lay like dormant chains, con-
stricting the heart of Revelstone.

Quaan berated himself to the High Lord. "I am a
fool," he articulated severely, "an old fool. Replace
me before I am mad enough to send the Warward itself out to die."

"Who can replace you?" Mhoram replied gently.
"It is the Despiser's purpose to make mad all
the defenders of the Land."

Quaan looked around him as if to measure with his
eyes the chill of Revelstone's travail. "He will
succeed. He requires no weapon but patience."

Mhoram shrugged. "Perhaps. But I think it is an
unsure tactic. Lord Foul cannot foretell the size of our
stores—or the extent of our determination."

"Then why does he wait?"

The High Lord did not need to be a seer to answer
this question. "*Samadhi* Raver awaits a sign—perhaps
from us—perhaps from the Despiser."

Glowering at the thought, Quaan went back to his duties. And Mhoram returned to a problem which had been nagging at him. For the third time, he went in search of Trell.

But once again he could not locate the tormented Gravelingas. Trell must have secreted himself somewhere. Mhoram found no trace, felt no emanation, and none of the other *rhadhamaerl* had seen the big Stonedownor recently. Mhoram ached at the thought of Trell in hiding, gnawing in cataleptic isolation the infested meat of his anguishes. Yet the High Lord could not afford either the time or the energy to dredge all Revelstone's private places for the sake of one embittered Gravelingas. Before he had completed even a cursory search, he was distracted by a group of Lorewardens who had irrationally decided to go and negotiate a peace with the Raver. Once again, he was compelled to put aside the question of Trell Atiaranmate.

On the twenty-fourth day, Lord Trevor forsook his duties altogether. He sealed himself in his study like a penitent, and refused all food and drink. Loerya could get no response from him, and when the High Lord spoke to him, he said nothing except that he wished his wife and daughters to have his ration of food.

"Now even I am a cause of pain to him," Loerya murmured with hot tears in her eyes. "Because I have given some of my food to my daughters, he believes that he is an insufficient husband and father, and must sacrifice himself." She gave Mhoram one desperate glance, like a woman trying to judge the cost of abdication, then hurried away before he could reply.

On the twenty-fifth day, Lord Amatin strode up to Mhoram and demanded without preface or explanation that he reveal to her his secret knowledge.

"Ah, Amatin," he sighed, "are you so eager for burdens?"

She turned at once and walked fragilely away as if he had betrayed her.

When he went to stand his solitary watch on the tower, a dull vermeil mood was on him, and he felt that he had in fact betrayed her; he had withheld dangerous knowledge from her as if he judged her unable to bear it. Yet nowhere in his heart could he find the courage to give his fellow Lords the key to the Ritual of Desecration. That key had a lurid, entrancing weight. It urged him to rage at Trevor, pummel the pain from Loerya's face, shake Amatin's frail shoulders until she understood, call down fire from the hidden puissance of the skies on Satansfist's head —and refused to let him speak.

On the twenty-seventh day, the first of the storerooms was emptied. Together, the chief cook and the most experienced Healer reported to Mhoram that the old and infirm would begin to die of hunger in a few days.

When he went to his chambers to rest, he felt too cold to sleep. Despite the warm graveling, Lord Foul's winter reached through the stone walls at him as if the gray, unfaltering wind were tuned to his most vulnerable resonances. He lay wide-eyed on his pallet like a man in a fever of helplessness and imminent despair.

The next night he was snatched off his bed shortly after midnight by the sudden thrill of trepidation which raced through the walls like a flame in the extreme tinder of the Keep's anticipation. He was on his way before any summons could reach him; with his staff clenched whitely in his hand, he hastened toward the highest eastward battlements of the main Keep. He focused on Quaan's dour presence, found the Warmark on a balcony overlooking the watchtower and the night soot of Satansfist's army.

As Mhoram joined him, Quaan pointed one rigid arm like an indictment away toward the east. But the High Lord did not need Quaan's gesture; the sight seemed to spring at him out of the darkness like a bright abomination on the wind.

Running from the east toward Revelstone was a rift of the clouds, a break that stretched out to the north and south as far as Mhoram could see. The rift appeared wide, assertive, but the clouds behind it were as impenetrable as ever.

It was so clearly visible because through it streamed light as green as the frozen essence of emerald.

Its brightness made it seem swift, but it moved like a slow, ineluctable tide across the ice-blasted fields beyond the foothills. Its green, radiant swath swept like a blaze of wrong over the ground, igniting invisible contours into brilliance and then quenching them again. Mhoram watched it in stunned silence as it lit the Raver's army and rushed on into the foothills of the plateau. Like a tsunami of malignant scorn, it rolled upward and broke across the Keep.

People screamed when they saw the full emerald moon leering evilly at them through the rift. The High Lord himself flinched, raised his staff as if to ward off a nightmare. For a horrific moment while the rift moved, Lord Foul's moon dominated the clear, starless abysm of the sky like an incurable wound, a maiming of the very Law of the heavens. Emerald radiance covered everything, drowned every heart and drenched Revelstone's every upraised rock in thetic, green defeat.

Then the rift passed; sick light slid away into the west. Lord's Keep sank like a broken sea-cliff into irreparable night.

"Melenkurion!" Quaan panted as if he were suffocating. *"Melenkurion!"*

Slowly, Mhoram realized that he was grimacing like a cornered madman. But while the darkness crashed and echoed around him, he could not relax his features; the contortion clung to his face like the grin of a skull. A long, taut time seemed to pass before he thought to peer through the night at Satansfist's army.

When at last he compelled himself to look, he saw that the army had come to life. It sloughed off its uneasy repose and began to seethe, bristling in the darkness like reanimated lust.

"Ready the Warward," he said, fighting an unwonted tremor in his rough voice. "The Raver has been given his sign. He will attack."

With an effort, Warmark Quaan brought himself

back under control and left the balcony, shouting orders as he moved.

Mhoram hugged his staff to his chest and breathed deeply, heavily. At first, the air shuddered in his lungs, and he could not pull the grimace off his face. But slowly he untied his muscles, turned his tension into other channels. His thoughts gathered themselves around the defense of the Keep.

Calling on the Hearthralls and the other Lords to join him, he went to the tower to watch what *samadhi* Raver was doing.

There, in the company of the two shaken sentries, he could follow the Raver's movements. Satansfist held his fragment of the Illearth Stone blazing aloft, an oriflamme of gelid fire, and its stark green illumination revealed him clearly as he moved among his forces, barking orders in a hoarse, alien tongue. Without haste he gathered ur-viles about him until their midnight forms spread out under his light like a lake of black water. Then he forged them into two immense wedges, one on either side of him, with their tips at his shoulders, facing Revelstone. In the garish Stone light, the loremasters looked like roynish, compact power, fatal and eager. Waves of other creatures fanned out beyond them on either side as they began to approach the Keep.

Following the Raver's fire, they moved deliberately straight out of the southeast toward the knuckled and clenched gates at the base of the watchtower.

High Lord Mhoram tightened his grip on his staff and tried to prepare himself for whatever might happen.

At his back, he felt Lord Amatin and Hearthrall Borillar arrive, followed shortly by Tohrm and then Quaan. Without taking his eyes off Satansfist's approach, the Warmark reported.

"I have ordered two Eoward into the tower. More would serve no purpose—they would block each other. Half are archers. They are good warriors," he added unnecessarily, as if to reassure himself, "and all their Hafts and Warhafts are veterans of the war against Fleshharrower.

"The archers bear *lor-liarill* shafts. They will begin at your signal."

Mhoram nodded his approval. "Tell half the archers to strike when the Raver enters arrow range. Hold the rest for my signal."

The Warmark turned to deliver these instructions, but Mhoram abruptly caught his arm. A chill tightened the High Lord's scalp as he said, "Place more archers upon the battlements above the court of the Gilden. If by some great ill Satansfist breaches the gates, the defenders of the tower will require aid. And —stand warriors ready to cut loose the crosswalks from the Keep."

"Yes, High Lord." Quaan was a warrior and understood the necessity for such orders. He returned Mhoram's grip firmly, like a clasp of farewell, then left the top of the tower.

"Breach the gates?" Borillar gaped as if the mere suggestion amazed him. "How is it possible?"

"It is not possible," Tohrm replied flatly.

"Nevertheless we must prepare." Mhoram braced his staff on the stone like a standard, and watched *samadhi* Sheol's approach.

No one spoke while the army marched forward. It was already less than a hundred yards below the gates. Except for the dead rumble of its myriad feet on the frozen ground, it moved in silence, as if it were stalking the Keep—or as if in spite of their driven hunger many of its creatures themselves dreaded what Satansfist meant to do.

Mhoram felt that he had only moments left. He asked Amatin if she had seen either Trevor or Loerya.

"No." Her whispered answer had an empty sound, like a recognition of abandonment.

Moments later, a flight of arrows thrummed from one of the upper levels of the tower. They were invisible in the darkness, and Satansfist gave no sign that he knew they had been fired. But the radiance of the Illearth Stone struck them into flame and knocked them down before they were within thirty feet of him.

Another flight, and another, had no effect except to light the front of the Raver's army, revealing in lurid green and orange the deadly aspect of its leaders.

Then *samadhi* halted. On either side of him, the ur-viles trembled. He coughed his orders. The wedges tightened. Snarling, the Cavewights and other creatures arranged themselves into formation, ready to charge.

Without haste or hesitation, the Giant-Raver clenched his fist, so that iridescent steam plumed upward from his fragment of the Stone.

Mhoram could feel the Stone's power mounting, radiating in tumid waves against his face.

Abruptly, a bolt of force lashed from the Stone and struck the ground directly before one of the loremasters. The blast continued until the soil and rock caught fire, burned with green flames, crackled like firewood. Then *samadhi* moved his bolt, drew it over the ground in a wide, slow arc toward the other loremaster. His power left behind a groove that flamed and smoldered, flared and groaned in earthen agony.

When the arc was complete, it enclosed Satansfist from side to side—a half-circle of emerald coals standing in front of him like a harness anchored by the two ur-vile wedges.

Remembering the vortex of trepidation with which Fleshharrower had attacked the Warward at Doriendor Corishev, Mhoram strode across the tower and shouted up at the Keep, "Leave the battlements! All but the warriors must take shelter! Do not expose yourselves lest the sky itself assail you!" Then he returned to Lord Amatin's side.

Below him, the two great loremasters raised their staves and jabbed them into the ends of the arc. At once, Demondim vitriol began to pulse wetly along the groove. The green flames turned black; they bubbled, spattered, burst out of the arc as if Satansfist had tapped a vein of EarthBlood in the ground.

By the time Warmark Quaan had returned to the tower, Mhoram knew that *samadhi* was not summoning a vortex. The Raver's exertion was like nothing he had ever seen before. And it was slower than he had expected it to be. Once the ur-viles had tied themselves to the arc, Satansfist started to work with his

Stone. From its incandescent core, he drew a fire that gushed to the ground and poured into the groove of the arc. This force combined with the black fluid of the ur-viles to make a mixture of ghastly potency. Soon black-green snake-tongues of lightning were flicking into the air from the whole length of the groove, and these bursts carried to the onlookers a gut-deep sense of violation, as if the rocky foundations of the foothills were under assault—as if the Despiser dared traduce even the necessary bones of the Earth.

Yet the power did nothing except grow. Tongues of lightning leaped higher, joined together, became gradually but steadily more brilliant and wrong. Their violence increased until Mhoram felt that the nerves of his skin and eyes could endure no more—and went on increasing. When dawn began to bleed into the night at Satansfist's back, the individual tongues had merged into three continuous bolts striking without thunder into the deepest darkness of the clouds.

The High Lord's throat was too dry; he had to swallow roughly several times before he could muster enough moisture to speak. "Hearthrall Tohrm"—still he almost gagged on the words—"they will attack the gates. This power will attack the gates. Send any Gravelingases who will go to the aid of the stone."

Tohrm started at the sound of his name, then hurried away as if he were glad to remove himself from the baleful glare of the arc.

While gray daylight spread over the siege, the three unbroken bolts jumped and gibbered maniacally, raged at the silent clouds, drew closer to each other. Behind them, the army began to howl as the pressure became more and more unendurable.

Lord Amatin dug her thin fingers into the flesh of Mhoram's arm. Quaan had crossed his arms over his chest, and was straining against himself to keep from shouting. Borillar's hands scrubbed fervidly over his features in an effort to erase the sensation of wrong. His staff lay useless at his feet. The High Lord prayed for them all and fought his dread.

Then, abruptly, the Raver whirled his Stone and, roaring, threw still more power into the arc.

The three great columns of lightning sprang together, became one.

The earth shook with thunder in answer to that single, prodigious bolt. At once, the lightning vanished, though *samadhi* and the ur-viles did not withdraw their power from the arc.

The thunder continued; tremors jolted the ground. In moments, the tower was trembling as if its foundations were about to crack open and swallow it.

Immensely, tortuously, the ground of the foothills began to shift. It writhed, jerked, cracked; and through the cracks, stone shapes thrust upward. To his horror, Mhoram saw the forms of humans and Giants and horses rip themselves out of the earth. The forms were blunt, misshapen, insensate; they were articulated stone, the ancient fossilized remains of buried bodies.

The memory of Asuraka's cry from Revelwood echoed in Mhoram's ears: *He resurrected the old death!*

By hundreds and then thousands, the stone shapes heaved up out of the ground. Amid the colossal thunder of the breaking earth, they thrust free of their millennia-long graves and lumbered blindly toward the gates of Revelstone.

"Defend the tower!" Mhoram cried to Quaan. "But do not waste lives. Amatin! Fight here! Flee if the tower falls. I go to the gates."

But when he spun away from the parapet, he collided with Hearthrall Tohrm. Tohrm caught hold of him, stopped him. Yet in spite of the High Lord's urgency, a long moment passed before Tohrm could bring himself to speak.

At last, he wrenched out, "The tunnel is defended."

"Who?" Mhoram snapped.

"The Lord Trevor ordered all others away. He and Trell Gravelingas support the gates."

"*Melenkurion!*" Mhoram breathed. "*Melenkurion abatha!*" He turned back to the parapet.

Below him, the dead, voiceless shapes had almost reached the base of the tower. Arrows flew at them from hundreds of bows, but the shafts glanced uselessly off the earthen forms and fell flaming to the ground without effect.

He hesitated, muttering to himself in extreme astonishment. The breaking of the Law of Death had consequences beyond anything he had imagined. Thousands of the gnarled shapes were already massed and marching, and at every moment thousands more struggled up from the ground, writhed into motion like lost souls and obeyed the command of Sheol Satansfist's power.

But then the first shape set its hands on the gates, and High Lord Mhoram sprang forward. Whirling his staff, he sent a blast down the side of the tower, struck the dead form where it stood. At the impact of his Lords-fire, it shattered like sandstone and fell into dirt.

At once, he and Lord Amatin set to work with all their might. Their staffs rang and fired, rained blue strength like hammer blows down on the marching shapes. And every blow broke the dead into sand. But every one that fell was replaced by a score of others. Across all the terrain between the watchtower and Satansfist's arc, the ground heaved and buckled, pitching new forms into motion like beings dredged up from the bottommost muck of a lifeless sea. First one by one, then by tens, scores, fifties, they reached the gates and piled against them.

Through the stone, Mhoram could feel the strain on the gates mounting. He could feel Trevor's fire and Trell's mighty subterranean song supporting the interlocked gates, while hundreds, thousands, of the blind, mute forms pressed against them, crushed forward in lifeless savagery like an avalanche leaping impossibly up out of the ground. He could feel the groaning retorts of pressure as if the bones of the tower were grinding together. And still the dead came, shambling out of the earth until they seemed as vast as the Raver's army and as irresistible as a cataclysm. Mhoram and Amatin broke hundreds of them and had no effect.

Behind the High Lord, Tohrm was on his knees, sharing the tower's pain with his hands and sobbing openly, "Revelstone! Oh, Revelstone, alas! Oh, Revelstone, Revelstone!"

Mhoram tore himself away from the fighting, caught hold of Tohrm's tunic, hauled the Hearthrall to his feet. Into Tohrm's broken face, he shouted, "Gravelingas! Remember who you are! You are the Hearthrall of Lord's Keep."

"I am nothing!" Tohrm wept. "Ah! the Earth—!"

"You are Hearthrall and Gravelingas! Hear me—I, High Lord Mhoram, command you. Study this attack —learn to know it. The inner gates must not fall. The *rhadhamaerl* must preserve Revelstone's inner gates!"

He felt the change in the attack. Satansfist's Stone now threw bolts against the gates. Amatin tried to resist, but the Raver brushed her efforts aside as if they were nothing. Yet Mhoram stayed with Tohrm, focused his strength on the Hearthrall until Tohrm met the demand of his eyes and hands.

"Who will mourn the stone if I do not?" Tohrm moaned.

Mhoram controlled his desire to yell. "No harm will receive its due grief if we do not survive."

The next instant, he forgot Tohrm, forgot everything except the silent screams that detonated through him from the base of the tower. Over Trell's shrill rage and the vehemence of Trevor's fire, the gates shrieked in agony.

A shattering concussion convulsed the stone. The people atop the tower fell, tumbled across the floor. Huge thunder like a howl of victory crashed somewhere between earth and sky, as if the very firmament of existence had been rent asunder.

The gates split inward.

Torrents of dead stone flooded into the tunnel under the tower.

Mhoram was shouting at Quaan and Amatin, "Defend the tower!" The shaking subsided, and he staggered erect. Pulling Tohrm with him, he yelled, "Come! Rally the Gravelingases! The inner gates must not fall." Though the tower was still trembling, he started toward the stairs.

But before he could descend, he heard a rush of

cries, human cries. An anguish like rage lashed through the roiling throng of his emotions. "Quaan!" he roared, though the old Warmark had almost caught up with him. "The warriors attack!" Quaan nodded bitterly as he reached Mhoram's side. "Stop them! They cannot fight these dead. Swords will not avail."

With Tohrm and Quaan, the High Lord raced down the stairs, leaving Amatin to wield her fire from the edge of the parapet.

Quaan went straight down through the tower, but Mhoram took Tohrm out over the courtyard between the tower and the Keep on the highest crosswalk. From there, he saw that Trell and Lord Trevor had already been driven back out of the tunnel. They were fighting for their lives against the slow, blind march of the dead. Trevor exerted an extreme force like nothing Mhoram had ever seen in him before, battering the foremost attackers, breaking them rapidly, continuously, into sand. And Trell wielded in both hands a massive fragment of one gate. He used the fragment like a club with such ferocious strength that even shapes vaguely resembling horses and Giants went down under his blows.

But the two men had no chance. Swords and spears and arrows had no effect on the marching shapes; scores of warriors who leaped into the tunnel and the courtyard were simply crushed underfoot; and the cries of the crushed were fearful to hear. While Mhoram watched, the dead pushed Trell and Trevor back past the old Gilden tree toward the closed inner gates.

Mhoram shouted to the warriors on the battlements below him, commanding them to stay out of the courtyard. Then he ran across to the Keep and dashed down the stairways toward the lower levels. With Tohrm behind him, he reached the first abutment over the inner gates in time to see Cavewights spill through the tunnel, squirming their way among the dead to attack the side doors which provided the only access to the tower.

Some of them fell at once with arrows in their throats and bellies, and others were cut down by the

few warriors in the court who had avoided being
crushed. But their thick, heavy jerkins protected them
from most of the shafts and swords. With their great
strength and their knowledge of stone, they threw
themselves at the doors. And soon the gangrel creatures were swarming through the tunnel in large numbers. The High Lord saw that the warriors alone could
not keep *samadhi*'s creatures out of the tower.

For a harsh moment, he pushed Trevor and Trell,
Cavewights, warriors, animated dead earth from his
mind, and faced the decision he had to make. If
Revelstone were to retain any viable defense, either
the tower or the inner gates must be preserved. Without the gates, the tower might still restrict Satansfist's
approach enough to keep Revelstone alive; without
the tower, the gates could still seal out Satansfist.
Without one or the other, Revelstone was defeated.
But Mhoram could not fight for both, could not be in
both places at once. He had to choose where to concentrate the Keep's defense.

He chose the gates.

At once, he sent Tohrm to gather the Gravelingases.
Then he turned to the battle of the courtyard. He
ignored the Cavewights, focused instead on the shambling dead as they trampled the Gilden tree and
pushed Trell and Trevor back against the walls.
Shouting to the warriors around him for *clingor,* he
hurled his Lords-fire down at the faceless shapes,
battered them into sand. Together, he and Trevor
cleared a space in which the trapped men could make
their escape.

Almost immediately, the sentries brought two tough
clingor lines, anchored them, tossed them down to
Trevor and Trell. But in the brief delay, a new wave
of Cavewights rode into the courtyard on the shoulders of the dead and joined the assault on the doors.
With a nauseating sound like the breaking of bones,
they tore the doors off the hinges, tossed the stone
slabs aside, and charged roaring into the tower. They
were met instantly by staunch, dour-handed warriors,
but the momentum and strength of the Cavewights
carried them inward.

When he saw the doors broken, Trell gave a cry of outrage, and tried to attack the Cavewights. Slapping aside the *clingor* line, he rushed the dead as if he believed he could fight his way through them to join the defense of the tower. For a moment, his granite club and his *rhadhamaerl* lore broke passage for him, and he advanced a few steps across the court. But then even his club snapped. He went down under the prodigious weight of the dead.

Trevor sprang after him. Aided by Mhoram's fire, the Lord reached Trell. One of the dead stamped a glancing blow along his ankle, but he ignored the pain, took hold of Trell's shoulders, dragged him back.

As soon as he was able to regain his feet, Trell pushed Trevor away and attacked the insensate forms with his fists.

Trevor snatched up one of the *clingor* lines and whipped it several times around his chest. Then he pounced at Trell's back. With his arms under Trell's, he gripped his staff like a bar across Trell's chest, and shouted for the warriors to pull him up. Instantly, ten warriors caught the line and hauled. While Mhoram protected the two men, they were drawn up the wall and over the parapet of the abutment.

With a sickening jolt, the dead thudded against the inner gates.

Amid the cries of battle from the tower, and the mute pressure building sharply against the gates, High Lord Mhoram turned his attention to Trell and Lord Trevor.

The Gravelingas struggled free of Trevor's hold and the hands of the warriors, thrust himself erect, and faced Mhoram as if he meant to leap at the High Lord's throat. His face flamed with exertion and fury.

"Intact!" he rasped horribly. "The tower lost— intact for Sheol's use! Is that your purpose for Revelstone? Better that we destroy it ourselves!"

Swinging his powerful arms to keep anyone from touching him, he spun wildly and lurched away into the Keep.

Mhoram's gaze burned dangerously, but he bit his

lips, kept himself from rushing after the Gravelingas. Trell had spent himself extravagantly, and failed. He could not be blamed for hating his inadequacy; he should be left in peace. But his voice had sounded like the voice of a man who had lost all peace forever. Torn within himself, Mhoram sent two warriors to watch over Trell, then turned toward Trevor.

The Lord stood panting against the back wall. Blood streamed from his injured ankle; his face was stained with the grime of battle, and he shuddered as the effort of breathing wracked his chest. Yet he seemed unconscious of his pain, unconscious of himself. His eyes gleamed with eldritch perceptions. When Mhoram faced him, he gasped, "I have felt it. I know what it is."

Mhoram shouted for a Healer, but Trevor shrugged away any suggestion that he needed help. He met the High Lord like a man exalted, and repeated, "I have felt it, Mhoram."

Mhoram controlled his concern. "Felt it?"

"Lord Foul's power. The power which makes all this possible."

"The Stone—" Mhoram began.

"The Stone does not suffice. This weather—the speed with which he became so mighty after his defeat in Garroting Deep—the force of this army, though it is so far from his command—these dead shapes, compelled from the very ground by power so vast—!

"The Stone does not suffice. I have felt it. Even Lord Foul the Despiser could not become so much more unconquerable in seven short years."

"Then how?" the High Lord breathed.

"This weather—this winter. It sustains and drives the army—it frees Satansfist—it frees the Despiser himself for other work—the work of the Stone. The work of these dead. Mhoram, do you remember Drool Rockworm's power over the weather—and the moon?"

Mhoram nodded in growing amazement and dread.

"I have felt it. Lord Foul holds the Staff of Law."

A cry tore itself past Mhoram's lips, despite his instantaneous conviction that Trevor was right. "How is it possible? The Staff fell with High Lord Elena under *Melenkurion* Skyweir."

"I do not know. Perhaps the same being who slew Elena bore the Staff to Foul's Creche—perhaps it is dead Kevin himself who wields the Staff on Foul's behalf, so that the Despiser need not personally use a power not apt for his control. But I have felt the Staff, Mhoram—the Staff of Law beyond all question."

Mhoram nodded, fought to contain the amazed fear that seemed to echo illimitably within him. The Staff! Battle raged around him; he could afford neither time nor strength for anything but the immediate task. Lord Foul held the Staff! If he allowed himself to think about such a thing, he might lose himself in panic. Eyes flashing, he gave Trevor's shoulder a hard clasp of praise and comradeship, then turned back toward the courtyard.

For a moment, he pushed his perceptions through the din and clangor, bent his senses to assess Revelstone's situation. He could feel Lord Amatin atop the tower, still waging her fire against the dead. She was weakening—her continuous exertions had long since passed the normal limits of her stamina— yet she kept her ragged blaze striking downward, fighting as if she meant to spend her last pulse or breath in the tower's defense. And her labor had its effect. Though she could not stop even a tenth of the shambling shapes, she had now broken so many of them that the unbound sand clogged the approaches to the tunnel. Fewer of the dead could plow forward at one time; her work, and the constriction of the tunnel, slowed their march, slowed the multiplication of their pressure on the inner gates.

But while she strove, battle began to mount up through the tower toward her. Few Cavewights now tried to enter through the doors. Their own dead blocked the corridors; and while they fought for access, they were exposed to the archers of the Keep. But enemies were breaching the tower somehow; Mhoram could hear loud combat surging upward through the tower's complex passages. With an effort, he ignored everything else around him, concentrated on the tower. Then through the hoarse commands, the clash of weapons, the raw cries of hunger and pain, the tumult of urgent feet, he sensed Satansfist's attack on the outer wall of the tower. The Raver threw fierce bolts of Illearth power at the exposed coigns and windows, occasionally at Lord Amatin herself; and under the cover of these blasts, his creatures threw up ladders against the wall, swarmed through the openings.

In the stone under his feet, High Lord Mhoram could feel the inner gates groaning.

Quickly, he turned to one of the warriors, a tense Stonedownor woman. "Go to the tower. Find Warmark Quaan. Say that I command him to withdraw from the tower. Say that he must bring Lord Amatin with him. Go."

She saluted and ran. A few moments later, he saw her dash over the courtyard along one of the crosswalks.

By that time, he had already returned to the battle. With Lord Trevor working doggedly at his side, he renewed his attack on the earthen pressure building against Revelstone's inner gates. While the supportive power of the Gravelingases vibrated in the stone under him, he gathered all his accumulated ferocity and drove it at the crush of dead. Now he knew clearly what he hoped to achieve; he wanted to cover the flagstones of the courtyard with so much sand that the blind, shambling shapes would have no solid footing from which to press forward. Trevor's aid seemed to uplift his effectiveness, and he shattered dead by tens and scores until his staff hummed in his hands and the air around him became so charged with blue force that he appeared to emanate Lords-fire.

Yet while he labored, wielded his power like a scythe through Satansfist's ill crop, he kept part of his attention cocked toward the crosswalks. He was watching for Quaan and Amatin.

A short time later, the first crosswalk fell. The battered remnant of an Eoman dashed along it out of the tower, rabidly pursued by Cavewights. Archers sent the Cavewights plunging to the courtyard, and as soon as the warriors were safe, the walk's cables were cut. The wooden span swung clattering down and crashed against the wall of the tower.

The tumult of battle echoed out of the tower. Abruptly, Warmark Quaan appeared on one of the upper spans. Yelling stridently to make himself heard, he ordered all except the two highest crosswalks cut.

Mhoram shouted up to the Warmark, "Amatin!"

Quaan nodded, ran back into the tower.

The next two spans fell promptly, but the sentries at the third waited. After a moment, several injured warriors stumbled out onto the walk. Supporting each other, carrying the crippled, they struggled toward the Keep. But then a score of Stone-born creatures charged madly out of the tower. Defying arrows and swords, they threw the injured off the span and rushed on across the walk.

Grimly, deliberately, the sentries cut the cables.

Every enemy that appeared in the doorways where the spans had been was killed or beaten back by a hail of fiery arrows. The higher crosswalks fell in swift succession. Only two remained for the survivors in the tower.

Now Lord Trevor was panting dizzily at the High Lord's side, and Mhoram himself felt weak with strain. But he could not afford to rest. Tohrm's Gravelingases would not be able to hold the gates alone.

Yet his flame lost its vehemence as the urgent moments passed. Fear for Quaan and Amatin disrupted his concentration. He wanted intensely to go after them. Warriors were escaping constantly across the last two spans, and he watched their flight with dread in his throat, aching to see their leaders.

One more span went down.

He stopped fighting altogether when Quaan appeared alone in the doorway of the last crosswalk.

Quaan shouted across to the Keep, but Mhoram could not make out the words. He watched with clenched breath as four warriors raced toward the Warmark.

Then a blue-robed figure moved behind Quaan— Amatin. But the two made no move to escape. When the warriors reached them, they both disappeared back into the tower.

Stifling in helplessness, Mhoram stared at the empty doorway as if the strength of his desire might bring the two back. He could hear the Raver's hordes surging constantly upward.

A moment later, the four warriors reappeared. Between them, they carried Hearthrall Borillar.

He dangled in their hands as if he were dead.

Quaan and Amatin followed the four. When they all had gained the Keep, the last crosswalk fell. It seemed to make no sound amid the clamor from the tower.

A mist passed across Mhoram's sight. He found that he was leaning heavily on Trevor; while he gasped for breath, he could not stand alone. But the Lord upheld him. When his faintness receded, he met Trevor's gaze and smiled wanly.

Without a word, they turned back to the defense of the gates.

The tower had been lost, but the battle was not done. Unhindered now by Amatin's fire, the dead were slowly able to push a path through the sand. The weight of their assault began to mount again. And the sensation of wrong that they sent shuddering through the stone increased. The High Lord felt Revelstone's pain growing around him until it seemed to come from all sides. If he had not been so starkly confronted with these dead, he might have believed that the Keep was under attack at other points as well. But the present need consumed his attention. Revelstone's only hope lay in burying the gates with sand before they broke.

He sensed Tohrm's arrival behind him, but did not turn until Quaan and Lord Amatin had joined the Hearthrall. Then he dropped his power and faced the three of them.

Amatin was on the edge of prostration. Her eyes ached in the waifish pallor of her face; her hair stuck to her face in sweaty strands. When she spoke, her voice quivered. "He took a bolt meant for me. Borillar—he—I did not see *samadhi*'s aim in time."

A moment passed before Mhoram found the self-mastery to ask quietly, "Is he dead?"

"No. The Healers—he will live. He is a Hirebrand —not defenseless." She dropped to the stone and slumped against the wall as if the thews which held her up had snapped.

"I had forgotten he was with you," Mhoram murmured. "I am ashamed."

"*You* are ashamed!" The rough croak of Quaan's voice caught at Mhoram's attention. The Warmark's face and arms were smeared with blood, but he appeared uninjured. He could not meet Mhoram's gaze. "The tower—lost!" He bit the words bitterly. "It is I who am ashamed. No Warmark would permit— Warmark Hile Troy would have found a means to preserve it."

"Then find a means to aid us," Tohrm groaned. "These gates cannot hold."

The livid desperation in his tone pulled all the eyes on the abutment toward him. Tears streamed down his face as if he would never stop weeping, and his hands flinched distractedly in front of him, seeking something impossible in the air, something that would not break. And the gates moaned at him as if they were witnessing to the truth of his distress.

"We cannot," he went on. "Cannot. Such force! May the stones forgive me! I am—we are unequal to this stress."

Quaan turned sharply on his heel and strode away, shouting for timbers and Hirebrands to shore up the gates.

But Tohrm did not seem to hear the Warmark. His wet gaze held Mhoram as he whispered, "We are prevented. Something ill maims our strength. We do not comprehend—High Lord, is there other wrong here? Other wrong than weight and dead violence? I hear—all Revelstone's great rock cries out to me of evil."

High Lord Mhoram's senses veered, and he swung into resonance with the gut-rock of the Keep as if he were melding himself with the stone. He felt all the weight of *samadhi*'s dead concentrated as if it were impending squarely against him; he felt his own soul gates groaning, detonating, cracking. For an instant, like an ignition of prophecy, he became the Keep, took its life and pain into himself, experienced the horrific might which threatened to rend it—and something else, too, something distinct, private, terrible. When he heard frantic feet clattering toward him along the main hall, he knew that Tohrm had glimpsed the truth.

One of the two men Mhoram had sent to watch over Trell dashed forward, jerked to a halt. His face was as white as terror, and he could hardly thrust words stuttering through his teeth.

"High Lord, come! He!—the Close! Oh, help him!"

Amatin covered her head with her arms as if she could not bear any more. But the High Lord said, "I hear you. Remember who you are. Speak clearly."

The man gulped sickly several times. "Trell—you sent—he immolates himself. He will destroy the Close."

A hoarse cry broke from Tohrm, and Amatin gasped, *"Melenkurion!"* Mhoram stared at the warrior as if he could not believe what he had heard. But he believed it; he felt the truth of it. He was appalled by the dreadful understanding that this knowledge also had come too late. Once again, he had failed of foresight, failed to meet the needs of the Keep. Spun by irrefusable exigencies, he wheeled on Lord Trevor and demanded, "Where is Loerya?"

For the first time since his rescue, Trevor's exaltation wavered. He stood in his own blood as if his injury had no power to hurt him, but the mention of his wife pained him like a flaw in his new courage. "She," he began, then stopped to swallow thickly. "She has left the Keep. Last night—she took the children upland—to find a place of hiding. So that they would be safe."

"By the Seven!" Mhoram barked, raging at all his failures rather than at Trevor. "She is needed!" Revelstone's situation was desperate, and neither Trevor nor Amatin were in any condition to go on fighting. For an instant, Mhoram felt that the dilemma could not be resolved, that he could not make these decisions for the Keep. But he was Mhoram son of Variol, High Lord by the choice of the Council. He had said to the warrior: *Remember who you are.* He had said it to Tohrm. He was High Lord Mhoram, incapable of surrender. He struck the stone with his staff so that its iron heel rang, and sprang to his work.

"Lord Trevor, can you hold the gates?"

Trevor met Mhoram's gaze. "Do not fear, High Lord. If they can be held, I will hold them."

"Good." The High Lord turned his back on the courtyard. "Lord Amatin—Hearthrall Tohrm—will you aid me?"

For answer, Tohrm met the outreach of Amatin's arm and helped her to her feet.

Taking the fear-blanched warrior by the arm, Mhoram hastened away into the Keep.

As he strode through the halls toward the Close, he asked the warrior to tell him what had happened. "He —it—" the man stammered. But then he seemed to draw a measure of steadiness from Mhoram's grip. "It surpassed me, High Lord."

"What has happened?" repeated Mhoram firmly.

"At your command, we followed him. When he learned that we did not mean to leave him, he reviled us. But his cursing showed us a part of the reason for your command. We were resolved to obey you. At last he turned from us like a broken man and led us to the Close.

"There he went to the great graveling pit and knelt beside it. While we watched over him from the doors, he wept and prayed, begging. High Lord, it is in my heart that he begged for peace. But he found no peace. When he raised his head, we saw—we saw abomination in his face. He—the graveling—flame came from the fire-stones. Fire sprang from the floor. We ran down to him. But the flames forbade us. They consumed my comrade. I ran to you."

The words chilled Mhoram's heart, but he replied to meet the pain and faltering in the warrior's face. "His Oath of Peace was broken. He lost self-trust,

and fell into despair. This is the shadow of the Gray
Slayer upon him."

After a moment, the warrior said hesitantly, "I have
heard—it is said—is this not the Unbeliever's doing?"

"Perhaps. In some measure, the Unbeliever is Lord
Foul's doing. But Trell's despair is also in part my
doing. It is Trell's own doing. The Slayer's great
strength is that our mortal weakness may be so turned
against us."

He spoke as calmly as he could, but before he was
within a hundred yards of the Close, he began to feel
the heat of the flames. He had no doubt that this was
the source of the other ill Tohrm had sensed. Hot
waves of desecration radiated in all directions from
the council chamber. As he neared the high wooden
doors, he saw that they were smoldering, nearly
aflame, and the walls shimmered as if the stone were
about to melt. He was panting for breath, wincing
against the heat, even before he reached the open
doorway and looked down into the Close.

An inferno raged within it. Floor, tables, seats—all
burned madly, spouted roaring flames like a convulsion of thunder. Heat scorched Mhoram's face, crisped
his hair. He had to blink tears away before he could
peer down through the conflagration to its center.

There Trell stood in the graveling pit like the core
of a holocaust, bursting with flames and hurling great
gouts of fire at the ceiling with both fists. His whole
form blazed like incarnated damnation, white-hot
torment striking out at the stone it loved and could not
save.

The sheer power of it staggered Mhoram. He was
looking at the onset of a Ritual of Desecration. Trell
had found in his own despair the secret which
Mhoram had guarded so fearfully, and he was using
that secret against Revelstone. If he were not stopped,
the gates would only be the first part of the Keep to
break, the first and last link in a chain of destruction
which might tear the whole plateau to rubble.

He had to be stopped. That was imperative. But
Mhoram was not a Gravelingas, had no stone-lore to

counter the might which made this fire possible. He turned to Tohrm.

"You are of the *rhadhamaerl!*" he shouted over the raving of the fire. "You must silence this flame!"

"Silence it?" Tohrm was staring, aghast, into the blaze; he had the stricken look of a man witnessing the ravage of his dearest love. "Silence it?" He did not shout; Mhoram could only comprehend him by reading his lips. "I have no strength to equal this. I am a Gravelingas of the *rhadhamaerl*—not Earthpower incarnate. He will destroy us all."

"Tohrm!" the High Lord cried. "You are the Hearthrall of Lord's Keep! You or no one can meet this need!"

Tohrm mouthed soundlessly, "How?"

"I will accompany you! I will give you my strength —I will place all my power in you!"

The Hearthrall's eyes rolled fearfully away from the Close and hauled themselves by sheer force of will into focus on the High Lord's face.

"We will burn."

"We will endure!"

Tohrm met Mhoram's demand for a long moment. Then he groaned. He could not refuse to give himself for the sake of the Keep's stone. "If you are with me," he said silently through the roar.

Mhoram whirled to Amatin. "Tohrm and I will go into the Close. You must preserve us from the fire. Put your power around us—protect us."

She nodded distractedly, pushed a damp strand of hair out of her face. "Go," she said weakly. "Already the table melts."

The High Lord saw that she was right. Before their eyes, the table slumped into magma, poured down to the lowest level of the Close and into the pit around Trell's feet.

Mhoram called his power into readiness and rested the shaft of his staff on Tohrm's shoulder. Together, they faced the Close, waited while Amatin built a defense around them. The sensation of it swarmed over their skin like hiving insects, but it kept back the heat.

When she signaled to them, they started down into

the Close as if they were struggling into a furnace.

Despite Amatin's protection, the heat slammed into them like the fist of a cataclysm. Tohrm's tunic began to scorch. Mhoram felt his own robe blackening. All the hair on their heads and arms shriveled. But the High Lord put heat out of his mind; he concentrated on his staff and Tohrm. He could feel the Hearthrall singing now, though he heard nothing but the deep, ravenous howl of the blaze. Turning his power to the pitch of Tohrm's song, he sent all his resources running through it.

The savage flames backed slightly away from them as they moved, and patches of unburned rock appeared like stepping-stones under Tohrm's feet. They walked downward like a gap in the hell of Trell's rage.

But the conflagration sealed behind them instantly. As they drew farther from the doors, Amatin's defense weakened; distance and flame interfered. Mhoram's flesh stung where his robe smoldered against it, and his eyes hurt so badly that he could no longer see. Tohrm's song became more and more like a scream as they descended. By the time they reached the level of the pit, where Loric's *krill* still stood embedded in its stone, Mhoram knew that if he did not take his strength away from Tohrm and use it for protection they would both roast at Trell's feet.

"Trell!" Tohrm screamed soundlessly. "You are a Gravelingas of the *rhadhamaerl!* Do not do this!"

For an instant, the fury of the inferno paused. Trell looked at them, seemed to see them, recognize them.

"Trell!"

But he had fallen too far under the power of his own holocaust. He pointed a rigid, accusing finger, then stooped to the graveling and heaved a double armful of fire at them.

At the same moment, a thrill of strength ran through Mhoram. Amatin's protection steadied, stiffened. Though the force of Trell's attack knocked Tohrm back into Mhoram's arms, the fire did not touch them. And Amatin's sudden discovery of power called up an answer in the High Lord. With a look like joy gleaming in his eyes, he swept aside all his self-

restraints and turned to his secret understanding of
desecration. That secret contained might—might
which the Lords had failed to discover because of
their Oath of Peace—might which could be used to
preserve as well as destroy. Despair was not the only
unlocking emotion. Mhoram freed his own passion
and stood against the devastation of the Close.

Power coursed vividly in his chest and arms and
staff. Power made even his flesh and blood seem like
invulnerable bone. Power shone out from him to oppose Trell's ill. And the surge of his strength restored
Tohrm. The Hearthrall regained his feet, summoned
his lore; with all of his and Mhoram's energy, he resisted Trell.

Confronting each other, standing almost face to
face, the two Gravelingases wove their lore-secret
gestures, sang their potent *rhadhamaerl* invocations.
While the fire raged as if Revelstone were about to
crash down upon them, they commanded the blaze,
wrestled will against will for mastery of it.

Tohrm was exalted by Mhoram's support. With the
High Lord's power resonating in every word and note
and gesture, renewing him, fulfilling his love for the
stone, he bent back the desecration. After a last convulsive exertion, Trell fell to his knees, and his fire
began to fail.

It ran out of the Close like the recession of a tide—
slowly at first, then faster, as the force which had
raised it broke. The heat declined; cool fresh air
poured around Mhoram from the airways of the Keep.
Sight returned to his scorched eyes. For a moment, he
feared that he would lose consciousness in relief.

Weeping with joy and grief, he went to help Tohrm
lift Trell Atiaran-mate from the graveling pit. Trell
gave no sign that he felt them, knew in any way that
they were present. He looked around with hollow
eyes, muttering brokenly, "Intact. There is nothing
intact. Nothing." Then he covered his head with his
arms and huddled into himself on the floor at
Mhoram's feet, shaking as if he needed to sob and
could not.

Tohrm met Mhoram's gaze. For a long moment,

they looked into each other's faces, measuring what they had done together. Tohrm's features had the burned aspect of a wilderland, a place that would never grin again. But his emotion was clear and clean as he murmured at last, "We will grieve for him. The *rhadhamaerl* will grieve. The time has come for mourning."

From the top of the stairs, an excited voice cried, "High Lord! The dead! They have all fallen into sand! Satansfist has exhausted this attack. The gates hold!"

Through his tears, Mhoram looked around the Close. It was badly damaged. The Lords' table and chairs had melted, the steps were uneven, and most of the lower tiers had been misshaped by the fire. But the place had survived. The Keep had survived. Mhoram nodded to Tohrm. "It is time."

His sight was so blurred with tears that he seemed to see two blue-robed figures moving down the stairs toward him. He blinked his tears away, and saw that Lord Loerya was with Amatin.

Her presence explained the protection which had saved him and Tohrm; she had joined her strength to Amatin's.

When she reached him, she looked gravely into his face. He searched her for shame or distress but saw only regret. "I left them with the Unfettered One at Glimmermere," she explained quietly. "Perhaps they will be safe. I returned—when I found courage."

Then something at Mhoram's side caught her attention. Wonder lit her face, and she turned him so that he was looking at the table which held Loric's *krill*.

The table was intact.

In its center, the gem of the *krill* blazed with a pure white fire, as radiant as hope.

Mhoram heard someone say, "Ur-Lord Covenant has returned to the Land." But he could no longer tell what was happening around him. His tears seemed to blind all his senses.

Following the light of the gem, he reached out his hand and clasped the *krill*'s haft. In its intense heat, he felt the truth of what he had heard. The Unbeliever had returned.

With his new might, he gripped the *krill* and pulled it easily from the stone. Its edges were so sharp that when he held the knife in his hand he could see their keenness. His power protected him from the heat.

He turned to his companions with a smile that felt like a ray of sunshine on his face.

"Summon Lord Trevor," he said gladly. "I have—a knowledge of power that I wish to share with you."

TWELVE: Amanibhavam

Hate.

It was the only thought in Covenant's mind. The weight of things he had not known crushed everything else.

Hate.

He clung to the unanswered question as he pried himself with the spear up over the rim of the hollow and hobbled down beyond the last ember-light of Pietten's fire.

Hate.

His crippled foot dragged along the ground, grinding the splintered bones of his ankle together until beads of excruciation burst from his pores and froze in the winter wind. But he clutched the shaft of the spear and lurched ahead, down that hillside and diagonally up the next. The wind cut against his right cheek, but he paid no attention to it; he turned gradually toward the right because of the steepness of the hill, not because he had any awareness of direction. When the convolution of the next slope bent him northward again, away from the Plains of Ra and his only friends, he followed it, tottered down it, fluttering in the wind like a maimed wildman, thinking only:

Hate.

Atiaran Trell-mate had said that it was the responsibility of the living to make meaningful the sacrifices of the dead. He had a whole Land full of death to make meaningful. Behind him, Lena lay slain in her own blood, with a wooden spike through her belly. Elena was buried somewhere in the bowels of *Melenkurion* Skyweir, dead in her private apocalypse because of his manipulations and his failures. She had never even existed. Ranyhyn had been starved and slaughtered. Bannor and Foamfollower might be dead or in despair. Pietten and Hile Troy and Trell and Triock were all his fault. None of them had ever existed. His pain did not exist. Nothing mattered except the one absolute question.

He moaned deep in his throat, "Hate?"

Nothing could have any meaning without the answer to that question. Despite its multitudinous disguises, he recognized it as the question which had shaped his life since the day he had first learned that he was subject to the law of leprosy. Loathing, self-loathing, fear, rape, murder, leper outcast unclean—they were all the same thing. He hobbled in search of the answer.

He was totally alone for the first time since the beginning of his experiences in the Land.

Sick gray dawn found him laboring vaguely northeastward—poling himself feverishly with the spear, and shivering in the bitter ague of winter. The dismal light seemed to rouse parts of him. He plunged into the shallow lee of a hillside and tried to take the measure of his situation.

The shrill wind gibed around him as he plucked with diseased and frozen fingers at his pant leg. When he succeeded in moving the fabric, he felt a numb surprise at the dark discoloration of his flesh above the ankle. His foot sat at a crooked angle on his leg, and through the crusted blood he could see slivers of bone protruding against the thongs of his sandals.

The injury looked worse than it felt. Its pain grated in his knee joint dully, gouged aches up through his thigh to his hip, but the ankle itself was bearable. Both his feet had been frozen senseless by the cold. And both were jabbed and torn and painlessly infected like the feet of a pilgrim. He thought blankly that he would probably lose the broken one. But the possibility carried no weight with him; it was just another part of his experience that did not exist.

There were things that he should have been doing for himself, but he had no idea what they were. He had no conception of anything except the central need which drove him. He lacked food, warmth, knowledge of where he was or where he was going. Yet he was already urgent to be moving again. Nothing but movement could keep his lifeblood circulating—nothing but movement could help him find his answer.

No tentative or half-unready answer would satisfy his need.

He levered himself up, then slipped and fell, crying out unconsciously at the unfelt pain. For a moment, the winter roared in his ears like a triumphant predator. His breathing rasped him as if claws of cold had already torn his air passages and lungs. But he braced the spear on the hard earth again, and climbed up it hand over hand until he was erect. Then he lurched forward once more.

He forced himself up the hill and beyond it to a low ridge lying across his way like a minor wall. His arms trembled at the strain of bearing his weight, and his hands slipped repeatedly on the smooth shaft of the spear. The ascent almost defeated him. When he reached the top, air whooped brokenly in and out of his frostbitten lungs, and icy vertigo made the whole winterscape cant raggedly from side to side. He rested, leaning on the spear. His respiration was so difficult that he thought the frozen sweat and vapor on his face might be suffocating him. But when he tried to break it, it tore away like a protective scab, hurting his skin, exposing new nerves to the cold. He let the rest of his

frozen mask remain, and stood panting until at last
his vision began to clear.

The hard barren region ahead of him was so dreary,
so wilderlanded by Foul's cruelty, that he could hardly
bear to look at it. It was gray cold and dead from
horizon to horizon under the gray dead clouds—not
the soft comfortable gray of twilit illusions, of unstark
colors blurring like consolation or complacency into
each other, but rather the gray of disconsolation and
dismay, paradoxically dull and raw, numb and poignant, a gray like the ashen remains of color and sap
and blood and bone. Gray wind drove gray cold over
the gray frozen hills; gray snow gathered in thin drifts
under the lees of the gray terrain; gray ice under-
scored the black, brittle, leafless branches of the trees
barely visible in the distance on his left, and stifled the
gray, miserable current of the river almost out of sight
on his right; gray numbness clutched at his flesh and
soul. Lord Foul the Despiser was everywhere.

Then for a time he remembered his purpose. He set
his ice-muzzled teeth into the teeth of the cold and
hobbled down from the ridge straight toward the
source of the winter. Half blinded by the opposition
of the wind, he stumped unheeding past slight shelters
and straggling *aliantha,* thrust his tattered way among
the hills, dragging his frozen foot like an accusation
he meant to bring against the Despiser.

But gradually the memory faded, lapsed from his
consciousness like everything else except his reiterat-
ing interrogation of hate. Some inchoate instinct kept
him from wending downward toward the river, but all
other sense of direction deserted him. With the wind
angling against his right cheek, he struggled slowly
upward, upward, as if it were only in climbing that he
could keep himself erect at all.

As the morning passed, he began to fall more often.
He could no longer retain his grip on the spear; his
hands were too stiff, too weak, and a slick sheen of
ice sweat made the spear too slippery. Amid the
crunch of ice and his own panting cries, he slipped
repeatedly to the ground. And after several convulsive
efforts to go on, he lay face down on the ruined earth

with his breath rattling in his throat, and tried to sl̲

But before long he moved again. Sleep was not wha̲
he wanted; it had no place in the one focused fragment of his consciousness. Gasping thickly, he levered
himself to his knees. Then, with an awkward abrupt-
ness, as if he were trying to take himself by surprise,
he put weight on his broken ankle.

It was numb enough. Pain jabbed the rest of his leg,
and his foot twisted under him. But his ankle was
numb enough.

Ignoring the fallen spear, he heaved erect, tottered
—and limped extremely into motion again.

For a long time, he went on that way, jerking on
his broken ankle like a badly articulated puppet commanded by clumsy fingers. He continued to fall; he
was using two hunks of ice for feet, and could not
keep his balance when the hillsides became too steep.
And these slopes grew gradually worse. For some
reason, he tended unevenly to his left, where the
ground rose up to meet black trees; so more and more
often he came to ascents and descents that affected
him like precipices, though they might have seemed
slight enough to a healthy traveler. He went up them
on hands and knees, clawing against the hard ground
for handholds, and plunged rolling helplessly down
them like one of the damned.

But after each fall he rested prone in the snow like
a penitent, and after each rest he staggered or crawled
forward once more, pursuing his private and inevitable
apotheosis, though he was entirely unable to meet it.

As the day waned into afternoon, his falls came
more and more often. And after falling he lay still and
listened to the air sob in and out of his lungs as if the
breaking of his ankle had fractured some essential
bone in him, some obdurate capacity for endurance—
as if at last even numbness failed him, proved in some
way inadequate, leaving him at the mercy of his injury. By degrees he began to believe that after all his
dream was going to kill him.

Sometime in the middle of the afternoon, he
slipped, rolled, came to rest on his back. He could not
muster the strength to turn over. Like a pinned insect,

he struggled for a moment, then collapsed into prostrate sleep—trapped there between the iron heavens and the brass earth.

Dreams roiled his unconsciousness, giving him no consolation. Again and again, he relived the double-fisted blow with which he had stabbed Pietten. But now he dealt that fierce blow at other hearts—Llaura, Manethrall Rue, Elena, Joan, the woman who had been killed protecting him at the battle of Soaring Woodhelven—why had he never asked anyone her name? In dreams he slew them all. They lay around him with gleams of light shining keenly out of their wounds like notes in an alien melody. The song tugged at him, urged—but before he could hear it, another figure hove across his vision, listing like a crippled frigate. The man was dressed in misery and violence. He had blood on his hands and the love of murder in his eyes, but Covenant could not make out his face. Again he raised the knife, again he drove it with all his might into that vulnerable breast. Only then did he see that the man was himself.

He lurched as if the blank sky had struck him, and flopped over onto his chest to hide his face, conceal his wound.

When he remembered the snow in which he lay, he got quavering to his feet and limped on into the late afternoon.

Before long, he came to a hillside he could not master. He flung himself at it, limped and crawled at it as hard as he could. But he was exhausted and crippled. He turned left and stumbled along the slope, seeking a place where he could ascend, but then inexplicably he found himself rolling downward. When he tumbled to a stop at the bottom, he rested for a while in confusion. He must have crossed the top without knowing it. He hauled himself up again, gasping, and went on.

The next hill was no better. But he had to master it. When he could not drive himself upward any farther, he turned to the left again, always left and up, though for some strange reason this seemed to take him down toward the river.

After a short distance he found a trail in the snow.

Part of him knew that he should be dismayed, but he felt only relief, hope. A trail meant that someone had passed this way—passed recently, or the wind would have effaced the marks. And that someone might help him.

He needed help. He was freezing, starving, failing. Under its crust of scab and ice, his ankle was still bleeding. He had reached the infinitude of his impotence, his inefficacy, the point beyond which he could not keep going, could not believe, envision, hope that continuation, life, was possible. He needed whoever or whatever had made that trail to decide his fate for him.

He followed it to the left, downward, into a hollow between hills. He kept his eyes on the trail immediately before him, fearing to look up and find that the maker of the trail was out of sight, out of reach. He saw where the maker had fallen, shed blood, rested, limped onward. Soon he met the next hill and began crawling up it along the crawling trail. He was desperate—alone and impoverished as he had never before been in the Land.

But at last he recognized the truth. When the trail turned, crawled away to the left, fell back down the hillside, he could no longer deny that he had been following himself, that the trail was his own, a circle between hills he could not master.

With a thick moan, he passed the boundary. His last strength fell out of him. Keen gleams winked across the dark gulf behind his closed eyes, but he could not answer them. He fell backward, slid down the hill into a low snowdrift.

Yet even then his ordeal continued. His fall uncovered something in the snow. While he lay gasping helplessly, felt his heart tremble toward failure in his chest, a smell intruded on him. Despite the cold, it demanded his notice; it rose piquant and seductive in his face, ran into him on every breath, compelled him to respond. He propped himself up on quivering arms, and wiped the snow away with dead fingers.

He found grass growing under the snowdrift. Somehow its potent life refused to be quenched; even a few yellow flowers blossomed under the weight of the snow. And their sharp aroma caught hold of him. His hands were useless for plucking, so he knocked some of the ice from around his mouth. Then he lowered his face to the grass, tore up blades with his teeth and ate them.

As he swallowed the grass, its juice seemed to flow straight to his muscles like the energy of madness. The suddenness of the infusion caught him unaware. As he bent for a fourth bite, a convulsion came over him, and he collapsed into a rigid fetal position while raw power raged through his veins.

For an instant, he screamed in agony. But at once he passed beyond himself into a bleak wilderland where nothing but winter and wind and malice existed. He felt Lord Foul's preternatural assault on a level that was not sight or hearing or touch, but rather a compaction of all his senses. The nerves of his soul ached as if they had been laid bare to the livid ill. And in the core of this perception, a thought struck him, stabbed into him as if it were the spear point of the winter. He identified the thing he did not understand.

It was *magic*.

A suggestion of keen gleams penumbraed the thought, then receded. Magic: eldritch power, theurgy. Such a thing did not exist, could not exist. Yet it was part of the Land. And it was denied to him. The thought turned painfully in him as cruel hands twisted the spear.

He had heard Mhoram say, *You are the white gold*. What did that mean? He had no power. The dream was his, but he could not share its life-force. Its life-force was what proved it to be a dream. Magic: power. It sprang from him, and he could not touch it. It was impossible. With the Land's doom locked in the irremediable white gold circle of his ring, he was helpless to save himself.

Gripped by an inchoate conviction, where prophecy and madness became indistinguishable, he flung himself around the contradiction and tried to contain it, make it all one within him.

But then it faded in a scatter of keen alien gleaming. He found himself on his feet without any knowledge of how he had climbed erect. The gleams danced about his head like silent melody. The wild light of the grass played through his veins and muscles, elevating inanition and cold to the stature of gaunt priests presiding over an unholy sacrifice. He laughed at the immense prospect of his futility. The folly of his attempts to survive alone amused him.

He was going to die a leper's death.

His laughter scaled up into high gibbering mirth. Stumbling, limping, falling, lurching up and limping again, he followed the music toward the dark trees.

He laughed every time he fell, unable to contain the secret humor of his distress; the frozen agony grinding in his ankle drew shrill peals from him like screams. But though he was impatient now for the end, eager for any blank damnable repose, still the keen gleams carried him along. Advancing and receding, urging, sprinkling his way like glaucous petals of ambergris, they made him rise after each fall and continue toward the outskirts of the forest.

After a while, he began to think that the trees were singing to him. The gleams which fraught the air fell about him in alien intervals, like moist, blue-green shines of woodsong. But he could neither see nor hear them; they were apparent only to the restless energy in his veins. When in his wildness he tried to pluck them as if they were *aliantha*, they strewed themselves beyond his reach, enticing him on and on again after each fall until he found himself among the first winter-black trunks.

As he wended through the marge of the forest, he felt an unexpected diminution of the cold. Daylight was dying out of the ashen sky behind him, and ahead lay nothing but the brooding bloom of the forest depths. Yet the winter seemed to ease rather than sharpen with the coming of night. Shambling onward, he soon discovered that the snow thinned as he moved deeper among the trees. In a few places, he even saw living leaves. They clung grimly to the branches, and the trees in turn clung to each other, interwove their branches and leaned on each other's shoulders like staunch, broad, black-wounded comrades holding themselves erect together. Through the thinning snow, animal tracks made light whorls that dizzied him when he tried to follow them. And the air grew warmer.

Gradually, a dim light spread around him. For a time, he did not notice it to wonder what it was; he walked like a ruin along the alien spangles, and did not see the pale ghost-light expanding. But then a wet strand of moss struck his face, and he jerked into awareness of his surroundings.

The tree trunks were glowing faintly, like moonlight mystically translated out of the blind sky into the forest. They huddled around him in stands and stretches and avenues of gossamer illumination; they were poised on all sides like white eyes, watching him. And through their branches hung draped, dangled curtains and hawsers of moist black moss.

Then in his madness, fear came upon him like a shout of ancient forestial rage, springing from the un-avenged slaughter of the trees; and he turned to flee. Wailing lornly, he slapped the moss away from him and tried to run. But his ankle buckled under him at every stride. And the music held him. Its former allure became a command, swinging him against his will so that his panic itself, his very flight, drove him deeper among the trees and the moss and the light. He had lost all possession of himself. The strength of the grass capered in him like poison; the gleams danced through their blue-green intervals, guiding him. He fled like the hunted, battering and recoiling against trunks, tangling himself in moss, tearing his hair in fear. Animals scampered out of his wailing path, and his ears echoed to the desolate cries of owls.

He was soon exhausted. His flesh could not bear any more. As his wailing turned to frenzy in his throat, a large hairy moth the size of a cormorant suddenly fluttered out of the branches, veered erratically, and crashed into him. The impact knocked him to the ground in a pile of useless limbs. For a moment, he thrashed weakly. But he could not regain his breath, steady himself, rise. After a brief struggle, he collapsed on the warm turf and abandoned himself to the forest.

For a time, the gleaming hovered over him as if it were curious about his immobility. Then it spangled away into the depths of the trees, leaving him clapped in dolorous dreams. While he slept, the light mounted until the trunks seemed to be reaching toward him with their illumination, seeking a way to absorb him, rid the ground of him, efface him from the sight of their hoary rage. But though they glowered, they did not harm him. And before long a feathery scampering came through the branches and the moss. The sound seemed to reduce the trees to baleful insentience; they withdrew their threatening as a host of spiders began to drop lightly onto Covenant's still form.

Guided by gleams, the spiders swarmed over him as if they were searching for a vital spot to place their stings. But instead of stinging him, they gathered around his wounds; working together, they started to weave their webs over him wherever he was hurt.

In a short time, both his feet were thickly wrapped in pearl-gray webs. The bleeding of his ankle was stanched, and its protruding bone-splinters were covered with gentle protection. A score of the spiders draped his frostbitten cheeks and nose with their threads, while others bandaged his hands, and still others webbed his forehead, though no injury was apparent there. Then they all scurried away as quickly as they had come.

He slept on. His dreams wracked him at odd moments, but for the most part he lay still, and so his ragged pulse grew steadier, and the helpless whimper faded from his breathing. In his gray webs, he looked like a cocooned wreck in which something new was aborning.

Much later that night, he stirred and found the keen gleams peering at him again through his closed eyelids. He was still far from consciousness, but the notes of the melody roused him enough to hear feet shuffling toward him across the grass. "Ah, mercy," an old woman's voice sighed over him, "mercy. So peace and

silence come to this. I left all thought of such work—
and yet my rest comes to this. Have mercy."

Hands cleared the gentle bindings from his head and
face.

"Yes I see—for this reason the Forest called
me from my old repose. Injured—cold-ill. And he has
eaten *amanibhavam*. Ah, mercy. How the world intrudes, when even Morinmoss bestirs itself for such
things as this. Well, the grass has kept life in him, whatever its penalty. But I mislike the look of his thoughts.
He will be a sore trial to me."

Covenant heard the words, though they did not penetrate the cold center of his sleep. He tried to open his
eyes, but they kept themselves closed as if out of fear
of what he might see. The old woman's hands as they
searched him for other injuries filled him with loathing;
yet he lay still, slumberous, shackled in mad dreams.
He had no volition with which to oppose her. So he
lurked within himself, hid from her until he could
spring and strike her down and free himself.

"Mercy," she mumbled on to herself, "mercy, indeed. Cold-ill and broken-minded. I left such work.
Where will I find the strength for it?" Then her deft
fingers bared his left hand, and she gasped, *"Melenkurion!* White gold? Ah, by the Seven! How has such a burden come to me?"

The need to protect his ring from her drew him
closer to consciousness. He could not move his hand,
could not even clench his fist around the ring, so he
sought to distract her.

"Lena," he croaked through cracked lips, without
knowing what he said. "Lena? Are you still alive?"

With an effort he pried open his eyes.

THIRTEEN: The Healer

STILL sleep shrouded his sight; at first he saw nothing except the compact, baleful light of the trees. But his ring was in danger from her. He was jealous of his white gold. Sleep or no sleep, he did not mean to give it up. He strove to focus his eyes, strove to come far enough out of hiding to engage her attention.

Then a soft stroke of her hand swept the cobwebs from his eyebrows, and he found that he could see her.

"Lena?" he croaked again.

She was a dusky, loamy woman, with hair like tangled brown grass, and an old face uneven and crude of outline, as if it had been inexpertly molded in clay. The hood of a tattered fallow-green cloak covered the crown of her head. And her eyes were the brown of soft mud, an unexpected and suggestive brown, as if the silt of some private devotion filled her orbs, effaced her pupils—as if the black, round nexus between her mind and the outside world were something that she had surrendered in exchange for the rare, rich loam of power. Yet there was no confidence, no surety, in her gaze as she regarded him; the life which had formed her eyes was far behind her. Now she was old, timorous. Her voice rustled like the creaking of antique parchment as she asked, "Lena?"

"Are you still alive?"

"Am I—? No, I am not your Lena. She is dead—if the look of you tells any truth. Mercy."

Mercy, he echoed soundlessly.

"This is the doing of the *amanibhavam*. Perhaps you have preserved your life in eating it—but surely you know that it is poison to you, a food too potent for human flesh."

"Are you still alive?" he repeated with cunning in his throat. Thus he disguised himself, protected that part of him which had come out of hiding and sleep to ward his ring. Only the damaged state of his features kept him from grinning at his own slyness.

"Perhaps not," she sighed. "But let that pass. You have no knowledge of what you say. You are cold-ill and poison-mad—and—and there is a sickness in you that I do not comprehend."

"Why aren't you dead?"

She brought her face close to his, and went on: "Listen to me. I know that the hand of confusion is upon you—but listen to me. Hear and hold my words. You have come in some way into Morinmoss Forest. I am —a Healer, an Unfettered One who turned to the work of healing. I will help you—because you are in need, and because the white gold reveals that great matters are afoot in the Land—and because the Forest found its voice to summon me for you, though that also I do not comprehend."

"I saw him kill you." The raw croak of Covenant's voice sounded like horror and grief, but in his depths he hugged himself for glee at his cunning.

She drew back her head but showed no other reaction to what he had said. "I came to this place from— from my life—because the Forest's unquiet slumber met my own long ache for repose. I am a Healer, and Morinmoss permits me. Yet now it speaks— Great matters, indeed. Ah, mercy. It is in my heart that the Colossus itself— Well, I wander. I have made my home here for many years. I am accustomed to speak only for my own pleasure."

"I saw."

"Do you not hear me?"

"He stabbed you with a wooden spike. I saw the blood."

"Mercy! Is your life so violent then? Well, let that

pass also. You do not hear me—you have fallen too far into the *amanibhavam*. But violent or not I must aid you. It is well that my eyes have not forgotten their work. I see that you are too weak to harm me, whatever your purpose."

Weak, he echoed to himself. What she said was true; he was too frail even to clench his fist for the protection of his wedding band. "Have you come back to haunt me?" he gasped. "To blame me?"

"Speak if you must," she said in a rustling tone, "but I cannot listen. I must be about my work." With a low groan, she climbed to her feet and moved stiffly away from him.

"That's it," he continued, impelled by his grotesque inner glee. "That's it, isn't it? You've come back to torture me. You're not satisfied that I killed him. I put that knife all the way into his heart but you're not satisfied. You want to hurt me some more. You want me to go crazy thinking about all the things I'm guilty of. I did Foul's work for him, and you came to torture me for it. You and your blood! Where were you when it would have made a difference what happens to me? Why didn't you try to get even with me after I raped you? Why wait until now? If you'd made me pay for what I did then, maybe I would have figured out what's going on before this. All that generosity—! It was cruel. Oh, Lena! I didn't even understand what I'd done to you until it was too late, too late, I couldn't help myself. What are you waiting for? Torture me! I need pain!"

"You need food," the Healer muttered as if he had disgusted her. With one hand she fixed his jaw in an odd compelling grip while the other placed two or three treasure-berries in his mouth. "Swallow the seeds. They, too, will sustain you."

He wanted to spit out the *aliantha,* but her grip made him chew in spite of himself. Her other hand stroked his throat until he swallowed, then fed him more of the berries. Soon she had coerced him to eat several mouthfuls. He could feel sustenance flowing into him, yet for some reason it seemed to feed his deep slumber rather than his cunning. Before long he could not remember what he had been saying. An involuntary drowsiness shone into him from the trees. He was unable to resist or comply when the Healer lifted him from the grass.

Grunting at the strain, she raised his limp form until he was half erect in her arms. Then she leaned him against her back with his arms over her shoulders, and gripped his upper arms like the handles of a burden. His feet dragged behind him; he dangled on her squat shoulders. But she bore his weight, carried him like a dead sack into the pale white night of Morinmoss.

While he drowsed, she took him laboriously farther and farther into the secret depths of the Forest. And as they left its borders behind, they passed into warmer air and greater health—a region where spring had not been quenched by Lord Foul's winter. Leaves multiplied and spread out around bird nests to cloak the branches; moss and grass and small woodland animals increased among the trees. A defying spirit was abroad in this place—resisting cold, nourishing growth, affirming Morinmoss's natural impulse toward buds and new sap and arousal. It was as if the ancient Forestals had returned, bringing with them the wood's old knowledge of itself.

Yet even in its secret heart Morinmoss was not impervious to the Despiser's fell influence. Temperatures rose above the freezing point, but failed to climb any higher. The leaves had no spring profusion; they grew thinly, in dark bitter greens rather than in hale verdancy. The animals wore their winter coats over bones that were too gaunt for true spring. If a Forestal had indeed returned to Morinmoss, he lacked the potency of his olden predecessors.

No, it was more likely that the monolithic Colossus of the Fall had shrugged off its brooding slumber to take a hand in the defenses of the Forest. And it was more likely still that Caerroil Wildwood was reaching out from his fastness in Garroting Deep, doing what he could across the distance to preserve old Morinmoss.

Nevertheless, this lessening of winter was a great boon to the trees, and to the denizens of the Forest. It kept alive many things which might have been among the first to die when Lord Foul interdicted spring. For that reason among others, the Unfettered Healer trudged onward with Covenant on her back. The defying spirit had not only tolerated both her and him; it had summoned her to him. She could not refuse. Though she was old, and found Covenant painfully heavy, she sustained herself by sucking moisture from the moss, and plodded under him toward her home among the secrets of the Forest.

The tree shine had lapsed into dim gray dawn before her journey ended at a low cave in the bank of a hill. Thrusting aside the moss which curtained its small entrance, she stooped and dragged Covenant behind her into the modest single chamber of her dwelling.

The cave was not large. It was barely deep enough for her to stand erect in its center, and its oval floor was no more than fifteen feet wide. But it was a cozy home for one person. It had comfort enough in the soft loam of its walls and its beds of piled dry leaves. It was warm, protected from the winter. And when other lights were withdrawn, it was lit in ghostly filigree by the tree roots which held its walls and ceiling. In its underground safety, her small cookfire was not a threat to the Forest.

In addition to the low embers which awaited her against one wall, she possessed a pot of graveling. Dropping Covenant wearily on the bed, she opened the graveling and used some of its heat to resurrect her fire. Then she set her stiff old bones on the floor and rested for a long time.

It was nearly midmorning when her fire threatened to die out. Sighing dryly, she roused herself to stoke up a blaze and cook a hot meal for herself. This she ate without a glance at Covenant. He was in no condition for solid food. She cooked and ate to gather strength for herself, because her peculiar power of healing required strength—so much strength that she had exhausted her reserves of courage before reaching middle age, and had left her work to rest in Morinmoss for the remainder of her days. Decades—four or five, she no longer knew—had passed since she had fled; and during that time she had lived in peace and reticence among the seasons of the Forest, believing that the ordeals of her life were over.

Yet now even Morinmoss had bestirred itself to bring her work back to her. She needed strength. She forced herself to eat a large meal, then rested again.

But at last she rallied herself to begin the task. She set her pot of fire-stones on a shelf in the wall so that its warm yellow light fell squarely over Covenant. He was still asleep, and this relieved her; she did not want to face either his mad talk or his resistance. But she was made afraid once again by the extent of his sickness. Something bone-deep had hold of him, something she could not recognize or understand. In its unfamiliarity, it reminded her of old nightmares in which she had terrified herself by attempting to heal the Despiser.

The acute fracture of his ankle she did understand; his cold-bitten and battered hands and feet were within her experience, and she saw that they might even heal themselves, if he were kept warm for a long convalescence; his cheeks and nose and ears, his cracked lips with the odd scar on one side, his uncleanly healed forehead, all did not challenge her. But the damage the *amanibhavam* had done to his mind was another matter. It made his sleeping eyes bulge so feverishly in their sockets that through their lids she could read every flick and flinch of his wild dreams; it knuckled his forehead in an extreme scowl of rage or pain; it locked his hands into awkward fists, so that even if she had dared to touch his white gold she could not have taken it from him. And his essential sickness was still another matter. She caught glimpses of the way in which it was interwoven with his madness. She dreaded to touch that ill with her power.

To steady herself, she hummed an old song under her breath:

> When last comes to last,
>   I have little power:
>   I am merely an urn.
> I hold the bone-sap of myself,
>   and watch the marrow burn.

When last comes to last,
   I have little strength:
  I am only a tool.
I work its work; and in its hands
   I am the fool.

When last comes to last,
   I have little life.
  I am simply a deed:
an action done while courage holds:
   a seed.

While she strove to master her faintheartedness, she made preparations. First she cooked a thin broth, using hot water and a dusty powder which she took from a leather pouch among her few belongings. This she fed to Covenant without awakening him. It deepened his repose, made rest and unconsciousness so thick in him that he could not have struggled awake to save his own life. Then, when he was entirely unable to interfere with her, she began to strip off his attire.

Slowly, using her own hesitation to enhance the thoroughness of her preparations, she removed all his raiment and bathed him from head to foot. After cleaning away the cobwebs and grime and old sweat and encrusted blood, she explored him with her hands, probed him gently to assure herself that she knew the full extent of his hurts. The process took time, but it was done too soon for her unready courage.

Still hesitating, she unwrapped from her belongings one of her few prized possessions—a long, cunningly woven white robe, made of a fabric both light and tough, easy to wear and full of warmth. It had been given to her decades ago by a great weaver from Soaring Woodhelven, whose life she had saved at severe cost to herself. The memory of his gratitude was precious to her, and she held the robe for a long time in hands that trembled agedly. But she was old now, old and alone; she had no need of finery. Her tattered cloak would serve her well enough as either apparel or cerement. With an expensive look in her loamy eyes, she took the robe to Covenant and dressed him tenderly in it.

The effort of moving his limp form shortened her breathing, and she rested again, muttering out of old habit, "Ah, mercy, mercy. This is work for the young—for the young. I rest and rest, but I do not become young. Well, let that pass. I did not come to Morinmoss in search of youth. I came because I had lost heart for my work. Have I not found it again—in all this time? Ah, but time is no Healer. The body grows old—and now cruel winter enslaves the world—and the heart does not renew itself. Mercy, mercy. Courage belongs to the young, and I am old—old.

"Yet surely great matters are afoot—great and terrible. White gold!—by the Seven! White gold. And this winter is the Despiser's doing, though Morinmoss resists. Ah, there are terrible purposes— The burden of this man was put upon me by a terrible purpose. I cannot—I must not refuse. Must not! Ah, mercy, but I am afraid. I am old—I have no need to fear—no, I do not fear death. But the pain. The pain. Have mercy—have mercy upon me, I lack the courage for this work."

Yet Covenant lay on her bed like an irrefusable demand molded of broken bone and blood and mind, and after she had dozed briefly, she came back to herself. "Well, that too I must set aside. Complaint also is no Healer. I must set it aside, and work my work."

Stiffly, she got to her feet, went to the far end of the cave to her supplies of firewood. Even now, she hoped in her heart that she would find she did not have enough wood; then she would need to hunt through the Forest for fallen dead branches and twigs before she could begin her main task. But her woodpile was large enough. She could not pretend that it justified any further delay. She carried most of the wood to her cookfire and faced the commencement of her ordeal.

First she took her graveling pot from the shelf above Covenant and made a place for it in the center of the fire, so that its heat and light were added to the core of the coals. Then, panting already at the thought of what she meant to do, she began to build up the fire. She stoked it, concentrated it with dry hard wood, until its

flames mounted toward the cave's ceiling and its heat
drew sweat from her old brows. And when the low
roar of its blaze sucked at the air, causing the moss curtains over the entrance to flutter in the draft, she returned to the pouch of powder from which she had
made the broth. With her fist clenched in the pouch,
she hesitated once more, faltering as if the next step
constituted an irretrievable commitment. "Ah, mercy,"
she breathed brittlely to herself. "I must remember—
remember that I am alone. No one else will tend him—
or me. I must do the work of two. For this reason eremites do not Heal. I must do the work."

Panting in dismay at her own audacity, she threw a
small quantity of the powder into the high fire.

At once, the blaze began to change. The flames did
not die down, but they muted themselves, translated
their energy into a less visible form. Their light turned
from orange and red and yellow to brown, a steadily
deepening brown, as if they sprang now from thick
loam rather than from wood. And as the brightness of
the fire dimmed, a rich aroma spread into the cave. It
tasted to the Healer like the breaking of fresh earth so
that seeds could be planted—like the lively imminence
of seeds and buds and spring—like the fructifying of
green things which had germinated in wealthy soil. She
could have lost herself in that brown fragrance, forget-
ful of Lord Foul's winter and the sick man and all pain.
But it was part of her work. Through her love for it, it
impelled her to Covenant's side. There she planted her
feet and took one last moment to be sure of what she
meant to do.

His hands and feet and face she would not touch.
They were not crucial to his recovery, not worth what
they would cost her. And the sickness in his mind was
too complex and multifarious to undertake until he was
physically whole enough to bear the strain of healing.
So she bent her loamy gaze toward his broken ankle.

As she concentrated on that injury, the light of the
fire became browner, richer, more potent and explicit,
until it shone like the radiance of her eyes between her
face and his ankle. The rest of the cave fell into gloom;
soon only the link of sight between her attention and

his pain retained illumination. It stretched between them, binding them together, gradually uniting their opposed pieces of need and power. Amid the heat and fragrancy of the fire, they became like one being, annealed of isolation, complete.

Blindly, tremulously, as if she were no longer aware of herself, she placed her hands on his ankle, explored it with her touch until she unconsciously knew the precise angle and acuteness of its fracture. Then she withdrew.

Her power subsumed her, made her independent flesh seem transient, devoid of significance; she became an involuntary vessel for her work, anchor and source of the bond which made her one with his wound.

When the bond grew strong enough, she retreated from him. Without volition or awareness, she stopped and picked up the smooth heavy stone which she used as a pestle; without volition or awareness, she held it like a weighty gift in both hands, offering it to Covenant. Then she raised it high over her head.

She blinked, and the brown link of oneness trembled.

With all her strength, she swung the stone down, slammed it against her own ankle.

The bones broke like dry wood.

Pain shot through her—pain like the splintering of souls, hers and his. She shrieked once and crumbled to the floor in a swoon.

Then time passed for her in a long agony that shut and sealed every other door of her mind. She lay on the floor while the fire died into dim embers, and the aroma of spring turned to dust in the air, and the ghostly fibers of the roots shone and waned. Nothing existed for her except the searing instant in which she had matched Covenant's pain—the instant in which she had taken all their pain, his and hers, upon herself. Night passed and came again; still she lay crumbled. Her breathing gasped hoarsely between her flaccid lips, and her heart fluttered along the verges of extinction. If she could have regained consciousness long enough to choose to die, she would have done so gladly, eagerly. But the pain sealed her within herself and had its way with her until it became all she knew of life or death.

Yet at last she found herself thinking that it had never been this bad when she was younger. The old power had not altogether failed her, but her ordeals at their worst had never been like this. Her body was wracked with thirst and hunger. And this, too, was not as it had ever been before. Where were the people who should have watched over her—who should have at least given her water so that she did not die of thirst before the agony passed? Where were the family or friends who brought the ill and injured to her, and who gladly did all they could to aid the healing?

In time, such questions led her to remember that she was alone, that she and the sick man were both untended. He, too, had been without food or water during the whole course of her ordeal; and even if her power had not failed, he was in no condition to endure such privation. He might be dead in spite of what she had survived for him.

With an effort that made her old body tremble exhaustedly, she raised herself from the floor.

On her hands and knees she rested, panting heavily. She needed to gather the feeble remnant of herself before she faced the sick man. Miserable tasks awaited her if he were dead. She would have to struggle through the Despiser's winter to take that white gold ring to the Lords of Revelstone. And she would have to live with the fact that her agony had been the agony of failure. Such possibilities daunted her.

Yet she knew that even this delay might make the difference, might prove fatal. Groaning, she tried to stand up.

Before she could get her legs under her, movement staggered toward her from the bed. A foot kicked her to the floor again. The sick man lumbered past her and thrashed through the curtain of moss while she sprawled on the packed earth.

The surprise of the blow hurt her more than the kick itself; the man was far too weak to do her any real harm. And his violence rekindled some of her energy. Panting blunt curses to herself, she stumbled stiffly upright and limped out of the cave after him.

She caught up with him within twenty feet of the

cave's mouth. The gleaming pale gaze of the tree trunks had stopped his flight. He reeled with fear whimpering in his throat, as if the trees were savage beasts crouched and waiting for him.

"You are ill," the Healer muttered wearily. "Understand that if you understand nothing else. Return to the bed."

He veered around to face her. "You're trying to kill me."

"I am a Healer. I do not kill."

"You hate lepers, and you're trying to kill me." His eyes bulged insanely in his haggard face. "You don't even exist."

She could see that inanition had only aggravated his *amanibhavam* confusion and his inexplicable sickness; they had become so dominant that she could no longer tell them apart. And she was too weak to placate him; she had no strength to waste on words or gentleness which would not reach him. Instead, she simply stepped close to him and jabbed her rigid fingers into his stomach.

While he fell gagging to the grass, she made her way to the nearest *aliantha*.

It was not far from the entrance to her cave, but her fatigue was so extreme that she nearly swooned again before she could pluck and eat a few of the treasure-berries. However, their tangy potency came to her aid as soon as she swallowed them. Her legs steadied. After a moment, she was able to throw the seeds aside and pick more berries.

When she had eaten half the ripe fruit, she picked the rest and took it back to Covenant. He tried to crawl away from her, but she held him down and forced him to eat. Then she went to a large sheet of moss hanging nearby, where she drank deeply of its rich green moisture. This refreshed her, gave her enough strength to wrestle the sick man back into the cave and control him while she put him back to sleep with a pinch of her rare powder.

Under other circumstances, she might have pitied the turgid panic with which he felt himself lapsing into helplessness again. But she was too weary—and too full of dread for the work she had yet to do. She did not know how to console him and made no attempt. When he fell into uneasy slumber, she only muttered "Mercy," over him, and turned away.

She wanted to sleep, too, but she was alone and had to bear the burden of care herself. Groaning at the unwieldiness of her old joints, she built another fire from the graveling and started a meal for herself and the sick man.

While the food heated, she inspected his ankle. She nodded dully when she saw that it was as whole as her own. Already his pale scars were fading. Soon his bones would be as well and sturdy as if they had never been fractured. Looking at the evidence of her power, she wished that she could take pleasure in it. But she had lost decades ago her capacity to be pleased by the results of her anguish. She knew with certainty that if she had comprehended when she was young what her decisions would cost, she would never have taken the Rites of Unfettering, never have surrendered to the secret power yearning for birth within her.

But power was not so easily evaded. Costs could not be known until they came to full fruition, and by that time the power no longer served the wielder. Then the wielder was the servant. No escape, no peace or reticence, could then evade the expense, and she could take no pleasure in healing. With the work she had yet to do lying stricken before her, she had no more satisfaction than choice.

Yet as she resumed her cooking, she turned her back on regret. "Let it pass," she murmured dimly. "Let it pass. Only let it be done purely—without failure." At least the work which remained would be a different pain altogether.

When the food was ready, she fed herself and Covenant, then gave him more of the soporific broth, so that he would not rise to strike her again. Then she banked her cookfire, pulled her tattered cloak tightly around her, and went agedly to sleep leaning against the pile of leaves that had been her bed.

In the days that followed, she rested, tended Covenant's madness, and tried to remember courage. His need made her heart quail in her old bosom. Even in his slumber she could see that his mind was being eaten away by its ingrown torments. As his body regained its strength, her potions slowly lost their ability to control the restlessness of his dream-ridden sleep. He began to flail his arms and jabber deliriously, like a man snared in the skein of a nightmare. At unexpected moments, his ring gave out white gleams of passion; and when by chance the Healer saw them squarely, they seemed to pierce her like a voice of misery, beseeching her to her work.

The Forest itself echoed his distress. Its mood bent in toward her like a demand, a compulsion as unmistakable as the summons which had called her to him in the beginning. She did not know why Morinmoss cared; she only felt its caring brush her cheek like the palm of authority, warning her. He needed to be healed. If it were not done in time, the essential fabric of his being would rot beyond all restitution.

At last she became aware of time; she felt in the brightness of the tree shine that somewhere behind the impenetrable clouds moved a dark moon, readying itself for a new phase of the Despiser's power. She forced herself to unclench her hesitations, one by one, and to face her work again.

Then she built her high blaze for the second time and made ready her rare powder. While the hard wood took fire, she set both water and food on the shelf above Covenant so that if he regained consciousness before she did, he would not have to search for what he needed. A fatal mood was on her, and she did not believe she would survive. "Mercy," she muttered as the fire mounted, "mercy." She uttered the word as if she were seeking a benediction for herself.

Soon the flames filled her cave with light and heat, flushing the withered skin of her cheeks. The time had come; she could feel the power limping in her like a sere lover, oddly frail and masterful, yearning for its chance to rise up once more and take her—yearning, and yet strangely inadequate, old, as if it could no longer match what it remembered of its desires. For a moment, her blood deserted her; weakness filled all her muscles, so that the leather pouch fell from her fingers. But then she stooped to regain it, thrust her trembling hand into it, threw its dust into the fire as if that gesture were her last, best approximation of courage.

As the potent aroma of the dust spread its arms, took all the air of the cave into its embrace, began its slow transubstantiation of the firelight, she stood near Covenant's head and locked her quavering knees. Staring brownly at his forehead while the heat and illumination of the blaze came into consonance with her attention, she passed beyond the verges of volition and became once more the vessel of her power. Around her the cave grew dim as the rich, loamy light of the bond wove itself between her pupilless orbs and his sick, mad mind. And before her Covenant tensed, stiffened —eyes staring gauntly, neck corded, knuckles white— as if her power clutched his very soul with fear.

Trembling, she reached out her hands, placed her palms flat against the gathered thunder of his forehead.

The next instant, she recoiled as if he had scalded her. "No!" she cried. Horror flooded her, she foundered in it. "You ask too much!" Deep within her, she fought to regain her self-command, fought to thrust down the power, deny it, return to herself so that she would not be destroyed. "I cannot heal this!" But the man's madness came upon her as if he had reached out and caught her wrists. Wailing helplessly, she returned to him, replaced her palms on his forehead.

The terror of it rushed into her, filled her until it burst between her lips like a shriek. Yet she could not withdraw. His madness pounded through her as she sank into it, trying not to see what lay at its root. And when at last it made her see, forced her to behold itself, the leering disease of its source, she knew that she was ruined. She wrenched her seared hands from his head and went hunting, scrabbling frantically among her possessions.

Still shrieking, she pounced upon a long stone cooking knife, snatched it up, aimed it at his vulnerable heart.

He lay under the knife like a sacrifice defiled with leprosy.

But before she could stab out his life, consummate his unclean pain in death, a host of glaucous, alien gleams leaped like music into the air around her. They fell on her like dew, clung to her like moist melody, stayed her hand; they confined her power and her anguish, held all things within her until her taut, soundless cry imploded. They contained her until she broke under the strain of things that could not be contained. Then they let her fall.

Gleaming like the grief of trees, they sang themselves away.

FOURTEEN: Only Those
Who Hate

COVENANT first awoke after a night and a day. But the stupor of essential sleep was still on him, and he only roused himself at the behest of a nagging thirst. When he sat up in the bed of leaves, he found a water jug on a shelf by his head. He drank deeply, then saw that a bowl of fruit and bread also occupied the shelf. He ate, drank again, and went back to sleep as soon as he had stretched himself out among the warm dry leaves once more.

The next time, he came languorously out of slumber amid the old gentle fragrance of the bed. When he opened his eyes, he discovered that he was looking up through a dim gloom of daylight at the root-woven roof of a cave. He turned his head, looked around the earthen walls until he located the moss-hung entrance which admitted so little light. He did not know where he was, or how he had come here, or how long he had slept. But his ignorance caused him no distress. He had recovered from fear. On the strength of unknown things which lay hidden behind the veil of his repose, he felt sure that he had no need to fear.

That feeling was the only emotion in him. He was calm, steady, and hollow—empty and therefore undisturbed—as if the same cleansing or apotheosis which had quenched his terror had also drained every other passion from him. For a time, he could not even remember what those passions had been; between him and his past lay nothing but sleep and an annealed gulf of extravagant fear.

Then he caught the first faint scent of death in the air. It was not urgent, and he did not react to it immediately. While he took its measure, made sure of it, he stretched his sleep-stiff muscles, feeling the flex of their revitalization. Whatever had brought him to this place had happened so long ago that even his body appeared to have forgotten it. Yet his recovery gave him little satisfaction. He accepted it with complete and empty confidence, for reasons that were hidden from him.

When he was ready, he swung his feet off the bed and sat up. At once, he saw the old brown woman lying crumpled on the floor. She was dead with an outcry still rigid on her lips and a blasted look in the staring loam of her eyes. In the dim light, she seemed like a wracked mound of earth. He did not know who she was—he gazed at her with an effort of recollection and could not remember ever having seen her before—but she gave him the vague impression that she, too, had died for him.

That's enough, he said dimly to himself. Other memories began to float to the surface like the dead seaweed and wreckage of his life. This must not happen again.

He looked down at the unfamiliar white robe for a moment, then pushed the cloth aside so that he could see his ankle.

It was broken, he thought in hollow surprise. He could remember breaking it; he could remember wrestling with Pietten, falling—he could remember using Pietten's spear to help him walk until the fracture froze. Yet now it showed no sign of any break. He tested it against the floor, half expecting its wholeness to vanish like an illusion. He stood up, hopped from foot to foot, sat down again. Muttering dully to himself, By hell, by hell, he gave himself his first VSE in many days.

He found that he was more healed than he would have believed possible. The damage which he had done to his feet was almost completely gone. His gaunt hands flexed easily—though they had lost flesh, and his ring hung loosely on his wedding finger. Except for a faint numbness at their tips, his ears and nose had recovered from frostbite. His very bones were full of deep, sustaining warmth.

But other things had not changed. His cheeks felt as stiff as ever. Along his forehead was the lump of a badly healed scar; it was tender to the touch, as if beneath the surface it festered against his skull. And his disease still gnawed its way remorselessly up the nerves of his hands and feet. His fingers were numb to the palms, and only the tops of his feet and the backs of his heels remained sensitive. So the fundamental condition of his existence remained intact. The law of his leprosy was graven within him, carved with the cold chisel of death as if he were made of dolomite or marble rather than bone and blood and humanity.

For that reason he remained unmoved in the hollow center of his healing. He was a leper and had no business exposing himself to the risks of passion.

Now when he looked back at the dead woman, he remembered what he had been doing before the winter had reft him of himself; he had been carrying a purpose of destruction and hate eastward, toward Foul's Creche. That purpose now wore the aspect of madness. He had been mad to throw himself against the winter alone, just as he had been mad to believe that he could ever challenge the Despiser. The path of his past appeared strewn with corpses, the victims of the process which had brought him to that purpose—the process of manipulation by which Lord Foul sought to produce the last fatal mistake of a direct challenge. And the result of that mistake would be a total victory for the Despiser.

He knew better now. The fallen woman taught him a kind of wisdom. He could not challenge the Despiser for the same reason that he could not make his way through the Despiser's winter alone: the task was impossible, and mortal human beings accomplished nothing but their own destruction when they attempted the impossible. A leper's end—prescribed and circumscribed for him by the law of his illness—awaited him not far down the road of his life. He would only hasten his journey toward that end if he lashed himself with impossible demands. And the Land would be utterly lost.

Then he realized that his inability to remember what had brought him to this place, what had happened to him in this place, was a great blessing, a giving of mercy so clear that it amazed him. Suddenly he understood at least in part why Triock had spoken to him of the *mercy* of new opportunities—and why Triock had refused to share his purpose. He put that purpose aside and looked around the cave for his clothes.

He located them in a heap against one wall, but a moment later he had decided against them. They seemed to represent participation in something that he now wished to eschew. And this white robe was a gift which the dead woman had given him as part and symbol of her larger sacrifice. He accepted it with calm, sad, hollow gratitude.

But he had already started to don his sandals before he realized how badly they reeked of illness. In days of walking, his infection had soaked into the leather, and he was loath to wear the unclean stench. He tossed the sandals back among his discarded apparel. He had come barefoot into this dream, and knew that he would go barefoot and sole-battered out of it again, no matter how he tried to protect himself. In spite of his reawakening caution, he chose not to worry about his feet.

The faint attar of death in the air reminded him that he could not remain in the cave. He drew the robe tight around him and stooped through the entrance to see if he could discover where he was.

Outside, under the gray clouds of day, the sight of the Forest gave him another surge of empty surprise. He recognized Morinmoss; he had crossed this wood once before. His vague knowledge of the Land's geography told him in general terms where he was, but he had no conception of how he had come here. The last thing in his memory was the slow death of Lord Foul's winter.

There was little winter to be seen here. The black trees leaned against each other as if they were rooted interminably in the first gray verges of spring; but the air was brisk rather than bitter, and tough grass grew sufficiently over the clear ground between the trunks. He breathed the Forest smells while he examined his unreasoning confidence, and after a moment he felt sure that Morinmoss also was something he should not fear.

When he turned to reenter the cave, he had chosen at least the first outlines of his new road.

He did not attempt to bury the woman; he had no digging tool and no desire to offer any injury to the soil of the Forest. He wore her robe in part to show his respect for her, but he could not think of any other gesture to make toward her. He wanted to apologize for what he was doing—for what he had done—but had no way to make her hear him. At last he placed her on her bed, arranged her stiff limbs as best he could to give her an appearance of dignity. Then he found a sack among her possessions and packed into it all the food he could find.

After that, he drank the last of her water and left behind the jug to save weight. With a pang of regret, he also left behind the pot of graveling; he knew he would want its warmth, but did not know how to tend it. The knife which lay oddly in the center of the floor he did not take because he had had enough of knives.

Remembering Lena, he lightly kissed the woman's cold, withered cheek. Then he shrugged his way out of the cave, muttering, as if the word were a talisman he had learned from her sacrifice, "Mercy."

He strode away into the day of his new comprehension.

He did not hesitate over the choice of directions. He knew from past experience that the terrain of Morinmoss sloped generally downward from northwest to southwest, toward the Plains of Ra. He followed the slopes with his sack over his shoulder and his heart hollow—steady because it was full of lacks, like the heart of a man who had surrendered himself to the prospect of a colorless future.

Before he had covered two leagues, daylight began to fail in the air, and night fell from the clouds like rain. But Morinmoss roused itself to light his way. And after his long rest, he did not need sleep. He slowed his pace so that he could move without disturbing the dark moss, and went on while the Forest grew lambent and restless around him. Its ancient uneasiness, its half-conscious memory of outrage and immense bereavement, was not directed at him—the perennial mood of the trees almost seemed to stand back as he passed, allowing him along his way—but he felt it nonetheless, heard it muttering through the breeze as if Morinmoss were breathing between clenched teeth. His senses remained truncated, winter-blurred, as they had been before his crisis with Pietten and Lena, but still he could perceive the Forest's sufferance of him. Morinmoss was aware of him and made a special exertion of tolerance on his behalf.

Then he remembered that Garroting Deep also had not raised its hand against him. He remembered Caerroil Wildwood and the Forestal's unwilling disciple. Though he knew himself suffered, permitted, he murmured, "Mercy," to the pale, shining trunks and strove to move carefully, avoiding anything which might give offense to the trees.

His caution limited his progress, and when dawn came he was still wending generally southeast within the woods. But now he was reentering the demesne of winter. Cold snapped in the air, and the trees were bleak. Grass had given way to bare ground. He could see the first thin skiffs of snow through the gloom ahead of him. And as dawn limped into ill day, he began to learn what a gift the white robe was. Its lightness made it easy to wear, yet its special fabric was warm and comfortable, so that it held out the harshness of the wind. He considered it a better gift than any knife or staff or *orcrest*-stone, and he kept it sashed gratefully around him.

Once the tree shine had subsided into daylight, he stopped to rest and eat. But he did not need much rest, and after a frugal meal he was up and moving again. The wind began to gust and flutter around him. In less than a league, he left the last black shelter of the Forest, and went out into Foul's uninterrupted spite.

The wilderness of snow and cold that met his blunt senses seemed unchanged. From the edges of the Forest, the terrain continued to slope gradually downward, through the shallow rumpling of old hills, until it reached the dull river flowing miserably into the northeast. And across his whole view, winter exerted its gray ruination. The frozen ground slumped under the ceaseless rasp of the wind and the weight of the snowdrifts until it looked like irreparable disconsolation or apathy, an abdication of loam and intended verdancy. In spite of his white robe and his recovered strength, he felt the cut of the cold, and he huddled into himself as if the Land's burden were on his shoulders.

For a moment he peered through the wind with moist eyes to choose his direction. He did not know where he was in relation to the shallows where he had crossed the river. But he felt sure that this river was in fact the Roamsedge, the northern boundary of the Plains of Ra. And the terrain off to his left seemed vaguely familiar. If his memory of the Quest for the Staff of Law did not delude him, he was looking down at the Roamsedge Ford.

Leaning against the wind, limping barefoot over the brutalized ground, he made for the Ford as if it were the gateway to his altered purpose.

But the distance was greater than it had appeared from the elevation of the Forest, and his movements were hampered by wind and snow and hill slopes. Noon came before he reached the last ridge west of the Ford.

When his gaze passed over the top of the ridge and down toward the river crossing, he was startled to see a man standing on the bank.

The man's visage was hidden by the hood of a Stonedownor cloak, but he faced squarely toward Covenant with his arms akimbo as if he had been impatiently awaiting the Unbeliever's arrival for some time. Caution urged Covenant to duck out of sight. But almost at once the man gestured brusquely, barking in tones that sounded like a distortion of a voice Covenant should have been able to recognize, "Come, Unbeliever! You have no craft for hiding or flight. I have watched your approach for a league."

Covenant hesitated, but in his hollow surety he was not afraid. After a moment, he shrugged, and started toward the Ford. As he moved down the hillside, he kept his eyes on the waiting man and searched for some clue to the man's identity. At first he guessed that the man represented a part of his lost experience in the Forest and the woman's cave—a part he might never be able to comprehend or evaluate. But then his eyes made out the pattern woven into the shoulders of the Stonedownor cloak. It was a pattern like crossed lightning.

"Triock!" he gasped under his breath. Triock?

He ran over the hard ground, hurried up to the man, caught him by the shoulders. "Triock." An awkward thickness in his throat constricted his voice. "Triock? What are you doing here? How did you get here? What happened?"

As Covenant panted questions at him, the man averted his face so that the hood sheltered his features. His hands leaped to Covenant's wrists, tore Covenant's hands off his shoulders as if their touch were noxious to him. With unmistakable ire, he thrust Covenant away from him. But when he spoke, his barking tone sounded almost casual.

"Well, ur-Lord Covenant, Unbeliever and white gold wielder." He invested the titles with a sarcastic twang. "You have not come far in so many days. Have you rested well in Morinmoss?"

Covenant stared and rubbed his wrists; Triock's anger left a burning sensation in them, like a residue of acid. The pain gave him an instant of doubt, but he recognized Triock's profile beyond the edge of the hood. In his confusion, he could not think of a reason for the Stonedownor's belligerence. "What happened?" he repeated uncertainly. "Did you get in touch with Mhoram? Did you find that Unfettered One?"

Triock kept his face averted. But his fingers flexed and curled like claws, hungry for violence.

Then a wave of sorrow effaced Covenant's confusion. "Did you find Lena?"

With the same hoarse casualness, Triock said, "I followed you because I do not trust your purpose—or your companions. I see that I have not misjudged."

"Did you find Lena?"

"Your vaunted aim against the Despiser is expensive in companions as well as in time. How was the Giant persuaded from your side? Did you leave him" —he sneered—"among the perverse pleasures of Morinmoss?"

"Lena?" Covenant insisted thickly.

Triock's hands jerked to his face as if he meant to claw out his eyes. His palms muffled his voice, made it sound more familiar. "With a spike in her belly. And a man slain at her side." Fierce trembling shook him. But abruptly he dropped his hands, and his tone resumed its mordant insouciance. "Perhaps you will ask me to believe that they slew each other."

Through his empty sorrow, Covenant replied, "It was my fault. She tried to save me. Then I killed him." He felt the incompleteness of this, and added, "He wanted my ring."

"The fool!" Triock barked sharply. "Did he believe he would be permitted to keep it?" But he did not give Covenant time to respond. Quietly again, he asked, "And the Giant?"

"We were ambushed. He stayed behind—so that Lena and I could get away."

A harsh laugh spat between Triock's teeth. "Faithful to the last," he gibed. The next instant, a wild sob convulsed him as if his self-control had snapped—as if a frantic grief had burst the bonds which held it down. But immediately he returned to sarcasm. Showing Covenant a flash of his teeth, he sneered, "It is well that I have come."

"Well?" Covenant breathed. "Triock, what happened to you?"

"Well, forsooth." The man sniffed as if he were fighting tears. "You have lost much time in that place of harm and seduction. With each passing day, the Despiser grows mightier. He straitly binds—" His teeth grinned at Covenant under the shadow of his hood. "Thomas Covenant, your work must be no longer delayed. I have come to take you to Ridjeck Thome."

Covenant gazed intensely at the man. A moment passed while he tested his hollow core and found that it remained sure. Then he bent all his attention toward Triock, tried to drive his truncated sight past its limits, its superficiality, so that he might catch some glimpse of Triock's inner estate. But the winter, and Triock's distraction, foiled him. He saw the averted face, the rigid flex and claw of the fingers, the baring of the white wet teeth, the turmoil, but he could not penetrate beyond them. Some stark travail was upon the Stonedownor. In sympathy and bafflement and self-defense, Covenant said, "Triock, you've got to tell me what happened."

"Must I?"

"Yes."

"Do you threaten me? Will you turn the wild magic against me if I refuse?" Triock winced as if he were genuinely afraid, and an oddly craven grimace flicked like a spasm across his lips. But then he shrugged sharply and turned his back, so that he was facing straight into the wind. "Ask, then."

Threaten? Covenant asked Triock's hunched shoulders. No, no. I don't want it to happen again. I've done enough harm.

"Ask!"

"Did you"—he could hardly get the words through his clogged throat—"did you find that Unfettered One?"

"Yes!"

"Did he contact Mhoram?"

"No!"

"Why not?"

"He did not suffice!"

The bitterness of the words barked along the bitter wind, and Covenant could only repeat, "Triock, what happened?"

"The Unfettered One lacked strength to match the *lomillialor*. He took it from me and could not match it. Yeurquin and Quirrel were lost—more companions lost while you dally and falter!"

Both lost.

"I didn't— How did you find me?"

"This is expensive blood, Covenant. When will it sate you?"

Sate me? Triock! The question hurt him, but he endured it. He had long ago lost the right to take umbrage at anything Triock might say. With difficulty, he asked again, "How did you find me?"

"I waited! Where else could you have gone?"

"Triock." Covenant covered himself with the void of his calm and said, "Triock, look at me."

"I do not wish to look at you."

"Look at me!"

"I have no stomach for the sight."

"Triock!" Covenant placed his hand on the man's shoulder.

Instantly, Triock spun and struck Covenant across the cheek.

The blow did not appear powerful; Triock swung shortly, as if he were trying to pull back his arm. But force erupted at the impact, threw Covenant to the ground several feet away. His cheek stung with a deep pain like vitriol that made his eyes stream. He barely saw Triock flinch, turn and start to flee, then catch himself and stop, waiting across the distance of a dozen yards as if he expected Covenant to hurl a spear through his back.

The pain roared like a rush of black waters in Covenant's head, but he forced himself to sit up, ignored his burning cheek, and said quietly, "I'm not going to Foul's Creche."

"Not?" Surprise spun Triock to face Covenant.

"No." Covenant was vaguely surprised by his own certitude. "I'm going to cross the river—I'm going to try to go south with the Ramen. They might—"

"You dare?" Triock yelled. He seemed livid with fury, but he did not advance toward Covenant. "You cost me my love! My comrades! My home! You slay every glad face of my life! And then you say you will deny the one promise which might recompense? Unbeliever! Do you think I would not kill you for such treachery?"

Covenant shrugged. "Kill me if you want to. It doesn't make any difference." The pain in his face interfered with his concentration, but still he saw the self-contradiction behind Triock's threat. Fear and anger were balanced in the Stonedownor, as if he were two men trapped between flight and attack, straining in opposite directions. Somewhere amid those antagonists was the Triock Covenant remembered. He resisted the roaring in his head and tried to explain so that this Triock might understand.

"The only way you can kill me is if I'm dying in my own world. You saw me—when you summoned me. Maybe you could kill me. But if I'm really dying, it doesn't matter whether you kill me or not. I'll get killed somehow. Dreams are like that.

"But before you decide, let me try to tell you why —why I'm not going to Foul's Creche."

He got painfully to his feet. He wanted to go to Triock, look deeply into the man's face, but Triock's conflicting passions kept him at a distance.

"I'm not exactly innocent. I know that. I told you it was my fault, and it is. But it isn't *all* my fault. Lena and Elena and Atiaran—and Giants and Ranyhyn and Ramen and Bloodguard—and you—it isn't all my fault. All of you made decisions for yourselves. Lena made her own decision when she tried to save me from punishment—after I raped her. Atiaran made her own decision when she helped me get to Revelstone. Elena made her own decision when she drank the EarthBlood. You made your own decision— you decided to be loyal to the Oath of Peace. None of it is entirely my doing."

"You talk as if we exist," Triock growled bitterly.

"As far as my responsibility goes, you do. I don't control my nightmares. Part of me—the part that's talking—is a victim, as you are. Just less innocent.

"But Foul has arranged it all. He—or the part of me that does the dreaming—has been arranging everything from the beginning. He's been manipulating me, and I finally figured out why. He wants this ring —he wants the wild magic. And he knows—knows! —that if he can get me feeling guilty and responsible and miserable enough I'll try to fight him on his own ground—on his own terms.

"I can't win a fight like that. I don't know how to win it. So he wants me to do it. That way he ends up with everything. And I end up like any other suicide.

"Look at me, Triock! Look! You can see that I'm diseased. I'm a leper. It's carved into me so loud anybody could see it. And lepers—commit suicide easily. All they have to do is forget the law of staying alive. That law is simple, selfish, practical caution. Foul's done a pretty good job of making me forget it—that's why you might be able to kill me now if you want to. But if I've got any choice left, the only way I can use it is by remembering who I am. Thomas Covenant, leper. I've got to give up these impossible ideas of trying to make restitution for what I've done. I've got to give up guilt and duty, or whatever it is I'm calling responsibility these days. I've got to give up trying to make myself innocent again. It can't be done. It's suicide to try. And suicide for me is the only absolute, perfect way Foul can win. Without it, he doesn't get the wild magic, and it's just possible that some-where, somehow, he'll run into something that can beat him.

"So I'm not going—I am not going to Foul's Creche. I'm going to do something simple and selfish and practical and cautious instead. I'm going to take care of myself as a leper should. I'll go into the Plains—I'll find the Ramen. They'll take me with them. The Ranyhyn—the Ranyhyn are probably going south already to hide in the mountains. The Ramen will take me with them. Mhoram doesn't know I'm here, so he won't be expecting anything from me.

"Please understand, Triock. My grief for you is— it'll never end. I loved Elena, and I love the Land. But if I can just keep myself alive the way I should— Foul can't win. He can't win."

Triock met this speech queerly across the distance between them. His anger seemed to fade, but it was not replaced by understanding. Instead, a mixture of cunning and desperation gained the upper hand on his desire to flee, so that his voice held a half-hysterical note of cajolery as he said, "Come, Unbeliever—do not take this choice hastily. Let us speak of it calmly. Let me urge"—he looked around as if in search of assistance, then went on hurriedly—"you are hungry and worn. That Forest has exacted a harsh penance— I see it. Let us rest here for a time. We are in no danger. I will build a fire—prepare food for you. We will talk of this choice while it may still be altered."

Why? Covenant wanted to ask. Why have you changed like this? But he already knew too many explanations. And Triock bustled away promptly in search of firewood as if to forestall any questions. The land on this side of the Roamsedge had been wooded at one time, and before long he had collected a large pile of dead brush and bushes, which he placed in the shelter of a hill a short distance from the Ford. All the time, he kept his face averted from Covenant.

When he was satisfied with his quantity of wood, he stooped in front of the pile with his hands hidden as if for some obscure reason he did not want Covenant to see how he started the fire. As soon as flames had begun to spread through the brush, he positioned himself on the far side of the fire and urged Covenant to approach its warmth.

Covenant acquiesced gladly enough. His robe could not keep the cold out of his hands and feet; he could hardly refuse a fire. And he could hardly refuse Triock's desire to discuss his decision. His debt to Triock was large—not easily borne. He sat down within the radiant balm of the fire opposite Triock and silently watched him prepare a meal.

As he worked, Triock mumbled to himself in a tone that made Covenant feel oddly uncomfortable. His movements seemed awkward, as if he were trying to conceal arcane gestures while he handled the food. He avoided Covenant's gaze, but whenever Covenant looked away, he could feel Triock's eyes flick furtively over him and flinch away. He was startled when Triock said abruptly, "So you have given up hate."

"Given up—?" He had not thought of the matter in those terms before. "Maybe I have. It doesn't seem like a very good answer. I mean, aside from the fact that there's no room for it in—in the law of leprosy. Hate, humiliation, revenge—I make a mistake every time I let them touch me. I risk my life. And love, too, if you want to know the truth. But aside from that. It doesn't seem that I could beat Foul that way. I'm just a man. I can't hate—forever—as he can. And"—he forced himself to articulate a new perception—"my hate isn't pure. It's corrupt because part of me always hates me instead of him. Always."

Triock placed a stoneware pot of stew in the fire to cook and said in a tone of eerie conviction, "It is the only answer. Look about you. Health, love, duty —none suffice against this winter. Only those who hate are immortal."

"Immortal?"

"Certainly. Death claims all else in the end. How else do the Despiser and—and his"—he said the name as if it dismayed him—"Ravers endure? They hate." In his hoarse, barking tone, the word took on a wide range of passion and violence, as if indeed it were the one word of truth and transcendence.

The savor of the stew began to reach Covenant. He found that he was hungry—and that his inner quiescence covered even Triock's queer asseverations. He stretched out his legs, reclined on one elbow. "Hate," he sighed softly, reducing the word to manageable dimensions. "Is that it, Triock? I think—I think I've spent this whole thing—dream, delusion, fact, whatever you want to call it—I've spent it all looking for a good answer to death. Resistance, rape—ridicule —love—hate? Is that it? Is that your answer?"

"Do not mistake me," Triock replied. "I do not hate death."

Covenant gazed into the dance of the fire for a moment and let the aroma of the stew remind him of deep, sure, empty peace. Then he said as if he were completing a litany, "What do you hate?"

"I hate life."

Brusquely, Triock spooned stew into bowls. When he handed a bowl around the fire to Covenant, his hand shook. But as soon as he had returned to his hooded covert beyond the flames, he snapped angrily, "Do you think I am unjustified? You, Unbeliever?"

No. No. Covenant could not lift up his head against the accusation in Triock's voice. Hate me as much as you need to, he breathed into the crackling of the fire and the steaming stew. I don't want anyone else to sacrifice himself for me. Without looking up, he began to eat.

The taste of the stew was not unpleasant, but it had a disconcerting under-flavor which made it difficult to swallow. Yet once a mouthful had passed his throat, he found it warm and reassuring. Slowly, drowsiness spread outward from it. After a few moments, he was vaguely surprised to see that he had emptied the bowl.

He put it aside and lay down on his back. Now the fire seemed to grow higher and hotter, so that he only caught glimpses of Triock watching him keenly through the weaving spring and crackle of the flames. He was beginning to rest when he heard Triock say through the fiery veil, "Unbeliever, why do you not resume your journey to Foul's Creche? Surely you do not believe that the Despiser will permit your flight— after he has striven so to bring about this confrontation of which you speak."

"He won't want me to get away," Covenant replied emptily, surely. "But I think he's too busy doing other things to stop me. And if I can slip through his fingers just once, he'll let me go—at least for a while. I've—I've already done so much for him. The only thing he still wants from me is the ring. If I don't threaten him with it, he'll let me go while he fights the Lords. And then he'll be too late. I'll be gone as far as the Ranyhyn can take me."

"But what of this—this Creator"—Triock spat the word—"who they say also chose you. Has he no hold upon you?"

Sleepiness only strengthened Covenant's confidence. "I don't owe him anything. He chose me for this—I didn't choose it or him. If he doesn't like what I do, let him find someone else."

"But what of the people who have died and suffered for you?" Triock's anger returned, and he ripped the words as if they were illustrations of meaning which he tore from the walls of a secret Hall of Gifts deep within him. "How will you supply the significance they have earned from you? They have lost themselves in bootless death if you flee."

I know, Covenant sighed to the sharp flames and the wind. We're all futile, alive or dead. He made an effort to speak clearly through his coming sleep. "What kind of significance will it give them if I commit suicide? They won't thank me for throwing away —something that cost them so much. While I'm alive" —he lost the thought, then recovered it—"while I'm alive, the Land is still alive."

"Because it is your dream!"

Yes. For that reason among others.

Covenant experienced a moment of stillness before the passion of Triock's response penetrated him. Then he hauled himself up and peered blearily through the fire at the Stonedownor. Because he could think of nothing else to say, he murmured, "Why don't you get some rest? You probably exhausted yourself waiting for me."

"I have given up sleep."

Covenant yawned. "Don't be ridiculous. What do you think you are? A Bloodguard?"

In answer, Triock laughed tautly, like a cord about to snap.

The sound made Covenant feel that something was wrong, that he should not have been so irresistibly sleepy. He should have had the strength to meet Triock's distress responsibly. But he could hardly keep his eyes open. Rubbing his stiff face, he said, "Why don't you admit it? You're afraid I'll sneak off as soon as you stop watching me."

"I do not mean to lose you now, Thomas Covenant."

"I wouldn't—do that to you." Covenant blinked and found his cheek resting against the hard ground. He could not remember having reclined. Wake up, he said to himself without conviction. Sleep seemed to be falling on him out of the grayness of the sky. He mumbled, "I still don't know how you found me." But he was asleep before the sound of his voice reached his ears.

He felt he had been unconscious for only a moment when he became aware on a half-subliminal level of darknesses thronging toward him out of the winter, as abysmal as death. Against them came faint alien gleams of music which he recognized and did not remember. They melodied themselves about him in blue-green intervals that he could neither hear nor see. They appeared weak, elusive, like voices calling to him across a great distance. But they were insistent; they nudged him, sang to him, plied him toward consciousness. Through his uncomprehending stupor, they danced a blind, voiceless warning of peril.

To his own surprise, he heard himself muttering: He drugged me. By hell! that crazy man drugged me. The assertion made no sense. How had he arrived at such a conclusion? Triock was an honest man, frank and magnanimous in grief—a man who clove to mercy and peace despite their cost to himself.

He drugged me.

Where had that conviction come from? Covenant fumbled with numb fingers through his unconsciousness, while an unshakable sense of peril clutched his heart. Darkness and harm crowded toward him. Behind his sleep—behind the glaucous music—he seemed to see Triock's campfire still burning.

How did he light that fire?

How did he find me?

The urgent gleams were trying to tell him things he could not hear. Triock was a danger. Triock had drugged him. He must get up and flee—flee somewhere—flee into the Forest.

He struggled into a sitting position, wrenched his eyes open. He faced the low campfire in the last dead light of evening. Winter blew about him as if it were salivating gall. He could smell the approach of snow; already a few fetid flakes were visible at the edges of the firelight. Triock sat cross-legged opposite him, stared at him out of the smoldering abomination of his eyes.

In the air before Covenant danced faint glaucous gleams, fragments of inaudible song. They were shrill with insistence: flee! flee!

"What is it?" He tried to beat off the clinging hands of slumber. "What are they doing?"

"Send it away," Triock answered in a voice full of fear and loathing. "Rid yourself of it. He cannot claim you now."

"What is it?" Covenant lurched to his feet and stood trembling, hardly able to contain the panic in his muscles. "What's happening?"

"It is the voice of a Forestal." Triock spoke simply, but every angle of his inflection expressed execration. He jumped erect and balanced himself as if he meant to give chase when Covenant began to run. "Garroting Deep has sent Caer-Caveral to Morinmoss. But he cannot claim you. I can"—his voice shook—"I cannot permit it."

"Claim? Permit?" The peril gripping Covenant's heart tightened until he gasped. Something in him that he could not remember urged him to trust the gleams. "You drugged me!"

"So that you would not escape!" White, rigid fear clenched Triock, and he stammered through drawn lips, "He urges you to destroy me. He cannot reach far from Morinmoss, but he urges—the white gold—! Ah!" Abruptly, his voice sharpened into a shriek. "Do not toy with me! I cannot—! Destroy me and have done! I cannot endure it!"

The cries cut through Covenant's own dread. His distress receded, and he found himself grieving for the Stonedownor. Across the urging of the gleams, he breathed thickly, "Destroy you? Don't you know that you're safe from me? Don't you understand that I haven't got one godforsaken idea how to use this—this white gold? I couldn't hurt you if that were my heart's sole desire."

"What?" Triock howled. "Still? Have I feared you for nothing?"

"For nothing," groaned Covenant.

Triock gaped bleakly out from under his hood, then threw back his head and began to laugh. Mordant glee barked through his teeth, making the music shiver as if its abhorrence were no less than his. "Powerless!" he laughed. "By the mirth of my master! Powerless!"

Chuckling savagely, he started toward Covenant.

At once, the silent song rushed gleaming between them. But Triock advanced against the lights. "Begone!" he growled. "You also will pay for your part in this." With a deft movement, he caught one spangle in each fist. Their wailing shimmered in the air as he crushed them between his fingers.

Ringing like broken crystal, the rest of the music vanished.

Covenant reeled as if an unseen support had been snatched away. He flung up his hands against Triock's approach, stumbled backward. But the man did not touch him. Instead, he stamped one foot on the hard ground. The earth bucked under Covenant, stretched him at Triock's feet.

Then Triock threw off his hood. His visage was littered with broken possibilities, wrecked faiths and loves, but behind his features his skull shone with pale malice. The backs of his eyes were as black as night, and his teeth gaped as if they were hungry for the taste of flesh. Leering down at Covenant, he smirked,

"No, groveler. I will not strike you again. The time for masquerading has ended. My master may frown upon me if I harm you now."

"Master?" Covenant croaked.

"I am *turiya* Rayer, also called Herem—and Kinslaughterer—and Triock." He laughed again grotesquely. "This guise has served me well, though 'Triock' is not pleased. Behold me, groveler! I need no longer let his form and thoughts disguise me. You are powerless. Ah, I savor that jest! So now I permit you to know me as I am. It was I who slew the Giants of Seareach—I who slew the Unfettered One as he sought to warn that fool Mhoram—I who have captured the white gold! Brothers! I will sit upon the master's right hand and rule the universe!"

As he gloated, he reached into his cloak and drew out the *lomillialor* rod. Brandishing it in Covenant's face, he barked, "Do you see it? High Wood! I spit on it. The test of truth is not a match for me." Then he gripped it between his hands as if he meant to break it, and shouted quick cruel words over it. It caught fire, blazed for an instant in red agony, and fell into cinders.

Gleefully, the Raver snarled at Covenant, "Thus I signal your doom, as I was commanded. Breathe swiftly, groveler. There are only moments left to you."

Covenant's muscles trembled as if the ground still pitched under him, but he braced himself, struggled to his feet. He felt stunned with horror, helpless. Yet in the back of his mind he strained to find an escape. "The ring," he panted. "Why don't you just take the ring?"

A black response leaped in Triock's eyes. "Would you give it to me?"

"No!" He thought desperately that if he could goad Triock into some act of power, Caer-Caveral's glaucous song might return to aid him.

"Then I will tell you, groveler, that I do not take your ring because the command of my master is too strong. He does not choose that I should have such power. In other times, he did not bind us so straitly, and we were free to work his will in our several ways. But he claims—and—I obey."

"Try to take it!" Covenant panted. "Be the ruler of the universe yourself. Why should he have it?"

For an instant, he thought he saw something like regret in Triock's face. But the Raver only snarled, "Because the Law of Death has been broken, and he is not alone. There are eyes of compulsion upon me even now—eyes which may not be defied." His leer of hunger returned. "Perhaps you will see them before you are slain—before my brother and I tear your living heart from you and eat it in your last sight."

He laughed harshly, and as if in answer the darkness around the campfire grew thicker. The night blackened like an accumulation of spite, then drew taut and formed discrete figures that came forward. Covenant heard their feet rustling over the cold ground. He whirled, and found himself surrounded by ur-viles.

When their eyeless faces felt his stricken stare, they hesitated for an instant. Their wide, drooling nostrils quivered as they tasted the air for signs of power, evidence of wild magic. Then they rushed forward and overwhelmed him.

Livid red blades wheeled above him like the shattering of the heavens. But instead of stabbing him, they pressed flat against his forehead. Red waves of horror crashed through him. He screamed once and went limp in the grasp of the ur-viles.

FIFTEEN: "Lord Mhoram's Victory"

THE exertion of hauling the dead forms from the ground and throwing them at Revelstone had exhausted *samadhi* Satansfist, drained him until he could no longer sustain that expenditure of force. He had seen High Lord's Furl torn from its flagpole atop the tower by his Cavewights. He knew he had met at least part of his master's objective in this assault. While his forces held the tower—while tons of sand blocked the inner gates of the Keep—while winter barrened the upland plateau above Revelstone—the Lords and all their people were doomed. They could not feed themselves within those stone walls indefinitely. If last came to last, the Giant-Raver knew that he could through patience alone make the great Keep into one reeking tomb or crypt. He let his dead collapse into sand.

Yet his failure to burst those inner gates enraged him, made him pant for recompense even though he lacked the strength to assail the walls himself. He was a Raver, insatiable for blood despite the mortal limits of the Giantish body he occupied. And other things compelled him also. There was an implacable coercion in the wind, a demand which brooked no failure, however partial or eventually meaningless.

As the dead fell apart, Satansfist ordered his long-leashed army to the attack.

With a howl that shivered the air, echoed savagely

off the carven walls, beat against the battlements like an ululation of fangs and claws and hungry blades, the Despiser's hordes charged. They swept up through the foothills like a shrill gray flood and hurled themselves at Revelstone.

Lord Foul's Stone-spawned creatures led the attack —not because they were effective against granite walls and abutments, but because they were expendable. The Raver's army included twice a hundred thousand of them, and more arrived every day, marching to battle from Foul's Creche through the Center Plains. So *samadhi* used them to absorb the defense of the Keep, thus protecting his Cavewights and ur-viles. Thousands of perverted creatures fell with arrows, spears, javelins jutting from them, but many many thousands more forged ahead. And behind them came the forces which knew how to damage Revelstone.

In moments, the charge hit. Rabid, rockwise Cavewights found crafty holds in the stone, vaulted themselves up onto the lowest battlements and balconies. Mighty ur-vile wedges used their black vitriol to wipe clear the parapets above them, then pounced upward on sturdy wooden ladders brought to the walls by other creatures. Within a short time, Revelstone was under assault all along its south and north faces.

But the ancient Giants who made Lord's Keep had built well to defend against such an attack. Even the lowest parapets were high off the ground; they could be sealed off, so that the attackers were denied access to the city; they were defended by positions higher still in the walls. And Warmark Quaan had drilled the Warward year after year, preparing it for just this kind of battle. The prearranged defenses of the Keep sprang into action instantly as alarms sounded throughout the city. Warriors left secondary tasks and ran to the battlements; relays formed to supply the upper defenses with arrows and other weapons; concerted Eoman charged the Cavewights and ur-viles which breached the lower abutments. Then came Lorewardens, Hirebrands, Gravelingases. Lorewardens repulsed the attacks with songs of power, while Hirebrands set fire to the ladders, and Gravelingases

braced the walls themselves against the strength of the
Cavewights.

As he commanded the struggle from a coign in the
upper walls, Quaan soon saw that his warriors could
have repulsed this assault if they had not been outnumbered thirty or more to one—if every life in his
army had not been so vital, and every life in the
Raver's so insignificant. But the Warward was outnumbered; it needed help. In response to the frag-
mentary reports which reached him from the Close—
reports of fire and power and immense relief—he sent
an urgent messenger to summon the Lords to Revelstone's aid.

The messenger found High Lord Mhoram in the
Close, but Mhoram did not respond to Quaan's call. It
only reached the outskirts of his mind, and he held it
gently distant, away from himself. When he heard one
of the guards explain to the messenger what had tran-
spired in the fire-ruined Close, he let his own awareness of the battle slip away—let all thought of the
present danger drop from him, and gave himself to
the melding of the Lords.

They sat on the slumped floor around the graveling
pit with their staffs on the stone before them—Trevor
and Loerya on Mhoram's left, Amatin on his right. In
his trembling hands, the *krill* blazed in hot affirmation
of white gold. Yet he barely saw the light; his eyes
were heat-scorched, and he was blinded by tears of
release that would not stop. Through the silent contact
of the meld, he spread strength about him, and shared
knowledge which had burdened him more than he
had ever realized. He told his fellow Lords how he
had been able to remove the *krill* from its stone rest,
and why now it did not burn his vulnerable flesh.

He could feel Amatin shrink from what he said,
feel Trevor shake with a pain that only in part came
from his injury, feel Loerya appraise his communication as she might have appraised any new weapon. To
each of them, he gave himself; he showed them his
conviction, his understanding, his strength. And he
held the proof in his hands, so that they could not
doubt him. With such evidence shining amid the rav-

age of the Close, they followed the process which had led him to his secret knowledge and shared the dismay which had taught him to keep it secret.

Finally, Lord Amatin framed her question aloud. It was too large for silence; it required utterance, so that Revelstone itself could hear it. She swallowed awkwardly, then floated words in the untarnished acoustics of the chamber. "So it is we—we ourselves who have— for so many generations the Lords themselves have inured themselves to the power of Kevin's Lore."

"Yes, Lord," Mhoram whispered, knowing that everyone in the Close could hear him.

"The Oath of Peace has prevented—"

"Yes, Lord."

Her breathing shuddered for a moment. "Then we are lost."

Mhoram felt the lorn dilemma in her words and stood up within himself, pulling the authority of his High Lordship about his shoulders. "No."

"Without power, we are lost," she countered. "Without the Oath of Peace, we are not who we are, and we are lost."

"Thomas Covenant has returned," responded Loerya.

Brusquely, Amatin put this hope aside. "Nevertheless. Either he has no power, or his power violates the Peace with which we have striven to serve the Land. Thus also we are lost."

"No," the High Lord repeated. "Not lost. We—and ur-Lord Covenant—must find the wisdom to attain both Peace and power. We must retain our knowledge of who we are, or we will despair as Kevin Landwaster despaired, in Desecration. Yet we must also retain this knowledge of power, or we will have failed to do our utmost for the Land. Perhaps the future Lords will find that they must turn from Kevin's Lore —that they must find lore of their own, lore which is not so apt for destruction. We have no time for such a quest. Knowing the peril of this power, we must cling to ourselves all the more, so that we do not betray the Land."

His words seemed to ring in the Close, and time

passed before Amatin said painfully, "You offer us things which contradict each other, and tell us that we must preserve both, achieve both together. Such counsel is easily spoken."

In silence, the High Lord strove to share with her his sense of how the contradiction might be mastered, made whole; he let his love for the Land, for Revelstone, for her, flow openly into her mind. And he smiled as he heard Lord Trevor say slowly, "It may be done. I have felt something akin to it. What little strength I have returned to me when the Keep's need became larger for me than my fear of the Keep's foe."

"Fear," Loerya echoed in assent.

And Mhoram added, "Fear—or hatred."

A moment later, Amatin began to weep quietly in comprehension. With Loerya and Trevor, Mhoram wrapped courage around her and held her until her dread of her own danger, her own capacity to Desecrate the Land, relaxed. Then the High Lord put down the *krill* and opened his eyes to the Close.

Dimly, blurrily, his sight made out Hearthrall Tohrm and Trell. Trell still huddled within himself, shirking the horror of what he had done. And Torhm cradled his head, commiserating in *rhadhamaerl* grief with the torment of soul which could turn a Gravelingas against beloved stone. They were silent, and Mhoram gazed at them as if he were to blame for Trell's plight.

But before he could speak, another messenger from Warmark Quaan arrived in the Close, demanded notice. When the High Lord looked up at him, the messenger repeated Quaan's urgent call for help.

"Soon," Mhoram sighed, "soon. Tell my friend that we will come when we are able. The Lord Trevor is wounded. I am"—with a brief gesture, he indicated the scalded skin of his head—"the Lord Amatin and I must have food and rest. And the Lord Loerya—"

"I will go," Loerya said firmly. "I have not yet fought as I should for Revelstone." To the messenger, she responded, "Take me to the place of greatest need, then carry the High Lord's reply to Warmark Quaan." Moving confidently, as if the new discovery of power answered her darkest doubts, she climbed the stairs and followed the warrior away toward the south wall of the Keep.

As she departed, she sent the guards to call the Healers and bring food. The other Lords were left alone for a short time, and Tohrm took that opportunity to ask Mhoram what was to be done with Trell.

Mhoram gazed around the ruined galleries as if he were trying to estimate the degree to which he had failed Trell. He knew that generations of *rhadhamaerl* work would be required to restore some measure of the chamber's useful rightness, and tears blurred his vision again as he said to Tohrm, "The Healers must work with him. Perhaps they will be able to restore his mind."

"What will be the good? How will he endure the knowledge of what he has done?"

"We must help him to endure. I must help him. We must attempt all healing, no matter how difficult. And I who have failed him cannot deny the burden of his need now."

"Failed him?" Trevor asked. The pain of his injury had drawn the blood from his face, but he had not lost the mood which had inspired him to bear such a great share of the Keep's defense. "In what way? You did not cause his despair. Had you treated him with distrust, you would have achieved nothing but the confirmation of his distress. Distrust—vindicates itself."

Mhoram nodded. "And I distrusted—I distrusted all. I kept knowledge secret even while I knew the keeping wrong. It is fortunate that the harm was no greater."

"Yet you could not prevent—"

"Perhaps. And perhaps—if I had shared my knowledge with him, so that he had known his peril—known — Perhaps he might have found the strength to remember himself—remember that he was a Gravelingas of the *rhadhamaerl*, a lover of stone."

Tohrm agreed stiffly, and his sympathy for Trell made him say, "You have erred, High Lord."

"Yes, Hearthrall," Mhoram replied with deep gentleness in his voice. "I am who I am—both human and mortal. I have—much to learn."

Tohrm blinked fiercely, ducked his head. The tautness of his shoulders looked like anger, but Mhoram had shared an ordeal with the Hearthrall, and understood him better.

A moment later, several Healers hurried into the Close. They brought with them two stretchers, and carefully bore Trell away in one. Lord Trevor they carried in the other, peremptorily ignoring his protests. Tohrm went with Trell. Soon Mhoram and Amatin were left with the warrior who brought their food, and a Healer who softly applied a soothing ointment to the High Lord's burns.

Once Mhoram's hurts had been treated, he dismissed the warrior and the Healer. He knew that Amatin would want to speak with him, and he cleared the way for her before he began to eat. Then he turned to the food. Through his weariness, he ate deliberately, husbanding his strength so that when he was done he would be able to return to his work.

Lord Amatin matched his silence; she seemed to match the very rhythm of his jaws, as if his example were her only support in the face of a previously unguessed peril. Mhoram sensed that her years of devotion to Kevin's Wards had left her peculiarly unprepared for what he had told her; her trust in the Lore of the Old Lords had been exceedingly great. So he kept silent while he ate; and when he was done, he remained still, resting himself while he waited for her to speak what was in her heart.

But her question, when it came, took a form he had not anticipated. "High Lord," she said with a covert nod toward the *krill*, "if Thomas Covenant has returned to the Land—who summoned him? How was that call performed? And where is he?"

"Amatin—" Mhoram began.

"Who but the Despiser could do such a thing?"

"There are—"

"And if this is not Lord Foul's doing, then where has Covenant appeared? How can he aid us if he is not here?"

"He will not aid us." Mhoram spoke firmly to stop the tumble of her questions. "If there is help to be found in him, it will be aid for the Land, not aid for us against this siege. There are other places from which he may serve the Land—yes, and other summoners also. We and Lord Foul are not the only powers. The Creator himself may act to meet this need."

Her waifish eyes probed him, trying to locate the source of his serenity. "I lack your faith in this Creator. Even if such a being lives, the Law which preserves the Earth precludes— Do not the legends say that if the Creator were to break the arch of Time to place his hand upon the Earth, then the arch and all things in it would come to an end, and the Despiser would be set free?"

"That is said," Mhoram affirmed. "I do not doubt it. Yet the doom of any creation is upon the head of its Creator. Our work is enough for us. We need not weary ourselves with the burdens of gods."

Amatin sighed. "You speak with conviction, High Lord. If I were to say such things, they would sound glib."

"Then do not say them. I speak only of what gives me courage. You are a different person and will have a different courage. Only remember that you are a Lord, a servant of the Land—remember the love that brought you to this work, and do not falter."

"Yes, High Lord," she replied, looking intensely into him. "Yet I do not trust this power which makes Desecration possible. I will not hazard it."

Her gaze turned him back to the *krill*. Its white gem flamed at him like the light of a paradox, a promise of life and death. Slowly, he reached out and touched its hilt. But his exaltation had faded, and the *krill*'s heat made him withdraw his hand.

He smiled crookedly. "Yes," he breathed as if he were speaking to the blade, "it is a hazard. I am very afraid." Carefully, he took a cloth from within his robe; carefully, he wrapped the *krill* and set it aside until it could be taken to a place where the Lorewardens could study it. Then he glanced up and saw that Amatin was trying to smile also.

"Come, sister Amatin," he said to her bravery, "we have delayed our work too long."

Together, they made their way to the battle, and with Lord Loerya they called fire from their staffs to throw back the hordes of the Despiser.

The three were joined late in the afternoon by a bandaged and hobbling Trevor. But by that time, Revelstone had survived the worst frenzy of Satansfist's assault. The Lords had given the Warward the support it needed. Under Quaan's stubborn command, the warriors held back the onslaught. Wherever the Lords worked, the casualties among the defenders dropped almost to nothing, and the losses of the attackers increased vastly. In this kind of battle, the ur-viles could not focus their power effectively. As a result, the Lords were able to wreak a prodigious ruin among the Cavewights and other creatures. Before the shrouded day had limped into night, *samadhi* Raver called back his forces.

But this time he did not allow the Keep to rest. His attacks began again shortly after dark. Under the cover of cold winter blackness, ur-viles rushed forward to throw liquid vehemence at the battlements, and behind them tight companies of creatures charged, carrying shields and ladders. Gone now was the haphazard fury of the assault, the unconcerted wild attempt to breach the whole Keep at once. In its place were precision and purpose. Growling with hunger, the hordes shaped themselves to the task of wearing down Revelstone as swiftly and efficiently as possible.

In the days that followed, there was no let to the fighting. Satansfist controlled his assaults so that his losses did not significantly outrun the constant arrival of his reinforcements; but he exerted pressure remorselessly, allowing the warriors no respite in which to recover. Despite Quaan's best efforts to rotate his Eoman and Eoward, so that each could rest in turn, the Warward grew more and more weary—and weary warriors were more easily slain. And those who fell could not be replaced.

But the Warward did not have to carry the burden of this battle alone. Gravelingases and Hirebrands and

Lorewardens fought as well. People who had no other urgent work—homeless farmers and Cattleherds, artists, even older children—took over supporting tasks; they supplied arrows and other weapons, stood sentry duty, ran messages. Thus many Eoman were freed for either combat or rest. And the Lords rushed into action whenever Quaan requested their aid. They were potent and compelling; in their separate ways, they fought with the hard strength of people who knew themselves capable of Desecration and did not intend to be driven to that extreme.

Thus Lord's Keep endured. Eoman after Eoman fell in battle every day; food stores shrank; the Healers' supplies of herbs and poultices dwindled. Strain carved the faces of the people, cut away comfortable flesh until their skulls seemed to be covered by nothing but pressure and apprehension. But Revelstone protected its inhabitants, and they endured.

At first, the Lords concentrated their attention on the needs of the battle. Instinctively, they shied away from their dangerous knowledge. They spent their energy in work and fighting, rather than in studying last resorts. But when the continuous adumbrations of assault had echoed through the Keep for six days, High Lord Mhoram found that he had begun to dread the moment when Satansfist would change his tactics —when the Raver and his master were ready to use the Stone and the Staff again. And during the seventh night, Mhoram's sleep was troubled by dim dreams like shadows of his former visionary nightmares. Time and again, he felt that he could almost hear somewhere in the depths of his soul the sound of an Unfettered One screaming. He awoke in an inchoate sweat, and hastened upland to see if anything had happened to the Unfettered One of Glimmermere.

The One was safe and well, as were Loerya's daughters. But this did not relieve Mhoram. It left a chill in the marrow of his bones like an echo of winter. He felt sure that someone, somewhere, had been slain in torment. Straightening himself against the shiver of dread, he called the other Lords to a Council, where for the first time he raised the question of how their new knowledge could be used against the Despiser.

His question sparked unspoken trepidations in them all. Amatin stared widely at the High Lord, Trevor winced, Loerya studied her hands—and Mhoram felt the acuteness of their reaction as if they were saying, *Do you think then that we should repeat the work of Kevin Landwaster?* But he knew they did not intend that accusation. He waited for them, and at last Loerya found her voice. "When you defended the Close—you worked against another's wrong. How will you control this power if you initiate it?"

Mhoram had no answer.

Shortly, Trevor forced himself to add, "We have nothing through which we could channel such might. It is in my heart that our staffs would not suffice—they would not be strong to control power of that extent. We lack the Staff of Law, and I know of no other tool equal to this demand."

"And," Amatin said sharply, "this knowledge in which you dare to put your faith did not suffice for High Lord Kevin son of Loric. It only increased the cost of his despair. I have—I have given my life to his Lore, and I speak truly. Such power is a snare and a delusion. It cannot be controlled. It strikes the hand that wields it. Better to die in the name of Peace than to buy one day of survival at the cost of such peril!"

Again, Mhoram had no answer. He could not name the reasons behind his question. Only the cold foreboding in his bones impelled him, told him that unknown horrors stalked the Land in places far distant from Revelstone. When Amatin concluded grimly, "Do you fear that ur-Lord Covenant may yet Desecrate us?" he could not deny that he was afraid.

So the Council ended without issue, and the Lords went back to the defense of the Keep.

Still the fighting went on without surcease. For four more days, the Lords wielded their staff fire with all the might and cunning they could conceive—and the Warward drove itself beyond its weariness as if it could not be daunted—and the other people of Revelstone did their utmost to hurl Cavewights, ur-viles, Stone-spawn, from the walls. But Satansfist did not relent. He pressed his assault as if his losses were meaningless, spent whole companies of his creatures to do any kind of damage to the city, however small. And the accumulating price that Lord's Keep paid for its endurance grew more terrible day by day.

During the fifth day, Mhoram withdrew from the battle to inspect the condition of the city. Warmark Quaan joined him, and when they had seen the fatal diminishment of the stores, had taken the toll of lost lives, Quaan met Mhoram's gaze squarely and said with a tremor in his brusque voice, "We will fall. If this Raver does not raise another finger against us, still we will fall."

Mhoram held his old friend's eyes. "How long can we hold?"

"Thirty days—at most. No more. Forty—if we deny food to the ill, and the injured, and the infirm."

"We will not deny food to any who yet live."

"Thirty, then. Less, if my warriors lose strength and permit any breach of the walls." He faltered and his eyes fell. "High Lord, does it come to this? Is this the end—for us—for the Land?"

Mhoram put a firm hand on Quaan's shoulder. "No, my friend. We have not come to the last of ourselves. And the Unbeliever—Do not forget Thomas Covenant."

That name brought back Quaan's war-hardness. "I would forget him if I could. He will—"

"Softly, Warmark," Mhoram interrupted evenly. "Do not be abrupt to prophesy doom. There are mysteries in the Earth of which we know nothing."

After a moment, Quaan murmured, "Do you yet trust him?"

The High Lord did not hesitate. "I trust that Despite is not the sum of life."

Quaan gazed back into this answer as if he were trying to find its wellspring. Some protest or plea moved in his face; but before he could speak, a messenger came to recall him to the fighting. At once, he turned and strode away.

Mhoram watched his stern back for a moment, then bestirred himself to visit the Healers. He wanted to know if any progress had been made with Trell Atiaran-mate.

In the low groaning hall which the Healers had made into a hospital for the hundreds of injured men and women, Mhoram found the big Gravelingas sprawled like a wreck on a pallet in the center of the floor. A fierce brain-fever had wasted him. To Mhoram's cold dread, he looked like the incarnated fate of all Covenant's victims—a fleshless future crouched in ambush for the Land. The High Lord's hands trembled. He did not believe he could bear to watch that ineluctable ravage happen.

"At first, we placed him near the wall," one of the attendants said softly, "so that he would be near stone. But he recoiled from it in terror. Therefore we have laid him here. He does not recover—but he no longer shrieks. Our efforts to succor him are confounded."

"Covenant will make restitution," Mhoram breathed in answer, as if the attendant had said something else. "He must."

Trembling, he turned away, and tried to find relief for his dismay in the struggle of Revelstone.

The next night, *samadhi* changed his tactics. Under cover of darkness, a band of Cavewights rushed forward and clambered up onto one of the main battlements, and when warriors ran out to meet the attack, two ur-vile wedges hidden in the night near the walls swiftly formed Forbiddings across the ends of the battlement, thus trapping the warriors, preventing any escape or rescue. Two Eoman were caught and slaughtered by the ur-viles before Lord Amatin was able to break down one of the Forbiddings.

The same pattern was repeated simultaneously at several points around the Keep.

Warmark Quaan had lost more than eightscore warriors before he grasped the purpose of these tactics. They were not intended to break into Revelstone, but rather to kill defenders.

So the Lords were compelled to bear the brunt of defending against these new assaults; a Forbidding was an exercise of power which only they were equipped to counter. As long as darkness covered the approach of the ur-viles, the attacks continued, allowing the Lords no chance to rest. And when dawn came, Sheol Satansfist resumed the previous strategy of his assault.

After four nights of this, Mhoram and his comrades were near exhaustion. Each Forbidding cost two of them an arduous exertion; one Lord could not counteract the work of three- or fivescore ur-viles swiftly enough. As a result, Amatin was now as pale and hollow-eyed as an invalid; Loerya's once-sturdy muscles seemed to hang like ropes of mortality on her bones; and Trevor's eyes flinched at everything he saw, as if even in the deepest safety of the Keep he was surrounded by ghouls. Mhoram himself felt that he had a great weight leaning like misery against his heart. They could all taste the accuracy of Quaan's dire predictions, and they were sickening on the flavor.

During a brief moment of dazed half-sleep late that fourth night, the High Lord found himself murmuring, "Covenant, Covenant," as if he were trying to remind the Unbeliever of a promise.

But the next morning the attacks stopped. A silence like the quietude of open graves blew into Revelstone on the wind. All the creatures had returned to their encampment, and in their absence Revelstone panted and quivered like a scourged prisoner between lashes. Mhoram took the opportunity to eat, but he put food into his mouth without seeing it and chewed without tasting it. In the back of his mind, he was trying to measure the remnant of his endurance. Yet he responded immediately when a messenger hastened up to him, informed him that *samadhi* Raver was approaching the Keep alone.

Protected by flanks of archers from any attack by the enemy occupying the tower, Mhoram and the other Lords went to one of the high balconies near the eastward point of the Keep and faced Satansfist.

The Giant-Raver approached sardonically, with a swagger of confidence and a spring of contempt in his stride. His huge fist gripped his fragment of the Stone, and it steamed frigidly in the freezing air. He stopped just beyond effective bow range, leered up at the Lords, and shouted stertorously, "Hail, Lords! I give you greeting! Are you well?"

"Well!" Quaan grated under his breath. "Let him come five paces nearer, and I will show him 'well.' "

"My master is concerned for you!" *samadhi* continued. "He fears that you have begun to suffer in this unnecessary conflict!"

The High Lord's eyes glinted at this gibe. "Your master lives for the suffering of others! Do you wish us to believe that he has eschewed Despite?"

"He is amazed and saddened that you resist him. Do you still not see that he is the one word of truth in this misformed world? His is the only strength—the one right. The Creator of the Earth is a being of disdain and cruelty! All who are not folly-blind know this. All who are not cowards in the face of the truth know that Lord Foul is the only truth. Has your suffering taught you nothing? Has Thomas Covenant taught you nothing? Surrender, I say! Give up this perverse and self-made misery—surrender! I swear to you that you will stand as my equals in the service of Lord Foul!"

In spite of his mordant sarcasm, the Raver's voice carried a strange power of persuasion. The might of the Stone was in his words, compelling his hearers to submit. As *samadhi* spoke, Mhoram felt that the flesh of his resistance was being carved away, leaving his bare bones exposed to the winter. His throat ached at the taste of abdication, and he had to swallow heavily before he could reply.

"*Samadhi* Sheol," he croaked, then swallowed again and focused all his skeletal resolve in his voice. "*Samadhi* Sheol! You mock us, but we are not mocked. We are not blind—we see the atrocity which underlies your persuasion. Begone! Foul-chattel! Take this army of torment and despication—return to your master. He has made your suffering—let him take joy in it while he can. Even as we stand here, the days of his might are numbered. When his end comes upon him, be certain he will do nothing to preserve your miserable being. Begone, Raver! I have no interest in your cheap taunts."

He hoped that the Raver would react with anger, do something which would bring him within reach of the archers. But Satansfist only laughed. Barking with savage glee, he turned away and gave a shout that sent his forces forward to renew their assault.

Mhoram turned also, pulled himself painfully around to face his fellow Lords. But they were not looking at him. They were intent on a messenger who stood trembling before them. Fear-sweat slicked his face despite the cold, and the muscles of his throat locked, clenched him silent. Mutely, he reached into his tunic, brought out a cloth bundle. His hands shook as he unwrapped it.

After a febrile moment, he exposed the *krill*.

Its gem was as dull as death.

Mhoram thought he heard gasps, groans, cries, but he could not be sure. Dread roared in his ears, made other sounds indistinguishable. He snatched up the *krill*. Staring aghast at it, he fell to his knees, plunged as if his legs had broken. With all the force of his need, he thrust his gaze into the gem, tried to find some gleam of life in it. But the metal was cold to his touch, and the edges of the blade were dull. Blind, lusterless winter filled the furthest depths of the jewel.

The hope of the wild magic was lost. Covenant was gone.

Now Mhoram understood why the Raver had laughed.

"Mhoram?"

"High Lord."

"Mhoram!"

Supplications reached toward him, asking him for strength, begging him, requiring. He ignored them. He shrugged off the hands of melding which plucked at his mind. The prophecy of his dread had come to pass. He had nothing left with which to answer supplications.

"Ah, High Lord!"

There were tears and despair in the appeals, but he had nothing left with which to answer.

He was only dimly aware that he rose to his feet, returned the *krill* to the messenger. He wanted it removed from his sight as if it were a treacher, yet that feeling occupied only a distant portion of him. With the rest, he tightened his frail blue robe as if he were still fool enough to believe it could protect him from the cold, and walked numbly away from the battlement. The short, stiff shock of his hair, newly grown after the fire in the Close, gave him a demented aspect. People came after him, beseeching, requiring, but he kept up his wooden pace, kept ahead of them so that he would not have to see their needy faces.

He gave no thought to where he was going until he reached a fork in the passage. There, the weight of decision almost crushed him to his knees again—left and down into the Keep, or right and out toward the upland plateau. He turned to the right because he could not bear the unintended recrimination of Revelstone—and because he was a man who already knew that he had no choice.

When he started up the long ascending road, the people behind him slowed, let him go. He heard them whispering:

"He goes to the Unfettered One—to the interpreter of dreams."

But that was not where he was going; he had no questions to ask an oracle. Oracles were for people to whom ambiguous visions could make a difference, but now the only things which could make a difference to High Lord Mhoram son of Variol were things which would give him courage.

In a stupor of dread, he climbed out into the wind which scythed across the open plateau. Above its chill ululations, he could hear battle crashing against the walls of the Keep, waves of assailants hurling themselves like breakers against a defiant and ultimately frangible cliff. But he put the sound behind him; it was only a symbol, a concentration, of the whole Land's abominable doom. Without Thomas Covenant—! Mhoram could not complete the thought. He walked up through the barren hills away from Revelstone, up toward the river and northward along it, with an abyss in his heart where the survival of the Land should have been. This, he told himself, was what Kevin Landwaster must have felt when Lord Foul overwhelmed Kurash Plenethor, making all responses short of Desecration futile. He did not know how the pain of it could be endured.

After a time, he found himself standing cold in the wind on a hill above Glimmermere. Below him, the rare, potent waters of the lake lay unruffled despite the buffeting of the wind. Though the skies above it were as gray as the ashes of the world's end, it seemed to shine with remembered sunlight. It reflected cleanly the hills and the distant mountains, and through its purity he could see its fathomless, rocky bottom.

He knew what he would have to do; he lacked courage, not comprehension. The last exactions of faith lay unrolled before him in his dread like the map of a country which no longer existed. When he stumbled frozenly down toward the lake, he did so because he had nowhere else to turn. There was Earthpower in Glimmermere. He placed his staff on the bank, stripped off his robe, and dropped into the lake, praying that its icy waters would do for him what he could not do for himself.

Though he was already numb with cold, the water seemed to burn instantly over all his flesh, snatch him out of his numbness like a conflagration in his nerves. He had had no thought of swimming when he had slipped into the depths, but the force of Glimmermere triggered reactions in him, sent him clawing up toward the surface. With a whooping gasp, he broke water, sculled for a moment to catch his breath against the fiery chill, then struck out for the bank where he had left his robe.

Climbing out onto the hillside, he felt aflame with cold, but he compelled himself to remain naked while the wind made ice of the water on his limbs and dried him. Then he pulled his robe urgently over his shoulders, hugged his staff to his chest so that its heat warmed him where he most needed warming. His feverish chill took some time to pass, and while he waited, he braced himself, strove to shore up his heart against the obstacles and the dismay which awaited him.

He had to do something which was obviously impossible. He had to slay *samadhi* Satansfist.

He would need help.

Putting grimly aside all his former scruples, he turned to the only possible source of help—the only aid whose faithfulness matched his need. He raised one cold hand to his lips and whistled shrilly three times.

The turbulent wind seemed to snatch the sound to pieces, tatter it instantly. In a place where echoes were common, his call disappeared without resonance or answer; the wind tore it away as if to undo his purpose, make him unheard. Nevertheless he summoned his trust, pried himself up the hillside to stand waiting on the vantage of the crest. A suspense like the either/or of despair filled him, but he faced the western mountains as if his heart knew neither doubt nor fear.

Long moments which sharpened his suspense to the screaming point passed before he saw a dull brown movement making its way toward him out of the mountains. Then his soul leaped up in spite of its burdens, and he stood erect with the wind snapping in his ears so that his stance would be becoming to the Ranyhyn that was answering his call.

The wait nearly froze the blood in his veins, but at last the Ranyhyn reached the hills around Glimmermere, and nickered in salutation.

Mhoram groaned at the sight. In order to answer his call, the Ranyhyn must have left the Plains of Ra scores of days ago—must have fled Satansfist's army to run straight across the Center Plains into the Westron Mountains, then found its pathless way among the high winter of the peaks northward to the spur of the range which jutted east and ended in the plateau of Revelstone. The long ordeal of the mountain trek had exacted a severe price from the great stallion. His flesh hung slack over gaunt ribs, he stumbled painfully on swollen joints, and his coat had a look of ragged misery. Still Mhoram recognized the Ranyhyn, and

greeted him with all the respect his voice could carry:
"Hail, Drinny, proud Ranyhyn! Oh, bravely done!
Worthy son of a worthy mother. Tail of the Sky, Mane
of the World, I am"—a clench of emotion caught his
throat, and he could only whisper—"I am honored."

Drinny made a valiant effort to trot up to Mhoram,
but when he reached the High Lord he rested his
head trembling on Mhoram's shoulder as if he needed
the support in order to keep his feet. Mhoram hugged
his neck, whispered words of praise and encouragement in his ear, stroked his ice-clogged coat. They
stood together as if in their differing weaknesses they
were making promises to each other. Then Mhoram
answered the nudging of Drinny's unquenchable pride
by springing onto the Ranyhyn's back. Warming the
great horse with his staff, he rode slowly, resolutely,
back toward Revelstone.

The ride took time—time made arduous and agon-
izing by the frailty of Drinny's muscles, his painful,
exhausted stumbling. While they passed down through
the hills, Mhoram's own weariness returned, and he
remembered his inadequacy, his stupefying dread.
But he had placed his feet on the strait path of his
faith; now he held the Ranyhyn between his knees
and bound himself in his determination not to turn
aside. Drinny had answered his call. While his
thoughts retained some vestige of Glimmermere's clarity, he made his plans.

Then at last his mount limped down into the wide
tunnel which led into Lord's Keep. The clop of hooves
echoed faintly against the smooth stone walls and ceiling—echoed and scurried ahead of the High Lord
like a murmurous announcement of his return. Soon
he could feel the voices of the Keep spreading word
of him, proclaiming that he had come back on a
Ranyhyn. People left their work and hastened to the
main passage of the tunnel to see him. They lined his
way, muttered in wonder or pain at the sight of the
Ranyhyn, whispered intently to each other about the
look of focused danger which shone in his eyes. Down
into the Keep he rode as if he were borne on a low
current of astonishment and hope.

After he had ridden a few hundred yards along the main ways of Revelstone, he saw ahead of him the other leaders of the city—the Lords Trevor, Amatin, and Loerya, Warmark Quaan, the two Hearthralls, Tohrm and Borillar. They awaited him as if they had come out together to do him honor. When the Ranyhyn stopped before them, they saluted the High Lord and his mount mutely, lacking words for what they felt.

He gazed back at them for a moment, studied them. In their separate ways, they were all haggard, needy, stained with battle. Quaan in particular appeared extravagantly worn. His bluff old face was knotted into a habitual scowl now, as if only the clench of constant belligerence held the pieces of his being together. And Amatin, too, looked nearly desperate; her physical slightness seemed to drain her moral stamina. Borillar's face was full of tears that Mhoram knew came from the loss of Thomas Covenant. Trevor and Loerya supported each other, unable to remain upright alone. Of them all, only Tohrm was calm, and his calm was the steadiness of a man who had already passed through his personal crisis. Nothing could be worse for him than the stone Desecration he had experienced in the Close—experienced and mastered. The others met Mhoram with concentrated hope and dismay and suspense and effectlessness in their faces—expressions which begged to know what this returning on a Ranyhyn meant.

He nodded to their silent salute, then dropped heavily from Drinny's back and moved a step or two closer to them. On the only level for which he had sufficient strength—the level of his authority—he answered them. He spoke softly, but his voice was raw with peril. "Hear me. I am Mhoram son of Variol, High Lord by the choice of the Council. I have taken my decision. Hear me and obey. Warmark Quaan, Drinny of the Ranyhyn must be given care. He must be fed and healed—he must be returned swiftly to his strength. I will ride him soon.

"Lords, Hearthralls, Warmark—the watchtower of Revelstone must be regained. The gates of the Keep must be cleared. Do it swiftly. Warmark, ready the horses of the Warward. Prepare all mounted warriors and as many unmounted as you deem fit—prepare them to march against *samadhi* Satansfist. We strike as soon as our way has been made clear."

He could see that his commands stunned them, that they were appalled at the mad prospect of attacking the Raver's army. But he did not offer them any aid, any reassurance. When the time came for the certain death of his purpose, he hoped to leave behind him men and women who had proved to themselves that they could meet extreme needs—leaders who had learned that they could do without him.

Yet he could not refuse to explain the reason for his commands. "My friends," he went on with the rawness livid in his tone, "the light of the *krill* has failed. You know the meaning of this. Thomas Covenant has left the Land—or has fallen to his death—or has been bereft of his ring. Therein lies our sole hope. If the Unbeliever lives—and while the wild magic has not been brought into use against us—we can hope that he will regain his ring.

"We must act on this hope. It is small—but all hopes are small in this extremity. It is our work to redeem victory from the blood and havoc of despair. We must act. Surely the Despiser knows that ur-Lord Covenant has lost the white gold—if it has been lost and not withdrawn from the Land or captured. Therefore his thoughts may be turned from us for a time. In that time we may have some hope of success against *samadhi* Raver. And if Lord Foul seeks to prevent the Unbeliever's recovery of his ring, we may give a distant aid to ur-Lord Covenant by requiring the Despiser to look toward us again."

He could not bear to watch the aghast supplications which wrung the faces of his friends. He put his arm over Drinny's neck and concluded as if he were speaking to the Ranyhyn, "This choice is mine. I will ride against Satansfist alone if I must. But this act must be made."

At last, Amatin found herself to gasp, *"Melenkurion! Melenkurion abatha!* Mhoram, have you learned

nothing from Trell Atiaran-mate—from the Bloodguard—from Kevin Landwaster himself? You beg
yourself to become a Desecrator. In this way, we learn
to destroy that which we love!"

High Lord Mhoram's reply had the sting of authority. "Warmark, I will take no warrior with me who
has not accepted this hazard freely. You must explain
to the Warward that the light of Loric's *krill* has
failed."

He ached to rush to his friends, ached to throw his
arms around them, hug them, show them in some way
his love and his terrible need for them. But he knew
himself; he knew he would be utterly unable to leave
them if they did not first show their independence to
themselves and him by meeting alone his extreme demands. His own courage hung too much on the verge
of faltering; he needed some demonstration from them
to help him follow the strait line of faith. So he contained himself by hugging Drinny tightly for a moment, then turned on his heel and walked stiffly away
to his private chambers.

He spent the next days alone, trying to rest—
searching himself for some resource which would en-
able him to bear the impossibility and the uselessness
of his decision. But a fever was on his soul. The foun-
dation of serenity which had sustained him for so long
seemed to have eroded. Whether he lay on his bed, or
ate, or paced his chambers, or studied, he could feel a
great emptiness in the heart of the Keep where the
krill's fire should have been. He had not realized how
much that white blaze had taught him to rely on the
Unbeliever. Its quenching left him face to face with
futile death—death for himself, for Drinny, for any
who dared follow him—death that could only be
trusted to foreshorten Revelstone's survival. So he
spent large stretches of the time on his hands and
knees on the floor, probing through the stone in an effort to sense how his commands were being met.

Without difficulty he read the preparations of the
Warward. The few hundred horses which had been
stabled in the Keep were being made ready. The duty
rotations of the warriors were changed so that those

who chose to follow the High Lord could rest and pre-pare. And as a result, the burden of resisting *samadhi*'s attacks fell on fewer shoulders. Soon the defense took on a febrile pitch which matched Mhoram's own fever. His commands had hastened the Warward's ineluctable decline into frenzy and desperation. He ground his teeth on that pain and hunted elsewhere in the city for the Lords.

He found that Lord Amatin had retreated to the isolation of the Loresraat's libraries, but Trevor, Loerya, and Hearthrall Tohrm were active. Together, Lord Trevor and Tohrm went down into one of the unfrequented caverns directly under the tower. There they combined their lore in a rite dangerously similar to Trell's destruction of the Close, and sent a surge of heat up through the stone into the passages of the tower. They stoked the heat for a day, raised it against the enemy until the Cavewights and creatures began to abandon the tower.

And when the lowest levels were empty, Lord Loerya led several Eoman in an assault. Under cover of darkness, they leaped from the main Keep into the sand, crossed the courtyard, and entered the tower to fight their way upward. By the dawn of the third day, they were victorious. Makeshift crosswalks were thrown up over the courtyard, and hundreds of archers rushed across to help secure the tower.

Their success gave Mhoram a pride in them that eased his distress for a time. He doubted that the tower could be held for more than a day or two, but a day or two would be enough, if the rest of his com-mands were equally met.

Then, during the third day, Amatin returned to work. She had spent the time in an intense study of certain arcane portions of the Second Ward which High Lord Mhoram himself had never grasped, and there she had found the rites and invocations she sought. Armed with that knowledge, she went to the abutments directly above the courtyard, made eldritch signs and symbols on the stone, wove rare gestures, chanted songs in the lost language of the Old Lords—and below her the sandy remains of the dead slowly parted. They pulled back far enough to permit the opening of the gates, far enough to permit an army to ride out of Revelstone.

Her achievement drew Mhoram from his chambers to watch. When she was done, she collapsed in his arms, but he was so proud of her that his concern was dominated by relief. When the Healers assured him she would soon recover if she were allowed to rest, he left her and went to the stables to see Drinny.

He found a Ranyhyn that hardly resembled the ragged, worn horse he had ridden into Revelstone. Good food and treatment had rekindled the light in Drinny's eyes, renewed his flesh, restored elasticity to his muscles. He pranced and nickered for Mhoram as if to show the High Lord he was ready.

Such things rejuvenated Mhoram. Without further hesitation, he told Warmark Quaan that he would ride out against the Raver the next morning.

But late that night, while Trevor, Loerya, and Quaan all struggled against a particularly fierce flurry of onslaughts, Lord Amatin came to Mhoram's rooms. She did not speak, but her wan, bruised aspect caught at his heart. Her labors had done something to her; in straining herself so severely, she had lost her defenses, left herself exposed to perils and perceptions for which she was neither willing nor apt. This vulnerability gave her a look of abjection, as if she had come to cast herself at Mhoram's feet.

Without a word, she raised her hands to the High Lord. In them she held the *krill* of Loric.

He accepted it without dropping his gaze from her face. "Ah, sister Amatin," he breathed gently, "you should rest. You have earned—"

But a spasm of misery around her eyes cut him off. He looked down, made himself look at the *krill*.

Deep in its gem, he saw faint glimmerings of emerald.

Without a word, Amatin turned and left him alone with the knowledge that Covenant's ring had fallen into the power of the Despiser.

When he left his rooms the next morning, he looked like a man who had spent the night wrestling in vain against his own damnation. His step had lost its conviction; he moved as if his very bones were loose and bending. And the dangerous promise of his gaze had faded, leaving his eyes dull, stricken. He bore the *krill* within his robe and could feel Lord Foul's sick emerald hold upon it growing. Soon, he knew, the cold of the green would begin to burn his flesh. But he was past taking any account of such risks. He dragged himself forward as if he were on his way to commit a perfidy which appalled him.

In the great entrance hall a short distance within Revelstone's still-closed gates, he joined the warriors. They were ranked by Eoman, and he saw at a glance that they numbered two thousand: one Eoward on horseback and four on foot—a third of the surviving Warward. He faltered at the sight; he had not expected to be responsible for so many deaths. But the warriors hailed him bravely, and he forced himself to respond as if he trusted himself to lead them. Then he moved in anguish to the forefront, where Drinny awaited him.

The Lords and Warmark Quaan were there with the Ranyhyn, but he passed by them because he could not meet their eyes, and tried to mount. His muscles failed him; he was half paralyzed by dread and could not leap high enough to gain Drinny's back. Shaking on the verge of an outcry, he clung to the horse for support, and beseeched himself for the serenity which had been his greatest resource.

Yet he could not make the leap; Drinny's back was too high for him. He ached to ask for help. But before he could force words through his locked throat, he felt Quaan behind him, felt Quaan's hand on his shoulder. The old Warmark's voice was gruff with urgency as he said, "High Lord, this risk will weaken Revelstone. A third of the Warward—two thousand lives wasted. High Lord—why? Have you become like Kevin Landwaster? Do you wish to destroy that which you love?"

"No!" Mhoram whispered because the tightness of his throat blocked any other sound. With his hands, he begged Drinny for strength. "I do not—I do not forget— I am the High Lord. The path of faith is clear. I must follow it—because it is not despair."

"You will teach us despair—if you fail."

Mhoram heard the pain in Quaan's voice, and he compelled himself to answer. He could not refuse Quaan's need; he was too weak, but he could not refuse. "No. Lord Foul teaches despair. It is an easier lesson than courage." Slowly, he turned around, met first Quaan's gaze, then the eyes of the Lords. "An easier lesson," he repeated. "Therefore the counsels of despair and hate can never triumph over Despite."

But his reply only increased Quaan's pain. While knuckles of distress clenched Quaan's open face, he moaned brokenly, "Ah, my Lord. Then why do you delay? Why do you fear?"

"Because I am mortal, weak. The way is only clear —not sure. In my time, I have been a seer and oracle. Now I—I desire a sign. I require to see."

He spoke simply, but almost at once his mortality, his weakness, became too much for him. Tears blurred his vision. The burden was not one that he could bear alone. He opened his arms and was swept into the embrace of the Lords.

The melding of their minds reached him, poured into him on the surge of their united concern. Folded within their arms and their thoughts, he felt their love soothe him, fill him like water after a long thirst, feed his hunger. Throughout the siege, he had given them his strength, and now they returned strength to him. With quiet diffidence, Lord Trevor restored his crippled sense of endurance in service—a fortitude which came, not from the server, but from the preciousness of the thing served. Lord Loerya shared with him her intense instinct for protection, her capacity for battle on behalf of children—loved ones who could not defend themselves. And Lord Amatin, though she was still frail herself, gave him the clear, uncluttered concentration of her study, her lore-wisdom—a rare gift which for his sake she proffered separate from her distrust of emotion.

In such melding, he began to recover himself. Blood seemed to return to his veins; his muscles uncramped; his bones remembered their rigor. He accepted the Lords deep into himself, and in response he shared with them all the perceptions which made his decision necessary. Then he rested on their love and let it assuage him.

His appetite for the meld seemed to have no bottom, but after a time the contact was interrupted by a strident voice so full of strange thrills that none of the Lords could refuse to hear it. A sentry raced into the hall clamoring for their attention, and when they looked at her she shouted, "The Raver is attacked! His army —the encampment—! It is under attack. By Waynhim! They are few—few—but the Raver had no defenses on that side, and they have already done great damage. He has called his army back from Revelstone to fight them!"

High Lord Mhoram whirled away, ordering the Warward to readiness as he moved. He heard Warmark Quaan echo his commands. A look full of dire consequences for the Raver passed between them; then Quaan leaped onto his own horse, a tough, mountain-bred mustang. To one side among the warriors, Mhoram saw Hearthrall Borillar mounting. He started to order Borillar down; Hirebrands were not fighters. But then he remembered how much hope Borillar had placed in Thomas Covenant, and left the Hearthrall alone.

Loerya was already on her way to aid the defenses of the tower, keep it secure so that the Warward would be able to reenter Revelstone. Trevor had gone to the gates. Only Amatin remained to see the danger shining in Mhoram's eyes. She held him briefly, then released him, muttering, "It would appear that the Waynhim have made the same decision."

Mhoram spun and leaped lightly onto Drinny's back. The Ranyhyn whinnied; peals of pride and defiance resounded through the hall. As the huge gates opened outward on the courtyard, Mhoram sent Drinny forward at a canter.

The Warward started into motion behind him, and at its head High Lord Mhoram rode out to war.

In a moment, he flashed through the gates, across the courtyard between steep banks of sand and earth, into the straight tunnel under the tower. Drinny

stretched jubilantly under him, exalted by health and
running and the scent of battle. As Mhoram passed
through the splintered remains of the outer gates, he
had already begun to outdistance the Warward.

Beyond the gates, he wheeled Drinny once, gave
himself an instant in which to look back up at the lofty
Keep. He saw no warriors in the tower, but he sensed
them bristling behind the fortifications and windows.
The bluff stone of the tower, with Revelstone rising
behind it like the prow of a great ship, answered his
gaze in granite permanence as if it were a prophecy
by the old Giants—a cryptic perception that victory
and defeat were human terms which had no meaning
in the language of mountains.

Then the riders came cantering through the throat
of the tower, and Mhoram turned to look at the enemy. For the first time, he saw *samadhi*'s army from
ground level. It stood blackly in the bleak winterscape around him like a garrote into which he had
prematurely thrust his neck. Briefly, he remembered other battles—Kiril Threndor, Doom's Retreat,
Doriendor Corishev—as if they had been child's play,
mere shadows cast by the struggle he now faced. But
he pushed them out of his mind, bent his attention
toward the movements in the foothills below him.

As the sentry had said, Revelstone's attackers were
pelting furiously back toward their encampment. It
was only a few hundred yards distant, and Mhoram
could see clearly why *samadhi*'s forces had been recalled. The Giant-Raver was under assault by a tight
wedge of ten- or fifteenscore Waynhim.

Satansfist himself was not their target, though he
fought against them personally with feral blasts of
green. The Waynhim struck against the undefended
rear of the encampment in order to destroy its food
supplies. They had already incinerated great long
troughs of the carrion and gore on which Lord Foul's
creatures fed; and while they warded off the scourge
of Satansfist's Stone as best they could, they assailed
other stores, flash-fired huge aggregations of hacked
dead flesh into cinders.

Even if they had faced the Raver alone, they would

have had no chance to survive. With his Giantish
strength and his fragment of the Illearth Stone—with
the support of the Staff of Law—he could have
beaten back ten or fifteen thousand Waynhim. And he
had an army to help him. Hundreds of ur-viles were
nearly within striking distance; thousands of other
creatures converged toward the fighting from all directions. The Waynhim had scant moments of life left.

Yet they fought on, resisted *samadhi*'s emerald ill
with surprising success. Like the ur-viles, they were
Demondim-spawn—masters of a dark and potent lore
which no Lord had ever touched. And they had not
wasted the seven and forty years since they had gone
into hiding. They had prepared themselves to resist
Despite. Yelping rare words of power, gesturing urgently, they shrugged off the Raver's blasts, and continued to destroy every trough and accumulation of
food they could reach.

All this High Lord Mhoram took in almost instantly. The raw wind hurt his face, made his eyes
burn, but he thrust his vision through the blur to see.
And he saw that, because of the Waynhim, he and the
Warward had not yet been noticed by Satansfist's
army.

"Warmark," he snapped, "we must aid the Waynhim! Give the commands."

Rapidly, Quaan barked his instructions to the
mounted warriors and the Hafts of the four unmounted Eoward as they came through the tunnel. At
once, a hundred riders positioned themselves on either
side of the High Lord. The remaining two hundred fell
into ranks behind him. Without breaking stride, the
unmounted warriors began to run.

Mhoram touched Drinny and started at a slow gallop straight down through the foothills toward the
Raver.

Some distant parts of the encampment saw the
riders before they had covered a third of the distance.
Hoarse cries of warning sprang up on all sides; ur-
viles, Cavewights, Stone-made creatures which had not
already been ordered to the Giant-Raver's aid, swept
like a ragged tide at the Warward. But the confusion

around the Waynhim prevented Satansfist's immediate forces from hearing the alarm. The Raver did not turn his head. Revelstone's counterattack was nearly upon him before he saw his danger. .

In the last distance, Warmark Quaan shouted an order, and the riders broke into full gallop. Mhoram had time for one final look at his situation. The forces around *samadhi* were still locked in their concentration on the Waynhim. The Raver's reinforcements were long moments away. If Quaan's warriors could hit hard enough, break through toward the Waynhim fast enough, the unmounted Eoward might be able to protect their rear long enough for them to strike once at the Raver and withdraw. That way, some of the warriors might survive to return to the Keep.

Mhoram sent Drinny forward at a pace which put him among the first riders crashing into Satansfist's unready hordes.

They impacted with a shock that shook the High Lord in his seat. Horses plunged, hacked with their hooves. Swords were brandished like metal lightning. Shrieks of surprised pain and rage shivered the air as disorganized ranks of creatures went down under the assault. Heaving their mounts forward, the warriors cut their way in toward the Raver.

But thousands of creatures milled between them and Satansfist. Though the hordes were in confusion, the sheer weight of their numbers slowed the Warward's charge.

Seeing this, Quaan gave new orders. On his command, the warriors flanking Mhoram turned outward on either side, cleared a space between them for the riders behind the High Lord. These Eoman sprinted forward. When they reached Mhoram, he called up the power of his staff. Blue fire raged ahead of him like the point of a lance, piercing the wall of enemies as he led the second rush of riders deeper into the turmoil of the Raver's army.

For a moment, he thought they might succeed. The warriors with him hacked their way swiftly through the enemy. And ahead of them, Satansfist turned from the Waynhim to meet this new threat. The Raver howled orders to organize his army, turned his forces against the Warward, surged a few furious strides in that direction. Mhoram saw the distance shorten. He wielded his Lords-fire fiercely, striving to reach his foe before the impossible numbers of the enemy broke his momentum.

But then the riders plowed into an obstacle. A band of Cavewights had had time to obey the Raver's commands; they had lined themselves across the path of the Warward, linked their strong earth-delvers' arms, braced themselves. When the riders plunged forward, they crashed into the creatures.

The strength of the Cavewights was so great that their line held. Horses were thrown down. Riders tumbled to the ground, both before and beyond the wall. The charge of the Warward was turned against itself as the horses which followed stumbled and trampled among the leaders.

Only Mhoram was not unhorsed. At the last instant, Drinny gathered himself, leaped; he hurdled the line easily, kicking at the heads of the Cavewights as he passed.

With the riders who had been thrown beyond the wall, Mhoram found himself faced by a massing wedge of ur-viles.

The Cavewights cut him off from the Warward. And the falling of the horses gave *samadhi*'s creatures a chance to strike back. Before Quaan could organize any kind of assault on the Cavewights, his warriors were fighting for their lives where they stood.

Wheeling Drinny, Mhoram saw that he would get no help from the riders. But if he went back to them, fought the wall himself, the ur-viles would have time to complete their wedge; they would have the riders at their mercy.

At once, he sent the warriors with him to attack the Cavewights. Then he flung himself like a bolt of Lords-fire at the ur-viles.

He was only one man against several hundred of the black, roynish creatures. But he had unlocked the secret of High Lord Kevin's Lore; he had learned the link between power and passion; he was mightier than he had ever been before. Using all the force his staff could bear, he shattered the formation like a battering ram, broke and scattered ur-viles like rubble. With Drinny pounding, kicking, slashing under him, he held his staff in both hands, whirled it about him, sent vivid blasts blaring like the blue fury of the cloud-damned heavens, shouting in a rapture of rage like an earthquake. And the ur-viles staggered as if the sky had fallen on them, collapsed as if the ground had bucked under their feet. He fired his way through them like a titan, and did not stop until he had reached the bottom of a low hollow in the hills.

There he spun, and discovered that he had completely lost the Warward. The riders had been thrown back; in the face of insuperable odds, Quaan had probably taken them to join the unmounted warriors so that they could combine their strength in an effort to save the High Lord.

On the opposite rim of the hollow, Satansfist stood glaring down at Mhoram. He held his Stone cocked to strike, and the mad lust of the Raver was in his Giantish face. But he turned away without attacking, disappeared beyond the rim as if he had decided that the Waynhim were a more serious threat than High Lord Mhoram.

"Satansfist!" Mhoram yelled. "*Samadhi* Sheol! Return and fight me! Are you craven, that you dare not risk a challenge?"

As he shouted, he hit Drinny with his heels, launched the Ranyhyn in pursuit of Satansfist. But in the instant that his attention was turned upward, the surviving ur-viles rallied. Instead of retreating to form a wedge, they flung themselves at him. He could not swing his staff; ravenous black hands clutched at him, clawed his arms, caught hold of his robe.

Drinny fought back, but he succeeded only in pulling himself out from under the High Lord. Mhoram lost his seat and went down under a pile of rabid black bodies.

Blood-red Demondim blades flared at him. But before any of the eldritch knives could bite his flesh, he mustered an eruption of force which blasted the ur-viles away. Instantly, he was on his feet again, wielding his staff, crushing every creature that came near him—searching fervidly for his mount.

The Ranyhyn was already gone, driven out of the hollow.

Suddenly, Mhoram was alone. The last ur-viles fled, leaving him with the dead and dying. In their place came a fatal silence that chilled his blood. Either the fighting had ended, or the livid wind carried all sounds away; he could hear nothing but the low cruel voice of Lord Foul's winter, and his own hoarse respiration.

The abrupt absence of clamor and turmoil kept him still also. He wanted to shout for Quaan but could not raise his voice through the horror in his throat—wanted to whistle for Drinny, but could not bring himself to break the awful quietude. He was too astonished with dread.

The next instant, he realized that the Raver had trapped him. He sprang into a run, moving away from the Warward, toward the Waynhim, hoping that this choice would take the trap by surprise.

It was too complete to be surprised. Before he had gone a dozen yards, creatures burst into view around the entire rim of the hollow. Hundreds of them let him see them; they stood leering down at him, pawing the ground hungrily, slavering at the anticipated taste of his blood and bones. The wind bore their throaty lust down to him as if they gave tongue to the animating spirit of the winter.

He was alone against them.

He retreated to the center of the hollow, hunted swiftly around the rim for some gap or weakness in the surrounding horde. He found none. And though he sent his perceptions ranging as far as he could through the air, he discovered no sign of the Warward; if the warriors were still alive, still fighting, they were blocked from his senses by the solid force of the trap.

As he grasped the utterness of his plight, he turned inward, retreated into himself as if he were fleeing. There he looked the end of all his hopes and all his Landservice in the face, and found that its scarred, terrible visage no longer appalled him. He was a fighter, a man born to fight for the Land. As long as something for which he could fight remained, he was impervious to terror. And something did remain; while he lived, at least one flame of love for the Land still burned. He could fight for that.

His crooked lips stretched into an extreme and perilous grin; hot, serene triumph shone in his eyes. "Come, then!" he shouted. "If your master is too much a coward to risk himself against me, then come for me yourselves! I do not wish to harm you, but if you dare me, I will give you death!"

Something in his voice halted them momentarily. They hesitated, moiling uneasily. But almost at once the grip of their malice locked like jaws. At the harsh shout of a command, they started down toward him from all sides like an avalanche.

He did not wait for them. He swung in the direction Satansfist had taken, intending to pursue the Raver as far as his strength would carry him. But some instinct or intuition tugged him at the last instant, deflected him to one side. He turned and met that part of the avalanche head-on.

Now the only thing which limited his might was his staff itself. That wood had been shaped by people who had not understood Kevin's Lore; it was not formed to bear the force he now sent blazing through it. But he had no margin for caution. He made the staff surpass itself, sent it bucking and crackling with power to rage against his assailants. His flame grew incandescent, furnace-hot; in brilliance and coruscation it sliced through his foes like a scythe of sun-fire.

In moments, their sheer numbers filled all his horizons, blocked everything but their dark assault out of his awareness. He saw nothing else, felt nothing but huge waves of misshapen fiends that sought to deluge him, knew nothing but their ravening lust for blood and his blue, fiery passion. Though they threw themselves at him in scores and hundreds, he met them, cut them down, blasted them back. Wading through their corpses as if they were the very sea of death, he fought them with fury in his veins, indomitability in his bones, extravagant triumph in his eyes.

Yet they outweighed him. They were too many. Any moment now, one of them would drive a sword into his back, and he would be finished. Through the savage clash of combat, he heard a high, strange cry of victory, but he hardly knew that he had made it himself.

Then, unexpectedly, he glimpsed the light of a fire through a brief gap in his attackers. It disappeared instantly, vanished as if it had never happened. But he had recognized it. He shouted again and began to fight toward it. Ignoring the danger at his back, he reaped a break in the avalanche ahead. There he saw the fire again.

It was the blaze of a Hirebrand.

On the rim of the hollow, Hearthrall Borillar and the last of the Waynhim fought together against Mhoram's foes. Borillar used his flaming staff like a mace, and the Waynhim supported him with their own powers. Together they struggled impossibly to rescue the High Lord.

At the sight of them, Mhoram faltered; he could see immense monsters rising up to smite them, and their peril interrupted his concentration. But he recovered, surged toward them, driving his staff until it screamed in his hands.

Too many creatures were pressed between him and his rescuers; he could not reach them in time. While he fought slipping and plowing through the blood, he saw Borillar slain, saw the formation of the Waynhim broken, scattered. He almost fell himself under his inability to help them.

But with their deaths they had purchased a thinning in the flood of attackers at that point. Through that thinning came Drinny of the Ranyhyn, bucking and charging to regain his rider.

His violent speed carried him down into the hollow. He crashed through creatures, leaped over them, hacked them out of his way. Before they could brace themselves to meet him, Drinny had reached the High Lord.

Mhoram sprang onto the Ranyhyn's back. From that vantage, he brought his power down on the heads of his assailants, while Drinny kicked and plunged back up the hillside. In moments, they crested the rim and broke into clearer ground beyond it.

As he guided Drinny ahead, Mhoram caught a glimpse of the Warward. It had rallied around Quaan and was struggling in the High Lord's direction. The riders charged to break up the ranks of the enemy, then the other warriors rushed to take advantage of the breach. But they were completely engulfed—a small, valiant island in the sea of Satansfist's army. Their progress was tortuous, their losses atrocious. High Lord Mhoram knew of only one effective way to help them, and he took Drinny toward it without an instant of hesitation.

Together, they pursued *samadhi* Raver.

Satansfist was only fifty yards away. He stood on a knoll from which he could direct the battle. And he was alone; all his forces were engaged elsewhere. He towered atop the hill like a monolith of hatred and destruction, wielding his army with the force of green ill.

Holding his staff ready, Mhoram sent the Ranyhyn lunging straight into the teeth of the winter—straight at *samadhi*. When he was scant strides away from his foe, he cried his challenge:

"Melenkurion abatha! Duroc minas mill khabaal!"

With all his strength, he leveled a blast of Lords-fire at the Raver's leering skull.

Satansfist knocked the attack down as if it were negligible; disdainfully, he slapped Mhoram's blue out of the air with his Stone and returned a bolt so full of cold emerald force that it scorched the atmosphere as it moved.

Mhoram sensed its power, knew that it would slay him if it struck. But Drinny dodged with a fleet, fluid motion which belied the wrenching change of his momentum. The bolt missed, crashed instead into the creatures pursuing the High Lord, killed them all.

That gave Mhoram the instant he needed. He corrected Drinny's aim, cocked his staff over his shoulder. Before *samadhi* could unleash another blast, the High Lord was upon him.

Using all Drinny's speed, all the strength of his body, all the violated passion of his love for the Land, Mhoram swung. His staff caught Satansfist squarely across the forehead.

The concussion ripped Mhoram from his seat like a dry leaf in the wind. His staff shattered at the blow, exploded into splinters, and he hit the ground amid a brief light rain of wood slivers. He was stunned. He rolled helplessly a few feet over the frozen earth, could not stop himself, could not regain his breath. His mind went blank for an instant, then began to ache as his body ached. His hands and arms were numb, paralyzed by the force which had burned through them.

Yet even in his daze, he had room for a faint amazement at what he had done.

His blow had staggered Satansfist, knocked him backward. The Giant-Raver had fallen down the far side of the knoll.

With a gasp, Mhoram began to breathe again. Spikes of sensation dug into his arms; dazzling pain filled his vision. He tried to move, and after a moment succeeded in rolling onto his side. His hands hung curled on the ends of his wrists as if they were crippled, but he shifted his shoulder and elbow, turned himself onto his stomach, then levered himself with his forearms until he gained his knees. There he rested while the pain of returning life stabbed its way down into his fingers.

The sound of heavy steps, heavy breathing, made him look up.

Samadhi Sheol stood over him.

Blood poured from Satansfist's forehead into his eyes, but instead of blinding him, it seemed only to enrich his raving ferocity. His lips were contorted with a paroxysm of savage glee; ecstatic rage shone on his wet teeth. In the interlocked clasp of his fists, the Ill-earth Stone burned and fumed as if it were on the brink of apotheosis.

Slowly, he raised the Stone over Mhoram's head like an ax.

Transfixed, stunned—as helpless as a sacrifice—

Mhoram watched his death rise and poise above him.

In the distance, he could hear Quaan shouting wildly, uselessly, "Mhoram! Mhoram!" On the ground nearby, Drinny groaned and strove to regain his feet. Everywhere else there was silence. The whole battle seemed to have paused in midblow to watch Mhoram's execution. And he could do nothing but kneel and regret that so many lives had been spent for such an end.

Yet when the change of the air came an instant later, it was so intense, so vibrant and thrilling, that it snatched him to his feet. It made Satansfist arrest his blow, gape uncomprehendingly into the sky, then drop his fists and whirl to shout strident curses at the eastern horizon.

For that moment, Mhoram also only gaped and gasped. He could not believe his senses, could not believe the touch of the air on his cold-punished face. He seemed to be tasting something which had been lost from human experience.

Then Drinny lurched up, braced himself on splayed legs, and raised his head to neigh in recognition of the change. His whinny was weak and strained, but it lifted Mhoram's heart like the trumpets of triumph.

While he and Satansfist and all the armies stared at it, the wind faltered. It limped, spurting and fluttering in the air like a wounded bird, then fell lifeless to the ground.

For the first time since Lord Foul's preternatural winter had begun, there was no wind. Some support or compulsion had been withdrawn from *samadhi* Satansfist.

With a howl of rage, the Raver spun back toward Mhoram. "Fool!" he screamed as if the High Lord had let out a shout of jubilation. "That was but one weapon of many! I will yet drink your heart's blood to the bottom!" Reeling under the weight of his fury, he lifted his fists again to deliver the executing blow.

But now Mhoram felt the fire which burned against his flesh under his robe. In a rush of exaltation, he understood it, grasped its meaning intuitively. As the

Stone reached its height over his head, he tore open his robe and grasped Loric's *krill*.

Its gem blazed like a hot white brazier in his hands. It was charged to overflowing with echoes of wild magic; he could feel its keenness as he gripped its hilt.

It was a weapon strong enough to bear any might.

His eyes met Satansfist's. He saw dismay and hesitation clashing against the Raver's rage, against *samadhi* Sheol's ancient malice and the supreme confidence of the Stone.

Before Satansfist could defend himself, High Lord Mhoram sprang up and drove the *krill* deep into his bosom.

The Raver shrieked in agony. With Mhoram hanging from the blade in his chest, he flailed his arms as if he could not find anything to strike, anywhere to exert his colossal outrage. Then he dropped to his knees.

Mhoram planted his feet on the ground and braced himself to retain his grip on the *krill*. Through the focus of that blade, he drove all his might deeper and deeper toward the Giant-Raver's heart.

Yet *samadhi* did not die. Faced with death, he found a way to resist. Both his fists clenched the Stone only a foot above the back of Mhoram's neck. With all the rocky, Giantish strength of his frame, he began to squeeze.

Savage power steamed and pulsed like the beating of a heart of ice—a heart laboring convulsively, pounding and quivering to carry itself through a crisis. Mhoram felt the beats crash against the back of his spine. They kept Satansfist alive while they strove to quench the power which drove the *krill*.

But Mhoram endured the pain, did not let go; he leaned his weight on the blazing blade, ground it deeper and still deeper toward the essential cords of *Samadhi*'s life. Slowly, his flesh seemed to disappear, fade as if he were being translated by passion into a being of pure force, of unfettered spirit and indomitable will. The Stone hammered at his back like a mounting cataclysm, and Satansfist's chest heaved against his hands in great, ragged, bloody gasps.

Then the cords were cut.

Pounding beyond the limits of control, the Illearth Stone exploded, annihilated itself with an eruption that hurled Mhoram and Satansfist tumbling inextricably together from the knoll. The blast shook the ground, tore a hole in the silence over the battle. One slow instant of stunned amazement gripped the air, then vanished in the dismayed shrieks of the Despiser's army.

Moments later, Warmark Quaan and the surviving remnant of his mounted Eoward dashed to the foot of the knoll. Quaan threw himself from his horse and leaped to the High Lord's side.

Mhoram's robe draped his bloodied and begrimed form in tatters; it had been shredded by the explosion. His hands as they gripped the *krill* were burned so badly that only black rags of flesh still clung to his bones. From head to foot, his body had the look of pain and brokenness. But he was still alive, still breathing faintly, fragilely.

Fear, weariness, hesitation dropped off Quaan as if they were meaningless. He took the *krill*, wrapped it, and placed it under his belt, then with celerity and care lifted the High Lord in his arms. For an instant, he looked around. He saw Drinny nearby, shaking his head and mane to throw off the effects of the blast. He saw the Despiser's army seething in confusion and carnage. He hoped that it would fall apart without the Raver's leadership and coercion. But then he saw also that the ur-viles were rallying, taking charge of the creatures around them, reorganizing the hordes.

In spite of the High Lord's weight, Quaan ran and vaulted onto Drinny's back. Shouting to the Warward, "Retreat! Return to the Keep! The Gray Slayer has not lost his hold!" he clapped Drinny with his heels and took the Ranyhyn at a full gallop toward the open gates of Revelstone.

SIXTEEN: Colossus

THERE were gaps in the darkness during which Covenant knew dimly that rank liquids were being forced into him. They nourished him despite their rancid taste; his captors were keeping him alive. But between these gaps nothing interrupted his bereavement, his loss of everything he could grasp or recognize. He was dismembered from himself. The shrill vermillion nail of pain which the ur-viles had driven through his forehead impaled his identity, his memory and knowledge and awareness. He was at the nadir—captured, conquered, bereft—and only that iron stab in his forehead stood between him and the last numbness of the end.

So when he began to regain consciousness, he jerked toward it like a half-buried corpse, striving to shift the weight which enfolded him like the ready arms of his grave. Cold ebbed into him from the abyss of the winter. His heart labored; shuddering ran through him like a crisis. His hands clutched uselessly at the frozen dirt.

Then rough hands flopped him onto his back. A grim visage advanced, receded. Something struck his chest. He gasped at the force of the blow. Yet it helped him; it seemed to break him free of imminent hysteria. He began to breathe more easily. In a moment, he became aware that he was beating the back of his head against the ground. With an effort, he stopped himself. Then he concentrated on trying to see.

He wanted to see, wanted to find some answer to the completeness of his loss. And his eyes were open —must have been open, or he would not have been able to perceive the shadowy countenance snarling over him. Yet he could not make it out. His eyeballs were dry and blind; he saw nothing but cold, universal gray smeared around the more compact gray of the visage.

"Up, Covenant," a harsh voice rasped. "You are of no use as you are."

Another blow knocked his head to the side. He lurched soddenly. Through the pain in his cheek, he felt himself gaping into the raw wind. He blinked painfully at the dryness of his eyes, and tears began to resolve his blindness into shapes and spaces.

"Up, I say!"

He seemed to recognize the voice without knowing whose it was. But he lacked the strength to turn his head for another look. Resting on the icy ground, he blinked until his sight came into focus on a high, monolithic fist of stone.

It was perhaps twenty yards from him and forty feet tall—an obsidian column upraised on a plinth of native rock, and gnarled at its top into a clench of speechless defiance. Beyond it he could see nothing; it stood against a background of clouds as if it were erect on the rim of the world. At first, it appeared to him a thing of might, an icon of Earthpower upthrust or set down there to mark a boundary against evil. But as his vision cleared, the stone seemed to grow shallow and slumberous, blank; while he blinked at it, it became as inert as any old rock. If it still lived, he no longer had the eyes to see its life.

Slowly, fragments of other senses returned to him. He discovered that he could hear the wind hissing ravenously past him like a river thrashing across rapids; and behind it was a deep, muffled booming like the thunder of a waterfall.

"Up!" the harsh voice repeated. "Must I beat you senseless to awaken you?"

Mordant laughter echoed after the demand as if it were a jest.

Abruptly, the rough hands caught hold of his robe and yanked him off the ground. He was still too weak to carry his own weight, too weak even to hold up his head. He leaned against the man's chest and panted at his pain, trying with futile fingers to grasp the man's shoulders.

"Where—?" he croaked at last. "Where—?"

The laughter ridiculed him again. Two unrecognizable voices were laughing at him.

"Where?" the man snapped. "Thomas Covenant, you are at my mercy. That is the only *where* which signifies."

Straining, Covenant heaved up his head and found himself staring miserably into Triock's dark scowl.

Triock? He tried to say the name, but his voice failed him.

"You have slain everything that was precious to me. Think on that, Unbeliever"—he invested the title with abysms of contempt—"if you require to know where you are."

Triock?

"There is murder and degradation in your every breath. Ah! you stink of it." A spasm of revulsion knotted Triock's face, and he dropped Covenant to the ground again.

Covenant landed heavily amid sarcastic mirth. He was still too dazed to collect his thoughts. Triock's disgust affected him like a command; he lay prostrate with his eyes closed, trying to smell himself.

It was true. He stank of leprosy. The disease in his hands and feet reeked, gave off a rotten effluvium out of all proportion to the physical size of his infection. And its message was unmistakable. The ordure in him, the putrefaction of his flesh, was spreading—expanding as if he were contagious, as if at last even his body had become a violation of the fundamental health of the Land. In some ways, this was an even more important violation than the Despiser's winter—or rather his stench was the crown of the wind, the apex of Lord Foul's intent. That intent would be complete when his illness became part of the wind, when ice and leprosy together extinguished the Land's last vitality.

Then, in one intuitive leap, he understood his sense
of bereavement. He identified his loss. Without looking to verify the perception, he knew that his ring had
been taken from him; he could feel its absence like
destitution in his heart.

The Despiser's manipulations were complete. The
coercion and subterfuge which had shaped Covenant's
experiences in the Land had borne fruit. Like a Stone-
warped tree, they had fructified to produce this unanswerable end. The wild magic was now in Lord Foul's
possession.

A wave of grief rushed through Covenant. The
enormity of the disaster he had precipitated upon the
Land appalled him. His chest locked in a clench of
sorrow, and he huddled on the verge of weeping.

But before he could release his pain, Triock was at
him again. The Stonedownor gripped the shoulders of
his robe, shook him until his bones rattled. "Awaken!"
Triock rasped viciously. "Your time is short. My time
is short. I do not mean to waste it."

For a moment, Covenant could not resist; inanition
and unconsciousness and grief crippled him. But then
Triock's gratuitous violence struck sparks into the forgotten tinder of Covenant's rage. Anger galvanized
him, brought back control to his muscles. He twisted
in Triock's grip, got an arm and a leg braced on the
ground. Triock released him, and he climbed unevenly
to his feet, panting, "Hell and blood! Don't touch me,
you—Raver!"

Triock stepped forward as Covenant came erect
and stretched him on the dirt again with one sharp
blow. Standing over Covenant, he shouted in a voice
full of outrage, "I am no Raver! I am Triock son of
Thuler!—the man who loved Lena Atiaran-child—the
man who took the part of a father for Elena daughter
of Lena because you abandoned her! You cannot deny
any blow I choose to strike against you!"

At that, Covenant heard laughter again, but he still
could not identify its source. Triock's blow made the
pain in his forehead roar; the noise of the hurt confused his hearing. But when the worst of the sound

passed, his eyes seemed to clear at last. He forced himself to look up steadily into Triock's face.

The man had changed again. The strange combination of loathing and hunger, of anger and fear, was gone; the impression he had created that he was using his own anguish cunningly was gone. In the place of such distortions was an extravagant bitterness, a rage not controlled by any of his old restraints. He was himself and not himself. The former supplication of his eyes—the balance and ballast of his long acquaintance with gall—had foundered in passion. Now his brows clenched themselves into a knot of violence above the bridge of his nose; the pleading lines at the corners of his eyes had become as deep as scars; and his cheeks were taut with grimaces. Yet something in his eyes themselves belied the focus of his anger. His orbs were glazed and milky, as if they were blurred by cataracts, and they throbbed with a vain intensity. He looked as if he were going blind.

The sight of him made Covenant's own rage feel incondign, faulty. He was beholding another of his victims. He had no justification for anger. "Triock!" he groaned, unable to think of any other response. "Triock!"

The Stonedownor paused, allowing him a chance to regain his feet, then advanced threateningly.

Covenant retreated a step or two. He needed something to say, something that could penetrate or deflect Triock's bitterness. But his thoughts were stunned; they groped ineffectually, as if they had been rendered fingerless by the loss of his ring. Triock swung at him. He parried the blow with his forearms, kept himself from being knocked down again. Words —he needed words.

"Hellfire!" he shouted because he could not find any other reply. "What happened to your Oath of Peace?"

"It is dead," Triock growled hoarsely. "It is dead with a spike of wood in its belly!" He swung again, staggered Covenant. "The Law of Death is broken, and all Peace has been laid waste."

Covenant regained his balance and retreated farther. "Triock!" he gasped. "I didn't kill her. She died trying to save my life. She knew it was my fault, and she still tried to save me. She would fight you now if she saw you like this! What did that Raver do to you?"

The Stonedownor advanced with slow ferocity.

"You're not like this!" Covenant cried. "You gave your whole life to prove you're not like this!"

Springing suddenly, Triock caught Covenant by the throat. His thumbs ground into Covenant's windpipe as he snarled, "You have not seen what I have seen!"

Covenant struggled, but he had no strength to match Triock's. His fingers clawed and clutched, and had no effect. The need for air began to hum in his ears.

Triock released one hand, cocked his fist deliberately, and hit Covenant in the center of his wounded forehead. He pitched backward, almost fell. But hands caught him from behind, yanked him upright, put him on his feet—hands that burned him like the touch of acid.

He jerked away from them, then whirled to see who had burned him. Fresh blood ran from his yammering forehead into his eyes, clogged his vision, but he gouged it away with numb fingers, made himself see the two figures that had caught him.

They were laughing at him together. Beat for beat, their ridicule came as one, matched each other in weird consonance; they sounded like one voice jeering through two throats.

They were Ramen.

He saw them in an instant, took them in as if they had been suddenly revealed out of midnight by a flash of dismay. He recognized them as two of Manethrall Kam's Cords, Lal and Whane. But they had changed. Even his truncated vision could see the alteration which had been wrought in them, the complete reversal of being which occupied them. Contempt and lust submerged the former spirit of their health. Only the discomfortable spasms which flicked their faces, and the unnecessary violence of their emanations, gave any indication that they had ever been unlike what they were now.

"Our friend Triock spoke the truth," they said together, and the unharmonized unison of their voices mocked both Covenant and Triock. "Our brother is not with us. He is at work in the destruction of Revelstone. But Triock will take his place—for a time. A short time. We are *turiya* and *moksha,* Herem and Jehannum. We have come to take delight in the ruin of things we hate. You are nothing to us now, groveler —Unbeliever." Again they laughed, one spirit or impulse uttering contempt through two throats. "Yet you —and our friend Triock—amuse us while we wait."

But Covenant hardly heard them. An instant after he comprehended what had happened to them, he saw something else, something that almost blinded him to the Ravers. Two other figures stood a short distance behind Whane and Lal.

The two people he had most ached to see since he had regained himself in Morinmoss: Saltheart Foamfollower and Bannor.

The sight of them filled him with horror.

Foamfollower wore a host of recent battle-marks among his older scars, and Bannor's silvering hair and lined face had aged perceptibly. But all that was insignificant beside the grisly fact that they were not moving.

They did not so much as turn their heads toward Covenant. They were paralyzed, clenched rigid and helpless, by a green force which played about them like a corona, enveloped them in coercion. They were as motionless as if even pulse and respiration had been crushed out of them by shimmering emerald.

And if they had been able to look at Covenant, they would not have seen him. Their eyes were like Triock's, but much more severely glazed. Only the faintest outlines of pupil and iris were visible behind the white blindness which covered their orbs.

Bannor! Covenant cried. Foamfollower! Ah!

While his body swayed on locked joints, he cowered inwardly. His arms covered his head as if to protect it from an ax. The plight of Bannor and Foamfollower dealt him an unendurable shock. He could not bear it. He quailed where he stood as if the ground were heaving under him.

Then Triock caught hold of him again. The Stone-downor bent him to the dirt, hunched furiously over him to pant, "You have not seen what I have seen. You do not know what you have done."

Weak, ringless, and miserable though he was, Covenant still heard Triock, heard the whelming passion with which Triock told him that even now he did not know the worst, had not faced the worst. And that communication made a difference to him. It pushed him deep into his fear, down to a place in him which had not been touched by either capture or horror. It drove him back to the calm which had been given to him in Morinmoss. He seemed to remember a part of himself that had been hidden from him. Something had been changed for him in the Forest, something which could not be taken away. He caught hold of it, immersed himself in the gift.

A moment later, he raised his head as if he had come through a dark gulf of panic. He was too weak to fight Triock; he had lost his ring; blood streamed from his damaged forehead into his eyes. But he was no longer at the mercy of fear.

Blinking rapidly to clear his vision, he gasped up at Triock, "What's happened to them?"

"You have not seen!" Triock roared. Once more, he raised his fist to hammer the Unbeliever's face. But before he could strike, a low voice commanded simply, "Stop."

Triock jerked, struggling to complete his blow.

"I have given you time. Now I desire him to know what I do."

The command held Triock; he could not strike. Trembling, he wrenched away from Covenant, then spun back to point lividly toward the stone column and shout, "There!"

Covenant lurched to his feet, wiped his eyes.

Midway between him and the upreared fist of stone stood Elena!

She was robed in radiant green velure, and she bore herself proudly, like a queen. She seemed swathed in

an aura of emeralds; her presence sparkled like gems
when she smiled. At once, without effort or assertion,
she showed that she was the master of the situation.
The Ravers and Triock waited before her like subjects
before their liege.

In her right hand she held a long staff. It was
metal-shod at both ends, and between its heels it was
intricately carved with the runes and symbols of
theurgy.

The Staff of Law.

But the wonder of its appearance there meant noth-
thing to Covenant compared with the miracle of Elena's
return. He had loved her, lost her. Her death at the
hands of dead Kevin Landwaster had brought his second sojourn in the Land to an end. Yet she stood now
scarcely thirty feet from him. She was smiling.

A thrill of joy shot through him. The love which had
tormented his heart since her fall rushed up in him
until he felt he was about to burst with it. Blood
streamed from his eyes like tears. Joy choked him so
that he could not speak. Half blinded, half weeping, he
shrugged off his travail and started toward her as if
he meant to throw himself down before her, kiss her
feet.

Before he had crossed half the distance, she made a
short gesture with the Staff, and at once a jolt of force
hit him. It drove the air from his lungs, pitched him to
his hands and knees on the hard ground.

"No," she said softly, almost tenderly. "All your
questions will be answered before I slay you, Thomas
Covenant, ur-Lord and Unbeliever—beloved." On her
cold lips, the word *beloved* impugned him. "But you
will not touch me. You will come no closer."

A great weight leaned against his shoulders, held
him to the ground. He retched for air, but when he
gasped it into his lungs, it hurt him as if he were inhaling disease. The atmosphere around him reeked
with her presence. She pervaded the air like rot. On a
scale that dwarfed him, she smelled as he did—
smelled like—leprosy.

He forced up his head, gaped gasping at her from
under the streaming spike of his wound.

With a smile like a smirk or leer, she extended her left hand toward him and opened it, so that he could see lying in her palm his white gold wedding band.

Elena! he retched voicelessly. Elena! He felt that he was being crushed under a burden of impenetrable circumstance. In supplication and futility, he reached toward her, but she only laughed at him quietly, as if he were a masque of impotence enacted for her pleasure.

A moment passed before his anguish permitted him to see her clearly, and while he groveled without comprehension, she shone defiantly before him like a soul of purest emerald. But slowly he recovered his vision. Like a reborn phoenix, she flourished in green loveliness. Yet in some way she reminded him of the specter of Kevin Landwaster—a spirit dredged out of its uneasy grave by commands of irrefusable cruelty. Her expression was as placid as power could make it; she radiated triumph and decay. But her eyes were completely lightless, dark. It was as if the strange bifurcation, the dualness, of her sight had gone completely to its other pole, away from the tangible things around her. She seemed not to see where or who she was, what she did; her gaze was focused elsewhere, on the secret which compelled her.

She had become a servant of the Despiser. Even while she stood there with the Staff and the ring in her hands, Lord Foul's eyes held her like the eyes of a serpent.

In her violated beauty, Covenant beheld the doom of the Land. It would be kept fair, so that Lord Foul could more keenly relish its ravishment—and it would be diseased to the marrow.

"Elena," he panted, then paused, gagging at the reek of her. "Elena. Look at me."

With a disdainful toss of her head, she turned away from him, moved a step or two closer to the stone pillar. "Triock," she commanded lightly, "answer the Unbeliever's questions. I do not wish him to be in ignorance. His despair will make a pretty present for the master."

At once, Triock strode stiffly forward, and stood so

that Covenant could see him without fighting the pressure which held him to the ground. The Stonedownor's scowl had not changed, not abated one muscle or line of its vehemence, but his voice carried an odd undertow of grief. He began roughly, as if he were reading an indictment: "You have asked where you are. You are at Landsdrop. Behind you lies the Fall of the River Landrider and the northmost reach of the Southron Range. Before you stands the Colossus of the Fall."

Covenant panted at this information as if it interfered with his ragged efforts to breathe.

"Perhaps the Lords"—Triock hissed the word *Lords* in rage or desperation—"have spoken to you of the Colossus. In ages long past, it uttered the power of the One Forest to interdict its enemies the three Ravers from the Upper Land. The Colossus has been silent for millennia—silent since men broke the spirit of the Forest. Yet you may observe that *turiya* and *moksha* do not approach the stone. While one Forestal still lives in the remnants of the Forest, the Colossus may not be altogether undone. Thus it remains a thorn in the Despiser's mastery.

"It is now Elena's purpose to destroy this stone."

Behind Covenant, both Ravers growled with pleasure at the thought.

"This has not been possible until now. Since this war began, Elena has stood here with the Staff of Law in support of the master's armies. With the Staff's power, she has held this winter upon the Land, thus freeing the master for other war work. This place was chosen for her so that she would be ready if the Colossus awoke—and so that she could destroy it if it did not awaken. But it has resisted her." The hardness in his voice sounded almost like rage at Elena. "There is Earth-power in it yet.

"But with the Staff and the wild magic, she will be capable. She will throw the rubble of the Colossus from its cliff. And when you have seen that no ancient bastion, however Earthpowerful and incorruptible, can stand against a servant of the master—then Elena Foul-wife will slay you where you kneel in your despair. She will slay us all." With a jerk of his head, he included Bannor and Foamfollower.

In horrific unison, the Ravers laughed.

Covenant writhed under the pressure which held him. "How?"

His question could have meant many things, but Triock understood him. "Because the Law of Death has been broken!" he rasped. Fury flamed in his voice; he could no longer contain it. He watched Elena as she moved gracefully toward the Colossus, preparing herself to challenge it, and his voice blared after her as if he were striving in spite of her coercion to find some way to restrain her. Clearly, he knew how he was being compelled, what was being done to him, and the knowledge filled him with torment. "Broken!" he repeated, almost shouting. "When she employed the Power of Command to bring Kevin Landwaster back from his grave, she broke the Law which separates life from death. She made it possible for the master to call her back in her turn—and with her the Staff of Law. Therefore she is his servant. And in her hands, the Staff serves him—though he would not use it himself, lest he share the fate of Drool Rockworm. Thus all Law is warped to his will!

"Behold her, Thomas Covenant! She is unchanged. Within her still lives the spirit of the daughter of Lena. Even as she readies herself for this destruction, she remembers what she was and hates what she is." His chest heaved as if he were strangling on bitterness. "That is the master's way. She is resurrected so that she may participate in the ruin of the Land—the Land she loves!"

He no longer made any pretense of speaking to Covenant; he hurled his voice at Elena as if his tone were the only part of him still able to resist her. "Elena Foul-wife"—he uttered the name with horror—"now holds the white gold. She is more the master's servant than any Raver. In the hands of *turiya* or *moksha,* that power would breed rebellion. With wild magic, any Raver would throw down the master if he could, and take a new seat in the thronehall of Ridjeck Thome. But Elena will not rebel. She will not use the wild magic to free herself. She has been commanded from the dead, and her service is pure!"

He raged the word *pure* at her as if it were the worst affront he could utter. But she was impervious to him, secure in power and triumph. She only smiled faintly, amused by his ranting, and continued to make her preparations.

With her back to Covenant and Triock, she faced the monolith. It towered over her as if it were about to fall and crush her, but her stance admitted to no possibility of danger. With the Staff and the ring, she was superior to every power in the Land. In radiance and might, she raised her hands, holding up the Staff of Law and the white gold. Her sleeves fell from her arms. Exulting and exalted, she began to sing her attack on the Colossus of the Fall.

Her song hurt Covenant's ears, exacerbating his raw helplessness. He could not bear her intent, and could not oppose it; her interdict kept him on his knees like fetters of humiliation. Though he was only a dozen yards from her, he could not reach her, could not interfere with her purpose.

His thoughts raced madly, scrambled for alternatives. He could not abide the destruction of the Colossus. He had to find another answer.

"Foamfollower!" he croaked in desperation. "I don't know what's happening to you—I don't know what's being done to you. But you've got to fight it! You're a Giant! You've got to stop her! Try to stop her! Foamfollower! Bannor!"

The Ravers met his plea with sardonic jeers, and Triock rasped without taking his eyes off Elena, "You are a fool, Thomas Covenant. They cannot help you. They are too strong to be mastered—as I have been mastered—and too weak to be masters. Therefore she has imprisoned them by the power of the Staff. The Staff crushes all resistance. Thus it is proven that Law does not oppose Despite. We are all mastered beyond redemption."

"Not you!" Covenant responded urgently. He fought the pressure until he feared his lungs would break, but he could not free himself. Without his ring, he felt as crippled as if his arms had been amputated. Without it, he weighed less than nothing in the scales of the Land's fate. "Not you!" he gasped again. "I can hear you, Triock! You! She isn't afraid of you—she isn't holding you. Triock! Stop her!"

Again the Ravers laughed. But this time Covenant heard the strain in their voices. Heaving against his captivity, he managed to wrench his head around far enough to look at Whane and Lal.

They still stood a safe distance from the Colossus. Neither made any move to help Covenant or oppose Elena. Both went on chuckling as if they could not help themselves. Yet their exertion was unmistakable. They were white-lipped and rigid; beads of effort ran down their faces. With all the long pride of their people, the Ramen were struggling to break free.

And behind them, Foamfollower and Bannor strove for freedom also. Somehow, both of them had found the strength to move slightly. Foamfollower's head was bowed, and he clenched his face with one hand as if he were trying to alter the shape of his skull. Bannor's fingers clawed at his sides; his face grew taut, baring his teeth. Urgently, desperately, they fought Elena's power.

Their ordeal felt terrible to Covenant—terrible and hopeless. Like the Ramen, they were beyond the limits of what they could do. Pressure mounted in them, radiated from them. It was so acute that Covenant feared their hearts would rupture. And they had no chance of success. The power of the Staff increased to crush every extravagance of their self-expenditure.

Their futility hurt Covenant more than his own. He was accustomed to impotence, inured to it, but Bannor and Foamfollower were not. The stark vision of their defeat almost made him cry out in anguish. He wanted to shout to them, beg them to stop before they drove themselves soul-mad.

But the next instant a surge of new hope shot through him as he suddenly understood what they were doing. They knew they could not escape, were not trying to escape. They fought toward another goal. Elena was paying no attention to them; she concentrated on preparing for the destruction of the Colossus. So she was not actively exerting herself to imprison them. She had simply left her compulsion in the air and turned her back.

Foamfollower and Bannor were drawing on this compulsion, using it—using it up. As the Giant and the Bloodguard strained for freedom, strove with all their personal might, Triock jerked his head from side to side, quivered in a fever of passion, snapped his jaws as if he were trying to tear hunks of domination out of the air—and began to move toward Elena.

The Ravers made no attempt to stop him. They could not; the struggles of the Ramen gave them no leeway in which to act.

Triock strained as he moved as if his bones were being torn asunder, and he quavered imploringly again and again, "Elena? Elena?" But he moved; he advanced step by step toward her.

Covenant watched him in an agony of suspense.

Before he came within arm's reach of her, she said severely, "Stop."

Swaying in a gale of conflicting demands, Triock halted.

"If you resist me one more step," she grated, "I will tear your heart from your pathetic old body and feed it to Herem and Jehannum while you observe them and beg me to let you die."

Triock was weeping now, shaking with importunate sobs. "Elena? Elena?"

Without even glancing at him, she resumed her song.

But the next instant, something snatched at her attention, spun her away from the Colossus. Her face pointed lividly toward the west. Surprise and anger contorted her features. For a moment, she stared in speechless indignation at the intrusion.

Then she brandished the Staff of Law. "The Lords strike back!" she howled furiously. *"Samadhi* is threatened! They dare!"

Covenant gaped at the information, at her knowledge of the siege of Revelstone. But he had no time to assimilate it.

"Foul's blood!" she raged. "Blast them, Raver!" Immense forces gathered in the Staff, mounting to be hurled across the distance to *samadhi* Sheol's aid.

For that instant, she neglected her compulsion of the people around her.

The blindness lost its hold on Bannor and Foamfollower. They tottered, lurched, started into motion. The Ravers tried to react, but could not move quickly enough against the resistance of the Ramen.

Covenant felt the pressure on his back ease. At once, he rolled out from under it. Springing to his feet, he launched himself toward Elena.

But Triock was the only one close enough to her to take advantage of her lapse. With a wild cry, he chopped both fists down at her left hand.

His hands passed through her spectral flesh and struck the ring. The unexpectedness of the blow tore the solid band from her surprised fingers. It dropped free.

He dove after it, got one hand on it, flicked it away toward Covenant as his body slapped the hard ground.

Elena's reaction came instantly. Before Triock could roll, try to evade her, she stabbed the Staff down at him, hit him in the center of his back. Power flared through him, shattering his spine.

Almost in the same motion, she swung the Staff up again, caught it in a combat grip as she whirled to face Covenant.

His start toward her almost made him miss the ring. It went past him on one side, but he skidded and pounced on it, scooped it up before she could stop him. With his wedding band clenched in his fist, he braced himself to meet her attack.

She regarded him momentarily, then chose not to exert herself against him. With one wave of the Staff, she reimprisoned Foamfollower and Bannor, quenched the rebellion of the Ramen. Then she dropped her guard as if she no longer needed it. Her voice shook with anger, but she was steady as she said, "It will not avail him. He knows not how to awaken its might. Herem, Jehannum—I leave him to you."

In horrid unison, the two Ravers snarled their satisfaction, their hunger for him. Together, they moved slowly toward him.

He was caught between them and Elena.

So that he would not lose his ring again, he pushed it onto his wedding finger. He had lost weight; his fingers were gaunt, and the ring hung on him insecurely, as if it might fall off at any moment. Yet his need for it had never been greater. He clenched his fist around it and retreated before the advance of the Ravers.

In the back of his mind, he was sure that Triock was not dead. Triock was his summoner; he would disappear from the Land as soon as the Stonedownor died. But Triock surely had only moments of life left. Without knowing how to do it, Covenant wanted to make those moments count.

He backed away from the Ravers, toward Elena. She stood at rest near the Colossus, observing him. Glee and anger were balanced in her face. The Ravers came at him step by slow step, with their arms extended hungrily, sarcastically, inviting him to abandon resistance and rush into the oblivion of their grasp.

They advanced; he retreated; she stood where she was, defying him to touch her. His ring hung lifeless on his finger as if it were a thing of metal and futility, nothing more—a talisman devoid of meaning in his hands. A rising tide of protest filled him with ineffectual curses.

Hellfire. Hellfire. Hell and blood!

Impulsively, without knowing why he did it, he shrieked into the gray wind, "Forestal! Help me!"

At once, the clenched crown of the Colossus burst into flame. For an instant while Herem and Jehannum yowled, the monolith blazed with verdant fire—a conflagration the color of leaves and grass flourishing, green that had nothing in common with Lord Foul's emerald Illearth Stone. Raw, fertile aromas crackled in the air like violent spring.

Abruptly, two bolts of force raged out of the blaze, sprang like lightning at the Ravers. In a coruscating welter of sparks and might, the bolts struck the chests of Lal and Whane.

The monolith's power flamed at their hearts until

the mortal flesh of the Ramen was incinerated, flash-burned into nothingness. Then the bolts dropped, the conflagration vanished.

Herem and Jehannum were gone.

The sudden blast and vanishing of the fire staggered Covenant. Forgetting his peril, he stared dumbly about him. The Ramen were dead. More blood, more lives sacrificed to his impotence. He wanted to cry out, No!

Some instinct warned him. He ducked, and the Staff of Law hissed past his head.

He jumped away, turned, caught his balance. Elena was advancing toward him. She held the Staff poised in both hands. Her face was full of murder.

She could have felled him with an exertion of the Staff's might, ravaged him where he stood by unleashing her power against him. But she was too mad with rage for such fighting. She wanted to crush him physically, beat him to death with the strength of her own arms. As he faced her, she gestured toward Foamfollower and Bannor without even glancing in their direction. They crumpled like puppets with cut strings, fell on their faces and lay still. Then she raised the Staff over his head like an ax and hacked at Covenant.

With a desperate fling of his arm, he deflected the Staff so that it slammed against his right shoulder rather than his head. The force of the blow seemed to paralyze his whole right side, but he grappled for the Staff with his left hand, caught hold of it, prevented her from snatching it back for another strike.

Quickly, she shifted her hands on the Staff and threw her weight onto the wood to take advantage of his defense. Bearing down on his shoulder, she drove him to his knees.

He braced his numb arm on the ground and strained to resist her, tried to get his feet under him. But he was too weak. She changed the direction of her pressure so that it jammed squarely against his throat. He had to fight the Staff with both hands to keep his larynx from being crushed. Slowly, almost effortlessly, she bent him back.

Then she had him flat on the ground. He pushed against the Staff with all his waning strength, but he could not stop her. His breathing was cut off. His bloodied eyes throbbed in their sockets as he stared at her ferocity.

Her gaze was focused on him as if he were food for the rankest hunger of her ill soul. Through it, he seemed to see the Despiser slavering in triumph and scorn. And yet her eyes showed something else as well. Triock had told the truth about her. Behind the savagery of her glare, he felt the last unconquerable core of her sobbing with revulsion.

He lacked the strength to save himself. If he could have hated her, met her fury with fury, he might have been capable of one convulsive heave, one thrust to buy himself another moment or two of life. But he could not. She was his daughter; he loved her. He had put her where she was as surely as if he had been a conscious servant of the Despiser all along. She was about to kill him, and he loved her. The only thing left for him was to die without breaking faith with himself.

He used his last air and his last resistance to croak, "You don't even exist."

His words inflamed her like an ultimate denial. In mad fury, she eased the pressure for an instant while she gathered all her force, all her strength, and all the power of the Staff, for one crush which would eradicate the offense of his life. She took a deep breath as if she were inhaling illimitable might, then threw her weight and muscle and power, her very Foul-given existence, through the Staff at his throat.

But his hands were clenched on the Staff. His ring pressed the wood. When her force touched his white gold, the wild magic erupted like an uncapped volcano.

His senses went blank at the immensity of the blast. Yet not one flame or thrust of it touched him; all the detonation went back through the Staff at Elena.

It did not hurl her off him; it was not that kind of power. But it tore through the rune-carved wood of the Staff like white sun-fire, rent the Staff fiber from fiber as if its Law were nothing but a shod bundle of splinters. A sharp riving shook the atmosphere, so that even the Colossus seemed to recoil from this unleashing of power.

The Staff of Law turned to ash in dead Elena's hands.

At once, the wind lurched as if the eruption of wild magic were an arrow in its bosom. With flutters and gusts and silent cries, it tumbled to the ground, came to an end as if the raw demon of winter had been stricken out of the air with one shaft.

A whirl of force sprang up around Elena, mounted like a wind devil with her in its center. Her death had come back for her; the Law she had broken was sucking her out of life again. As Covenant watched—stunned and uncomprehending, almost blinded by his reprieve—she began to dissipate. Particle by particle, her being vanished into the gyre, fled into dissolution. But while she faded and failed, lost her ill existence, she found the solidity for one final cry.

"Covenant," she called like a lorn voice of desolation. "Beloved! Strike a blow for me!"

Then she was gone, reabsorbed into death. The gyre grew pale, paler, until it had disappeared in unruffled air.

Covenant was left alone with his victims.

Involuntarily, through means over which he had no control, he had saved himself—and had allowed his friends to be struck down. He felt chastened, frail, as devoid of victory as if he had actively slain the woman he loved.

So many people had sacrificed themselves.

He knew that Triock was still alive, so he climbed painfully to his feet and stumbled over to the fallen Stonedownor. Triock's breathing rattled like blood in his throat; he would be dead soon. Covenant seated himself on the ground and lifted Triock so that the man's head rested on his lap.

Triock's face was disfigured by the force which had smashed him. His charred skin peeled off his skull in places, and his eyes had been seared. From the slack dark hole of his mouth came faint plumes of smoke like the fleeing wisps of his soul.

Covenant hugged Triock's head with both arms and began to weep.

After a time, the Stonedownor sensed in some way

who held him. Through the death thickening in his gullet, he struggled to speak. "Covenant."

His voice was barely audible, but Covenant fought back his tears to respond, "I hear you."

"You are not to blame. She was—flawed from birth."

That was as far as his mercy could go. After one final wisp, the smoke faded away. Covenant held him, and knew he had no pulse or breath of life left.

He understood that Triock had forgiven him. The Stonedownor was not to blame if his gift gave no consolation. In addition to everything else, Covenant was responsible for the flaw of Elena's birth. She was the daughter of a crime which could never be undone. So he could do nothing but sit with Triock's unanswerable head in his lap, and weep while he waited for the reversal of his summons, the end which would reave him of the Land.

But no end came. In the past, he had always begun to fail as soon as his summoner died; but now he remained. Moments passed, and still he was undiminished. Gradually, he realized that this time he would not disappear, that for reasons he did not understand, he had not yet lost his chance.

He did not have to accept Elena's fate. It was not the last word—not yet.

When Bannor and Foamfollower stirred, groaned, began to regain consciousness, he made himself move. Carefully, deliberately, he took his ring from his wedding finger and placed it on the index finger of his halfhand, so that it would be less likely to slip off.

Then, amid all his grief and regret, he stood up on bones that could bear anything, and hobbled over to help his friends.

SEVENTEEN: The Spoiled Plains

BANNOR recovered more quickly than Foamfollower. In spite of his advancing age, the toughness of the *Haruchai* was still in him; after Covenant had chafed his wrists and neck for a moment, he shrugged off his unconsciousness and became almost instantly alert. He met Covenant's teary gaze with characteristic dispassion, and together they went to do what they could for the Giant.

Foamfollower lay moaning on the ground in a fever of revulsion. Spasms bared his teeth, and his massive hands thrashed erratically against his chest as if he were trying to smite some fatal spot of wrong in himself. He seemed in danger of harming himself. So Bannor sat on the ground at the Giant's head, braced his feet on Foamfollower's shoulders, and caught his flailing arms by the wrists. Bannor held the Giant's arms still while Covenant sat on Foamfollower's chest and slapped his snarling face.

After a moment of resistance, Foamfollower let out a roar. Wrenching savagely, he heaved Bannor over Covenant's head, knocked the Unbeliever off his chest, and lurched panting to his feet.

Covenant retreated from the threat of Foamfollower's fists. But as the Giant blinked and panted, he recovered himself, recognized his friends. "Covenant?" he gritted, "Bannor?" as if he feared they were Ravers.

"Foamfollower," Covenant responded thickly. Tears of relief streamed down his gaunt cheeks. "You're all right."

Slowly, Foamfollower relaxed as he saw that his friends were unmastered and whole. "Stone and Sea!" he gasped weakly, shuddering as he breathed. "Ah! My friends—have I harmed you?"

Covenant could not answer; he was choked with fresh weeping. He stood where he was and let Foamfollower watch his tears; he had no other way to tell the Giant how he felt. After a moment, Bannor replied for him, "We are well—as well as may be. You have done us no injury."

"And the—the specter of High Lord Elena? The Staff of Law? How is it that we yet live?"

"Gone." Covenant fought to control himself. "Destroyed."

Foamfollower's face was full of sympathy. "Ah, no, my friend," he sighed. "She is not destroyed. The dead cannot be destroyed."

"I know. I know that." Covenant gritted his teeth, hugged his chest, until he passed the crest of his emotion. Then it began to subside, and he regained some measure of steadiness. "She's just dead—dead again. But the Staff—it was destroyed. By wild magic." Half fearing the reaction of his friends to this information, he added, "I didn't do it. It wasn't my doing. She—" He faltered. He had heard Mhoram say. *You are the white gold.* How could he be sure now what was or was not his doing?

But his revelation only drew a strange glint from Bannor's flat eyes. The *Haruchai* had always considered weapons unnecessary, even corruptive. Bannor found satisfaction rather than regret in the passing of the Staff. And Foamfollower shrugged the explanation aside, as if it were unimportant compared to his friend's distress. "Ah, Covenant, Covenant," he groaned. "How can you endure? Who can withstand such things?"

"I'm a leper," Covenant responded. He was surprised to hear himself say the word without bitterness. "I can stand anything. Because I can't feel it." He gestured with his diseased hands because his tears so obviously contradicted him. "This is a dream. It can't touch me. I'm"—he grimaced, remembering the belief which had first led Elena to break the Law of Death—"numb."

Answering tears blurred Foamfollower's cavernous eyes. "And you are very brave," he said in a thick voice. "You are beyond me."

The Giant's grief almost reopened Covenant's weeping. But he steadied himself by thinking of the questions he would have to ask, the things he would have to say. He wanted to smile for Foamfollower, but his cheeks were too stiff. Then he felt he had been caught in the act of a perennial failure, a habitual inadequacy of response. He was relieved to turn away when Bannor called their attention to the weather.

Bannor made him aware of the absence of wind. In his struggle with Elena, he had hardly noticed the change. But now he could feel the stillness of the atmosphere like a palpable healing. For a time, at least, Lord Foul's gelid frenzy was gone. And without the wind to drive it, the gray cloud-cover hung sullen and empty overhead, like a casket without a corpse.

As a result, the air felt warmer. Covenant half expected to see dampness on the ground as the hard earth thawed, half expected spring to begin on the spot. In the gentle stillness, the sound of the waterfall reached him clearly.

Bannor's perceptions went further; he sensed something Covenant had missed. After a moment, he took Covenant and Foamfollower to the Colossus to show them what he had found.

From the obsidian monolith came a soft emanation of heat.

This warmth held the true promise of spring; it smelled of buds and green grass, of *aliantha* and moss and forest-loam. Under its influence, Covenant found that he could relax. He put aside misery, fear, unresolved need, and sank down gratefully to sit with his back against the soothing stone.

Foamfollower hunted around the area until he located the sack of provisions he had carried with him from the Ramen covert. He took out food and his pot of graveling. Together, he, Bannor, and Covenant ate a silent meal under the fist of the Colossus as if they were sharing a communion—as if they accepted the stone's warmth and shelter to do it honor. They had no other way to express their thanks.

Covenant was hungry; he had had nothing but Demondim-drink to sustain him for days. Yet he ate the food, absorbed the warmth, with a strange humility, as if he had not earned them, did not deserve them. He knew in his heart that the destruction of the Staff purchased nothing more than a brief respite for the Land, a short delay in the Despiser's eventual triumph. And that respite was not his doing. The reflex which had triggered the white gold was surely as unconscious, as involuntary, as if it had happened in his sleep. And yet another life had been spent on his account. That knowledge humbled him. He fed and warmed himself because all his work had yet to be done, and no other being in the Land could do it for him.

When the frugal meal was finished, he began his task by asking his companions how they had come to the Colossus.

Foamfollower winced at the memory. He left the telling of it to Bannor's terseness. While Bannor spoke, the Giant cleaned and tended Covenant's forehead.

In short sentences, Bannor indicated that the Ramen had been able to defeat the attack on their covert, thanks to the Giant's prodigious aid. But the battle had been a long and costly one, and the night was gone before Bannor and Foamfollower could begin to search for Covenant and Lena. ("Ur-viles!" Foamfollower muttered at Covenant's injury. "This will not heal. To make you captive, they put their mark upon you.") The Manethralls permitted only two Cords, Whane and Lal, to aid in the search. For during the night, a change had come over the Ranyhyn. To the surprise and joy of the Ramen, the great horses had unexpectedly started south toward the sanctuary of the mountains. The Ramen followed at once. Only their mixed awe and concern for the Ringthane induced them to give Bannor and Foamfollower any aid at all.

So the four of them began the hunt. But they had lost too much time; wind and snow had obscured the trail. They lost it south of the Roamsedge and could find no trace of Covenant. At last they concluded that he must have gained other aid to take him eastward. Together the four made what haste they could toward the Fall of the River Landrider.

The journey was made slow and arduous by *kresh* packs and marauders, and the four feared that Covenant would have left the Upper Land days ago. But when they neared the Colossus, they came upon a band of ur-viles accompanied by the Raver, Herem-Triock. Then the four were dismayed to see that the band bore with it the Unbeliever, prostrate as if he were dead.

The four attacked, slew the ur-viles. But they could not prevent the call which Herem sent. And before they could defeat Herem, rescue Covenant, and retrieve the ring, that call was answered by the dead Elena, wielding the Staff of Law. She mastered the four effortlessly. Then she gave Whane to Herem, so that Triock's anguish would be more poignant. When Jehannum came to her, that Raver entered Lal. Covenant knew the rest.

Bannor and Foamfollower had seen no sign of Lena. They did not know what had delayed Covenant's arrival at Landsdrop.

As Bannor finished, Foamfollower growled in angry disgust, "Stone and Sea! She has made me unclean. I must bathe—I will need a sea to wash away this coercion."

Bannor nodded. "I, also."

But neither of them moved, though the River Landrider was nearby beyond a low line of hills. Covenant knew they were holding themselves at his disposal; they seemed to sense that he needed them. And they had questions of their own. But he felt unready for the things he would have to say. After a silence, he asked painfully, "Triock summoned me—and he's dead. Why am I still here?"

Foamfollower mused briefly, then said, "Perhaps because the Law of Death has been broken—perhaps it was that Law which formerly sent you from the Land when your summoner died. Or perhaps it is because I also had a hand in this call."

Yes, Covenant sighed to himself. His debt to Triock was hardly less than what he owed Foamfollower.

He could not shirk the responsibility any longer; he forced himself to describe what had happened to Lena.

His voice was dull as he spoke of her—an old woman brought to a bloody and graveless end because in her confusion she clung to the man who had harmed her. And her death was only the most recent tragedy in her family. First and last, her people had borne the brunt of him: Trell Gravelingas, Atiaran Trell-mate, High Lord Elena, Lena herself—he had ruined them all. Such things altered him, made a different man of him. That made it possible for him to ask another question after he had told all he knew of his own tale.

"Foamfollower"—he framed his inquiry as carefully as he could—"it's none of my business. But Pietten said some terrible things about you. Or he meant them to be terrible. He said—" But he could not say the words. No matter how he uttered them, they would sound like an accusation.

The Giant sighed, and his whole frame sagged. He studied his intertwined hands as if somewhere in their clasped gentleness and butchery were a secret he could not unclose, but he no longer evaded the question. "He said that I betrayed my kinfolk—that the Giants of Seareach died to the last child at the hands of *turiya* Raver because I abandoned them. It is true."

Foamfollower! Covenant moaned. My friend! Sorrow welled up in him, almost made him weep again.

Abstractedly, Bannor said, "Many things were lost in The Grieve that day."

"Yes." Foamfollower blinked as if he were trying to hold back tears, but his eyes were dry, as parched as a wilderland. "Yes—many things. Among them I was the least.

"Ah, Covenant, how can I tell you of it? This tongue has no words long enough for the tale. No word can encompass the love for a lost homeland, or the anguish of diminishing seed, or the pride—the pride in fidelity — That fidelity was our only reply to our extinction. We could not have borne our decline if we had not taken pride.

"So my people—the Giants—I also, in my own way —the Giants were filled with horror—with abhorrence so deep that it numbed the very marrow of their bones—when they saw their pride riven—torn from them like rotten sails in the wind. They foundered at the sight. They saw the portent of their hope of Home —the three brothers—changed from fidelity to the most potent ill by one small stroke of the Despiser's evil. Who in the Land could hope to stand against a Giant-Raver? Thus the Unhomed became the means to destroy that to which they had held themselves true. And in horror at the naught of their fidelity, their folly practiced through long centuries of pride, they were transfixed. Their revulsion left no room in them for thought or resistance or choice. Rather than behold the cost of their failure—rather than risk the chance that more of them would be made Soulcrusher's servants—they—they elected to be slain.

"I also—in my way, I was horrified as well. But I had already seen what they had not, until that moment. I had seen myself become what I hated. Alone of all my kindred, I was not surprised. It was not the vision of a Giant-Raver which horrified me. It was my —my own people.

"Ah! Stone and Sea! They appalled me. I stormed at them—I ran through The Grieve like a dark sea of madness, howling at their abandonment, raging to strike one spark of resistance in the drenched tinder of their hearts. But they—they put away their tools, and banked their fires, and made ready their homes as if in preparation for departure—" Abruptly, his suppressed passion broke into a cry. "My people! I could not bear it! I fled them with abjection crowding at my heart—fled them lest I, too, should fall into their dismay. Therefore they were slain. I who might have

fought the Raver deserted them in the deepest blackness of their need." Unable to contain himself any
longer, he heaved to his feet. His raw, scourged voice
rasped thickly in his throat. "I am unclean. I must—
wash."

Holding himself stiffly upright, he turned and lumbered away toward the river.

The helplessness of Covenant's pain came out as
anger. His own voice shook as he muttered to Bannor,
"If you say one word to blame him, I swear—"

Then he stopped himself. He had accused Bannor
unjustly too often in the past; the Bloodguard had
long ago earned better treatment than this from him.
But Bannor only shrugged. "I am a *Haruchai*," he
said. "We also are not immune. Corruption wears
many faces. Blame is a more enticing face than others,
but it is none the less a mask for the Despiser."

His speech made Covenant look at him closely.
Something came up between them that had never been
laid to rest, neither on Gallows Howe nor in the
Ramen covert. It wore the aspect of habitual Bloodguard distrust, but as he met Bannor's eyes, Covenant
sensed that the issue was a larger one.

Without inflection, Bannor went on: "Hate and vengeance are also masks."

Covenant was struck by how much the Bloodguard
had aged. His mortality had accelerated. His hair was
the same silver as his eyebrows; his skin had a sere appearance, as if it had started to wither; and his wrinkles looked oddly fatal, like gullies of death in his
countenance. Yet his steady dispassion seemed as complete as ever. He did not look like a man who had
deserted his sworn loyalty to the Lords.

"Ur-Lord," he said evenly, "what will you do?"

"Do?" Covenant did his best to match the Bloodguard, though he could not look at Bannor's aging
without remorse. "I still have work to do. I've got to
go to Foul's Creche."

"For what purpose?"

"I've got to stop him."

"High Lord Elena also strove to stop him. You have
seen the outcome."

"Yes." Covenant did full justice to Bannor's statement. But he did not falter. "I've got to find a better answer than she did."

"Do you make this choice out of hate?"

He met the question squarely. "I don't know."

"Then why do you go?"

"Because I must." That *must* carried the weight of an irrefusable necessity. The escape he had envisioned when he had left Morinmoss did not suffice. The Land's need held him like a harness. "I've done so many things wrong. I've got to try to make them right."

Bannor considered this for a moment, then asked bluntly, "Do you know then how to make use of the wild magic?"

"No," Covenant answered. "Yes." He hesitated, not because he doubted his reply, but because he was reluctant to say it aloud. But his sense of what was unresolved between him and Bannor had become clearer; something more than distrust was at stake. "I don't know how to call it up, do anything with it. But I know how to trigger it." He remembered vividly how Bannor had compelled him to help High Lord Prothall summon the Fire-Lions of Mount Thunder. "If I can get to the Illearth Stone—I can do something."

The Bloodguard's voice was hard. "The Stone corrupts."

"I know." He understood Bannor's point vividly. "I know. That's why I have to get to it. That's what this is all about—everything. That's why Foul has been manipulating me. That's why Elena—why Elena did what she did. That's why Mhoram trusted me."

Bannor did not relent. "Will it be another Desecration?"

Covenant had to steady himself before he could reply. "I hope not. I don't want it to be."

In answer, the Bloodguard got to his feet. Looking soberly down at the Unbeliever, he said, "Ur-Lord Covenant, I will not accompany you for this purpose."

"Not?" Covenant protested. In the back of his mind, he had been counting on Bannor's companionship.

"No. I no longer serve Lords."

More harshly than he intended, Covenant rasped, "So you've decided to turn your back?"

"No." Bannor denied the charge flatly. "What help I can, I will give. All the Bloodguard knowledge of the Spoiled Plains, of Kurash Qwellinir and Hotash Slay, I will share with you. But Ridjeck Thome, Corruption's seat—there I will not go. The deepest wish of the Bloodguard was to fight the Despiser in his home, pure service against Corruption. This desire misled. I have put aside such things. My proper place now is with the Ranyhyn and their Ramen, in the exile of the mountains."

Covenant seemed to hear an anguish behind the inflectionless tone of the speech—an anguish that hurt him in the same way that this man always hurt him. "Ah, Bannor," he sighed. "Are you so ashamed of what you were?"

Bannor cocked a white eyebrow at the question, as if it came close to the truth. "I am not shamed," he said distinctly. "But I am saddened that so many centuries were required to teach us the limits of our worth. We went too far, in pride and folly. Mortal men should not give up wives and sleep and death for any service—lest the face of failure become too abhorrent to be endured." He paused almost as if he were hesitating, then concluded, "Have you forgotten that High Lord Elena carved our faces as one in her last marrowmeld work?"

"No." Bannor had moved him. His response was both an assertion and a promise. "I will never forget."

Bannor nodded slowly. Then he said, "I, too, must wash," and strode away toward the river without a backward glance.

Covenant watched him go for a moment, then leaned his head back against the warmth of the Colossus and closed his sore eyes. He knew that he should not delay his departure any longer, that he increased his risks every moment he remained where he was. Lord Foul was certain to know what had happened; he would feel the sudden destruction of the Staff, and would search until he found the explanation, perhaps by compelling Elena once more out of her death to answer his questions. Then preparations would be made against the Unbeliever; Foul's Creche would be defended; hunting parties would be sent out. Any delay might mean defeat.

But Covenant was not ready. He still had one more confession to make—the last and hardest thing he would have to tell his friends. So he sat absorbing the heat of the Colossus like sustenance while he waited for Bannor and Foamfollower to return. He did not want to carry the weight of any more dishonesty with him when he left the place where Triock had died.

Bannor was not gone long. He and Foamfollower returned dripping to dry themselves in the heat of the stone. Foamfollower had regained his composure. His teeth flashed through his stiff wet beard as if he were eager to be on his way—as if he were ready to fight his way through a sea of foes for one chance to strike a blow at the Despiser. And Bannor stood dourly at the Giant's side. They were equals, despite the difference in size. They both met Covenant's gaze when he looked up at them. For an odd moment he felt torn between them, as if they represented the opposing poles of his dilemma.

But odder than this torn feeling was the confidence which came with it. In that fleeting moment, he seemed to recognize where he stood for the first time. While the impression lasted, his fear or reluctance or uncertainty dropped from him. "There's one more thing," he said to both his friends at once, "one more thing I've got to tell you."

Then, because he did not want to see their reactions until he had given them the whole tale, he sat gazing into the lifeless circle of his ring while he described how High Lord Mhoram had summoned him to Revelstone, and how he had refused.

He spoke as concisely as he could without minimizing the plight of Revelstone as he had seen it then, or the danger of the little girl for whom he had denied Mhoram's appeal, or the hysteria which had been on him when he had made his choice. He found as he spoke that he did not regret the decision. It seemed to have nothing to do with either his regret or his volition; he simply could not have chosen otherwise. But the Land had many reasons for regret—a myriad reasons, one for every life which had been lost, one for every day which had been added to the winter, because he had not given himself and his ring into Mhoram's hands. He explained what he had done so that Bannor and Foamfollower at least would not be able to reproach him for dishonesty.

When he was done, he looked up again. Neither Bannor nor Foamfollower met his eyes at first; in their separate ways, they appeared upset by what they had heard. But finally Bannor returned Covenant's gaze and said levelly, "A costly choice, Unbeliever. Costly. Much harm might have been averted—"

Foamfollower interrupted him. "Costly! Might!" A fierce grin stretched his lips, echoed out of his deep eyes. "A child was saved! Covenant—my friend— even reduced as I am, I can hear joy in such a choice. Your bravery—Stone and Sea! It astounds me."

Bannor was not swayed. "Call it bravery, then. It is costly nonetheless. The Land will bleed under the expense for many years, whatever the outcome of your purpose in Foul's Creche."

Once again, Covenant was forced to say, "I know." He knew with a vividness that felt terrible to him. "I couldn't do anything else. And—and I wasn't ready then. I'm ready now—readier." I'll never be ready, he thought. It's impossible to be ready for this. "Maybe I can do something now that I couldn't do then."

Bannor held his eyes for another moment, then nodded brusquely. "Will you go now?" he asked without expression. "Corruption will be ahunt for you."

Covenant sighed, and pushed himself to his feet. "Yes." He did not want to leave the comfort of the Colossus. "Ready or not. Let's get on with it."

He walked between Bannor and Foamfollower, and they took him up the last of the hills to a place where he could look down the cliff of Landsdrop to the Spoiled Plains.

The precipice seemed to leap out from behind the

hill as if it had been hiding in ambush for Covenant—
abruptly, he found himself looking over the edge and
down two thousand feet—but he gripped the arms of
his friends on either side and breathed deeply to hold
back his vertigo. After a moment, the suddenness of
the view faded, and he began to notice details.

At the base of the hill on his right, the River Landrider swooped downward in a final rush to pour heavily over the lip of Landsdrop. The tumult of its roar
was complex. In this region, the cliff broke into four
or five ragged stairs, so that the waterfall went down
by steps, all pounding simultaneously, anharmonically.
From the bottom of the Fall, it angled away south-
eastward into the perpetual wasteland of the Spoiled
Plains.

"There," said Bannor, "there begins its ordeal.
There the Landrider becomes the Ruinwash, and
flows polluted toward the Sea. It is a murky and repelling water, unfit for use by any but its own unfit
denizens. But it is your way for a time. It will provide
a path for you through much of these hazardous
Plains. And it will place you south of Kurash
Qwellinir.

"You know"—he nodded to Foamfollower—"that
the Spoiled Plains form a wide deadland around the
promontory of Ridjeck Thome, where Foul's Creche
juts into the Sea. Within that deadland lies Kurash
Qwellinir, the Shattered Hills. Some say that these
Hills were formed by the breaking of a mountain—
others, that they were shaped from the slag and refuse
of Corruption's war caverns, furnaces, breeding dens.
However they were made, they are a maze to be-
wilder the approach of any foe. And within them lies
Gorak Krembal—Hotash Slay. From Sea-cliff to
Sea-cliff about the promontory, it defends Corruption's seat with lava, so that none may pass that way
to gain the one gateless maw of the Creche.

"Corruption's creatures make their way to and from
Ridjeck Thome through tunnels which open in secret
places among Kurash Qwellinir. But it is in my heart
that such an approach will not avail you. I do not
doubt that a Giant may find a tunnel within the maze.

But on that road all Corruption's defending armies stand before you. You cannot pass.

"I will tell you of a passage through the Shattered Hills on their southward side. The narrowest point of Hotash Slay is there, where the lava pours through a gash in the cliff into the Sea. A Giant may find crossing in that place." He spoke as if he were discussing a convenient path among mountains, not an approach to the Corrupter of the Bloodguard. "In that way, it may be that you will take Ridjeck Thome by surprise."

Foamfollower absorbed this information, and nodded. Then he listened closely while Bannor detailed his route through the maze of Kurash Qwellinir. Covenant tried to listen also, but his attention wandered. He seemed to hear Landsdrop calling to him. Imminent vertigo foiled his concentration. Elena, he breathed to himself. He called her up in his mind, hoping that her image would steady him. But the emerald radiance of her fate made him wince and groan.

No! he averred into the approach of dizziness. It doesn't have to be that way. It's my dream. I can do something about it.

Foamfollower and Bannor were looking at him strangely. His fingers gripped them feebly, urgently. He could not take his eyes off the waterfall's rush. It called him downward like the allure of death.

He took a deep breath. Finger by finger, he forced himself to release his friends. "Let's get going," he murmured. "I can't stand any more waiting."

The Giant hefted his sack. "I am ready," he said. "Our supplies are scant—but we have no recourse. We must hope for *aliantha* on the Lower Land."

Without looking away from the Fall, Covenant addressed Bannor. He could not ask the Bloodguard to change his decision, so he said, "You'll bury Triock? He's earned a decent grave."

Bannor nodded, then said, "I will do another thing also." He reached one hand into his short robe and drew out the charred metal heels of the Staff of Law. "I will bear these to Revelstone. When the time of my end comes upon me, I will return to the mountain

home of the *Haruchai*. On the way, I will visit
Revelstone—if the Lords and Lord's Keep still stand.
I know not what value may remain in this metal, but
perhaps the survivors of this war will find some use
for it."

Thank you, Covenant whispered silently.

Bannor put the bands away and bowed once briefly
to Covenant and Foamfollower. "Look for help wherever you go," he said. "Even in the Spoiled Plains,
Corruption is not entirely master." Before they could
reply, he turned and trotted away toward the Colossus. As he passed over the hilltop, his back told them
as clearly as speech that they would never see him
again.

Bannor! Covenant groaned. Was it that bad? He
felt bereft, deserted, as if half his support had been
taken away.

"Gently, my friend," Foamfollower breathed. "He
has turned his back on vengeance. Two thousand
years and more of pure service were violated for him
—yet he chooses not to avenge them. Such choices
are not easily made. They are not easily borne. Retribution—ah, my friend, retribution is the sweetest of
all dark sweet dreams."

Covenant found himself still staring at the waterfall.
The complex plunge of the river had a sweetness all its
own. He shook himself. "Hellfire." The emptiness of
his curses seemed appropriate to his condition. "Are
we going to do it or aren't we?"

"We will go." Covenant felt the Giant's gaze on him
without meeting it. "Covenant—ur-Lord—there is no
need for you to endure this descent. Close your eyes,
and I will bear you as I did from Kevin's Watch."

Covenant hardly heard himself answer, "That was
a long time ago." Vertigo was beginning to reel in his
head. "I've got to do this for myself." For a moment,
he let slip his resistance and almost fell to his knees.
As the suction tugged at his mind, he comprehended
that he would have to go into it rather than away
from it, that the only way to master vertigo was to
find its center. Somewhere in the center of the spinning
would be an eye, a core of stability. "Just go ahead—

so you can catch me." Only in the eye of the whirl could he find solid ground.

Foamfollower regarded him dubiously, then started down to the edge of the cliff near the Fall. With Covenant limping in his wake, he went to the rim, glanced down to pick the best place for a descent, then lowered himself out of sight over the edge.

Covenant stood for a moment teetering on the lip of Landsdrop. The Fall yawed abysmally from side to side; it beckoned to him like relief from delirium. It was such an easy answer. As his vertigo mounted, he did not see how he could refuse it.

But its upsurge made his pulse hammer in his wounded forehead. He spun around that pain as if it were a pivot, and found that the seductive panic of the plunge was fading. The simple hope that vertigo had a firm center seemed to make his hope come true. The whirl did not stop, but its hold on him receded, withdrew into the background. Slowly, the pounding in his forehead eased.

He did not fall.

He felt as weak as a starving penitent—hardly able to carry his own weight. But he knelt on the edge, lowered his legs over the rim. Clinging to the top of the cliff with his arms and stomach, he began to hunt blindly for footholds. Soon he was crawling backward down Landsdrop as if it were the precipice of his personal future.

The descent took a long time, but it was not particularly difficult. Foamfollower protected him all the way down each stage of the broken cliff. And the steeper drops were moderated by enough ledges and cracks and hardy scrub brush to make that whole stretch of the cliff passable. The Giant had no trouble finding a route Covenant could manage, and Covenant eventually gained a measure of confidence, so that he was able to move with less help down the last stages to the foothills.

When at last he reached the lower ground, he took his drained nerves straight to the pool at the foot of the Fall and dropped into the chill waters to wash away the accumulated sweat of his fear.

While Covenant bathed, Foamfollower filled his water jug and drank deeply at the pool. This might be the last safe water they would find. Then the Giant set out the graveling for Covenant. As the Unbeliever dried himself, he asked Foamfollower how long their food supplies would last.

The Giant grimaced. "Two days. Three or four, if we find *aliantha* a day or two into the Spoiled Plains. But we are far from Foul's Creche. Even if we were to run straight into Soulcrusher's arms, we would have three or four foodless days within us before he made sustenance unnecessary." Then he grinned. "But it is said that hunger teaches many things. My friend, a wealth of wisdom awaits us on this journey."

Covenant shivered. He had had some experience with hunger. And now the possibility of starvation lay ahead of him; his forehead had been reinjured; he would have to walk a long distance on bare feet. One by one, the conditions of his return to his own life were being met. As he tightened the sash of his robe, he muttered sourly, "I heard Hyrim say once that wisdom is only skin-deep. Or something like that. Which means that lepers must be the wisest people in the world."

"Are they?" the Giant asked. "Are you wise, Unbeliever?"

"Who knows? If I am—wisdom is overrated."

At this, Foamfollower's grin broadened. "Perhaps it is—perhaps it is. My friend, we are the two wisest hearts in the Land—we who march thus weaponless and unredeemed into the very bosom of the Despiser. Verily, wisdom is like hunger. Perhaps it is a very fine thing—but who would willingly partake of it?"

Despite the absence of the wind, the air was still wintry. Knuckles of ice clenched the rocky borders of the pool where the spray of the Fall had frozen, and Foamfollower's breath plumed wetly in the humid air. Covenant needed to move to warm himself, keep up his courage. "It's not fine," he grated, half to himself. "But it's useful. Come on."

Foamfollower repacked his graveling, then swung

the sack onto his broad shoulder, and led Covenant
away from Landsdrop along the river.

Night stopped them when they had covered only
three or four leagues. But by that time they had left
behind the foothills and the last vestiges of the un-
Spoiled flatland which had at one time, ages ago in
the history of the Earth, stretched from the Southron
Wastes north to the Sarangrave and Lifeswallower, the
Great Swamp. They were down in the bosque of the
Ruinwash.

Gray, brittle, dead brush and trees—cottonwoods,
junipers, once-beautiful tamarisks—stood up out of the
dried mud on both sides of the stream, occupying
ground which had once been part of the riverbed. But
the Ruinwash had shrunk decades or centuries ago,
leaving partially fertile mud on either side—mud in
which a scattering of tough trees and brush had
eked out a bare existence until Lord Foul's preternatural winter had blasted them. As darkness soaked into
the air as if it were oozing out of the ground, the trees
became spectral shapes of forbidding which made the
bosque almost impassable. Covenant resigned himself to
camping there for the night, though the dried mud had
an old, occluded reek, and the river made a slithering
noise like an ambush in its course. He knew that he
and Foamfollower would be safer if they traveled at
night, but he was weary and did not believe the Giant
could find his way in the cloud-locked dark.

Later, however, he found that the river gave off a
light like lambent verdigris; the whole surface of the
water glowed dimly. This light came, not from the
water, but from the hot eels which flicked back and
forth across the current. They had a hungry aspect,
and their jaws were rife with teeth. Yet they made it
possible for him and Foamfollower to resume their
journey.

Even in the cynosural eel light, they did not go
much farther. The destruction of the Staff had changed
the balance of Lord Foul's winter; without the wind
to hold them, the massed energies of the clouds recoiled. In the deeper chill of darkness, they triggered
rain out of the blind sky. Soon torrents fell through

the damaged grasp of the clouds, crashed straight down onto the Lower Land as if the vaulting which held up the heavens had broken. Under those conditions, Foamfollower could not find his way. He and Covenant had no choice but to huddle together for warmth in the mud and try to sleep while they waited.

With the coming of dawn, the rain stopped, and Covenant and Foamfollower went on along the Ruinwash in the blurred light of morning. During that day, they saw the last of the *aliantha;* as they penetrated into the Spoiled Plains, the mud became too dead for treasure-berries. The travelers kept themselves going on scant shares of their dwindling supplies. At night, the rains came again, soaking them until they seemed to have its dankness in the marrow of their bones.

The next day, an eagle spotted them through a gap in the gray trees. It cycled twice close over their heads, then soared away, screaming in mockery like a voice from the dead, "Foamfollower! Kinabandoner!"

"They're after us," said Covenant.

The Giant spat violently. "Yes. They will hunt us down." He found a smooth stone the size of Covenant's two fists and carried it with him to throw at the eagle if it returned.

It did not come back that day, but the next—after another torrential downpour avalanched the Plains as if the cloud lid over the Land were a shattered sea— Lord Foul's bird circled them twice, morning and afternoon. The first time, it taunted them until Foamfollower had hurled all the stones he could find nearby, then it slashed close to bark scornfully, "Kinabandoner! Groveler!"

The second time, Foamfollower kept one stone hidden. He waited until the eagle had swooped lower to jeer, then threw at it with deadly force. It survived by breaking the blow with its wings, but it flew limping away, barely able to stay aloft.

"Make haste," Foamfollower growled. "That ill bird has been guiding the pursuit toward us. It is not far off."

At the best pace Covenant could manage on his

numb, battered feet, he pushed ahead through the bosque.

They stayed under tree cover as much as possible to ward against spying birds. This caution slowed them somewhat, but the largest drag on their progress was Covenant's weariness. His injury and the ordeal of the Colossus appeared to have drained some essential resilience out of him. He got little sleep in the cold wet nights, and he felt that he was slowly starving on his share of the food. In dogged silence he shambled along league after league as if his fear of the hunt were the only thing that kept him moving. And that evening, in the gloaming verdigris of the eel fire, he consumed the last of Foamfollower's supplies.

"Now what?" he muttered vaguely when he was done.

"We must resign ourselves. There is no more."

Ah, hell! Covenant groaned to himself. He remembered vividly what had happened to him in the woods behind Haven Farm, when his self-imposed inanition had made him hysterical. The memory filled him with cold dread.

In turn, that dread called up other memories—recollections of his ex-wife, Joan, and his son, Roger. He felt an urge to tell Foamfollower about them, as if they were spirits he could exorcise by simply saying the right thing about them to the right person. But before he could find the words, his thoughts were scattered by the first attack of the hunt.

Without warning, a band of apelike creatures came crashing through the bosque from the south side of the Ruinwash. Voiceless, like the rush of a nightmare, they broke through the brittle wood and the eel light. They threw themselves from the low bank and heaved across the current toward their prey.

Either they did not know their danger, or they had forgotten it. Without one shout or cry, they all vanished under a sudden, hot, seething of blue-green iridescence. None of them reappeared.

At once, Covenant and Foamfollower started on their way again. While the crepuscular light lasted, they put as much distance as possible between themselves and the place of the attack.

A short time later the rain began. It fell on them like the collapse of a mountain, made the whole night impenetrable. They were forced to stop. They hunched together like waifs under the scant, leafless shelter of a tree, trying to sleep and hoping that the hunt could not follow them in this weather.

After a while, Covenant dozed. He was hovering near the true depths of sleep when Foamfollower shook him awake.

"Listen!"

Covenant could hear nothing but the uninterrupted smash of the rain.

The Giant's ears were keener. "The Ruinwash rises! There will be a flood."

Straggling like blind men, thrashing their way against unseen trees and brush, slipping through water that already reached above their ankles, they tried to climb out of the bosque toward higher ground. After a long struggle, they worked clear of the old river-bed. But the water continued to mount, and the terrain did not. Now beyond the rain, Covenant could hear the deeper roar of the flood; it seemed to tower above them in the night. He was stumbling knee-deep in muddy water, and could see no way to save himself.

But Foamfollower dragged him onward. Some time later, they waded into an erosion gully. Its walls were slick, and the water poured down through it like flowing silt, but the Giant did not hesitate. He attached Covenant to him with a short *clingor* line and began to forge up the gully.

Covenant clung to Foamfollower for a distance that seemed as long as leagues. But at last he could feel that they were climbing. The walls of the gully narrowed. Foamfollower used his hands to help him ascend.

When they reached an open hillside where the flow of water hardly covered their feet, they stopped. Covenant sank exhausted into the mud. The rain faltered to an end, and he went numbly to sleep until another cold gray dawn smeared its way across the clouds from the east.

At last he rubbed the caked fatigue out of his eyes and sat up. Foamfollower was gazing at him with amusement. "Ah, Covenant," the Giant said, "we are a pair. You are so bedraggled and sober— And I fear my own appearance is not improved." He struck a begrimed pose. "What is your opinion?"

For a moment, Foamfollower looked as gay and carefree as a playing child. The sight gave Covenant a pang. How long had it been since he had heard the Giant laugh? "Wash your face," he croaked with as much humor as he could manage. "You look ridiculous."

"You honor me," Foamfollower returned. But he did not laugh. As his amusement faded, he turned away and splashed a little water on his face to clean it.

Covenant followed his example, though he was too tired to feel dirty. He drank three swallows from the jug for breakfast, then pried himself unsteadily to his feet.

In the distance, he could see a few treetops sticking out of the broad brown swath of the flood. No other signs remained visible to mark the bosque of the Ruinwash.

Opposite the flood, in the direction he and Foamfollower would now have to take, lay a long ridge of hills. They piled in layers above him until they seemed almost as high as mountains, and their scarred sides looked as desolate as if their very roots had been dead for aeons.

He groaned at the prospect. His worn flesh balked. But he had no choice; the lowlands of the Ruinwash were no longer passable.

With nothing to sustain them but frugal rations of water, he and the Giant began to climb.

The ascent was shallower than it had appeared. If Covenant had been well fed and healthy, he would not have suffered. But in his drained condition, he could hardly drag himself up the slopes. The festering wound on his forehead ached like a heavy burden attached to his skull, pulling him backward. The thick humid air seemed to clog his lungs. From time to time, he found himself lying among the stones and could not remember how he had lost his feet.

Yet with Foamfollower's help he kept going. Late that day, they crested the ridge of hills, started their descent.

Since leaving the Ruinwash, they had seen no sign of pursuit.

The next morning, after a night's rain as ponderous and rancid as if the clouds themselves were stagnant, they moved down out of the hills. As Covenant's gaunt flesh adjusted to hunger, he grew steadier—not stronger, but less febrile. He made the descent without mishap, and from the ridge he and Foamfollower traveled generally eastward out into the barren landscape.

After a foodless and dreary noon, they came to an eerie wilderness of thorns. It occupied the bottom of a wide lowland; for nearly a league, dead thorn-trees with limbs like arms and gray barbs as hard as iron stood in their way. The whole bottom looked like a ruined orchard where sharp spikes and hooks had been grown for weapons; the thorns stood in crooked rows as if they had been planted there so that they could be tended and harvested. Here and there, gaps appeared in the rows, but from a distance Covenant could not see what caused them.

Foamfollower did not want to cross the valley. Higher ground bordered the thorn wastes on both sides, and the barren trees offered no concealment; while they were down in the bottom, they could be easily seen. But again they had no choice. The wastes extended far to the north and south. They would need time to circumvent the thorns—time in which hunger could overcome them, pursuit overtake them.

Muttering to himself, Foamfollower scanned all the terrain as far as he could see, searching for any sign of the hunt. Then he led Covenant down the last slope into the thorns.

They found that the lowest branches of the trees were six or seven feet above the ground. Covenant could move erect along the crooked rows of trunks, but Foamfollower had to crouch or bend almost double to keep the barbs from ripping open his torso and head. He risked injury if he moved too quickly. As a result, their progress through the wastes was dangerously slow.

Thick dust covered the ground under their feet. All the rain of the past nights seemed to have left this valley untouched. The lifeless dirt faced the clouds as if years of torrents could never assuage the thirst of its ancient ruin. Choking billows rose up from the strides of the travelers, filled their lungs and stung their eyes —and plumed into the sky to mark their presence as clearly as smoke.

Soon they came to one of the gaps in the thorns. To their surprise, they found that it was a mud pit. Damp clay bubbled in a small pool. In contrast to the dead dust all around it, it seemed to be seething with some kind of muddy life, but it was as cold as the winter air. Covenant shied away from it as if it were dangerous, and hurried on through the thorns as fast as Foamfollower could go.

They were halfway to the eastern edge of the valley when they heard a hoarse shout of discovery in the distance behind them. Whirling, they saw two large bands of marauders spring out of different parts of the hills. The bands came together as they charged in among the thorn-trees, howling for the blood of their prey.

Covenant and Foamfollower turned and fled.

Covenant sprinted with the energy of fear. In the first surge of flight, he had room in his mind for nothing but the effort of running, the pumping of his legs and lungs. But shortly he realized that he was pulling away from Foamfollower. The Giant's crouched stance cramped his speed; he could not use his long legs effectively without tearing his head off among the thorns. "Flee!" he shouted at Covenant. "I will hold them back!"

"Forget it!" Covenant slowed to match the Giant's pace. "We're in this together."

"Flee!" Foamfollower repeated, flailing one arm urgently as if to hurl the Unbeliever ahead.

Instead of answering, Covenant rejoined his friend. He heard the savage outcry of the pursuit as if it were clawing at his back, but he stayed with Foamfollower. He had already lost too many people who were important to him.

Abruptly, Foamfollower lurched to a halt. "Go, I say! Stone and Sea!" He sounded furious. "Do you believe I can bear to see your purpose fail for my sake?"

Covenant wheeled and stopped. "Forget it," he panted again. "I'm good for nothing without you."

Foamfollower spun to look at the charging hunters. "Then you must find the way of your white gold now. They are too many."

"Not if you keep moving! By hell! We can still beat them."

The Giant swung back to face Covenant. For an instant, his muscles bunched to carry him forward again. But then he went rigid; his head jerked up. He stared hotly through the branches into the distance past Covenant's head.

A new dread seized Covenant. He turned, followed the Giant's gaze.

There were ur-viles on the eastern slope of the valley. They rushed in large numbers toward the wastes as if they were swarming, and as they moved, they coalesced into three wedges. Covenant could see them clearly through the thorns. When they reached the bottom, they halted, wielded their staves. All along the eastern edge of the forest, they set fire to the dead trees.

The thorns flared instantly. Flames leaped up with a roar, spread rapidly through the branches from tree to tree. Each trunk became a torch to light its neighbors. In moments, Covenant and Foamfollower were cut off from the east by a wall of conflagration.

Foamfollower snatched his gaze back and forth between the fire and the charging hunters, and his eyes shot gleams of fury like battle-lust from under his massive brows. "Trapped!" he shouted as if the impossibility of the situation outraged him. But his anger had a different meaning. "They have erred! I am not so vulnerable to fire. I can break through and attack!"

"I'm vulnerable," Covenant replied numbly. He watched the Giant's rising rage with a nausea of apprehension in his guts. He knew what his response should have been. Foamfollower was far better equipped than he to fight the Despiser. He should have said, Take my ring and go. You can find a way to use it. You can get past those ur-viles. But his throat would not form the words. And the fear that Foamfollower would ask for his wedding band churned in him, inspired him to find an alternative. He croaked, "Can you swim in quicksand?"

The Giant stared at him as if he had said something incomprehensible.

"The mud pits! We can hide in one of them—until the fire passes. If you can keep us from drowning."

Still Foamfollower stared. Covenant feared that the Giant was too far gone in rage to understand what he said. But a moment later Foamfollower took hold of himself. With a sharp convulsion of will, he mastered his desire to fight. "Yes!" he snapped. "Come!" At once, he scuttled away toward the fire.

They raced to find a pool of the bubbling clay near the fire before the hunters caught up with them. Covenant feared that they would be too late; even through the wild roar of the fire, he could hear his pursuers howling. But the blaze moved with frightful rapidity. While the creatures were still several hundred yards distant, he slapped into the heat of the flames and veered aside, searching for one of the pits.

He could not find one. The rush of heat stung his eyes, half blinded him. He was too close to the fire. It chewed its way through the treetops toward him like a world-devouring beast. He called to Foamfollower, but his voice made no sound amid the tumult of the blaze.

The Giant caught his arm, snatched him up. Running crouched like a cripple, he headed toward a pool directly under the wall of flame. The twigs and thorns nearest the pit were already bursting into hot orange flower as if they had been brought back to life by fire.

Foamfollower leaped into the mud.

His impetus carried them in over their heads, but with the prodigious strength of his legs he thrust them to the surface again. The mounting heat seemed to scorch their faces instantly. But Covenant was more afraid of the mud. He thrashed frantically for a moment, then remembered that the swiftest way to die in quicksand was to struggle. Straining against his instinctive panic, he forced himself limp. At his back, he felt Foamfollower do the same. Only their heads protruded from the mud.

They did not sink. The fire swept over them while they floated, and long moments of pain seared Covenant's face as he hung in the wet clay, hardly daring to breathe. His intense helplessness seemed to increase as the fire passed.

When the flames were gone, he and Foamfollower would be left floating in mire to defend themselves as best they could against three wedges of ur-viles without so much as moving their arms.

He tried to draw a large enough breath to shout to Foamfollower. But while he was still inhaling, hands deep in the mud pit caught his ankles and pulled him down.

EIGHTEEN: The Corrupt

HE struggled desperately, trying to regain the surface. But the mud clogged his movements, sucked at his every effort, and the hands on his ankles tugged him downward swiftly. He grappled toward Foamfollower, but found nothing. Already, he felt he was far beneath the surface of the pit.

He held his breath grimly. His obdurate instinct for survival made him keep on fighting though he knew that he could never float to the surface from this cold depth. Straining against the mud, he bent, worked his hands down his legs in an effort to reach the fingers which held him. But he could not find them. They pulled him downward—he felt their wet clench on his ankles—but his own hands passed through where those hands should have been, must have been.

In his extremity, he seemed to feel the white gold pulsing for an instant. But the pulse gave him no sensation of power, and it disappeared as soon as he reached toward it with his mind.

The air in his lungs began to fail. Red veins of light intaglioed the insides of his eyelids. He began to cry wildly, Not like this! Not like this!

The next moment, he felt that he had changed directions. While his lungs wailed, the hands pulled him horizontally, then began to take him upward. With a damp sucking noise, they heaved him out of the mud into dank, black air.

405

He snatched at the air in shuddering gasps. It was stale and noisome, like the air in a wet crypt, but it was life, and he gulped it greedily. For a long moment, the red blazonry in his brain blinded him to the darkness. But as his respiration subsided into dull panting, he squeezed his eyes free of mud and blinked them open, tried to see where he was.

The blackness around him was complete.

He was lying on moist clay. When he moved, his left shoulder touched a muddy wall. He got to his knees and reached up over his head; an arm's length above him, he found the ceiling. He seemed to be against one wall of a buried chamber in the clay.

A damp voice near his ear said, "He cannot see." It sounded small and frightened, but the surprise of it startled him, made him jerk away and slip panting against the wall.

"That is well," another timorous voice responded. "He might harm us."

"It is not well. Provide light for him." This voice seemed more resolute, but it still quavered anxiously.

"No! No, no." Covenant could distinguish eight or ten speakers protesting.

The sterner voice insisted. "If we did not intend to aid him, we should not have saved him."

"He may harm us!"

"It is not too late. Drown him."

"No." The sterner voice stiffened. "We chose this risk."

"Oh! If the Maker learns—!"

"We chose, I say! To save and then slay—that would surely be Maker-work. Better that he should harm us. I will"—the voice hesitated fearfully—"I will provide light myself if I must."

"Stand ready!" speakers chorused, spreading an alarm against Covenant.

A moment later, he heard an odd slippery noise like the sound of a stick being thrust through mud. A dim red glow the color of rocklight opened in the darkness a few feet from his face.

The light came from a grotesque figure of mud standing on the floor of the chamber. It was about two feet tall, and it faced him like a clay statue formed by the unadept hands of a child. He could discern awkward limbs, vague misshapen features, but no eyes, ears, mouth, nose. Reddish pockets of mud in its brown form shone dully, giving off a scanty illumination.

He found that he was in the end of a tunnel. Near him was a wide pit of bubbling mud, and beyond it the walls, floor, and ceiling came together, sealing the space. But in the opposite direction the tunnel stretched away darkly.

There, at the limit of the light, stood a dozen or more short clay forms like the one in front of him.

They did not move, made no sound. They looked inanimate, as if they had been left behind by whatever creature had formed the tunnel. But the tunnel contained no one or nothing else that might have spoken. Covenant gaped at the gnarled shapes, and tried to think of something to say.

Abruptly, the mud pit began to seethe. Directly in front of Covenant, several more clay forms hopped suddenly out of the mire, dragging two huge feet with them. The glowing shape quickly retreated down the tunnel to make room for them. In an instant, they had heaved Foamfollower out onto the floor of the tunnel and had backed away from him to join the forms which stood watching Covenant.

Foamfollower's Giantish-lungs had sustained him; he needed no time at all to recover. He flung himself around in the constricted space and lurched snarling toward the clay forms with rage in his eyes and one heavy fist upraised.

At once, the sole light went out. Amid shrill cries of fear, the mud creatures scudded away down the tunnel.

"Foamfollower!" Covenant shouted urgently. "They saved us!"

He heard the Giant come to a stop, heard him panting hoarsely. "Foamfollower," he repeated. "Giant!"

Foamfollower breathed deeply for a moment, then said, "My friend?" In the darkness, his voice sounded cramped, too full of suppressed emotions. "Are you well?"

"Well?" Covenant felt momentarily unbalanced on the brink of hysteria. But he steadied himself. "They didn't hurt me. Foamfollower—I think they saved us."

The Giant panted a while longer, regaining his self-command. "Yes," he groaned. "Yes. Now I have taught them to fear us." Then, projecting his voice down the tunnel, he said, "Please pardon me. You have indeed saved us. I have little restraint—yes, I am quick to anger, too quick. Yet without purposing to do so you wrung my heart. You took my friend and left me. I feared him dead—despair came upon me. Bannor of the Bloodguard told us to look for help wherever we went. Fool that I was, I did not look for it so near to Soulcrusher's demesne. When you took me also, I had no thought left but fury. I crave your pardon."

Empty silence answered him out of the darkness.

"Ah, hear me!" he called intently. "You have saved us from the hands of the Despiser. Do not abandon us now."

The silence stretched, then broke. "Despair is Maker-work," a voice said. "It was not our intent."

"Do not trust them!" other voices cried. "They are hard."

But the shuffling noise of feet came back toward Covenant and Foamfollower, and several of the clay forms lit themselves as they moved, so that the tunnel was filled with light. The creatures advanced cautiously, stopped well beyond the Giant's reach. "We also ask your pardon," said the leader as firmly as it could.

"Ah, you need not ask," Foamfollower replied. "It may be that I am slow to recognize my friends—but when I have recognized them, they have no cause to fear me. I am Saltheart Foamfollower, the"—he swallowed as if the words threatened to choke him—"the last of the Seareach Giants. My friend is Thomas Covenant, ur-Lord and bearer of the white gold."

"We know," the leader said. "We have heard. We are the *jheherrin*—the *aussat jheherrin Befylam*. The

Maker-place has no secret that the *jheherrin* have not heard. You were spoken of. Plans were made against you. The *jheherrin* debated and chose to aid you."

"If the Maker learns," a voice behind the leader quavered, "we are doomed."

"That is true. If he guesses at our aid, he will no longer suffer us. We fear for our lives. But you are his enemies. And the legends say—"

Abruptly, the leader stopped, turned to confer with the other *jheherrin*. Covenant watched in fascination as they whispered together. From a distance, they all looked alike, but closer inspection revealed that they were as different as the claywork of different children. They varied in size, shape, hue, timidity, tone of voice. Yet they shared an odd appearance of unsolidity. They bulged and squished when they moved as if they were only held together by a fragile skin of surface tension—as if any jar or blow might reduce them to amorphous wet mud.

After a short conference, the leader returned. Its voice quivered as if it were afraid of its own audacity as it said, "Why have you come? You dare— What is your purpose?"

Foamfollower answered grimly, so that the *jheherrin* would believe him, "It is our purpose to destroy Lord Foul the Despiser."

Covenant winced at the bald statement. But he could not deny it. How else could he describe what he meant to do?

The *jheherrin* conferred again, then announced rapidly, anxiously, "It cannot be done. Come with us."

The suddenness of this made it sound like a command, though the leader's voice was too tremulous to carry much authority. Covenant felt impelled to protest, not because he had any objection to following the *jheherrin,* but because he wanted to know why they considered his task impossible. But they forestalled him by the celerity of their withdrawal; before he could frame a question, half the lights were gone and the rest were going.

Foamfollower shrugged and motioned Covenant ahead of him down the tunnel. Covenant nodded. With a groan of weariness, he began to crouch along behind the *jheherrin*.

They moved with unexpected speed. Bulging and oozing at every step, they half trotted and half poured their way down the tunnel. Covenant could not keep up with them. In his cramped crouch, his lungs ached on the stale air, and his feet slipped erratically in the slimy mud. Foamfollower's pace was even slower; the low ceiling forced him to crawl. But some of the *jheherrin* stayed behind with them, guiding them past the bends and intersections of the passage. And before long the tunnel began to grow larger. As the number and complexity of the junctions increased, the ceiling rose. Soon Covenant was able to stand erect, and Foamfollower could move at a crouch. Then they traveled more swiftly.

Their journey went on for a long time. Through intricate clusters of intersections where tunnels honeycombed the earth, and the travelers caught glimpses of other creatures, all hastening the same way, through mud so wet and thick that Covenant could barely wade it and shiny coal-lodes reflecting the rocklight of the *jheherrin* garishly, they tramped for leagues with all the speed Covenant could muster. But that speed was not great, and it became steadily less as the leagues passed. He had been two days without food and closer to ten without adequate rest. The caked mud throbbed like fever on his forehead. And the numbness in his hands and feet—a lack of sensation which had nothing to do with the cold—was spreading.

Yet he trudged on. He was not afraid that he would cripple himself; in his weariness, that perpetual leper's dread had lost its power over him. Feet, head, hunger —the conditions for his return to his own world were being met. It was not the fear of leprosy which drove him. He had other motivations.

The conditions of the trek gradually improved. Rock replaced the mud of the tunnel; the air grew slowly lighter, cleaner; the temperature moderated. Such things helped Covenant keep going. And whenever he faltered, Foamfollower's concern and encouragement steadied him. League after league, he went on as if he were trying to erase the troublesome numbness of his feet on the bare rock.

At last he lapsed into somnolence. He took no more notice of his surroundings or his guides or his exhaustion. He did not feel the hand Foamfollower placed on his shoulder from time to time to direct him. When he found himself unexpectedly stationary in a large, rock-lit cavern full of milling creatures, he stared at it dumbly as if he could not imagine how he had arrived there.

Most of the creatures stayed a safe distance from him and Foamfollower, but a few dragged themselves forward, carrying clay bowls of water and food. As they approached, they oozed with instinctive fear. Nevertheless, they came close enough to offer the bowls.

Covenant reached out to accept, but the Giant stopped him.

"Ah, *jheherrin*," Foamfollower said in a formal tone, "your hospitality honors us. If we could, we would return honor to you by accepting. But we are not like you—our lives are unalike. Your food would do us harm rather than help."

This speech roused Covenant somewhat. He made himself look into the bowls and found that Foamfollower was right. The food had the appearance of liquefied marl, and it reeked of old rot, as if dead flesh had moldered in it for centuries.

But the water was fresh and pure. Foamfollower accepted it with a bow of thanks, drank deeply, then handed it to Covenant.

For the first time, Covenant realized that Foamfollower's sack had been lost in the thorn wastes.

The rush of cold water into his emptiness helped him shake off more of his somnolence. He drank the bowl dry, savoring the purity of the water as if he believed he would never taste anything clean again. When he returned it to the waiting, trembling *jheherrin,* he did his best to match Foamfollower's bow.

Then he began to take stock of his situation. The cavern already held several hundred creatures, and more were arriving constantly. Like the *jheherrin* who had rescued him, they all appeared to be made of animated mud. They were grotesquely formed, like monsters ridiculed for their monstrosity; they lacked any sense organs that Covenant could recognize. Yet he was vaguely surprised to see that they came in several different types. In addition to the short erect forms he had first seen, there were two or three distinct beast-shapes, which looked like miserably failed attempts to mold horses, wolves, Cavewights in mud, and one oddly serpentine group of belly crawlers.

"Foamfollower?" he murmured. A painful intuition twisted in him. "What are they?"

"They name themselves in the tongue of the Old Lords," Foamfollower replied carefully, as if he were skirting something dangerous, "according to their shapes. Those who rescued us are the *aussat Befylam* of the *jheherrin*. Other *Befylam* you see—the *fael Befylam*"—he pointed to the crawlers—"and the *roge*" —he indicated the Cavewight-like creatures. "I have heard portions of their talk as we marched," he explained. But he did not continue.

Covenant felt nauseated by the thrust of his guess. He insisted, "What are they?"

Under the mud which darkened his face, Foamfollower's jaw muscles knotted. His voice quivered slightly as he said, "Ask them. Let them speak of it if they will." He stared around the cavern, did not meet Covenant's gaze.

"We will speak," a cold, dusky voice said. One of the *fael jheherrin Befylam* crawled a short distance toward them. It slopped wetly over the rock as it moved, and when it halted, it lay panting and gasping like a landed fish. Resolution and fear opposed each other in every heave of its length. But Covenant was not repelled. He felt wrung with pity for all the *jheherrin*. "We will speak," the crawler repeated. "You are hard —you threaten us all."

"They will destroy us," a host of voices whimpered.

"But we have chosen to aid."

"The choice was not unopposed!" voices cried.

"We have chosen. You are—the legend says—" It faltered in confusion. "We accept this risk." Then a wave of misery filled its voice. "We beg you—do not turn against us."

Evenly, firmly, Foamfollower said, "We will never willingly harm the *jheherrin*."

A silence like disbelief answered him from every part of the cavern. But then a few voices said in a tone of weary self-abandonment, "Speak, then. We have chosen."

The crawler steadied itself. "We will speak. We have chosen. White gold human, you ask what we are. We are the *jheherrin*—the soft ones—Maker-work." As it spoke, the rocklight pulsed in the air like sorrow.

"The Maker labors deep in the fastness of his home, breeding armies. He takes living flesh as you know living flesh, and works his power upon it, shaping power and malice to serve his own. But his work does not always grow to his desires. At times the result is weakness rather than strength. At times his making is blind —or crippled—or stillborn. Such spawn he casts into a vast quagmire of fiery mud to be consumed."

A vibration of remembered terror filled the cavern.

"But there is another potency in that abysm. We are not slain. In agony we become the *jheherrin*—the soft ones. We are transformed. From the depths of the pit we crawl."

"We crawl," voices echoed.

"In lightless combs lost even to the memory of the Maker—"

"Lost."

"—we supplicate our lives."

"Lives."

"From the mud of the thorn wastes to the very walls of the Maker-place, we wander in soil and fear, searching—"

"Searching."

"—listening—"

"Listening."

"—waiting."

"Waiting."

"The surface of the Earth is denied to us. We would perish in dust if the light of the sun were to touch us.

And we cannot delve—we cannot make new tunnels to lead us from this place. We are soft."

"Lost."

"And we dare not offend the Maker. We live in sufferance—he smiles upon our abjection."

"Lost."

"Yet we retain the shapes of what we were. We are"—the voice shuddered as if it feared it would be stricken for its audacity—"not servants of the Maker."

Hundreds of the *jheherrin* gasped in trepidation.

"Many of our combs border the passages of the Maker. We search the walls and listen. We hear—the Maker has no secret. We heard his enmity against you, his intent against you. In the name of the legend, we debated and chose. Any aid that could be concealed from the Maker, we choose to give."

As the crawler finished, all the *jheherrin* fell silent, and watched Covenant while he groped for a response. Part of him wanted to weep, to throw his arms around the monstrous creatures and weep. But his purpose was rigid within him. He felt that he could not bend to gentleness without breaking. To destroy Lord Foul, he grated silently. Yes! "But you," he responded harshly, "they said it's impossible. Cannot be done."

"Cannot," the crawler trembled. "The passages of the Maker under Kurash Qwellinir are guarded. Kurash Qwellinir itself is a maze. The fires of Gorak Krembal ward the Maker-place. His halls swarm with malice and servants. We have heard. The Maker has no secret."

"Yet you aided us." The Giant's tone was thoughtful. "You have dared the Maker's rage. You did not do this for any small reason."

"That is true." The speaker seemed afraid of what Foamfollower might say next.

"Surely there are other aids which you can give."

"Yes—yes. Of Gorak Krembal we do not speak—there is nothing. But we know the ways of Kurash Qwellinir. And—and in the Maker-place also—there is something. But—" The speaker faltered, fell silent.

"But," Foamfollower said steadily, "such aid is not

the reason for the aid you have already given. I am
not deaf or blind, *jheherrin.* Some other cause has led
you to this peril."

"The legend—" gulped the speaker, then slithered
away to confer with the creatures behind it. An intensely whispered argument followed, during which
Covenant tried to calm his sense of impending crisis.
For some obscure reason, he hoped that the creatures
would refuse to speak of their legend. But when the
crawler returned to them, Foamfollower said deliberately, "Tell us."

A silence of dread echoed in the cavern, and when
the speaker replied fearfully, "We will," a chorus of
shrieks pierced the air. Several score of the *jheherrin*
fled, unable to bear the risk. "We must. There is no
other way."

The crawler approached a few feet, then slumped
wetly on the floor, gasping as if it could not breathe.
But after a moment, it lifted up its quavering voice
and began to sing. The song was in an alien tongue
that Covenant did not comprehend, and its pitches
were made so uncertain by fear that he could not
discern the melody. Yet—more in the way the *jheherrin* listened than in the song itself—he sensed something of its potency, its attractiveness for the creatures.
Without understanding anything about it, he was
moved.

It was a short song, as if long ages of grim or abject
use had reduced it to its barest bones. When it was
done, the speaker said weakly, "The legend. The one
hope of the *jheherrin*—the sole part of our lives that
is not Maker-work, the sole purpose. It tells that the
distant forebearers of the *jheherrin,* the Un-Maker-
made, were themselves Makers. But they were not
seedless as he is—as we are. They were not driven to
breed upon the flesh of others. From their bodies came
forth young who grew and in turn made young. Thus
the world was constantly renewed, in firmness and re-
plenishment. Such things cannot be imagined.

"But the Makers were flawed. Some were weak,
some blind, others incautious. Among them the Maker
was born, seedless and bitter, and they did not see

or fear what they had done. Thus they fell into his power. He captured them and took them to the deep fastnesses of his home, and used them to begin the work of forming armies.

"We are the last vestige of these flawed un-Maker-made. Their last life is preserved in us. In punishment for their flaws, we are doomed to crawl the combs in misery and watchfulness and eternal fear. Mud is our sun and blood and being, our flesh and home. Fear is our heritage, for the Maker could bring us to an end with one word, living as we do in the very shadow of his home. But we are watchful in the name of our one hope. For it is said that some un-Maker-made are still free of the Maker—that they still bring forth young from their bodies. It is said that when the time is ready, a young will be birthed without flaw—a pure offspring impervious to the Maker and his making— unafraid. It is said that this pure one will come bearing tokens of power to the Maker's home. It is said that he will redeem the *jheherrin* if they prove—if he finds them worthy—that he will win from the Maker their release from fear and mud—if—if—" The crawler could not go on. Its voice stumbled into silence, left the cavern aching for a reply to fill the void of its misery.

But Covenant could not bend without breaking. He felt all the attention of the *jheherrin* focused on him. He could feel them voicelessly asking him, imploring, Are you the pure one? If we help you, will you free us? But he could not give them the answer they wanted. Their living death deserved the truth from him, not a false hope.

Deliberately, he sacrificed their help. His voice was harsh; he sounded angry as he said, "Look at me. You know the answer. Under all this mud, I'm sick—diseased. And I've done things— I'm not pure. I'm corrupt."

One last pulse of silence met his denial—one still moment while the intent, tremulous hope around him shattered. Then a shrill wail of despair tore through the multitude of the *jheherrin*. All the light vanished at once. Shrieking in darkness like desolated ghouls, the creatures ran.

Foamfollower caught hold of Covenant to protect him against an attack. But the *jheherrin* did not attack; they fled. The sound of their movement rushed through the cavern like a loud wind of loss, and died away. Soon the silence returned, fell limp at the feet of Covenant and Foamfollower like empty cerements, the remains of a violated grave.

Covenant's chest shook with dry spasms like sobs, but he clenched himself into union with the silence. He could not bend; he would break if the rictus of his determination were forced to bend. Foul! he jerked. Foul! You're too cruel.

He felt the attempted consolation of the Giant's hand on his shoulder. He wanted to respond, wanted to utter in some way the violence of his resolve. But before he could speak, the silence seemed to flow and concentrate itself into the sound of soft weeping.

The sound grew on him as he listened. Forlorn and miserable, it rose up into the darkness like irremediable grief, made the hollow air throb. He yearned to go to the weeper, yearned to comfort it in some way. But when he moved, it found words to halt him, desolate accusation. "Despair is Maker-work."

"Forgive me," Covenant groaned. "How could I lie to you?" He searched for the right reply, then said on intuition, "But the legend hasn't changed. I haven't touched the legend. I don't deny your worth. You are worthy. I'm just—not the pure one. He hasn't come yet. I don't have anything to do with your hope."

The weeper did not answer. Its sobs ached on in the air; having started, its old unanodyned misery could not stop. But after a moment it brought up a glimmer of rocklight. Covenant saw that it was the crawler who had spoken for the *jheherrin*.

"Come," it wept. "Come." Shaking with sorrow, it turned and crept out of the cavern.

Covenant and the Giant followed without hesitation. In the presence of the creature's grief, they silently accepted whatever it intended for them.

It led them back into the combs—away from their

earlier route, upward through a complex chain of tunnels. Soon the rock walls had become cold again, and the air began to smell faintly of brimstone. A short time later—little more than half a league from the cavern—their guide halted.

They kept themselves a respectful distance from the creature and waited while it tried to control its sobs. Its dim, rocklit struggle was painful to watch, but they contained their own emotions, waited. Covenant was prepared to allow the creature any amount of time. Patience seemed to be the only thing he could offer the *jheherrin*.

It did not keep them waiting long. Forcing down its grief, it said thickly, "This tunnel—it ends in Kurash Qwellinir. At every turn choose—the way toward the fire. You must pass a passage of the Maker. It will be guarded. Beyond it take each turn away from the fire. You will find Gorak Krembal. You cannot cross—you must cross it. Beyond it is the rock of the Maker-place.

"Its mouth is guarded, but has no gate. Within it swarms— But there are secret ways—the Maker has secret ways, which his servants do not use. Within the mouth is a door. You cannot see it. You must find it. Press once upon the center of the lintel. You will find many ways and hiding places."

The crawler turned and began to shuffle back down the tunnel. Its light flickered and went out, leaving Covenant and Foamfollower in darkness. Out of the distance of the hollow comb, the creature moaned, "Try to believe that you are pure." Then the sound of its grief faded, and it was gone.

After a long moment of silence, Foamfollower touched Covenant's shoulder. "My friend—did you hear it well? It has given us precious aid. Do you remember all it said?"

Covenant heard something final in the Giant's tone. But he was too preoccupied with the bitter rictus of his own intent to ask what that tone signified. "You remember it," he breathed stiffly. "I'm counting on you. You just get me there."

"My friend—Unbeliever," the Giant began dimly,

then stopped, let drop whatever he had been about to say. "Come, then." He steered Covenant by the shoulder. "We will do what we can."

They climbed on up the tunnel. It made two sharp turns and began to ascend steeply, narrowing as it rose. Soon Covenant was forced to his hands and knees by the angle of the cold stone slope. With Foamfollower breathing close behind him, helping him with an occasional shove, he pulled and scraped upward, kept on scrambling while the rock grew more and more constricted.

Then the tunnel ended in a blank wall. Covenant searched around with his numb hands. He found no openings—but he could not touch the ceiling. When he looked upward, he saw a faint window of red light out of reach above his head.

By pressing against each other, he and Foamfollower were able to stand in the end of the tunnel. The dim opening was within the stretch of Foamfollower's arms. Carefully, he lifted Covenant, boosted him through the window.

Covenant climbed into a vertical slit in the rock. Crawling along its floor, he went forward and looked out around its edges into what appeared to be a short, roofless corridor. Its walls were sheer stone, scores of feet high. It looked as if it had been rough-adzed out of raw, black, igneous rock—a passage leading senselessly from one blank wall to another. But as his eyes adjusted to the light, he discerned intersections at both ends of the corridor.

The light came from the night sky. Along one rim of the walls was a dull red glow—the shine of a fire in the distance. The air was acrid and sulfurous; if it had not been cold, Covenant would have guessed that he was already near Hotash Slay.

When he was sure that the corridor was empty, he called softly to Foamfollower. With a leap, the Giant thrust his head and shoulders through the opening into the slit, then squirmed up the rest of the way. In a moment, he was at Covenant's side.

"This is Kurash Qwellinir," he whispered as he looked around, "the Shattered Hills. If I have not lost all my reckoning, we are far from the passage which Bannor taught us. Without the aid of the *jheherrin,* we would be hard pressed to find our way." Then he motioned for Covenant to follow him. "Stay at my back. If we are discovered, I must know where you are."

Gliding forward as smoothly as if he were rested and eager for stealth, he started toward the fiery glow, and Covenant limped along behind him on bare numb feet. Near the end of the corridor, they pressed themselves cautiously against one wall. Covenant held his breath while Foamfollower peered around the corner. An instant later, the Giant signaled. They both hurried into the next passage, taking the turn toward the red sky-shine.

This second corridor was longer than the first. The ones beyond it were crooked, curved; they reversed directions, twisted back on themselves, writhed their way through the black, rough rock like tormented snakes. Covenant soon lost all sense of progress. Without the instructions of the *jheherrin,* he would have attempted to recover lost ground, correct apparent errors. Once again, he realized how much his survival had from the beginning depended on other people. Atiaran, Elena, Lena, Bannor, Triock, Mhoram, the *jheherrin*—he would have arrived nowhere, done nothing, without them. In return for his brutality, his raging and incondign improvidence, they had kept him alive, given him purpose. And now he was wholly dependent upon Saltheart Foamfollower.

It was not a good omen for a leper.

He trudged on under the aegis of dolorous portents. His wound felt like a weight under which he could no longer lift up his head; the brimstone air seemed to sap the strength from his lungs. In time he began to feel numb and affectless, as if he were wandering in confusion.

Yet he noticed the increase of light near a sharp turn in one corridor. The brightening was brief—it opened and shut like a door—but it plunged him into alertness. He dogged the Giant's feet like a shadow as they approached the corner.

They heard guttural voices from beyond the turn. Covenant flinched at the thought of pursuit, then steadied himself. The voices lacked the urgency or stealth of hunting.

Foamfollower put his head to the corner, and Covenant crouched under him to look as well.

Beyond it, the corridor opened into a wide area faintly lit by two small stones of rocklight, one near each entrance to the open space. Against the far wall midway between the two stones stood a dark band of half-human creatures. Covenant counted ten of them. They held spears and stood in relaxed or weary postures, talking to each other in low rough voices. Then five of them turned to the wall behind them. A section of the stone opened, letting out a stream of red light. Covenant glimpsed a deep tunnel behind the opening. The five creatures passed through the entrance and closed the stone behind them. The door closed so snugly that no crack or gleam of light revealed the tunnel's existence.

"Changing the watch," Foamfollower breathed. "We are fortunate that the light warned us."

With the door closed, the guards placed themselves against the darkness of the wall where they were nearly invisible, and fell silent.

Covenant and Foamfollower backed a short distance away from the corner. Covenant felt torn; he could not think of any way past the guards, yet in his fatigue he dreaded the prospect of hunting through the maze for another passage. But Foamfollower showed no hesitation. He put his mouth to Covenant's ear and whispered grimly, "Stay hidden. When I call, cross this open space and turn away from Hotash Slay. Wait for me beyond one turn."

Trepidation beat in Covenant's head. "What are you going to do?"

The Giant grinned. But his mud-dark face held no humor, and his eyes glinted hungrily. "I think I will strike a blow or two against these Maker-work creatures." Before Covenant could respond, he returned to the corner.

With both hands, Foamfollower searched the wall

until he found a protruding lump of stone. His great muscles strained momentarily, and the lump came loose in his hands.

He sighted for an instant past the turn, then lofted the stone. It landed with a loud clatter in the far corridor.

One guard snapped a command to the others. Gripping their spears, they started toward the noise.

Foamfollower gave them a moment in which to move. Then he launched himself at them.

Covenant jumped to the corner, saw Foamfollower charge the guards. They were looking the other way. Foamfollower's long legs crossed the distance in half a dozen silent strides. They only caught a glimpse of him before he fell on them like the side of a mountain.

They were large, powerful fighters. But he was a Giant. He dwarfed them. And he took them by surprise. One blow, two, three—in instant succession, he crushed three of them, skull or chest, and sprang at the fourth.

The creature dodged backward, tried to use its spear. Foamfollower tore the spear from its hands and broke the guard's head with one slap of the shaft.

But that took an instant too long; it allowed the fifth guard to reach the entrance of the tunnel. The door sprang open. Light flared. The guard disappeared down the bright stone throat.

Foamfollower wheeled to the opening. In his right hand, he balanced the spear. It looked hardly larger than an arrow in his fist, but he cocked it over his shoulder like a javelin, and flung it at the fleeing guard.

A strangled shout of pain echoed from the tunnel.

The Giant whirled toward Covenant. "Now!" he barked. "Run!"

Covenant started forward, impelled by the Giant's urgency; but he could not run, could not force his limbs to move that fast. His friend transfixed him. Foamfollower stood in the vivid rocklight with blood on his hands, and he was grinning. Savage delight corrupted his bluff features; glee flashed redly from the caves of his eyes.

"Foamfollower?" Covenant whispered as if the name hurt his throat. "Giant?"

"Go!" the Giant shouted, then turned back to the tunnel. With one sweep of his arm, he slammed the stone door shut.

Covenant stood blinking in the relative darkness and watched as Foamfollower snatched up the three remaining spears, took them to the doorway, then broke them in pieces and jammed the pieces into the cracks of the door to wedge it shut.

When he was done, he started away from the wall. Only then did he realize that Covenant had not obeyed him. At once, he pounced on the Unbeliever, caught him by the arm. "Fool!" he snapped, swinging Covenant toward the far passage. "Do you mock me?" But his hand was slick with blood. He lost his hold, accidentally sent Covenant reeling to jolt heavily against the stone.

Covenant slumped down the wall, gasping to regain his breath. "Foamfollower—what's happened to you?"

Foamfollower reached him, gripped his shoulders, shook him. "Do not mock me. I do such things for you!"

"Don't do them for me," Covenant protested. "You're not doing them for me."

With a snarl, the Giant picked up Covenant. "You are a fool if you believe we can survive in any other way." Carrying the Unbeliever under his arm like an obdurate child, he loped into the maze toward Hotash Slay.

Now he turned away from the fiery sky-glow at every intersection. Covenant flopped in his grasp, demanding to be put down; but Foamfollower did not accede until he had put three turns and as many switchbacks behind him. Then he stopped and set Covenant on his feet.

Covenant staggered, regained his balance. He wanted to shout at the Giant, rage at him, demand explanations. But no words came. In spite of himself, he understood Saltheart Foamfollower. The last of the Unhomed had struck blows which could not be called back or stopped; Covenant could not pretend that he did not understand. Yet his heart cried out. He needed some other answer to his own extremity.

A moment passed before he heard the sound that consumed Foamfollower's attention. But then he caught it—a distant, reiterated boom like the impact of a battering ram on stone. He guessed what it was; the Despiser's creatures were trying to break out of their tunnel into the maze. An instant later, he heard a sharp, splintering noise and shouts.

The Giant put a hand on his shoulder. "Come."

Covenant broke into a run to keep pace with Foamfollower's trot. Together, they hurried through the corridors.

They discarded all caution now, made no attempt to protect themselves from what might lie ahead. At every junction of the maze, they swung away from the mounting red glow, and in every curve and switchback of the corridors, they moved closer to the fire, deeper into the thick, acrid atmosphere of Gorak Krembal. Covenant felt heat in the air now, a dry, stifling heat like the windless scorching of a desert. As it grew, it sent rivulets of sweat running down his back. He panted hoarsely on the air, stumbled across the rough rock, kept running. At odd intervals, he could hear shouts of pursuit echoing over the walls of Kurash Qwellinir.

Whenever he tripped, the Giant picked him up and carried him a short way. This happened more and more often. His fatigue and inanition affected him like vertigo. In his falls, he battered himself until he felt benumbed with bruises from head to foot.

When he reached it, the change was so sudden that it almost flattened him. One moment he was lurching through a blind series of corridors, the next he was out on the shores of Hotash Slay.

He slapped into the heat and light of the lava and stopped. The Hills ended sharply; he found himself on a beach of dead ash ten yards from a moiling red river of molten stone.

Under the blank dome of night, Hotash Slay curved away from him out of sight on both sides. It bubbled and seethed, sent up flaring spouts of lava and brimstone into the air, swirled as if it were boiling where it stood rather than flowing. Yet it made no sound; it hit Covenant's ears silently, as if he had been stricken deaf. He felt that the flesh was being scorched from his bones, felt that he was suffocating on hot sulfur, but the lava seethed weirdly across his gaze as if it were inaudible—a nightmare manifestation, impossibly vivid and unreal.

At first, it dominated his sight, stretched from this ashen shore to the farthest limit of any horizon. But when he blinked back the damp heat-blur from his eyes, he saw that the lava was less than fifty yards wide. Beyond it, he could make out nothing but a narrow marge of ash. The hot red light cast everything else into darkness, made the night on the far side look as black and abysmal as the open throat of hell.

He groaned at that prospect, at the thought of Foul's Creche standing murderous and hidden beyond this impassable fire. Here all his purpose and pain came to nothing. Hotash Slay could not be crossed. Then a burst of echoed yelps jerked him around. He expected to see creatures pouring out of the maze.

The sound died again as the pursuit charged into less resonant corridors. But it could not be far behind them. "Foamfollower!" Covenant cried, and his voice cracked with fear despite his efforts to control it. "What do we do?"

"Listen to me!" Foamfollower said. A fever of urgency was on him. "We must cross now—before we are seen. If you are seen—if Soulcrusher knows that you have crossed—he will hunt for you on the far side. He will capture you."

"Cross?" Covenant gaped. "Me?"

"If we are not seen, he will not guess what we have done. He will judge that you are elsewhere in the maze—he will hunt you there, not on the promontory of Ridjeck Thome."

"Cross that? Are you crazy? What do you think I am?" He could not believe what he was hearing. In the past, he had assumed that he and Foamfollower would somehow get beyond Hotash Slay, but he had made that assumption because he had not visualized this moat of lava around Foul's dwelling place, had not conceived the true immensity of the obstacle. Now he saw his folly. He felt that if he went two steps closer to the lava, his skin would begin to char.

"No," replied Foamfollower. His voice was full of fatality. "I have striven to prepare myself. It may be that in doing this I will anneal the long harm of my life before I die. My friend, I will bear you across."

At once, he lifted Covenant into the air, placed him sitting upon his broad shoulders.

"Put me down!" Covenant protested. "What the hell are you doing?"

The Giant swung around to face the fiery liquefaction of the stone. "Do not breathe!" he barked fiercely. "My strength will help you to endure the heat, but it will sear your lungs if you breathe!"

"Damnation, Giant! Put me down! You're going to kill us!"

"I am the last of the Giants," Foamfollower grated. "I will give my life as I choose."

Before Covenant could say another word, Foamfollower sprinted down the ashen beach toward the lava of Hotash Slay.

From the last edge of the shore, he leaped mightily out over the molten stone. As his feet touched the lava, he began to run with all his great Giantish strength toward the far shore.

The swift blast of heat almost snuffed out Covenant's consciousness. He heard a distant wailing, but moments passed before he realized that it came from his throat. The fire blinded him, wiped everything but red violence out of his sight. It tore at him as if it were flailing the flesh from his bones.

But it did not kill him. Endurance flowed into him from the Giant. And his ring ached on his halfhand as if it were absorbing his torment, easing the strain on his flesh.

He could feel Foamfollower sinking under him. The lava was thicker than mud or quicksand, but with each stride the Giant fell deeper into it. By the time his long surging strides had covered half the distance, he was in over his thighs. Yet he did not falter. Agony shot up through his shoulders at Covenant. Still he thrust himself forward, stretching every sinew past all limits in his effort to reach the far bank.

Covenant stopped wailing to hold his breath, though Foamfollower's pain seemed to burn him worse than the heat of the lava. He tried to grasp the white gold with his mind, pull strength from it to aid the Giant. But he could not tell whether or not he succeeded. The red fire blinded his perceptions. In another two strides, Foamfollower had sunk to his waist. He gripped Covenant's ankles, boosted him up so that the Unbeliever was standing on his shoulders. Covenant wavered on that heaving perch, but Foamfollower's hold on his ankles was as strong as iron, kept him erect.

Two more strides—the lava reached Foamfollower's chest. He mastered his pain for one instant to gasp out over the silent fire, "Remember the *jheherrin!*" Then he began to howl, driven beyond his endurance by red molten agony.

Covenant could see nothing, did not know how far they had come. Reeling over the lava, he held his breath, kept himself from joining Foamfollower's terrible scream. The Giant went on, propelled himself with his tortured legs as if he were treading water.

But finally he floundered to a stop. The weight and pain of the lava halted him. He could not wade any farther.

With one last, horrific exertion, he thrust himself upward, reared back, concentrated all his strength in his shoulders. Heaving so hard that he seemed to tear his arms from their sockets, he hurled Covenant toward the bank.

Covenant arched through the blazing light for an instant, clenched himself against the sudden pain of incineration.

He landed on dead cinders five feet from the edge of Hotash Slay. The ashes crunched under him, gave slightly, absorbed some of the impact. Gasping for breath, he rolled, staggered to his knees. He could not see; he was blind with tears. He gouged water out of his eyes with numb fingers, blinked furiously, forced his vision into focus.

Ten or more yards out in the lava, he saw one of Foamfollower's hands still above the surface. It clenched uselessly for a moment, trying to find a grip on the brimstone air. Then it followed the Giant into the molten depths.

Foamfollower! Covenant cried soundlessly. He could not find enough air to scream aloud. Foamfollower!

The heat beat back at him furiously. And through the pounding blaze came dim shouts—the approaching clamor of pursuit.

Before we are seen, Covenant remembered dumbly. Foamfollower had done this for him so that he would not be seen—so that Foul would not know that he had crossed Hotash Slay. He wanted to kneel where he was until he dissolved in heat and grief, but he stumbled to his feet.

Foamfollower! My friend!

Lumbering stiffly, he turned his back on the lava as if it were the grave of all his victims, and moved away into darkness.

After a short distance, he crossed a low, barren ridge, fell into the shallow gully beyond it. At once, a landfall of weariness buried him, and he abandoned himself to sleep. For a long time, he lay in his own night, dreaming of impossible sunlight.

NINETEEN: Ridjeck Thome

HE awoke with the acrid taste of brimstone in his mouth, and ashes in his heart. At first, he could not remember where he was; he could not identify the ruined ground on which he lay, or the rasp of sulfur in his throat, or the sunless sky; he could not recollect the cause of his loneliness. How could anyone be so alone and still go on breathing? But after a time he began to notice a smell of sweat and disease under the brimstone. Sweat, he murmured. Leprosy. He remembered.

Frailly, he levered himself into a sitting position in the gully, then leaned his back against one crumbling wall and tried to grasp his situation.

His thoughts hung in tatters from the spars of his mind, shredded by a gale of inanition and loss. He knew that he was starving. That's right, he said to himself. That's the way it was. His feet were battered, scored with cuts, and his forehead hurt as if a spike had been driven through his skull. He nodded in recognition. That's right. That's the way it was. But his dirty skin was not burned, and his mud-stained robe showed no signs of heat damage. For a while, he sat without moving, and tried to understand why he was still alive.

Foamfollower must have saved him from the heat by exerting power through him, in the same way that the Giants propelled boats by exerting power through Gildenlode rudders. He shook his head at Foamfollower's valor. He did not know how he could go on without the help of a friend.

Yet he shed no tears over the Giant. He felt barren of tears. He was a leper and had no business with joy or grief. None, he claimed flatly. The crisis at the Colossus had taken him beyond himself, drawn responses from him which he did not properly possess. Now he felt that he had returned to his essential numbness, regained the defining touchstone of his existence. He was done pretending to be anything more than what he was.

But his work was not done. He needed to go on, to confront the Despiser—to complete, if he could, the purpose which had brought him here. All the conditions of his release from the Land had not yet been fulfilled. For good or ill, he would have to bring Lord Foul's quest for white gold to an end.

And he would have to do it as Bannor and Foamfollower would have done it—dispassionately and passionately, fighting and refusing to fight, both at once —because he had learned one more reason why he would have to seek out the Despiser. Surrounded in his mind by all his victims, he found that there was only one good answer still open to him.

That answer was a victory over Despite.

Only by defeating Lord Foul could he give meaning to all the lives which had been spent in his name, and at the same time preserve himself, the irremediable fact of who he was.

Thomas Covenant: Unbeliever. Leper.

Deliberately, he looked at his ring. It hung loosely on his emaciated finger—dull, argent, and intractable. He groaned, and started to wrestle himself to his feet.

He did not know why he was still in the Land after Foamfollower's death—and did not care. Probably the explanation lay somewhere in the breaking of the Law of Death. The Despiser could do anything. Covenant was prepared to believe that in Lord Foul's demesne all the former Law of the Earth had been abrogated.

He began to make his way up the far side of the gully. He had no preparations to make, no supplies or plans or resources to get ready—no reason why he should not simply begin his task. And the longer he delayed, the weaker he would become.

As he neared the crest of the hill, he raised his head to look around.

There he got his first sight of Foul's Creche.

It stood perhaps half a league away across a cracked, bare lowland of dead soil and rock, a place which had lain wrecked and riven for so long that it had forgotten even the possibility of life. From the vantage of the hill—the last elevation between him and Foul's Creche—he could see that he was at the base of Ridjeck Thome's promontory. Several hundred yards away from him on either side, the ground fell off in sheer cliffs which drew closer to each other as they jutted outward until they met at the tip of the promontory. In the distance, he heard waves thundering against the cliffs, and far beyond the lips of the wedge he could see the dark, gray-green waters of the Sea.

But he gave little attention to the landscape. His eyes were drawn by the magnet of the Creche itself. He had guessed from what he had heard that most of Lord Foul's home lay underground, and now he saw that this must be true. The promontory rose to a high pile of rock at its tip, and there the Creche stood. Two matched towers, as tall and slender as minarets, rose several hundred feet into the air, and between them at ground level was the dark open hole of the single entrance. Nothing else of the Despiser's abode was visible. From windows atop the towers, Lord Foul or his guards could look outward beyond the promontory, beyond Hotash Slay, beyond even the Shattered Hills, but the rest of his demesne—his breeding dens, storehouses, power works, barracks, thronehall—had to be underground, delved into the rock, accessible only through that one mouth and the tunnels hidden among Kurash Qwellinir.

Covenant stared across the promontory; and the dark windows of the towers gaped blindly back at him like soulless eyes, hollow and abhorred. At first, he was simply transfixed by the sight, stunned to find himself so close to such a destination. But when that emotion faded, he began to wonder how he could reach the Creche without being spotted by sentries. He did not believe that the towers would be as empty as they appeared. Surely the Despiser would not leave any approach unwatched. And if he waited for dark to conceal him, he might fall off a cliff or into one of the cracks.

He considered the problem for some time without finding any answer. But at last he decided that he would have to take his chances. They were no more impossible than they had ever been. And the ground he had to cross was blasted and rough, scarred with slag pits, ash heaps, crevices; he would be able to find cover for much of the distance.

He began by returning to the gully and following it south until it began to veer down toward the cliff. He could hear and see the ocean clearly now, though the lava's brimstone still overwhelmed any smell of salt in the air; but he took notice of it only to avoid the danger of the cliff. From there he climbed the hill again, and peered over it to study the nearby terrain.

To his relief, he saw more gullies. From the base of the hill, they ran like a web of erosion scars over that part of the lowland. If he could get into them without being seen, he would be safe for some distance.

He congratulated himself grimly on the filthiness of his robe, which blended well into the ruined colors of the ground. For a moment, he gathered his courage, steadied himself. Then he sprinted, tumbled down the last slope, rolled into the nearest gully.

It was too shallow to allow him to move erect, but by alternately crawling and crouching, he was able to work his way into the web. After that, he made better progress.

But beyond the heat of Hotash Slay, the air turned cold and wet like an exhalation from a dank crypt; it soaked into him despite his robe, made his sweat hurt like ice on his skin, drained his scant energies. The ground was hard, and when he crawled, his knees felt muffled ill beating up through the rock. Hunger ached precipitously within him. But he drove himself onward.

Beyond the gullies, he moved more swiftly for a time by limping between slag pits and ash heaps. But after that he came to a flat, shelterless stretch riddled with cracks and crevices. Through some he could hear the crashing of the Sea; from others came rank blasts of air, ventilation for the Creche. He had to scuttle unprotected across the flat, now running between wide gaps in the ground, now throwing himself in dizzy fear over cracks across his path. When at last he reached the foot of the rugged, upraised rock which led to the towers, he dropped into the shelter of a boulder and lay there, gasping, shivering in the damp cold, dreading the sound of guards.

But he heard no alarms, no shout or rush of pursuit—nothing but his own hoarse respiration, the febrile pulse of his blood, the pounding of the waves. Either he had not been seen or the guards were preparing to ambush him. He mustered the vestiges of his strength and began to clamber up through the rocks.

As he climbed, he grew faint. Weakness like vertigo filled his head, made his numb hands powerless to grasp, his legs powerless to thrust. Yet he went on. Time and again, he stopped with his heart lurching because he had heard—or thought he had heard—some clink of rock or rustle of apparel which said that he was being stalked. Still he forced himself to continue. Dizzy, weak, alone, trembling, vulnerable—he was engaged in a struggle that he could understand. He had come too far for any kind of surrender.

Now he was so high that he could seldom hide completely from the towers. But the angle was an awkward one for any guards that might have been at the windows. So as he gasped and scraped up the last ascents, he worried less about concealment. He needed all his attention, energy, just to move his hands and feet, lift his body upward, upward.

At last he neared the top. Peering through a gap between two boulders, he caught his first close look at the mouth of Foul's Creche.

It was smooth and symmetrical, unadorned, perfectly made. The round opening stood in a massive abutment of wrought stone—a honed and polished fortification which cupped the entrance as if it led to a sacred crypt. Its sheen echoed the clouded sky exactly, reflected the immaculate gray image of the parapets.

One figure as tall as a Giant stood before the cave. It had three heads, three sets of eyes so that it could watch in all directions, three brawny legs forming a tripod to give it stability. Its three arms were poised in constant readiness. Each held a gleaming broadsword, each was protected with heavy leather bands. A long leather buckler girded its torso. At first, Covenant saw no movement to indicate that the figure was alive. But then it blinked, drew his attention to its fetid yellow eyes. They roamed the hilltop constantly, searching for foes. When they flicked across the gap through which he peered, he recoiled as if he had been discovered.

But if the figure saw him, it gave no sign. After a moment, he calmed his apprehension. The warder was not placed to watch any part of the promontory except the last approaches to the cave; virtually all his trek from Hotash Slay had been out of the figure's line of sight. So he was safe where he crouched. But if he wanted to enter Foul's Creche, he would have to pass that warder.

He had no idea how to do so. He could not fight the creature. He could not think of any way to trick it. And the longer he waited for some kind of inspiration, the larger his fear and weakness became.

Rather than remain where he was until he paralyzed himself, he squirmed on his belly up through the boulders to the fortification on one side of the entrance. Hiding behind the parapet almost directly below and between the twin towers, he clenched himself to quiet his breathing, and tried to muster his courage for the only approach he could conceive—drop over the parapet into the entryway and try to outrun the warder. He was so close to the figure now that he felt sure it could smell his sweat, hear the reel of his dizziness and the labor of his heart.

Yet he could not move. He felt utterly exposed to the towers, though he was out of sight of the windows; yet he could not make himself move. He was afraid. Once he showed himself—once the warder saw him—

Foul's Creche would be warned. All Foamfollower's effort and sacrifice, all the aid of the *jheherrin,* would be undone in an instant. He would be alone against the full defenses of Ridjeck Thome.

Damnation! he panted to himself. Come on, Covenant! You're a leper—you ought to be used to this by now.

Foul's Creche was a big place. If he could get past the warder, he might be able to avoid capture for a while, might even be able to find the secret door of which the *jheherrin* had spoken. This *if* was no greater than any other. He was trapped between mortal inadequacy and irrefusable need; he had long ago lost the capacity to count costs, measure chances.

He braced his hands on the stone, breathed deeply for a moment.

Before he could move, something crashed into him, slammed him down. He struggled, but a grip as hard as iron locked his arms behind his back. Weight pinned his legs. In fury and fear, he tried to yell. A hand clamped over his face.

He was helpless. His attacker could have broken his back with one swift wrench. But the hands only held him still—asserting their mastery over him, waiting for him to relax, submit.

With an effort, he forced his muscles to unclench.

The hand did not uncover his mouth, but he was suddenly flipped onto his back.

He found himself looking up into the warm, clean face of Saltheart Foamfollower.

The Giant made a silencing gesture, then released him.

At once, Covenant flung his arms around Foamfollower's neck, hugged him, clung to his strong neck like a child. A joy like sunrise washed the darkness out of him, lifted him up into hope as if it were the pure, clear dawn of a new day.

Foamfollower returned the embrace for a moment, then disentangled it and moved stealthily away. Covenant followed, though his eyes were so full of tears that he could hardly see where he was going. The Giant led him from the abutment to the far side of one of the towers. There they were hidden from the warder, and the rumble of the waves covered their voices. Grinning happily, Foamfollower whispered, "Please pardon me. I hope I have not harmed you. I have been watching for you, but did not see you. When you gained the parapet, I could not call without alerting that Foul-spawn. And I feared that in your surprise, you might betray your presence."

Covenant blinked back his tears. His voice shook with joy and relief as he said, "Pardon you? You scared me witless."

Foamfollower chuckled softly, hardly able to contain his own pleasure. "Ah, my friend, I am greatly glad to see you once again. I feared I had lost you in Hotash Slay—feared you had been taken prisoner—feared—ah! I had a host of fears."

"I thought you were dead." Covenant sobbed once, then caught hold of himself, steadied himself. Brusquely, he wiped his eyes so that he could look at the Giant.

Foamfollower appeared beautifully healthy. He was naked—he had lost his raiment in the fires of the Slay—and from head to foot his flesh was clean and well. The former extremity of his gaze had been replaced by something haler, something serene; his eyes gleamed with laughter out of their cavernous sockets. The alabaster strength of his limbs looked as solid as marble; and except for a few recent scrapes received while scrambling from Hotash Slay to the Creche, even his old battle-scars were gone, effaced by a fire which seemed to have refined him down to the marrow of his bones. Nothing about him showed that he had been through agony.

Yet Covenant received an impression of agony, of a transcending pain which had fundamentally altered the Giant. Somehow in Hotash Slay, Foamfollower had carried his most terrible passions through to their apocalypse.

Covenant steadied himself with sea air, and repeated, "I thought you were dead."

The Giant's happiness did not falter. "As did I. This outcome is an amazement to me, just as it is to you.

Stone and Sea! I would have sworn that I would die. Covenant, the Despiser can never triumph entirely over a world in which such things occur."

That's true, Covenant said to himself. In that kind of world. Aloud, he asked, "But how—how did you do it? What happened?"

"I am not altogether certain. My friend, I think you have not forgotten the Giantish *caamora,* the ritual fire of grief. Giantish flesh is not harmed by ordinary fire. The pain purges, but does not burn. In that way the Unhomed from time to time found relief from the extravagance of their hearts.

"In addition—it will surprise you to hear that I believe your wild magic succored me in some degree. Before I threw you from my shoulders, I felt—some power sharing strength with me, just as I shared strength with you."

"Hellfire." Covenant gaped at the blind argent band on his finger. Hellfire and bloody damnation. Again he remembered Mhoram's assertion, *You are the white gold.* But still he could not grasp what the High Lord had meant.

"And—in addition," the Giant continued, "there are mysteries alive in the Earth of which Lord Foul, Satansheart and Soulcrusher, does not dream. The Earthpower which spoke to befriend Berek Halfhand is not silent now. It speaks another tongue, perhaps—perhaps its ways have been forgotten by the people who live upon the Earth—but it is not quenched. The Earth could not exist if it did not contain good to match such banes as the Illearth Stone."

"Maybe," Covenant mused. He hardly heard himself. The thought of his ring had triggered an entirely different series of ideas in him. He did not want to recognize them, hated to speak of them, but after a moment he forced himself to say, "Are you—are you sure you haven't been—resurrected—like Elena?"

A look of laughter brightened the Giant's face. "Stone and Sea! That has the sound of the Unbeliever in it."

"Are you sure?"

"No, my friend," Foamfollower chuckled, "I am not

sure. I neither know nor care. I am only glad that I have been given one more chance to aid you."

Covenant consumed Foamfollower's answer, then found his response. He did his best to measure up to the Giant as he said, "Then let's do something about it while we still can."

"Yes." Gravity slowly entered Foamfollower's expression, but it did not lessen his aura of ebullience and pain. "We must. At our every delay, more lives are lost in the Land."

"I hope you have a plan." Covenant strove to repress his anxiety. "I don't suppose that warder is just going to wave us through if we ask it nicely."

"I have given some thought to the matter." Carefully, Foamfollower outlined the results of his thinking.

Covenant considered for a moment, then said, "That's all very well. But what if they know we're coming? What if they're waiting for us—inside there?"

The Giant shook his head, and explained that he had spent some time listening through the rock of the towers. He had heard nothing which would indicate an ambush, nothing to show that the towers were occupied at all. "Perhaps Soulcrusher truly does not believe that he can be approached in this way. Perhaps this warder is the only guard. We will soon know."

"Yes, indeed," Covenant muttered. "Only I hate surprises. You never know when one of them is going to ruin your life."

Grimly, Foamfollower replied, "Perhaps now we will be able to return a measure of ruin to the ruiner."

Covenant nodded. "I certainly hope so."

Together, they crept back toward the entrance, then separated. Following the Giant's instructions, Covenant worked his way down among the boulders and rubble, trying to get as close as he could to the front of the cave without being seen. He moved with extreme caution, took a circuitous route. When he was done, he was still at least forty yards from the abutment. The distance distressed him, but he could find no alternative. He was not trying to sneak past the warder; he only wanted to make it hesitate.

Come on, Covenant, he snarled. Get on with it. This is no place for cowards.

He took a deep breath, cursed himself once more as if this were his last chance, and stepped out of his hiding place.

At once, he felt the warder's gaze spring at him, but he tried to ignore it, strove to pick his way up toward the cave with at least a semblance of nonchalance. Gripping his hands behind him, whistling tunelessly through his teeth, he walked forward as if he expected free admittance to Foul's Creche.

He avoided the warder's stare. That gaze felt hot enough to lay bare his purpose, expose him for what he was. It made his skin crawl with revulsion. But as he passed from the rubble onto the polished stone apron of the entryway, he forced himself to look into the figure's face.

Involuntarily, he faltered, stopped whistling. The yellow ill of the warder's gaze smote him with chagrin. Those eyes seemed to know him from skin to soul, seemed to know everything about him and hold everything they knew in the utterest contempt. For a fraction of an instant, he feared that this being was the Despiser himself. But he knew better. Like so many of the marauders, this creature was made of warped flesh—a victim of Lord Foul's Stonework. And there was uncertainty in the way it held itself.

Feigning cockiness, he strode up the apron until he was almost within sword reach of the warder. There he stopped, deliberately scrutinized the figure for a moment. When he had surveyed it from head to foot, he met its powerful gaze again, and said with all the insolence he could muster, "Don't tell Foul I'm here. I want to surprise him."

As he said *surprise him,* he suddenly snatched his hands from behind his back. With his ring exposed on the index finger of his right hand, he lunged forward as if to attack the warder with a blast of wild magic.

The warder jumped into a defensive stance. For an instant, all three of its heads turned toward Covenant.

In that instant, Foamfollower came leaping over the abutment above the entrance to the Creche.

The warder was beyond his reach; but as he landed, he dove forward, rolled at it, swept its feet from under it. It went down in a whirl of limbs and blades.

At once, he straddled it. It was as large as he, perhaps stronger. It was armed. But he hammered it so mightily with his fists, pinned it so effectively with his body, that it could not defend itself. After he dealt it a huge two-fisted blow at the base of its necks, it went limp.

Quickly, he took one of its swords to behead it.

"Foamfollower!" Covenant protested.

Foamfollower thrust himself up from the unconscious figure, faced Covenant with the sword clenched in one fist.

"Don't kill it."

Panting slightly at his exertion, the Giant said, "It will alert the Creche against us when it recovers." His expression was grim, but not savage.

"There's been enough killing," Covenant replied thickly. "I hate it."

For a moment, Foamfollower held Covenant's gaze. Then he threw back his head and began to laugh.

Covenant felt suddenly weak with gratitude. His knees almost buckled under him. "That's better," he mumbled in relief. Leaning against one wall of the entry, he rested while he treasured the Giant's mirth.

Shortly, Foamfollower subsided. "Very well, my friend," he said quietly. "The death of this creature would gain time for us—time in which we might work our work and then seek to escape. But escape has never been our purpose." He dropped the sword across the prostrate warder. "If its unconsciousness allows us to reach our goal, we will have been well enough served. Let escape fend for itself." He smiled wryly, then went on: "However, it is in my heart that I can make a better use of this buckler." Bending over the warder, he stripped off its garment, and used the leather to cover his own nakedness.

"You're right," Covenant sighed. He did not intend to escape. "But there's no reason for you to get yourself killed. Just help me find that secret door—then get out of here."

"Abandon you?" Foamfollower adjusted the ill-fitting buckler with an expression of distaste. "How could I leave this place? I will not attempt Hotash Slay again."

"Jump into the Sea—swim away—I don't know." A sense of urgency mounted in him; they could not afford to spend time debating at the very portal of Foul's Creche. "Just don't make me responsible for you too."

"On the contrary," the Giant replied evenly, "it is I who am responsible for you. I am your summoner."

Covenant winced. "I'm not worried about that."

"Nor am I," Foamfollower returned with a grin. "But I mislike this talk of abandonment. My friend— I am acquainted with such things."

They regarded each other gravely; and in the Giant's gaze Covenant saw as clearly as words that he could not take responsibility for his friend, could not make his friend's decisions. He could only accept Foamfollower's help and be grateful. He groaned in pain at the outcome he foresaw. "Then let's go," he said dismally. "I'm not going to last much longer."

In answer, the Giant took his arm, supported him. Side by side, they turned toward the dark mouth of the cave.

Side by side, they penetrated the gloom of Foul's Creche.

To their surprise, the darkness vanished as if they had passed through a veil of obscurity. Beyond it, they found themselves in the narrow end of an egg-shaped hall. It was coldly lit from end to end as if green sea-ice were aflame in its walls; the whole place seemed on the verge of bursting into frigid fire.

Involuntarily, they paused, stared about them. The hall's symmetry and stonework were perfect. At its widest point, it opened into matched passages which led up to the towers, and the floor of its opposite end sank flawlessly down to form a wide, spiral stairway into the rock. Everywhere the stone stretched and met without seams, cracks, junctures; the hall was as smooth

carved, polished, and even, as unblemished by orna-
ment, feature, error, as if the ideal conception of its
creator had been rendered into immaculate stone
without the interference of hands that slipped, minds
that misunderstood. It was obviously not Giant-work;
it lacked anything which might intrude on the absolute
exaction of its shape, lacked the Giantish enthusiasm
for detail. Instead, it seemed to surpass any kind of
mortal craft. It was preternaturally perfect.

Covenant gaped at it. While Foamfollower tore himself away to begin searching the side walls for the door
of which the *jheherrin* had spoken, Covenant moved
out into the hall, wandered as if aimlessly toward the
great stairway. There was old magic here, might treasured by hate and hunger; he could feel it in the cere-
mental light, in the sharp cold air, in the immaculate
walls. This fiery, frigid place was Lord Foul's home,
seat and root of his power. The whole soulless demesne
spoke of his suzerainty, his entire and inviolate rule.
This empty hall alone made mere gnats and midges
out of his enemies. Covenant remembered having heard
it said that Foul would never be defeated while Ridjeck Thome still stood. He believed it.

When he reached the broad spiral of the stairway,
he found that its open center was like a great well,
curving gradually back into the promontory as it descended. The stair itself was large enough to carry fifteen or twenty people abreast. Its circling drew his gaze
down into the bright hole until he was leaning out from
the edge to peer as far as he could; and its symmetry
lent impetus to the surge of his vertigo, his irrational
love and fear of falling.

But he had learned the secret of that dizziness and
did not fall. His eyes searched the stairwell. And a
moment later, he saw something which shook away his
dangerous fascination.

Running soundlessly up out of the depths was a
̶ ̶ ̶ band of ur-viles.

̶ ̶led himself backward. "You better find it
̶ ̶called to Foamfollower. "They're coming."

̶ ̶ollower did not interrupt his scrutiny of the
̶ ̶s he searched the stone with his hands and

eyes, probed it for any sign of a concealed entrance, he muttered, "It is well hidden. I do not know how it is possible for stone to be so wrought. My people were not children in this craft, but they could not have dreamed such walls."

"They had too many nightmares of their own," gritted Covenant. "Find it! Those ur-viles are coming fast." Remembering the creature that had caused his fall in the catacombs under Mount Thunder, he added, "They can smell white gold."

"I am a Giant," answered Foamfollower. "Stonework is in the very blood of my people. This doorway cannot be concealed from me."

Then his hands found a section of the wall which felt hollow. Swiftly, he explored the section, measured its dimensions, though no sign of any door was visible in that immaculate wall.

When he had located the entrance as exactly as possible, he pressed once on the center of its lintel.

Glimmering with green tracery, the lintel appeared in the blank wall. Doorposts spread down from it to the floor as if they had at that instant been created out of the rock, and between them the door swung noiselessly inward.

Foamfollower rubbed his hands in satisfaction. Chuckling, "As you commanded, ur-Lord," he motioned for Covenant to precede him through the doorway.

Covenant glanced toward the stairs, then hastened into the small chamber beyond the door. Foamfollower came behind him, ducking for the lintel and the low ceiling of the chamber. At once, he closed the door, watched it dissolve back into featureless stone. Then he went ahead of Covenant to the corridor beyond the chamber.

This passage was as bright and cold as the outer hall. Foamfollower and Covenant could see that it sloped steeply downward, straight into the depths of the promontory. Looking along it, Covenant hoped that it would take him where he needed to go; he was to weak to sneak all through the Creche hunting for doom.

Neither of them spoke; they did not want to risk being heard by the ur-viles. Foamfollower glanced at Covenant, shrugged once, and started down into the tunnel.

The low ceiling forced Foamfollower to move in a crouch, but he traveled down the corridor as swiftly as he could. And Covenant kept pace with him by leaning against the Giant's back and simply allowing gravity to pull his strengthless legs from stride to stride. Like twins, brothers connected to each other despite all their differences by a common umbilical need, they crouched and shambled together through the rock of Ridjeck Thome.

As they descended, Covenant fell several times. His sense of urgency, his fear, grew in the constriction of the corridor; but it drained rather than energized him, left him as slack as if he had already been defeated. Livid cold drenched him, soaked into his bones like the fire of an absolute chill, surrounded him until he began to feel strangely comfortable in it—comfortable and drowsy, as if, like an exhausted sojourner, he were at last arriving home, sinking down before his rightful hearth. Then at odd moments he caught glimpses of the spirit of this place, the uncompromising flawlessness which somehow gave rise to, affirmed, the most rabid and insatiable malice. In this air, contempt and comfort became the same thing. Foul's Creche was the domain of a being who understood perfection—a being who loathed life, not because it was any threat to him, but because its mortal infestations offended the defining passion of his existence. In those glimpses, Covenant's numb, lacerated feet seemed to miss the stone, and he fell headlong at Foamfollower's back.

But they kept moving, and at last they reached the end of the tunnel. It opened into a series of unadorned, unfurnished apartments—starkly exact and symmetrical—which showed no sign that they had ever been, ̅ ̅ ̅would be, occupied by anyone. Yet the cold, ̅ ̅ ̅one everywhere, and the air was as sharp ̅ ̅ ̅ls. Foamfollower's sweat formed a clus- ̅ ̅ ̅lds in his beard, and he was shivering, ̅ ̅ ̅ormal immunity to temperature.

Beyond the apartments, they found a chain of stairs which took them downward through blank halls, empty caverns large enough to house the most fearsome banes, uninhabited galleries where an orator could have stormed at an audience of thousands. Here again they found no sign of any occupation. All this part of the Creche was for Lord Foul's private use; no ur-viles or other creatures intruded, had ever intruded. Foamfollower hastened Covenant through the eerie perfection. Down they went, always down, seeking the depths in which Lord Foul would cherish the Illearth Stone. And around them, the ancient ill of Ridjeck Thome grew heavier and more dolorous at each deeper level. In time, Foamfollower became too cold to shiver; and Covenant shambled along at his side as if only an insistent yearning to find the Creche's chillest place, the point of absolute ice, kept him from falling asleep where he was.

The instinct which took them downward at every opportunity did not mislead them. Gradually, Foamfollower began to sense the location of the Stone; the radiance of that bane became palpable to his sore nerves.

Eventually, they reached a landing in the wall of an empty pit. There he found another hidden door. Foamfollower opened it as he had the first one, and ducked through it into a high round hall. After Covenant had stumbled across the sill, Foamfollower closed the door and moved warily out into the center of the hall.

Like the other halls the Giant had seen, this one was featureless except for its entrances. He counted eight large doorways, each perfectly spaced around the wall, perfectly identical to the others, each sealed shut with heavy stone doors. He could sense no life anywhere near him, no activity beyond any of the doors. But all his nerves shrilled in the direction of the Stone.

"There," Foamfollower breathed softly, pointing at one of the entrances. "There is the thronehall of Ridjeck Thome. There Soulcrusher holds the Illearth Stone."

Without looking at his friend, he went over

door, placed his hands on it to verify his perception. "Yes," he whispered. "It is here." Dread and exultation wrestled together in him. Moments passed before he realized that Covenant had not answered him.

He pressed against the door to measure its strength. "Covenant," he said over his shoulder, "my friend, the end is near. Cling to your courage for one moment longer. I will break open this door. When I do, you must run at once into the thronehall. Go to the Stone —before any power intervenes." Still Covenant did not reply. "Unbeliever! We are at the end. Do not falter now."

In a ghastly voice, Covenant said, "You don't need to break it down."

Foamfollower whirled, springing away from the door.

The Unbeliever stood in the center of the hall. He was not alone.

An ur-vile loremaster stood before him, slavering from its gaping nostrils. In its hands, it held chains, shackles.

As Foamfollower watched in horror, it locked the shackles onto Covenant's wrists. Leading him by the chain, it took him to the door of the thronehall.

The Giant started toward his friend. But Covenant's terrible gaze stopped him. In the dark, starved bruises of Covenant's eyes, he read something that he could not answer. The Unbeliever was trying to tell him something, something for which he did not have words. Foamfollower had studied the injury which other ur-viles had done to Covenant, but he could not fathom the depth of a misery which could make a man surrender to Demondim-spawn.

"Covenant!" he cried in protest.

Deliberately, Covenant's gaze flicked away from the Giant—bored intensely into him and then jumped ꓽꓽꓽ pulling Foamfollower's eyes with it.

꓿꓿꓿ turned in spite of himself, and saw an꓿꓿꓿ ꓿anding across the hall from him. The ꓿꓿sts were clenched on his hips, and he ꓿꓿꓿savagely. Foamfollower recognized him ꓿꓿was one of the three brothers who had fallen victim to the Ravers. Like Elena, this tormented soul had been resurrected to serve Soulcrusher.

Before Foamfollower could react, the door to the thronehall opened, then closed behind Covenant.

At the same time, all the other doors leaped open, pouring Stone-made monsters into the hall.

TWENTY: The Unbeliever

FOAMFOLLOWER wheeled around, saw that he had been surrounded. Scores of creatures had entered the hall; they were more than enough to deluge him, bury him under their weight if they did not choose to slay him with their weapons. But they did not attack. They spread out along the wall, bunched in tight formations before the doors, so that he could not escape. There they stopped. With the doors closed behind them, they stood leaning eagerly forward as if they yearned to hack him to pieces. But they left him to the dead Giant.

Foamfollower swung back to face the specter.

It advanced slowly, jeering at him with its malevolent grin. "Greetings, Foamfollower," it spat. "Kinabandoner. Comrade! I have come to congratulate you. You serve the master well. Not content merely to desert our people in their time of doom, so that our entire race was extirpated from the Land, you have now delivered this groveler and his effectless white gold into the hands of the Despiser, Satansheart a^r Soulcrusher. Oh, well done! I give you greeting praise, comrade!" It ejaculated the word *comrade* as if it were a supreme affront. "I am Kinslaughterer. It was I who slew—adult and child—every Giant in The Grieve. Behold the fruit of your life, Kinabandoner. Behold and despair!"

Foamfollower retreated a few steps, but his eyes did not for an instant quail from the dead Giant.

"Retribution!" Kinslaughterer sneered. "I see it in your face. You do not think of despair—you are too blind to perceive what you have done. By the master! You do not even think of your despicable friend. You have retribution in your heart, comrade! You behold me, and believe that if all else in your life fails, you have now at least been made able to exact vengeance for your loss. For your crime! Kinabandoner, I see it in you. It is the dearest desire of your heart to rend me limb from limb with your own hands. Fool! Do I have the appearance of one who fears you?"

While he held the specter's gaze, Foamfollower gauged his position, measured distances around him. Kinslaughterer's words affected him. In them, he saw the sweetness of retribution. He knew the fury of killing, the miserable, involuntary delight of crushing flesh with his hands. He quivered as if he were eager, poised the gnarled might of his muscles for a leap.

"Attempt me, then," the dead Giant went on. "Unleash the lust which fills you. Do you believe you can vindicate yourself against me? Are you so blind? Comrade! There is nothing that justifies you. If you shed blood enough to wash the Land from east to west, you cannot wash out the ill of yourself. Imbecile! Anile fool! If the master did not control you, you would do his work for him so swiftly that he would be unable to take pleasure in it. Come then, comrade! Attempt me. I am slain already. How will you bring me to death again?"

"I will attempt it," Foamfollower grated softly, "in ___." The specter's unnecessary goading told ___ needed to know. The creatures could ___ him at any time—yet they waited while ___ erer strove to provoke him. Therefore Soul- ___ ll had something to gain from him; therefore

Covenant was still alive, still unbeaten. Perhaps Lord Foul hoped to use Foamfollower himself against the Unbeliever.

But Foamfollower had survived the *caamora* of Hotash Slay. He poised himself, his whole body tensed. Yet when he sprang suddenly into motion, he did not attack Kinslaughterer. Straining mightily, thrusting with all the power of his legs, he launched himself at the guards before the door of the thronehall.

They ducked under the suddenness of his assault. He dove headlong over them, forearms braced, so that his entire force struck the doors.

They had not been made to withstand such an impact. With a sharp cry of splintering stone, they burst inward.

Foamfollower fell in a flurry of door shards, somersaulted, snapped to his feet in the thronehall of Ridjeck Thome.

The room was a wide round hall like the one he had just left, but it had fewer doors, and its ceiling was far higher, as if to accommodate the immense powers which occupied it. Opposite Foamfollower was the great throne itself. On a low mound against the far wall, old grisly rock had been upreared to form the Despiser's seat in the shape of jaws, raw hooked teeth bared to grip and tear. It and its base were the only things he had seen in Foul's Creche which were not perfectly carved, utterly polished. It appeared to have been irremediably crippled, grotesqued, by the age-long weight of Lord Foul's malice. It looked like a prophecy or foretaste of ultimate doom for all Ridjeck Thome's immaculate rock.

Set into the floor directly before it was the Illearth Stone.

The Stone was not as large as Foamfollower had expected it to be; it did not appear so big or heavy that he could not have lifted it in his arms. Yet its radiance staggered him like the blow of a prodigious fist. It was not extremely bright—its illumination in the thronehall was only a little stronger than the light elsewhere—but it blazed in its setting like an incarnation of absolute cold. It pulsed like a mad heart, sent out unfetterable gouts and flares of force, radiated violently its power for corruption. Foamfollower slammed into the glare and stopped as if he could already feel the gelid emerald turning his skin to ice.

He stared at the Stone for a moment, horrified by its strength. But then his staggered senses became aware of another might in the thronehall. This power seemed oddly subdued in comparison to the Stone. But it was only subtler, more insidious—not weaker. As Foamfollower turned toward it, he knew that it was the Stone's master.

Lord Foul.

He located the Despiser more by tactile impression than by sight. Lord Foul was essentially invisible, though he cast an impenetrable blankness in the air like the erect shadow of a man—a shadow of absence rather than presence which showed where he would have been if he had been physically corporeal—and around the shadow shone a penumbra of glistering green. From within it, he reeked of attar.

He stood to one side of the Stone, with his back to the door and the Giant. And before him, facing Foamfollower, was Thomas Covenant.

They were alone; after delivering Covenant, the urvile had left the thronehall.

Covenant seemed unaware of the chains shackling his wrists. He did not appear to be struggling at all. He was already in the last stages of starvation and cold. Pain dripped like dank sweat down his emaciated cheeks; and his gaunt, desolate eyes met Lord Foul as if the Despiser's power were clenched in the ugly wound on his forehead.

Neither of them took any notice of Foamfollower's loud entrance; they were concentrated on each other to the exclusion of everything else. Some interchange had taken place between them—something Foamfollower had missed. But he saw the result. Just as he focused his attention on Lord Foul and Covenant, the Despiser raised one penumbral arm and struck Covenant across the mouth.

With a roar, Foamfollower charged to his friend's aid.

Before he had taken two strides, an avalanche of creatures rushed through the shattered doorway and fell on him. They pounded him to the floor, pinned him under their weight, secured his limbs. He fought wildly, extravagantly, but his opponents were many and strong. They mastered him in a moment. They dragged him to the side wall and fettered him there with chains so massive that he could not break them. When the creatures left him, hurried out of the throne-hall, he was helpless.

The dead Giant was not with them. Already it had served or failed its purpose; it had been banished again.

He had been placed in a position where he could watch Lord Foul and Covenant—where their conflict would be enacted with him as its audience.

As soon as the creatures had departed, the Despiser turned toward him for the first time. When the gleaming green penumbra had shifted itself to face him, he saw the Despiser's eyes. They were the only part of Lord Foul that was visible within his aura.

He had eyes like fangs, carious and yellow—fangs so vehement in malice that they froze Foamfollower's voice, gagging him on the encouragement he had tried to shout for Covenant's sake.

"Be silent," Lord Foul said venomously, "or I will roast you before your time."

Foamfollower obeyed without volition. He gaped as if he were choking on ice and watched with helpless passion in his throat.

The Despiser's eyes blinked in satisfaction. He turned his attention back to Covenant.

Covenant had been knocked from his feet by Lord Foul's blow, and he knelt now with his shackled hands covering his face in a gesture of the most complete abjection. His fingers seemed entirely numb; they pressed blindly against his face, as incapable as dead sticks of exploring his injury, of even identifying the dampness of his blood. But he could feel the disease gnawing at his nerves as if Lord Foul's presence amplified it, made the senseless erosion tangible; and he knew that his leprosy was in full career now, that the fragile arrest on which his life depended had been broken.

Illness reached down into his soul like tendrils of affectlessness, searching like tree roots in a rock for cracks, flaws, at which the rock could be split asunder. He was as weak and weary as any nightmare could make him without causing the labor of his heart to stop.

But when he lowered his bloodied hands—when the swift poison of Foul's touch made his lip blacken and swell so acutely that he could no longer bear to touch it—when he looked up again toward the Despiser, he was not abject. He was unbeaten.

Damn you, he muttered dimly. Damn you. It's not that easy.

Deliberately, he closed his fingers of his halfhand around his ring.

The Despiser's eyes raged at him, but Lord Foul controlled himself to say in a sneering, fatherly tone, "Come, Unbeliever. Do not prolong this unpleasantness. You know that you cannot stand against me. In my own name I am wholly your superior. And I possess the Illearth Stone. I can blast the moon in its course, compel the oldest dead from their deep graves, spread ruin at my whim. Without effort I can tear every fiber of your being from its moor and scatter the wreck of your soul across the heavens."

Then do it, Covenant muttered.

"Yet I choose to forbear. I do not purpose harm against you. Only place your ring in my hand, and all your torment will be at an end. It is a small price to pay, Unbeliever."

It's not that easy.

"And I am not powerless to reward you. If you wish to share my rule over the Land, I will permit you. You will find I am not an uncongenial master. If you wish to preserve the life of your friend Foamfollower, I will not demur—though he has offended me." Foamfollower thrashed in his chains, struggled to protest, but he could not speak. "If you wish health, that also I can and will provide. Behold!"

He waved one penumbral arm, and a ripple of distortion passed over Covenant's sense. At once, feeling flooded back into his hands and feet; his nerves returned to life in an instant. While they flourished, all his distress—all pain and hunger and weakness—sloughed off him. His body seemed to crow with triumphant life.

He was unmoved. He found his voice, breathed wearily through his teeth. "Health isn't my problem. You're the one who teaches lepers to hate themselves."

"Groveler!" Lord Foul snapped. Without transition, Covenant became leprous and starved again. "You are on your knees to me! I will make you plead for the veriest fragments of life! Do lepers hate themselves? Then they are wise. I will teach you the true stature of hatred!"

For a moment, the Despiser's own immitigable hate gouged down at Covenant from his carious eyes, and Covenant braced himself for an onslaught. But then Lord Foul began to laugh. His scorn shone from him, shook the air of the thronehall like the sound of great boulders crushing each other, made even the hard stone of the floor seem as insidious as a quagmire. And when he subsided, he said, "You are a dead man before me, groveler—as crippled of life as any corpse. Yet you refuse me. You refuse health, mastery, even friendship. I am interested—I am forbearant. I will allow you time to think better of your madness. Tell me why you are so rife with folly."

Covenant did not hesitate. "Because I loathe you."

"That is no reason. Many men believe that they loathe me because they are too craven to despise stupidity, foolhardiness, pretension, subservience. I am not misled. Tell me why, groveler."

"Because I love the Land."

"Oh, forsooth!" Lord Foul jeered. "I cannot believe that you are so anile. The Land is not your world—it has no claim upon your small fidelity. From the first, it has tormented you with demands you could not meet, honor you could not earn. You portray yourself as a man who is faithful unto death in the name of a fashion of apparel or an accident of diet—loyal to filthy robes and sand. No, groveler. I am unconvinced. Again, I say, tell me why." He pronounced his *why* as if with that one syllable he could make Covenant's entire edifice founder.

The Land is beautiful, Covenant breathed to himself. You're ugly. For a time, he felt too weary to respond. But at last he brought out his answer.

"Because I don't believe."

"No?" the Despiser shouted with glee. "Still?" His laughter expressed perfect contempt. "Groveler, you are pathetic beyond price. Almost I am persuaded to keep you at my side. You would be a jester to lighten my burdens." Still he catechized Covenant. "How is it possible that you can loathe or love where you do not believe?"

"Nevertheless."

"How is it possible to disbelieve where you loathe or love?"

"Still."

Lord Foul laughed again. "Do my ears betray me? Do you—after my Enemy has done all within his power to sway you—do you yet believe that this is a dream?"

"It isn't real. But that doesn't matter. That's not important."

"Then what is, groveler?"

"The Land. You."

Once more, the Despiser laughed. But his mirth was short and vicious now; he sounded disturbed, as if there were something in Covenant which he could not understand. "The Land and Unbelief," he jeered. "You poor, deranged soul! You cannot have both. They preclude each other."

But Covenant knew better; after all that he had been through, he knew better. Only by affirming them both, accepting both poles of the contradiction, keeping them both whole, balanced, only by steering himself not between them but with them, could he preserve them both, preserve both the Land and himself, find the place where the parallel lines of his impossible dilemma met. The eye of the paradox. In that place lay the reason why the Land had happened to him. So he said nothing as he stared up at the blank shadow and the emerald aura and the incalculable might of the Despiser. But in himself, he gritted, No they don't, Foul.

You're wrong. It's not that easy. If it were easy, I would have found it long ago.

"But I grow weary of your stupid assertions," Lord Foul went on after a moment. "My patience is not infinite. And there are other questions I wish to ask. I will set aside the matter of your entry into my demesne. It is a small matter, easily explained. In some manner unknown to me, you suborned a number of my chattel, so that twice I received false reports of your death. But set it aside. I will flay the very souls from their bones, and learn the truth. Answer this question, groveler." He moved closer to Covenant, and the intensity of his voice told Covenant that the Despiser had reached the heart of his probing. "This wild magic is not a part of your world. It violates your Unbelief. How can you use this power in which you do not believe?"

There Covenant found the explanation of Lord Foul's forbearance. The Despiser had spent his time interrogating Covenant rather than simply ripping the fingers off his hand to take the ring because he, Lord Foul, feared that Covenant had secretly mastered the wild magic—that he had concealed his power, risked death in the Spoiled Plains and Hotash Slay and Kurash Qwellinir, permitted himself to be taken captive, so that he could surprise the Despiser, catch Lord Foul from a weak or blind side.

Foul had reason for this fear. The Staff of Law had been destroyed.

For an instant, Covenant thought he might use this apprehension to help himself in some way. But then he saw that he could not. For his own sake, so that his defense would not be flawed by his old duplicity, he told the truth.

"I don't know how to use it." His voice stumbled thickly past his swollen lip. "I don't know how to call it up. But I know it is real in the Land. I know how to trigger it. I know how to bring this bloody icebox down around your ears."

The Despiser did not hesitate, doubt. He seemed to expand in Covenant's sight as he roared savagely, "You will trigger nothing! I have endured enough of your insolence. Do you say that you are a leper? I will show you leprosy!"

Power swarmed around Covenant like a thousand thousand mad wasps. Before him, the Despiser's blank shadow grew horribly, swept upward larger and larger until it dwarfed Covenant, dwarfed Foamfollower, dwarfed the thronehall itself; it filled the air, the hall, the entire Creche. He felt himself plunging into the abyss of it. He cried out for help, but no help came. Like a stricken bird, he plummeted downward. The speed of his fall roared in his ears as if it were trying to suck him out of himself. He could sense the rock on which he would be shattered, unutterably far below him.

In the void, an attar-laden voice breathed, "Worship me and I will save you."

Giddy terror-lust rushed up in him. A black whirlwind hurled him at the rock as if all the puissance of the heavens had come to smash him against the unbreakable granite of his fate. Despite screamed in his mind, demanding admittance, demanding like the suicidal paradox of vertigo to overwhelm him. But he clung to himself, refused. He was a leper; the Land was not real; this was not the way he was going to die.

He clenched his fist on the ring with all the frail strength of his arm.

At the crash of impact, pain detonated in his skull. Incandescent agony yowled and yammered through his head, shredded him like claws ferociously tearing the tissue of his brain. Foul rode the pain as if it were a tidal wave, striving to break down or climb over the seawall of his will. But he was too numb to break. His hands and feet were blind, frozen; his forehead was already inured to harm; and the black swelling in his lip was familiar to him. The green, ghastly cold could not bend the rigor of his bones. Like a dead man, he was stiff with resistance.

Lord Foul tried to enter him, tried to merge with him. The offer was seductively sweet—a surcease from pain, a release from the long unrest which he had miscalled his life. But he was harnessed to himself in a way that allowed no turning aside, no surrender. He was Thomas Covenant, Unbeliever and leper. He refused.

Abruptly, his pain fell into darkness. Harm, injury, crushing, assault—all turned to ashes and blew away on windless air. In their place came his own numbness, his irreparable lack of sensation. In the great, unillumined abyss, he found that he could see himself.

He was standing nowhere, surrounded by nothing; he was staring as if in dumb incomprehension at his hands.

At first they seemed normal. They were as gaunt as sticks, and the two missing digits of his right hand gave him a sense of loss, unwholeness, that made him groan. But his ring was intact; it hung inertly on his index finger, an argent circle as perfect and inescapable as if it had some meaning.

But as he watched, dim purple spots began to appear on his hands—on his fingers, the backs of his knuckles, the heels of his palms. Slowly, they spread and started to suppurate; they bulged slightly like blisters, then opened to show abscesses under his skin. Fluid oozed from the sores as they grew and spread. Soon both his hands were covered with infection.

They became gangrenous, putrescent; the cloying stench of live, rotten flesh poured from them like the effluvium of some gnawing fungus, noisome and cruel. And under the infection, the bones of his fingers began to gnarl. Unmarrowed, flawed by rot, stressed by tendons whose nerves had died, leaving them perpetually taut, perpetually clenched against each other, the bones twisted, broke, and froze at crooked angles. In the rot and the disease, his hands maimed themselves. And the black, sick swelling of gangrene began to eat its way up his wrists.

The same pressures, the same fetid and uncontrollable tension of muscles and thews—bereft of volition by the rot in his nerves—bowed his forearms so that they hung grotesquely from his elbows. Then pus began to blossom like sweat from the abscessed pores of his upper arms. When he twitched his robe aside, he found that his legs were already contorted to the knees.

The assault horrified him, buried him in misery and

self-loathing. He was wearing his own future, the outcome of his illness—the destination of the road down which every leper fared who did not either kill himself or fight hard enough to stay alive. He was seeing the very thing which had first determined him to survive, all those long months ago in the leprosarium, but now it was upon him, virulent and immedicable. His leprosy was in full rank flower, and he had nothing left for which to fight.

Nevertheless he was on his home ground. He knew leprosy with the intimacy of a lover; he knew that it could not happen so swiftly, so completely. It was not real. And it was not all of him. This heinous and putrescent gnawing was not the sum total of his being. Despite what the doctors said—despite what he saw in himself—he was more than that, more than just a leper.

No, Foul! he panted bitterly. It's not that easy.

"Tom. Tom!" a stricken voice cried. It was familiar to him—a voice as known and beloved as health. "Give it up. Don't you see what you're doing to us?"

He looked up, and saw Joan standing before him. She held their infant son, Roger, in her hands, so that the child was half extended like an offering toward him. Both of them appeared just as they had been when he had last seen them, so long ago; Joan had the same look of torn grief in her face, the expression that begged him to understand why she had already decided to divorce him. But she was inexplicably naked. His heart wept in him when he saw the lost love of her loins, the unwillingness of her breasts, the denied treasure of her face.

As he gazed at her, purple stains began to show through the warmth of her skin. Abscesses suppurated on her breasts; sickness oozed from her nipples like milk.

Roger was puling pathetically in her hands. When he turned his helpless infant head toward his father, Covenant saw that his eyes were already glazed and cataractal, half blinded by leprosy. Two dim magenta spots tainted his cheeks.

Foul! Covenant shrieked. Damn you!

Then he saw other figures pressing forward behind Joan. Mhoram was there; Lena and Atiaran were there; Bannor and Hile Troy were there. Mhoram's whole face had fallen into yellow rot and running chancrous sores; his eyes cried out through the infection as if they were drowning in a quagmire of atrocious wrong. All Lena's hair had fallen out, and her bald scalp bristled with tubercular nodules. Atiaran's eyes were drowning in milky blindness. The grotesque gnarling of Bannor's limbs entirely crippled him. Troy's eyeless face was one puckered mass of gangrene, as if the very brain within his skull were festering.

And behind these figures stood more of the people Covenant had known in the Land. All were mortally ill, rife and hideous with leprosy. And behind them crowded multitudes more, numberless victims—all the people of the Land stricken and destitute, abominable to themselves, as ruined as if Covenant had brought a plague of absolute virulence among them.

At the sight of them, he erupted. Fury at their travail spouted up in him like lava. Volcanic anger, so long buried under the weight of his complex ordeal, sent livid, fiery passion geysering into the void.

Foul! he screamed. Foul! You can't do this!

"I will do it," came the mocking reply. "I am doing it."

Stop it!

"Give me the ring."

Never!

"Then enjoy what you have brought to pass. Behold! I have given you companions. The solitary leper has remade the world in his own image, so that he will not be alone."

I won't let you!

The Despiser laughed sardonically. "You will aid me before you die."

"Never! Damn you! Never!"

Fury exalted Covenant—fury as hot as magma. A rage for lepers carried him beyond all his limits. He took one last look at the victims thronging innumerably before him. Then he began to struggle for freedom like a newborn man fighting his way out of an old skin.

He seemed to be standing in the nowhere nothingness of the abyss, but he knew that his physical body still knelt on the floor of the thronehall. With a savage effort of will, he disregarded all sensory impressions, all appearances that prevented him from perceiving where he was. Trembling, jerking awkwardly, he levered his gaunt frame to its feet. The eyes of his body were blind, still caught in Lord Foul's control, but he grated fiercely, "I see you, Foul." He did not need eyes. He could sense with the nerves of his stiff cheeks the emanations of power around him.

He took three lumbering, tottering steps, and felt Foul suddenly surge toward him, rush to stop him. Before the Despiser could reach him, he raised his hands and fell fists-first at the Illearth Stone.

The instant his wedding band struck the Stone, a hurricane of might exploded in his hand. Gales of green and white fire blasted through the air, shattered it like a bayamo. The veil of Lord Foul's assault was shredded in a moment and blown away. Covenant found himself lying on the floor with a tornado of power gyring upward from his halfhand.

He heaved to his feet. With one flex of his arms, he freed his wrists as if the shackles were a skein of lies.

Foul's penumbral shadow crouched in battle-readiness across the Stone from him. The Despiser brandished his carious eyes as if he were frantic to drive them into Covenant's heart. "Fool!" he howled shrilly. "Groveler! It is I who rule here! Alone I am your rightful master—and I command the Stone! I will destroy you. You will not so much as touch me!"

As he yelled, he threw out a flare of force which struck Covenant's hand, embedded itself deep in the core of his ring. Amid its raging gale, the white gold was altered. Cold ill soaked into the metal, forced itself into the ring until all the argent had been violated by green. Again, Covenant felt himself falling out of the thronehall.

Without transition, he found himself on Kevin's Watch. He stood on the stone platform like a titan, and with his malefic band he alone levied a new Ritual of Desecration upon the Land. All health withered before him. Great Gilden trees splintered and broke. Flowers died. *Aliantha* grew barren and became dust. Soil turned to sand. Rivers ran dry. Stonedowns and Woodhelvens were overthrown. Starvation and homelessness slew every shape of life that walked upon the earth. He was the Lord of a ruin more absolute than any other, a desolation utterly irreparable.

Never!

With one violent thrust of his will, he struck the green from his ring and returned to the thronehall. His wedding band was immaculate silver, and the slashing wind of its power was wild beyond all emerald mastery.

He almost laughed. The Stone could not corrupt him; he was already as fundamentally diseased as any corruption could make him.

To the Despiser, he rasped, "You've had your chance. You've used your filthy power. Now it's my turn. You can't stop me. You've broken too many Laws. And I'm outside the Law. It doesn't control wild magic—it doesn't control me. But it was the only thing that might have stopped me. You could have used it against me. Now it's just me—it's my will that makes the difference." He was panting heavily; he could not find enough air to support the extremity of his passion. "I'm a leper, Foul. I can stand anything."

At once, the Despiser attacked him. Foul put his hands on the Illearth Stone, placed his power on the pulsing heart of its violence. He sent green might raving at Covenant.

It fell on him like the collapse of a mountain, piled onto him like tons of wrecked stone. At first he could not focus the ring on it, and it drove him staggering backward. But then he found his error. He had tried to use the wild magic like a tool or weapon, something which could be wielded. But High Lord Mhoram had told him, *You are the white gold.* It was not a thing to be commanded, employed well or ill as skill or awkwardness allowed. Now that it was awake, it was a part of him, an expression of himself. He did not need to focus it, aim it; bone and blood, it arose from his passion.

With a shout, he threw back the attack, shattered it into a million droplets of rank fever.

Again Lord Foul struck. Power that fried the air between them sprang at Covenant, strove to interrupt the white, windless gale of the ring. Their conflict coruscated through the thronehall like a mad gibberish of lightning, green and white blasting, battering, devouring each other like all the storms of the world gone insane.

Its sheer immensity daunted Covenant, tried like a landslide to sweep the feet of his resolve from under him. He was unacquainted with power, unadept at combat. But his rage for lepers, for the Land, for the victims of Despite, kept him upright. And his Unbelief enabled him. He knew more completely than any native of the Land could have known that Lord Foul was not unbeatable. In this manifestation, Despite had no absolute reality of existence. The people of the Land would have failed in the face of Despite because they were convinced of it. Covenant was not. He was not overwhelmed; he did not believe that he had to fail. Lord Foul was only an externalized part of himself—not an immortal, not a god. Triumph was possible.

So he threw himself heart and soul and blood and bone into the battle. He did not think of defeat; the personal cost was irrelevant. Lord Foul beat him back until he was pressed to the wall at Foamfollower's side. The savagery of the Stone made a holocaust around him, tore every last flicker of warmth from the air, shot great lurid icicles of hatred at him. But he did not falter. The wild magic was passionate and unfathomable, as high as Time and as deep as Earth—raw power limited only by the limits of his will. And his will was growing, raising its head, blossoming on the rich sap of rage. Moment by moment, he was becoming equal to the Despiser's attack.

Soon he was able to move. He forged away from the wall, waded like a strong man through the tempest toward his enemy. White and green blasts scalded the atmosphere; detonations of savage lightning shattered against each other. Lord Foul's fiery cold and Covenant's gale tore at each other's throats, rent each other, renewed themselves and tore again. In the virulence of the battle, Covenant thought that Ridjeck Thome would surely come crashing down. But the Creche stood; the thronehall stood. Only Covenant and Lord Foul shook in the thunderous silence of the power storm.

Abruptly, he succeeded in driving Lord Foul back from the Stone. At once, his own fire blazed still higher. Without direct contact, the Despiser's control over his emerald bane was less perfect. His exertions became more frenzied, erratic. Unmastered force rocked the throne, tore ragged hunks of stone from the ceiling, cracked the floor. He was screaming now in a language Covenant could not understand.

The Unbeliever grabbed his opportunity. He moved forward, rained furious gouts and bolts of wild magic at the Despiser, then suddenly began to form a wall of might between Lord Foul and the Stone. Lord Foul shrieked, tried frantically to regain the Stone. But he was too late. In an instant, Covenant's force had surrounded Lord Foul.

With all the rage of his will, he pressed his advantage. He pounced like a hawk, clenched power around the Despiser. Whitely, brutally, he began to penetrate the penumbra.

Lord Foul's aura resisted with shrieks and showers of sparks. It was tough, obdurate; it shed Covenant's feral bolts as if they were mere show, incandescent child's play. But he refused to be denied. The dazzling of his wild magic flung shafts and quarrels of might at the emerald glister of the aura until one prodigious blast pierced it.

It ruptured with a shock which jarred the thronehall like an earth tremor. Waves of concussion pealed at Covenant's head, hammered at his sore and feverish skull. But he clung to his power, did not let his will wince.

The whole penumbra burst into flame like a skin of green tinder, and as it burned it tore, peeled away, fell in hot shreds and tatters to the floor.

Within Covenant's clench, Lord Foul the Despiser began to appear. By faint degrees, he became material, drifted from corporeal absence to presence. Perfectly molded limbs, as pure as alabaster, grew slowly visible—an old, grand, leonine head, magisterially crowned and bearded with flowing white hair—an enrobed, dignified trunk, broad and solid with strength. Only his eyes showed no change, no stern, impressive surge of incarnation; they lashed constantly at Covenant like fangs wet with venom.

When he was fully present, Lord Foul folded his arms on his chest and said harshly, "Now you do in truth see me, groveler." His tone gave no hint of fear or surrender. "Do you yet believe that you are my master? Fool! I grew beyond your petty wisdom or belief long before your world's babyhood. I tell you plainly, groveler—Despite such as mine is the only true fruit of experience and insight. In time you will not do otherwise than I have done. You will learn contempt for your fellow beings—for the small malices which they misname their loves and beliefs and hopes and loyalties. You will learn that it is easier to control them than to forbear—easier and better. You will not do otherwise. You will become a shadow of what I am —you will be a despiser without the courage to despise. Continue, groveler. Destroy my work if you must— slay me if you can—but make an end! I am weary of your shallow misperception."

In spite of himself, Covenant was moved. Lord Foul's lordly mien, his dignity and resignation, spoke more vividly than any cursing or defiance. Covenant saw that he still had answers to find, regardless of all he had endured.

But before he could respond, try to articulate the emotions and intuitions which Lord Foul's words called up in him, a sudden clap of vehemence splintered the silence of the thronehall. A great invisible door opened in the air at his back; without warning, strong presences, furious and abhorring, stood behind him. The violence of their emanations almost broke his concentrated hold on Lord Foul.

He clenched his will, steadied himself to face a shock, and turned.

He found himself looking up at tall figures like the one he had seen in the cave of the EarthBlood under

Melenkurion Skyweir. They towered above him, grisly and puissant; he seemed to see them through the stone rather than within the chamber.

They were the specters of the dead Lords. He recognized Kevin Landwaster son of Loric. Beside Kevin stood two other livid men whom he knew instinctively to be Loric Vilesilencer and Damelon Giantfriend. There were Prothall, Osondrea, a score of men and women Covenant had never met, never heard named. With them was Elena daughter of Lena. And behind and above them all rose another figure, a dominating man with hot prophetic eyes and one halfhand: Berek Earthfriend, the Lord-Fatherer.

In one voice like a thunder of abomination—one voice of outrage that shook Covenant to the marrow of his bones—they cried, "Slay him! It is within your power. Do not heed his treacherous lies. In the name of all Earth and health, slay him!"

The intensity of their passion poured at him, flooded him with their extreme desire. They were the sworn defenders of the Land. Its glory was their deepest love. Yet in one way or another, Lord Foul had outdone them all, seen them all taken to their graves while he endured and ravaged. They hated him with a blazing hate that seemed to overwhelm Covenant's individual rage.

But instead of moving him to obey, their vehemence washed away his fury, his power for battle. Violence drained out of him, giving place to sorrow for them—a sorrow so great that he could hardly contain it, hardly hold back his tears. They had earned obedience from him; they had a right to his rage. But their demand made his intuitions clear to him. He remembered Foamfollower's former lust for killing. He still had something to do, something which could not be done with rage. Anger was only good for fighting, for resistance. Now it could suborn the very thing he had striven to achieve.

In a voice thick with grief, he answered the Lords, "I can't kill him. He always survives when you try to kill him. He comes back stronger than ever the next time. Despite is like that. I can't kill him."

His reply stunned them. For a moment, they trembled with astonishment and dismay. Then Kevin asked in horror, "Will you let him live?"

Covenant could not respond directly, could not give a direct answer. But he clung to the strait path of his intuition. For the first time since his battle with the Despiser had begun, he turned to Saltheart Foamfollower.

The Giant stood chained to the wall, watching avidly everything that happened. The bloody flesh of his wrists and ankles showed how hard he had tried to break free, and his face looked as if it had been wrung dry by all the things he had been forced to behold. But he was essentially unharmed, essentially whole. Deep in his cavernous eyes, he seemed to understand Covenant's dilemma. "You have done well, my dear friend," he breathed when Covenant met his gaze. "I trust whatever choice your heart makes."

"There's no choice about it," Covenant panted, fighting to hold back his tears. "I'm not going to kill him. He'll just come back. I don't want that on my head. No, Foamfollower—my friend. It's up to you now. You—and them." He nodded toward the livid, spectral Lords. "Joy is in the ears that hear—remember? You told me that. I've got joy for you to hear. Listen to me. I've beaten the Despiser—this time. The Land is safe—for now. I swear it. Now I want—Foamfollower!" Involuntary tears blurred his sight. "I want you to laugh. Take joy in it. Bring some joy into this bloody hole. Laugh!" He swung back to shout at the Lords, "Do you hear me? Let Foul alone! Heal yourselves!"

For a long moment that almost broke his will, there was no sound in the thronehall. Lord Foul blazed contempt at his captor; the Lords stood aghast, uncomprehending; Foamfollower hung in his chains as if the burden were too great for him to bear.

"Help me!" Covenant cried.

Then slowly his plea made itself felt. Some prophecy in his words touched the hearts that heard him. With a terrible effort, Saltheart Foamfollower, the last of the Giants, began to laugh.

It was a gruesome sound at first; writhing in his fetters, Foamfollower spat out the laugh as if it were a curse. On that level, the Lords were able to share it. In low voices, they aimed bursts of contemptuous scorn, jeering hate, at the beaten Despiser. But as Foamfollower fought to laugh, his muscles loosened. The constriction of his throat and chest relaxed, allowing a pure wind of humor to blow the ashes of rage and pain from his lungs. Soon something like joy, something like real mirth, appeared in his voice.

The Lords responded. As it grew haler, Foamfollower's laugh became infectious; it drew the grim specters with it. They began to unclench their hate. Clean humor ran through them, gathering momentum as it passed. Foamfollower gained joy from them, and they began to taste his joy. In moments, all their contempt or scorn had fallen away. They were no longer laughing to express their outrage at Lord Foul; they were not laughing at him at all. To their own surprise, they were laughing for the pure joy of laughter, for the sheer satisfaction and emotional ebullience of mirth.

Lord Foul cringed at the sound. He strove to sustain his defiance, but could not. With a cry of mingled pain and fury, he covered his face and began to change. The years melted off his frame. His hair darkened, beard grew stiffer; with astonishing speed, he was becoming younger. And at the same time he lost solidity, stature. His body shrank and faded with every undone age. Soon he was a youth again, barely visible.

Still the change did not stop. From a youth he became a child, growing steadily younger as he vanished. For an instant, he was a loud infant, squalling in his ancient frustration. Then he disappeared altogether.

As they laughed, the Lords also faded. With the Despiser vanquished, they went back to their natural graves—ghosts who had at last gained something other than torment from the breaking of the Law of Death. Covenant and Foamfollower were left alone.

Covenant was weeping out of control now. The exhaustion of his ordeal had caught up with him. He felt too frail to lift his head, too weary to live any longer. Yet he had one more thing to do. He had promised that the Land would be safe. Now he had to ensure its safety.

"Foamfollower?" he wept. "My friend?" With his voice, he begged the Giant to understand him; he lacked the strength to articulate what he had to do.

"Do not fear for me," Foamfollower replied. He sounded strangely proud, as if Covenant had honored him in some rare way. "Thomas Covenant, ur-Lord and Unbeliever, brave white gold wielder—I desire no other end. Do whatever you must, my friend. I am at Peace. I have beheld a marvelous story."

Covenant nodded in the blindness of his tears. Foamfollower could make his own decisions. With the flick of an idea, he broke the Giant's chains, so that Foamfollower could at least attempt to escape if he chose. Then all Covenant's awareness of his friend became ashes.

As he shambled numbly across the floor, he tried to tell himself that he had found his answer. The answer to death was to make use of it rather than fall victim to it—master it by making it serve his goals, beliefs. This was not a good answer. But it was the only answer he had.

Following the nerves of his face, he reached toward the Illearth Stone as if it were the fruit of the tree of the knowledge of life and death.

As soon as he touched it, his ring's waning might reawoke. Immense white-green fire pillared upward, towered out of the Stone and his ring like a pinnacle tall enough to pierce the heavens. As he felt its power tearing through the battered hull or conduit of his being, he knew that he had found his fire, the fire for which he was apt like autumn leaves or a bad manuscript. In the heart of the whirling gale, the pillar of force, he knelt beside the Stone and put his arms around it like a man embracing immolation. New blood from his poisoned lip ran down his chin, dripped into the green and was vaporized.

With each moment, the conjunction of the two powers produced more and more might. Like a lifeless and indomitable heart of fury, the Illearth Stone pulsed in Covenant's arms, laboring in mindless, automatic reflex to destroy him rather than be destroyed. And he hugged it to his breast like a chosen fate. He could not slay the Corruption, but he could at least try to break this corruptive tool; without it, any surviving remnant of the Despiser would have to work ages longer to regain his lost power. Covenant embraced the Stone, gave himself to its fire, and strove with the last tatters of his will to tear it asunder.

The green-white, white-green holocaust grew until it filled the thronehall, grew until it hurricaned up through the stone out of the bowels of Ridjeck Thome. Like fighters locked mortally at each other's throats, emerald and argent galed and blasted, gyring upward at velocities which no undefended granite could withstand. In long pain, the roots of the promontory trembled. Walls bent; great chunks of ceiling fell; weaker stones melted and ran like water.

Then a convulsion shook the Creche. Gaping cracks shot through the floors, sped up the walls, as if they were headlong in mad flight. The promontory itself began to quiver and groan. Muffled detonations sent great clouds of debris up through the cracks and crevices. Hotash Slay danced in rapid spouts. The towers leaned like willows in a bereaving wind.

With a blast that jolted the Sea, the whole center of the promontory exploded into the air. In a rain of boulders, Creche fragments as large as homes, villages, the wedge split open from tip to base. Accompanied by cataclysmic thunder, the rent halves toppled in ponderous, monumental agony away from each other into the Sea.

At once, ocean crashed into the gap from the east, and lava poured into it from the west. Their impact obscured in steam and fiery sibilation the seething caldron of Ridjeck Thome's collapse, the sky-shaking fury of sea and stone and fire—obscured everything except the power which blazed from the core of the destruction.

It was green-white—savage, wild—mounting hugely toward its apocalypse.

But the white dominated and prevailed.

TWENTY-ONE: Leper's End

I<small>N</small> that way, Thomas Covenant kept his promise.

For a long time afterward, he lay in a comfortable grave of oblivion; buried in utter exhaustion, he floated through darkness—the disengaged no-man's-land between life and death. He felt that he was effectively dead, insensate as death. But his heart went on beating as if it lacked the wit or wisdom to stop when it had no more reason to go on. Raggedly, frailly, it kept up his life.

And deep within him—in a place hidden somewhere, defended, inside the hard bone casque of his skull—he retained an awareness of himself. That essential thing had not yet failed him, though it seemed to be soaking slowly away into the warm soft earth of his grave.

He wanted rest; he had earned rest. But the release which had brought him to his present dim peace had been too expensive. He could not approve.

Foamfollower is dead, he murmured silently.

There was no escape from guilt. No answer covered everything. For as long as he managed to live, he would never be clean.

He did not think that he could manage to live very long.

Yet something obdurate argued with him. That wasn't your fault, it said. You couldn't make his deci-

470

sions for him. Beyond a certain point, this responsibility of yours is only a more complex form of suicide.

He acknowledged the argument. He knew from experience that lepers were doomed as soon as they began to feel that they were to blame for contracting leprosy, were responsible for being ill. Perhaps guilt and mortality, physical limitation, were the same thing in the end—facts of life, irremediable, useless to protest. Nevertheless Foamfollower was gone, and could never be restored. Covenant would never hear him laugh again.

"Then take peace in your other innocence," said a voice out of the darkness. "You did not choose this task. You did not undertake it of your own free will. It was thrust upon you. Blame belongs to the chooser, and this choice was made by one who elected you without your knowledge or consent."

Covenant did not need to ask who was speaking; he recognized the voice. It belonged to the old beggar who had confronted him before his first experience in the Land—the old man who had urged him to keep his wedding band, and had made him read a paper on the fundamental question of ethics.

Dimly, he replied, "You must have been sure of yourself."

"Sure? Ah, no. There was great hazard—risk for the world which I made—risk even for me. Had my enemy gained the white wild magic gold, he would have unloosed himself from the Earth—destroyed it so that he might hurl himself against me. No, Thomas Covenant. I risked my trust in you. My own hands were bound. I could not touch the Earth to defend it without thereby undoing what I meant to preserve. Only a free man could hope to stand against my enemy, hope to preserve the Earth."

Covenant heard sympathy, respect, even gratitude in the voice. But he was unconvinced. "I wasn't free. It wasn't my choice."

"Ah, but you were—free of my suasion, my power, my wish to make you my tool. Have I not said that the risk was great? Choiceless, you were given the power of choice. I elected you for the Land but did not compel you to serve my purpose in the Land. You were free to damn Land and Earth and Time and all, if you chose. Only through such a risk could I hope to preserve the rectitude of my creation."

In his darkness, Covenant shrugged. "I still wasn't free. That singer—who called me Berek. That revival. The kid who got herself snakebit. Maybe you left me free in the Land, but you didn't leave me alone in my own life."

"No," the voice responded softly. "I had no hand in those chances. Had I done anything at all to shape you, you would have been my tool—effectless. Without freedom, you could not have mastered my enemy —without independence—without the sovereignty of your own allegiance. No, I risked too much when I spoke to you once. I interfered in no other way."

Covenant did not like to think that he had been so completely free to ruin the Land. He had come so close! For a while, he mused numbly to himself, measuring the Creator's risk. Then he asked, "What made you think I wouldn't just collapse—wouldn't give up in despair?"

The voice replied promptly. "Despair is an emotion like any other. It is the habit of despair which damns, not the despair itself. You were a man already acquainted with habit and despair—with the Law which both saves and damns. Your knowledge of your illness made you wise."

Wise, Covenant murmured to himself. Wisdom. He could not understand why his witless heart went on beating.

"Further, you were in your own way a creator. You had already tasted the way in which a creator may be impotent to heal his creation. It is ofttimes this impotence which teaches a creation to despair."

"What about the creator? Why doesn't he despair?"

"Why should he despair? If he cannot bear the world he has made, he can make another. No, Thomas Covenant." The voice laughed softly, sadly. "Gods and creators are too powerful and powerless for despair."

Yes, Covenant said with his own sadness. But then

he added almost out of habit, It's not that easy. He wanted the voice to go away, leave him alone with his oblivion. But though it was silent, he knew it had not left him. He drifted along beside it for a time, then gathered himself to ask, "What do you want?"

"Thomas Covenant"—the voice was gentle—"my unwilling son, I wish to give you a gift—a guerdon to speak my wordless gratitude. Your world runs by Law, as does mine. And by any Law I am in your debt. You have retrieved my Earth from the brink of dissolution. I could give you precious gifts a dozen times over, and still not call the matter paid."

A gift? Covenant sighed to himself. No. He could not demean himself or the Creator by asking for a cure to leprosy. He was about to refuse the offer when a sudden excitement flashed across him. "Save the Giant," he said. "Save Foamfollower."

In a tone of ineffable rue, the voice answered, "No, Thomas Covenant—I cannot. Have I not told you that I would break the arch of Time if I were to put my hand through it to touch the Earth? No matter how great my gratitude, I can do nothing for you in the Land or upon that Earth. If I could, I would never have permitted my enemy to do so much harm."

Covenant nodded; he recognized the validity of the answer. After a moment of emptiness, he said. "Then there's nothing you can do for me. I told Foul I don't believe in him. I don't believe in you either. I've had the chance to make an important choice. That's enough. I don't need any gifts. Gifts are too easy—I can't afford them."

"Ah! but you have earned—"

"I didn't earn anything." Faint anger stirred in him. "You didn't give me a chance to earn anything. You put me in the Land without my approval or consent—even without my knowledge. All I did was see the difference between health and—disease. Well, it's enough for me. But there's no particular virtue in it."

Slowly, the voice breathed. "Do not be too quick to judge the makers of worlds. Will you ever write a story for which no character will have cause to reproach you?"

"I'll try," said Covenant. "I'll try."

"Yes," the voice whispered. "Perhaps for you it is enough. Yet for my own sake I wish to give you a gift. Please permit me."

"No." Covenant's refusal was weary rather than belligerent. He could not think of anything he would be able to accept.

"I can return you to the Land. You could live out the rest of your life in health and honor, as befits a great hero."

"No." Have mercy on me. I couldn't bear it. "That's not my world. I don't belong there."

"I can teach you to believe that your experiences in the Land have been real."

"No." It's not that easy. "You'll drive me insane."

Again the voice was silent for a while before it said in a tone made sharp by grief, "Very well. Then hear me, Thomas Covenant, before you refuse me once more. This I must tell you.

"When the parents of the child whom you saved comprehended what you had done, they sought to aid you. You were injured and weak from hunger. Your exertions to save the child had hastened the poison in your lip. Your condition was grave. They bore you to the hospital for treatment. This treatment employs a thing which the Healers of your world name 'antivenin.' Thomas Covenant, this antivenin is made from the blood of horses. Your body loathes—you are allergic to the horse serum. It is a violent reaction. In your weak state, you cannot survive it. At this moment, you stand on the threshold of your own death.

"Thomas Covenant—hear me." The voice breathed compassion at him. "I can give you life. In this time of need, I can provide to your stricken flesh the strength it requires to endure."

Covenant did not answer for some time. Somewhere in his half-forgotten past, he had heard that some people were allergic to rattlesnake antivenin. Perhaps the doctors at the hospital should have tested for the allergy before administering the full dosage; probably he had been so far gone in shock that they had not had time for medical niceties. For a moment, he considered the thought of dying under their care as a form of retribution.

But he rejected the idea, rejected the self-pity behind it. "I'd rather survive," he murmured dimly. "I don't want to die like that."

The voice smiled. "It is done. You will live."

By force of habit, Covenant said, "I'll believe it when I see it."

"You will see it. But there is first one other thing that you will see. You have not asked for this gift, but I give it to you whether or not you wish it. I did not ask your approval when I elected you for the Land, and do not ask now."

Before Covenant could protest, he sensed that the voice had left him. Once again, he was alone in the darkness. Oblivion swaddled him so comfortably that he almost regretted his decision to live. But then something around him or in him began to change, modulate. Without sight or hearing or touch, he became aware of sunlight, low voices, a soft warm breeze. He found himself looking down as if from a high hill at Glimmermere.

The pure waters of the lake reflected the heavens in deep burnished azure, and the breeze smelled gently of spring. The hills around Glimmermere showed the scars of Lord Foul's preternatural winter. But already grass had begun to sprout through the cold-seared ground, and a few tough spring flowers waved bravely in the air. The stretches of bare earth had lost their gray, frozen deadness. The healing of the Land had begun.

Hundreds of people were gathered around the lake. Almost immediately, Covenant made out High Lord Mhoram. He stood facing east across Glimmermere. He bore no staff. His hands were heavily bandaged. On his left were the Lords Trevor and Loerya, holding their daughters, and on his right was Lord Amatin. All of them seemed solemnly glad, but Mhoram's serene gaze outshone them, testified more eloquently than they could to the Land's victory.

Behind the Lords stood Warmark Quaan and Hearthrall Tohrm—Quaan with the Hafts of his Warward, and Tohrm with all the Hirebrands and Gravelingases of Lord's Keep. Covenant saw that Trell Atiaran-mate was not among them. He understood intuitively; Trell had carried his personal dilemma to its conclusion, and was either dead or gone. Again, the Unbeliever found that he could not argue away his guilt.

All around the lake beyond the Lords were Lorewardens and warriors. And behind them were the survivors of Revelstone—farmers, Cattleherds, horsetenders, cooks, artisans, Craftmasters—children and parents, young and old—all the people who had endured. They did not seem many, but Covenant knew that they were enough; they would be able to commence the work of restoration.

As he watched, they drew close to Glimmermere and fell silent. High Lord Mhoram waited until they were all attentive, ready. Then he lifted up his voice.

"People of the Land," he said firmly, "we are gathered here in celebration of life. I have no long song to sing. I am weak yet, and none of us is strong. But we live. The Land has been preserved. The mad riot and rout of Lord Foul's army shows us that he has fallen. The fierce echo of battle within the *krill* of Loric shows us that the white gold has done combat with the Illearth Stone, and has emerged triumphant. That is cause enough for celebration. Enough? My friends, it will suffice for us and for our children, while the present age of the Land endures.

"In token of this, I have brought the *krill* to Glimmermere." Reaching painfully into his robe, he drew out the dagger. Its gem showed no light or life. "In it, we see that ur-Lord Thomas Covenant, Unbeliever and white gold wielder, has returned to his world, where a great hero was fashioned for our deliverance.

"Well, that is as it must be, though my heart regrets his passing. Yet let none fear that he is lost to us. Did not the old legends say that Berek Halfhand would come again? And was not that promise kept in the person of the Unbeliever? Such promises are not made in vain.

"My friends—people of the Land—Thomas Cove-

nant once inquired of me why we so devote ourselves
to the Lore of High Lord Kevin Landwaster. And now,
in this war, we have learned the hazard of that Lore.
Like the *krill,* it is a power of two edges, as apt for
carnage as for preservation. Its use endangers our Oath
of Peace.

"I am Mhoram son of Variol, High Lord by the
choice of the Council. I declare that from this day forth
we will not devote ourselves to any Lore which precludes Peace. We will gain lore of our own—we will
strive and quest and learn until we have found a lore
in which the Oath of Peace and the preservation of the
Land live together. Hear me, you people! We will
serve Earthfriendship in a new way."

As he finished, he lifted the *krill* and tossed it high
into the air. It arced glinting through the sunlight,
struck water in the center of Glimmermere. When it
splashed the potent water, it flared once, sent a burn
of white glory into the depths of the lake. Then it was
gone forever.

High Lord Mhoram watched while the ripples faded.
Then he made an exultant summoning gesture, and all
the people around Glimmermere began to sing in celebration:

> Hail, Unbeliever! Keeper and Covenant,
> Unoathed truth and wicked's bane,
> Ur-Lord Illender, Prover of Life:
> Hail! Covenant!
> Dour-handed wild magic wielder,
> Ur-Earth white gold's servant and Lord—
> Yours is the power that preserves.
> Sing out, people of the Land—
> Raise obeisance!
> Hold honor and glory high to the end of days:
> Keep clean the truth that was won!
> Hail, Unbeliever!
> Covenant!
> Hail!

They raised their staffs and swords and hands to
him, and his vision blurred with tears. Tears smeared

Glimmermere out of focus until it became only a smudge of light before his face. He did not want to lose it. He tried to clear his sight, hoping that the lake was not gone. But then he became conscious of his tears. Instead of wetting his cheeks, they ran from the corners of his eyes down to his ears and neck. He was lying on his back in comfort. When he refocused his sight, pulled it into adjustment like the resolution of a lens, he found that the smear of light before him was the face of a man.

The man peered at him for a long moment, then withdrew into a superficial haze of fluorescence. Slowly, Covenant realized that there were gleaming horizontal bars on either side of the bed. His left wrist was tied to one of them, so that he could not disturb the needle in his vein. The needle was connected by a clear tube to an IV bottle above his head. The air had a faint patina of germicide.

"I wouldn't have believed it if I hadn't seen it," the man said. "That poor devil is going to live."

"That's why I called you, doctor," the woman said. "Isn't there anything we can do?"

"Do?" the doctor snapped.

"I didn't mean it like that," the woman replied defensively. "But he's a leper! He's been making people in this town miserable for months. Nobody knows what to do about him. Some of the other nurses want —they want overtime pay for taking care of him. And look at him. He's so messed up. I just think it would be a lot better for everyone—if he—"

"That's enough." The man was angry. "Nurse, if I hear another word like that out of you, you're going to be looking for a new job. This man is ill. If you don't want to help people who are ill, go find yourself some other line of work."

"I didn't mean any harm," the nurse huffed as she left the room.

After she was gone, Covenant lost sight of the doctor for a while; he seemed to fade into the insensitive haze of the lighting. Covenant tried to take stock of his situation. His right wrist was also tied, so that he lay in the bed as if he had been crucified. But the restraints did not prevent him from testing the essential facts about himself. His feet were numb and cold. His fingers were in the same condition—numb, chill. His forehead hurt feverishly. His lip was taut and hot with swelling.

He had to agree with the nurse; he was in rotten shape.

Then he found the doctor near him again. The man seemed young and angry. Another man entered the room, an older doctor whom Covenant recognized as the one who had treated him during his previous stay in the hospital. Unlike the younger man, this doctor wore a suit rather than a white staff jacket. As he entered, he said, "I hope you've got good reason for calling me. I don't give up church for just anyone—especially on Easter."

"This is a hospital," the younger man growled, "not a bloody revival. Of course I've got good reason."

"What's eating you? Is he dead?"

"No. Just the opposite—he's going to live. One minute he's in allergic shock, and dying from it because his body's too weak and infected and poisoned to fight back—and the next— Pulse firm, respiration regular, pupillary reactions normal, skin tone improving. I'll tell you what it is. It's a goddamn miracle, that's what it is."

"Come, now," the older man murmured. "I don't believe in miracles—neither do you." He glanced at the chart, then listened to Covenant's heart and lungs for himself. "Maybe he's just stubborn." He leaned close to Covenant's face. "Mr. Covenant," he said, "I don't know whether you can hear me. If you can, I have some news which may be important to you. I saw Megan Roman yesterday—your lawyer. She said that the township council has decided not to rezone Haven Farm. The way you saved that little girl—well, some people are just a bit ashamed of themselves. It's hard to take a hero's home away from him.

"Of course, to be honest I should tell you that Megan performed a little legerdemain for you. She's a sharp lawyer, Mr. Covenant. She thought the council might think twice about evicting you if it knew that a national news magazine was going to do a human interest story on the famous author who saves children from rattlesnakes. None of our politicians were very eager for headlines like 'Town Ostracizes Hero.' But the point is that you'll be able to keep Haven Farm."

The older man receded. After a moment, Covenant heard him say to the other doctor, "You still haven't told me why you're in such high dudgeon."

"It's nothing," the younger man replied as they left the room. "One of our Florence Nightingales suggested that we should kill him off."

"Who was it? I'll get the nursing superintendent to transfer her. We'll get decent care for him from somewhere."

Their voices drifted away, left Covenant alone in his bed.

He was thinking dimly, A miracle. That's what it was.

He was a sick man, a victim of Hansen's disease. But he was not a leper—not just a leper. He had the law of his illness carved in large, undeniable letters on the nerves of his body; but he was more than that. In the end, he had not failed the Land. And he had a heart which could still pump blood, bones which could still bear his weight; he had himself.

Thomas Covenant: Unbeliever.

A miracle.

Despite the stiff pain in his lip, he smiled at the empty room. He felt the smile on his face, and was sure of it.

He smiled because he was alive.

Glossary

Acence: a Stonedownor, sister of Atiaran
ahamkara: Hoerkin, "the Door"
Ahanna: painter, daughter of Hanna
aliantha: treasure-berries
amanibhavam: horse-healing grass, poisonous to men
Amatin: a Lord, daughter of Matin
Amok: mysterious guide and servant to ancient Lore
Amorine: First Haft, later Hiltmark
anundivian yajña: "lost" Ramen craft of bone-sculpting
Asuraka: Staff-Elder of the Loresraat
Atiaran Trell-mate: a Stonedownor, mother of Lena
aussat Befylam: child-form of the *jheherrin*

Banas Nimoram: the Celebration of Spring
Bann: a Bloodguard, assigned to Lord Trevor
Bannor: a Bloodguard, assigned to Thomas Covenant
Baradakas: a Hirebrand of Soaring Woodhelven
Berek Halfhand: Heartthew, founder of the Line of
  Lords, first of the Old Lords
Bhrathair: a people met by the wandering Giants
Birinair: a Hirebrand; later a Hearthrall of Lord's Keep
Bloodguard: the defenders of the Lords
bone-sculpting: ancient Ramen craft, marrowmeld
Borillar: a Hirebrand and Hearthrall of Lord's Keep
Brabha: a Ranyhyn, Korik's mount

caamora: Giantish ordeal of grief by fire
Caer-Caveral: apprentice Forestal of Morinmoss Forest
Caerroil Wildwood: Forestal of Garroting Deep

481

Callindrill Faer-mate: a Lord

Cavewights: evil creatures existing under Mount Thunder

Celebration of Spring: the Dance of the Wraiths of Andelain on the dark of the moon in the middle night of spring

Cerrin: a Bloodguard, assigned to Lord Shetra

Circle of elders: Stonedown leaders

clingor: adhesive leather

Close, the: council chamber of Lord's Keep

Colossus, the: ancient stone figure guarding the Upper Land

Cord: second Ramen rank

Cording: ceremony of becoming a Cord

Corimini: Eldest of the Loresraat

Corruption: Bloodguard name for Lord Foul

Creator, the: legendary Timelord and Landsire, enemy of Lord Foul

Crowl: a Bloodguard

Damelon Giantfriend: Old High Lord, son of Berek Halfhand

Dance of the Wraiths: Celebration of Spring

Demondim: spawners of ur-viles and Waynhim

Desolation, the: era of ruin in the Land, after the Ritual of Desecration

Despiser, the: Lord Foul

Despite: Power of Evil

dharmakshetra: "to brave the enemy," Waynhim name

diamondraught: Giantish liquor

Doar: a Bloodguard

Drinishok: Sword-Elder of the Loresraat

Drinny: a Ranyhyn, Lord Mhoram's mount, foal of Hynaril

Drool Rockworm: a Cavewight, later leader of the Cavewights, finder of the Staff of Law

dukkha: "victim," Waynhim name

Dura Fairflank: a mustang, Thomas Covenant's mount

Earthfriend: title first given to Berek Halfhand

Earthpower, the: the source of all power in the Land

Elena: High Lord during first attack by Lord Foul;
daughter of Lena
Elohim: people met by the wandering Giants
Eoman: twenty warriors plus a Warhaft
Eoward: twenty Eoman plus a Haft

fael Befylam: serpent-form of the *jheherrin*
Faer: mate of Lord Callindrill
Fangthane the Render: Ramen name for Lord Foul
Fire-Lions: fire-flow of Mount Thunder
fire-stones: graveling
First Haft: third-in-command of the Warward
First Mark: the Bloodguard commander
First Ward of Kevin's Lore: primary knowledge left by
Lord Kevin
Fleshharrower: a Giant-Raver, Jehannum, *moksha*
Forbidding: a repelling force, a wall of power
Forestal: a protector of the Forests of the Land
Foul's Creche: the Despiser's home
Furl Falls: waterfall at Revelstone
Furl's Fire: warning fire at Revelstone

Gallows Howe: place of execution in Garroting Deep
Garth: Warmark of the Warward of Lord's Keep
Gay: a Winhome of the Ramen
Giantclave: Giantish conference
Giants: the Unhomed, ancient friends of the Lords
Gilden: a maplelike tree with golden leaves
Gildenlode: a power-wood formed from Gilden trees
Glimmermere: a lake on the upland above Revelstone
Gorak Krembal: Hotash Slay
Grace: a Cord of the Ramen
graveling: fire-stones, made to glow by stone-lore
Gravelingas: a master of stone-lore
Gravin Threndor: Mount Thunder
Gray Slayer: plains name for Lord Foul
Grieve, The: *Coercri,* Giant city
griffin: lionlike beast with wings

Haft: commander of an Eoward
Haruchai, the: original race of the Bloodguard
Healer: a physician

Hearthrall of Lord's Keep: a steward responsible for light, warmth, and hospitality

Heart of Thunder: cave of power in Mount Thunder

Heartthew: Berek Halfhand

heartwood chamber: Woodhelven meeting place

Heer: leader of a Woodhelven

Herem: a Raver, Kinslaughterer, *turiya*

High Lord: leader of the Council of Lords

High Lord's Furl: banner of the High Lord

High Wood: *lomillialor,* offspring of the One Tree

Hile Troy: Warmark of High Lord Elena's Warward

Hiltmark: second-in-command of the Warward

Hirebrand: a master of wood-lore

Hoerkin: a Warhaft

Home: original homeland of the Giants

Howor: a Bloodguard, assigned to Lord Loerya

Hurn: a Cord of the Ramen

hurtloam: a healing mud

Huryn: a Ranyhyn, Terrel's mount

Hynaril: a Ranyhyn, mount of Tamarantha and Mhoram

Hyrim: a Lord, son of Hoole

Illearth Stone: stone found under Mount Thunder, source of evil power

Imoiran Tomal-mate: a Stonedownor

Irin: a warrior of the Third Eoman of the Warward

Jain: a Manethrall of the Ramen

Jehannum: a Raver, Fleshharrower, *moksha*

jheherrin: soft ones, living by-products of Foul's misshaping

Kam: a Manethrall of the Ramen

Kelenbhrabanal: Father of Horses in Ranyhyn legends

Kevin Landwaster: son of Loric Vilesilencer, last High Lord of the Old Lords

Kevin's Lore: knowledge of power left by Kevin in the Seven Wards

Kinslaughterer: a Giant-Raver, Herem, *turiya*

Kiril Threndor: chamber of power deep under Mount Thunder, Heart of Thunder

Koral: a Bloodguard, assigned to Lord Amatin

Korik: a Bloodguard, a commander of the original *Haruchai* army

kresh: savage, giant, yellow wolves

krill, **the:** enchanted sword of Loric, a mystery to the New Lords, wakened to power by Thomas Covenant

Kurash Plenethor: region once called Stricken Stone and later Trothgard

Kurash Qwellinir: the Shattered Hills

Lal: a Cord of the Ramen

Land, the: generally, area found on the Map

Law of Death, the: the separation of the living and the dead

Lena: a Stonedownor, daughter of Atiaran and Trell; mother of Elena

Lifeswallower: the Great Swamp

lillianrill: wood-lore, or masters of wood-lore

Lithe: a Manethrall of the Ramen

Llaura: Heer of Soaring Woodhelven

Loerya Trevor-mate: a Lord

lomillialor: High Wood, a wood of power

Lord: master of the Sword and Staff parts of Kevin's Lore

Lord-Fatherer: Berek Halfhand

Lord Foul: the enemy of the Land

"Lord Mhoram's Victory": a painting by Ahanna

Lords-fire: staff fire used by the Lords

Lord's Keep: Revelstone

loremaster: ur-vile leader

Loresraat: Trothgard school at Revelwood where Kevin's Lore is studied

Lorewarden: teacher at the Loresraat

loreworks: Demondim power laboratory

Loric Vilesilencer: Old High Lord, son of Damelon Giantfriend

lor-liarill: Gildenlode

Lower Land, the: land east of Landsdrop

Maker, the: *jheherrin* name for Lord Foul

Maker-place: Foul's Creche

Malliner: Woodhelven Heer, son of Veinnin
Mane: a Ranyhyn
Maneing: ceremony of becoming a Manethrall
Manethrall: highest Ramen rank
Manhome: main dwelling place of the Ramen
Marny: a Ranyhyn, Tuvor's mount
marrowmeld: bone-sculpting
Mehryl: a Ranyhyn, Hile Troy's mount
Melenkurion abatha: phrase of invocation or power
Mhoram: a Lord, later High Lord, son of Variol
moksha: a Raver, Jehannum, Fleshharrower
Morin: First Mark of the Bloodguard, commander in
    original *Haruchai* army
Morril: a Bloodguard, assigned to Lord Callindrill
Murrin Odona-mate: a Stonedownor
Myrha: a Ranyhyn, Elena's mount

Oath of Peace: oath by the people of the Land against
    needless violence
Odona Murrin-mate: a Stonedownor
Old Lords: Lords prior to the Ritual of Desecration
Omournil: Woodhelven Heer, daughter of Mournil
One Forest, the: ancient forest which covered most of
    the Land
One Tree, the: mystic tree from which the Staff of Law
    was made
orcrest: a stone of power
Osondrea: a Lord, later High Lord, daughter of
    Sondrea

Padrias: Woodhelven Heer, son of Mill
Peak of the Fire-Lions: Mount Thunder
Pietten: Woodhelven child damaged by Lord Foul's
    minions, son of Soranal
Porib: a Bloodguard
Power of Command: Seventh Ward of Kevin's Lore
Pren: a Bloodguard
Prothall: High Lord, son of Dwillian
Puhl: a Cord of the Ramen

Quaan: Warhaft of the Third Eoman of the Warward,
    later Hiltmark, then Warmark

Quest, the: the search to rescue the Staff of Law
Quirrel: a Stonedownor, companion of Triock

Ramen: people who serve the Ranyhyn
Ranyhyn: the great, free horses of the Plains of Ra
Ravers: Lord Foul's three ancient servants
Revelstone: Lord's Keep, mountain city of the Lords
Revelwood: seat of the Loresraat
rhadhamaerl: stone-lore or masters of stone-lore
Ridjeck Thome: Foul's Creche
rillinlure: healing wood dust
Ringthane: Ramen name for Thomas Covenant
Rites of Unfettering: the ceremony of becoming Unfettered
Ritual of Desecration: act of despair by which High Lord Kevin destroyed the Old Lords and ruined most of the Land
Rockbrother, Rocksister: terms of affection between men and Giants
roge Befylam: Cavewight-form of the *jheherrin*
Rue: a Manethrall, formerly named Gay
Ruel: a Bloodguard, assigned to Hile Troy
Runnik: a Bloodguard
Rustah: a Cord of the Ramen

sacred enclosure: Vespers hall at Revelstone
Saltheart Foamfollower: a Giant, friend of Thomas Covenant
samadhi: a Raver, Sheol, Satansfist
Sandgorgons: monsters described by the Giants
Satansfist: a Giant-Raver, Sheol, *samadhi*
Satansheart Soulcrusher: Giantish name for Lord Foul
Seven Wards, the: collection of knowledge left by Lord Kevin
Seven Words, the: power-words
Sheol: a Raver, Satansfist, *samadhi*
Shetra Verement-mate: a Lord
Shull: a Bloodguard
Sill: a Bloodguard, assigned to Lord Hyrim
Slen Terass-mate: a Stonedownor
Soranal: Woodhelven Heer, son of Thiller
Soulcrusher: Giantish name for Lord Foul

Sparlimb Keelsetter: a Giant, father of triplets
springwine: a mild, refreshing liquor
Staff, the: a branch of Kevin's Lore studied at the Loresraat
Staff of Law, the: formed by Berek from the One Tree
Stonedown: a stone-village
Stonedownor: one who lives in a stone-village
Stricken Stone: region of Trothgard before renovation
suru-pa-maerl: a stone craft
Sword, the: a branch of Kevin's Lore studied at the Loresraat
Sword-Elder: chief Lorewarden of the Sword at the Loresraat

Tamarantha Variol-mate: a Lord, daughter of Enesta
Terass Slen-mate: an elder of Mithil Stonedown, daughter of Annoria
Terrel: a Bloodguard, assigned to Lord Mhoram, a commander of the original *Haruchai* army
test of truth, the: test of veracity by *lomillialor* or *orcrest*
Thew: a Cord of the Ramen
Thomin: a Bloodguard, assigned to Lord Verement
Tohrm: a Gravelingas and Hearthrall of Lord's Keep
Tomal: a Stonedownor craftmaster
treasure-berries: *aliantha,* nourishing fruit found throughout the Land
Trell Atiaran-mate: Gravelingas of Mithil Stonedown, father of Lena
Trevor Loerya-mate: a Lord
Triock: a Stonedownor, son of Thuler
Tull: a Bloodguard
turiya: a Raver, Herem, Kinslaughterer
Tuvor: First Mark of the Bloodguard, a commander of the original *Haruchai* army

Unbeliever, the: Thomas Covenant
Unfettered, the: lore-students freed from conventional responsibilities
Unhomed, the: the Giants
upland: plateau above Revelstone
Upper Land: land west of Landsdrop

ur-Lord: title given to Thomas Covenant
ur-viles: Demondim-spawn, evil creatures of power

Vailant: former High Lord
Vale: a Bloodguard
Valley of Two Rivers: site of Revelwood
Variol Farseer Tamarantha-mate: a Lord, later High Lord, son of Pentil, father of Mhoram
Verement Shetra-mate: a Lord
viancome: meeting place at Revelwood
Viles: sires of the Demondim
Vow, the: Bloodguard oath of service to the Lords

Ward: a unit of Kevin's Lore
Warhaft: commander of an Eoman
Warlore: "Sword" knowledge in Kevin's Lore
Warmark: commander of the Warward
Warrenbridge: entrance to the catacombs under Mount Thunder
Warward, the: army of Lord's Keep
Wavenhair Haleall: a Giant, wife of Sparlimb Keel-setter, mother of triplets
Waynhim: tenders of the Waymeets, Demondim-spawn but opponents of the ur-viles
Whane: a Cord of the Ramen
Wightwarren: home of the Cavewights under Mount Thunder
Winhome: lowest Ramen rank
Woodhelven: wood-village
Woodhelvennin: inhabitants of a wood-village
Word of Warning: a powerful, destructive forbidding
Wraiths of Andelain: creatures of living light that perform the Dance at the Celebration of Spring

Yeurquin: a Stonedownor, companion of Triock
Yolenid: daughter of Loerya

About the Author

Born in 1947 in Cleveland, Ohio, **Stephen R. Donaldson** makes his publishing debut with The Covenant Trilogy. From ages three to sixteen, he lived in India, where his father, an orthopedic surgeon, worked extensively with lepers. (It was after hearing one of his father's speeches on the subject of leprosy that he conceived the character of Thomas Covenant as protagonist for an epic fantasy.) He graduated from the College of Wooster (Ohio) in 1968, served two years as a conscientious objector doing hospital work in Akron, then attended Kent State University, where he received his M.A. in English in 1971. He now lives in Albuquerque, New Mexico.